ABOUT THE AUTHOR

Judith Almond is a pen name of Judith Taylor.

Judith was born and raised in Yorkshire, and now lives with her husband in London and Kent. After qualifying as a librarian, she worked as a volunteer in Sri Lanka; on her return she worked with overseas students at the University of London. Later, she moved into staff development and training in higher education. During this time she wrote a number of books on aspects of careers and training. She has completed the Certificate in Creative Writing at Birkbeck College, University of London, and is a member of an active and supportive writing group.

To my family

COUSINS

Judith Almond

Published in 2014 by FeedARead.com Publishing – Arts Council funded

Copyright © Judith Almond

First Edition

A CIP catalogue record for this title is available from the British
Library

CONTENTS

1954

It was late on a January night, two weeks after Christmas. The parties were over, the cards and decorations taken down. Months of cold winds and grey skies lay ahead, and no sign of any new work. There was nothing for Fay to do but stay at home and look after the child. And she didn't do that very well, she'd allowed her to get ill. Poor little Elisabeth, poor little baby bird. Fay brooded, gazing into the gas fire, a coat around her shoulders for additional warmth. The room was lit by the street light outside the window and a small lamp which cast a soft glow above her head. The buoyancy she had felt earlier that day had gone, gone as soon as Hugh left for the theatre. When she and Elisabeth stood at the door to wave him goodbye the daylight was fading and she knew that there would be hours of darkness before he came home again. Depression for Fay was never black, but grey, like winter fog, impossible to find your way through. It seeped into her veins, into her head, made worse by the contrast with Hugh's life; she knew (because she used to share it) that he would be enjoying himself among the lights and glitter and colour of the pantomime, acting, making friends, having fun. It was Saturday, there would probably be a party or drinks after the show. It would be hours before she saw him again.

She had tried to hold the fog at bay. She had delayed Elisabeth's bedtime as long as she could. She told her stories, acted some of the parts, waltzed around the room with Elisabeth in her arms. "Let's pretend we're in a ballroom! There are lights, and music, and beautiful ladies in long silk dresses. Handsome gentlemen in stiff white shirts! Come on, baby, let's dance!" She skipped over to the radio, found dance music and they waltzed round the room again. Elisabeth, holding on to her mother's shoulder with one arm, whimpered a little as they span round. Fay's burst of energy disappeared as quickly as it had arrived. She put her small daughter on the settee and sank down beside her, put her head in her hands and said "God, oh God, what's to become of us?" Elisabeth screwed up her face and her legs kicked against the settee.

After a time Fay sat up and wiped away her tears. "You're tired. I shouldn't keep you up, but oh baby, I'm so tired of being on my own." She gave the child some bread and milk, washed her face and brushed her teeth, and put her to bed. She spent some time in the bedroom, talking to her, kissing her, tucking then un-tucking and re-tucking the

5

blankets around her thin little shoulders. Elisabeth, half asleep, put her arm around her mother's neck.

"'Night, Mummy," she whispered. Fay hugged her tight then kissed her face, and hugged her again.

"Do you love me, darling? Do you love your mummy?"

"Yes, Mummy."

"Do you, darling? Really, really love me?"

"Yes, Mummy." Fay gazed into Elisabeth's eyes, tears running down her face, then hugged her again. Gently, she kissed the polio-wasted left arm. "My baby, little damaged daughter. Little bird, why couldn't I have saved you from this?" Finally she settled her back on her pillow, smoothing the hair away from her face. "Your hair is so beautiful, darling, you must never cut it. Promise me!" Elisabeth's sleepy eyes followed her mother as she wandered about the room, picking up objects and putting them down again. Fay pulled aside the curtain to look out, but there was nothing to be seen but the dark basement yard. She sighed, and sat down on Elisabeth's bed, smoothing her hair again. "Go to sleep now, little bird," she said, but continued to sit on the bed. Then she jumped up and went into the kitchenette.

She started to make a cup of tea, then remembered that she had given Elisabeth the last of the milk. The store cupboard was almost empty; somehow, despite her empty days, Fay never found the time to do any shopping. There was Marmite but no bread; tea but no milk; a tin of soup but she couldn't find a tin opener. Lower down were half a dozen wizened, sprouting potatoes, and an onion. A bottle of whisky stood on the floor of the cupboard; Hugh liked a glass when he got home from the theatre. He told her it was good for you, especially in winter, it sent the blood running more quickly in your veins. Fay wasn't tempted, she had never been a drinker. She wandered back to the living room, and turned the radio up. It was the Light Programme, playing music from the shows and she hummed along before remembering that she had lost her singing voice and in any case there was no one to listen to her. She went over to the mirror; it was old and gave a distorted image, but close up she could gaze into her large dark eyes (tragic eyes, she thought to herself, the eyes of Tosca or Mimi or even Butterfly). She went back into the bedroom to look for her handbag, and returned to the mirror to try out a new lipstick. It was dark red, and looked dramatic against her dark hair and eyes and pale oval face. "Poor Fay," she whispered to herself. "Poor, poor Fay."

Then, impatient, she rubbed the lipstick off with the back of her hand, running into the bathroom to scrub her mouth with wet toilet paper. She thrust the lipstick back into the bag. She felt cold. She went again into the bedroom, to pull an eiderdown off the bed that she and Hugh shared. She bent over Elisabeth, and kissed her cheek.

The rented flat had everything they needed in a practical sense but, apart from the radio, there was nothing to entertain her and pass the time. No piano, for example. Hugh had told her to come to the theatre to practise, but she couldn't see herself singing her songs while the pantomime was being rehearsed around her. She'd feel out of place. She picked up a magazine, but there was nothing in it to interest her.

Suddenly tired, she slumped back into the chair and sat for a long time without moving, trapped inside a darkness that was within herself as well as outside. After a time there was a pop and the fire went out. Fay continued to sit while the room grew colder. Finally, sluggishly, she roused herself to look at the clock on the mantelpiece. It was quarter to eleven. Hugh should have been home long before this; pantomime was usually over by half past nine. He must have gone out drinking, or to a party. Fay could no longer sit still. She jumped to her feet and picked up Elisabeth from her bed, wrapping her in the eiderdown, and carried her across the corridor to the flat opposite. Her neighbour, Annie, answered the door in her dressing gown with her hair in curlers and a smear of cold cream on her face.

"Do you know what time it is?"

"Yes, I do. Hugh's not back, I've got to fetch him."

"Why, for Pete's sake?"

"I just have. Look after Elisabeth for me, will you?" She thrust the bundle towards Annie.

Elisabeth in the eiderdown stirred and woke.

"Leave her if you must but you're wasting your time. Hugh can look after himself."

"I can't go on sitting here." Fay smoothed her daughter's hair from her face, then kissed her cheek.

"Then go to bed."

"It's no good. I need to know what he's doing."

"It's freezing out there, you'll catch your death."

"I'll be alright."

"Well, don't come banging on my door at three o'clock in the morning."

"No, no, she'll stay until morning if you'll have her. Thanks, Annie, you're a pal."

Fay turned and ran out of the building into the cold January night. Annie stayed in the doorway, looking after her, until the child stirred again and she took her inside and tucked her up on the settee.

Hugh had intended to go straight home and miss the party, but they'd sounded so disappointed he said he'd go for half an hour. But the half hour became an hour, and then two hours, and one way and another it was past midnight before he noticed the time, and then it was really too late to disturb Fay and Elisabeth. It was cold outside, and he'd had a drink or two, better to sleep it off and go back in the morning. It was Sunday, he didn't have to work, he'd make it up to them, take them out somewhere. He would stay the night with his friend Johnnie, even though Jessie, one of the dancers, was keen to get close, he was in enough trouble already, what with Fay telling him yesterday she thought she was pregnant again. That was worrying, he didn't want another child. Elisabeth was one thing, good as gold, went off to sleep wherever you put her, but he didn't want another. His little Lizzie. Hugh felt sentimental and thought perhaps he would go home. But Johnnie came up to him and said they were going dancing, and if there was one thing Hugh loved it was dancing. That was how he and Fay had met, just after the War, dancing to forget the gloom of postwar Britain.

So Hugh spent what remained of the night with Johnnie, and when he finally got home found the front door unlocked and the flat empty. While he stood there, wondering, Annie came across the corridor to tell him she had Elisabeth. She told him that Fay had gone out, late at night, and she hadn't seen her since.

"It's bloody freezing out there, you'd better go and look for her."

"Where did she go?"

"Looking for you, she said. Where the hell were you?"

"Stayed the night with Johnnie."

Elisabeth appeared in the doorway, small and pale. Her eyes were pink and her hair tousled. Hugh picked her up and gave her a big hug. Elisabeth rubbed her face against his moustache, wrinkling up her nose as she smelt the stale cigarette smoke and alcohol.

"Sorry, pet, I'll have a wash but first we must find Mummy."

"Christ, Hugh, don't take her out in the cold. I can keep her a bit longer. I've got a friend coming round this afternoon, though, you'll have to take her then."

Hugh ran up the stairs to the street and looked around him. The overnight clouds had cleared and it was bright and frosty. Where should he start? He tried the theatre first, then walked towards Jessie's flat. He knew Fay suspected him of having an affair with Jessie, so she may have been watching out for them. It wasn't true, of course; he may have flirted, and even found himself in her bed on one drunken occasion, but that didn't mean he was having an affair with her. But there was no sign of Fay at either place.

By the afternoon he had run out of ideas. He couldn't think where Fay might have gone. She had a bit of housekeeping money, he thought, perhaps she'd found a room in an hotel somewhere. She had no family, and no friends in this part of the country. They moved about so much, it was difficult to keep up with people. Belatedly, he realised that it must be a lonely existence for her. She worried about Elisabeth, too, blamed herself for her daughter's polio. When she got back he'd make it up to her, take her out dancing. It occurred to him that she might have returned home during the time he'd been out, and hurried home, optimistic again, but the flat was as he'd left it. He went to collect Elisabeth, and said to Annie that he didn't know what to do next.

"It was bloody freezing out there last night. She might have got into trouble. You'd better get the police." Hugh was reluctant to go to the police but Fay had never disappeared for as long as this, and Annie was right, it was very cold. Little drops of ice had formed on his moustache while he was walking about. So he and Elisabeth made their way to the nearest police station, where he told his story. The office on duty didn't seem too concerned. "She'll have found somewhere to stay. No-one in their right minds would stay out in weather like this." Hugh cheered up. The officer took down a few details.

"Occupation?"

"Actor," said Hugh.

"In the panto, are you?"

"That's right."

"Took the grandchildren on Boxing Day. They loved it. We'll find your missus for you, don't worry."

9

Hugh and Elisabeth went home again. By this time it was getting dark, and there didn't seem to be anything else they could do. It was Sunday so Hugh and Elisabeth spent the evening together; Hugh said that Fay had gone away for a little while but would soon be back. He was sure she'd be staying with someone, hadn't thought to leave a note.

Early on Monday morning the police came to tell Hugh that they had found her. There were steps leading to the canal a few streets away that were slippery with moss, and it seemed that she had lost her balance and fallen into the water. In that cold she wouldn't have lasted more than a minute or two, at most. Her body had drifted across the water to the steps at the far side, and lodged there. Hugh said that her heart had always been a little weak.

He went back inside to tell his daughter. She didn't understand at first, but when he said her mother wouldn't be coming back, she started to cry, and Hugh cried with her. They talked about Fay and her prettiness and love of music and tried to understand that she had gone away for ever. To Hugh it seemed like a scene from a play, he couldn't believe that his wife had drowned and now lay dead, in a police mortuary. Elisabeth asked him to tell her stories about her mother which he did, adding details each time. Over time memories of the real woman faded, and were replaced by a Fay of Hugh's imagination, a beautiful woman with a wonderful voice but a weak heart, whose fate was to die young before her talent could be recognised. She would live on in their hearts, said Hugh, they would never forget her. He told her they had each other, and he would always look after her. "I'll look after you too," said Elisabeth.

Hugh had to identify the body. He had to sign papers, and write letters. He had to attend the inquest, and arrange the funeral. He left Elisabeth with Annie when he could, taking her with him when he couldn't. He managed to do all the evening performances, though he had to miss a couple of matinees, one of them the day of the funeral. It seemed to him essential for both him and his daughter that he should work. Start letting people down and the word gets round very quickly that you're unreliable. It wasn't easy finding work.

He thought of asking his family for help, but his parents no longer communicated with him, and his sisters were not much better. He told them what had happened and both sent letters of sympathy although neither of them was able to come to the funeral. They lived in a different part of the country and had small children of their own. Irene

10

had always disapproved of him, like his father, and Phyllis had married a silent, surly kind of fellow, and no longer kept up with him. They hardly knew Fay. Irene did offer to have Elisabeth to stay for a few weeks, but Hugh said no. He couldn't bear the thought of losing her so soon after her mother's death. She was devoted to him. She was as good as gold if he had to take her to the theatre. She'd curl up in a corner of the dressing room and was no trouble at all. She was everyone's pet. Between them, they managed the arm which had been weakened by polio. Jessie, the dancer, taught her some arm movements, and Elisabeth did them every day in order to build up her muscles. They made a bit of a joke about it, experimented, had fun.

After the pantomime finished Hugh found bits of work to keep him going until the summer. If there was no theatre work he helped out in a bar, or tried to sell washing machines. He didn't really mind what he did to fill in. He could sign up for the dole, but they asked too many questions. He got the feeling that they didn't trust actors. In the summer, however, there was revue and rep at holiday resorts. He enjoyed that, and it was good for Elisabeth to be at the seaside. Summer was good. They would be alright.

PATTIE

1

Three years later Although it was cold on top of the cliffs the sky was blue and cloudless, and the children knew that the beach, sheltered from the wind, would be warm. Pattie and Lesley raced down the zig-zag path, shouting to each other as they skidded round corners. Heather followed more decorously, although as they neared the sand she too started to run, forgetting the dignity of her twelve years. Every so often round, worn footholds in the rock face made short cuts between the zig zags of the path, and the children liked to climb down these. At the bottom of one of these short cuts Pattie, more careless than her cousins, stumbled and fell. She got up at once and tried to pretend that she hadn't hurt herself, but the blood trickled down her leg and onto her sandal. Her aunt soon noticed, and hauled her into the ladies' lavatories at the foot of the cliff, where it was always cold and the floor was sandy and notices decreeing that changing into swimwear was forbidden were regularly ignored. The graze was washed with cold water, which stung, and dried with toilet paper. Auntie Irene spoke ominously of Germolene and sticking plaster and the dangers of getting sand into the wound, but Uncle Bertrand, hovering in the doorway, produced a clean white handkerchief which he tied round Pattie's knee, and said that salt water would stop it bleeding. Irene looked doubtful.

"It's not very clean, Bertrand."

Lesley and Heather were dancing about impatiently on the edge of the sand. It was unbearable to be hanging about when other children were already undressed and playing in the sea, or building sand castles. Irene gave in.

"Can we take our sandals off now?" shouted Heather.

"I've already taken mine off!" shrieked Lesley.

They jumped over the muddy brown channel made across the sand by water trickling from a drain pipe in the rock above. Auntie Irene always looked at this with distaste and insisted that they bathed at least two breakwaters away from it, although Uncle Bertrand said that it was nothing worse than an overflow pipe for rainwater. The children, scampering ahead, could not understand the adults' lack of urgency. To them it was vital to get to the beach as early as possible, to secure their 'spot', to glare at other families who threatened to sit too close, to wriggle out of their shorts and into their swim suits and to be ready for anything the day might offer.

14

Today it was donkeys. Pattie's heart began to thump with excitement as soon as she saw them standing meekly in line, heads bowed, bells silent. They were not on this part of the beach every day.

"Look, Lesley," she said, still in her shorts and tee shirt.

Lesley, struggling into her swimsuit, turned her head. "Ooh, yes!" she said, continuing to tie her straps.

"The donkeys are here this morning, Auntie Irene," Pattie tried again. She was longing to have a ride. She had decided that this holiday she would be best at riding donkeys. Her cousins were so much better than her at everything, even though she and Lesley were more or less the same age. Lesley was only five months older. They were better at swimming, running, cricket, throwing balls and catching them, building sand castles - not to mention spelling and sums and all those things. Pattie was not a jealous child, but she longed to be best at something.

It did seem as if she might have a chance with donkeys. Heather was frightened of them, and wouldn't ride. Lesley would ride, because she liked to do everything, but she wasn't keen. Pattie was sure that the donkeys could tell if someone liked them; she had read somewhere that horses always knew if a rider was afraid, and played up; she was sure it would be the same with donkeys, docile though they seemed. She sniffed the air and caught the sharp exciting scent - a mixture of straw, dung, and warm fur. She wondered which one she would ride. She liked the red headband worn by one, but on the other hand the donkey with the green headband was looking invitingly at her. The gipsy boy in charge saw her gazing across. He winked at her. Pattie was about to wink back, then remembered that she had been told it was wrong and that only common children winked. She envied the gipsy boy his life. To spend all day on the beach, looking after donkeys, giving rides to children, disappearing who knew where when dusk fell - it seemed a wonderfully romantic life. There was a woman with him, she seemed old, as brown as the boy but with hard, apple red cheeks. She wore a long, dark skirt and a shawl, and smoked a little pipe. She sat on a stool and took the money.

The green donkey was definitely looking at her. "Auntie..." she said imploringly. Her aunt, settled on the rug with her magazine, looked up and smiled. "Just look at the child. I suppose we'll have no peace until you've had a ride. Are you going, Lesley?"

"I'd rather swim first," mused Lesley, "if we ride in our wet costumes we'll dry in the wind."

"You can't ride wet."

"Why not?"

"They wouldn't like it."

"Who wouldn't?"

"The donkeys."

"They wouldn't know. You sit on a saddle, silly."

Pattie twisted one leg round the other, and scowled.

"You'd better go now if you're going," intervened Uncle Bertrand, for once taking Pattie's side. "You never know, they might have moved on by the time you've had your swim. The sea will stay put. And you'll give it chance to warm up." He gave the short, vigorous laugh he always gave when he amused himself. It was the kind of laugh that encouraged others to join in although afterwards it was not always clear what the joke was. He had made himself comfortable on a folding chair, had rolled up his shirt sleeves and removed his tie, and he was already wearing sandals. He would read the paper for a bit and then he would go for a walk around town. Then he might take them to the amusement arcade and Auntie Irene would look round the shops.

"You're as bad as she is," complained Irene, "you're both afraid the world will collapse if you don't act immediately. It's only half past ten. You'll run out of things to do by twelve."

Pattie could bear no more. "Please, oh please."

"Goodness me, child. Well, go and get it done with. You go too, Lesley. She'll fall off if she's left alone."

Pattie was too excited to respond to the last comment. A little shyly, she and Lesley approached the placid grey line. They handed their sixpences to the gipsy woman, who put them in the pocket of her skirt. The boy held the bridles of the two donkeys they picked out, saying "Whoa there!" and "Steady!", although the animals stood motionless with bowed heads. Bertrand came to help them into the saddles and see them off. Pattie sat on the donkey with the green headband and Lesley on the one with the red band. Each had a felt saddle with a pommel in front for small children to hold on to. Being older, they were allowed to use the reins. "Wait a minute!" said Bertrand, and took a photograph.

The boy walked the donkeys at something uncomfortably between a walk and a trot to the next breakwater, then turned them round and sent them back with a tap from his stick on their rumps. He tapped Lesley's mount first, with the result that it had a slight lead over Pattie's. Although no-one had suggested that it should be a race, Pattie

16

was desperate to get back before her cousin. She jabbed her heels in the donkey's fat sides, Uncle Bertrand's handkerchief falling to her ankle, but it was no good. Lesley, flapping her reins and doing it all wrong, reached the gipsy woman first.

"Hey," the boy came running up behind, "there's no call to go kicking him like that. He won't go no faster."

"He's stupid," muttered Pattie, sliding off into the sand.

"No, he ain't. No more'n you any road."

Lesley intervened, saying thank you in the firm way her mother had of making it clear there was to be no further discussion. She caught up with Pattie as the latter trudged up the beach, kicking the sand as she went.

"Why did you kick the donkey?"

"Didn't."

"Yes you did."

"Didn't."

"Oh," Lesley rolled her eyes and shrugged her shoulders, a gesture she admired in one of her teachers, "I s'pose you wanted yours to beat mine."

"Didn't." The shame of having been criticised by a boy of her own age made Pattie feel hot and miserable. Heather wanted to know what he had said to her. Pattie kicked up more sand and muttered "Nothing," giving a sideways glance at Lesley who looked superior but said nothing. She didn't tell tales.

Lesley and Heather went off to play in the sea. Pattie decided not to join them. She couldn't swim and Heather was always told to keep an eye on her and not let her go in too deep. Heather did not object to this. She liked to have someone under her care and Lesley would not tolerate elder sister bossiness. Pattie sat on the sand and examined her knee. The bleeding had stopped and it wasn't much more than a scratch. Still, she liked the idea of having a bandage and pulled the handkerchief up to tie it more securely round her knee. Then she decided to start building her sandcastle, usually an afternoon activity. If she began now she might just possibly finish at the same time as the others. By the time her cousins were out of the sea and wrapped up in towels she had almost forgotten the donkey incident and was back to her usual sunny self.

Almost but not quite. Pattie's conscience pricked her for the rest of the day. The donkeys had gone but they might be back tomorrow. Pattie could go up to the one with the green headband and give him a pat and say she hadn't meant to hurt him. She hadn't really hurt him, she was sure of that. She had just got carried away with the excitement of racing against Lesley. If she told the donkey, he would understand.

Next morning they were all at breakfast in the small dark dining room of the boarding house where they were staying, one of a series of stone built terraced houses climbing up the hillside. Their landlady, Mrs Rix, was a stout, unsmiling woman who wore skirts that were unfashionably long and a cardigan buttoned up to her chin even in the middle of summer. The family felt that she didn't like visitors, which was odd, as Bertrand said, as that was how she made her living. She frowned at their sandals when they came in from the beach, and looked at the clock as they came down the stairs for breakfast. House rules propped up against the marmalade pot and in the bedrooms reinforced the message. Lights must not be left on, beds should be made, shoes and sandals cleaned of sand before entering the house, and they were expected to vacate their rooms between breakfast and tea time.

The children sniggered behind their hands when they read the notice. Irene frowned at them. She was disappointed. The place had been recommended by a neighbour. "I don't think we'll come here again," she whispered.

"I've stayed in worse," said Bertrand, "during the war." The children rolled their eyes at each other, anticipating another of their father's stories. They couldn't take Mrs Rix seriously. They were on holiday. Everything was fun.

Irene poured the tea, strong for Bertrand and weaker for the girls. She helped herself to two lumps of sugar ("thank goodness it's off ration, one thing I could never get used to was tea without sugar.") Pattie, thinking about what she would say to the donkey, reached absentmindedly into the bowl and took a handful.

"Pattie!" said her aunt, "you are surely not going to put all those in your tea." Obediently, Pattie reached out to put them back.

"You can't put them back," Heather said fastidiously, "they've been in your hand." Pattie hesitated. At that moment Mrs Rix came in to see if they had finished. Quickly, Pattie put her hand under the table and emptied a fistful of sugar lumps into her shorts pocket.

"We'll be another few minutes, thank you, Mrs Rix," said Irene firmly, glaring at the children. Lesley spluttered into her tea and Heather choked on a crumb of toast. Pattie sat, wide eyed. An idea

18

had just come to her. When the others left the room she hung back in order to empty the rest of the sugar bowl into her pocket.

Later that morning they were sitting on the beach in their usual spot. Pattie knelt in the sand with her bucket and spade. The day was hot but she was reluctant to take off her shorts as the pockets were full of sugar lumps. They were intended for the donkeys; Pattie's idea was to make up for kicking the donkey by giving him a treat. However, the donkeys were not on their part of the beach that morning. Pattie looked up the beach as far as the rocks, and down as far as the pier; there were family groups all along the golden sand, and even one or two dogs, but there were no donkeys to be seen. Pattie pounded sand into her bucket with her spade and thought hard.

A little later her opportunity came. Bertrand and Heather went off to the park to have a game of tennis. Irene studied the sky and decided that she would have a swim. She had had the foresight to put her costume on under her dress, so there was no need for awkward manoeuvrings with the towels while she changed. Lesley went down to the water with her. The sea sparkled in the sunshine and the waves rippled, white and foamy, encouraging participation and Irene was seduced; otherwise she might have been suspicious of Pattie's willingness to stay quietly on the sand.

Once they had gone Pattie scrambled to her feet. She looked left towards the rocks which continued as far as she could see; after that the cliffs came down and you couldn't walk any further along the beach; it was unlikely that the donkeys were there. But beyond the pier to the right was the little harbour, and it was just possible that she would find them there. Pattie picked up her sandals and shuffled off through the soft sand. With any luck she'd be there and back in ten minutes and no-one would notice she was gone.

But by the time she had pushed her way through the crowds watching the fishing boats, and been frightened by screaming gulls, wheeling just above her head, climbed over coils of ropes and been shouted at for treading on nets that were drying, and been diverted by stalls selling cockles and whelks, and shops with seaside rock and candyfloss, and finally found the place she was looking for, Pattie was tired. And the donkeys weren't there. Her enthusiasm for giving them a present was abating. She took a few lumps of sugar out of her pocket and crunched them between her teeth.

Maybe they'd be there tomorrow. She could get more sugar. Pattie decided to go back. She thought she could take a short cut through the

19

town, and crossed the road, but almost immediately was attracted by the amusement arcade. She wandered in, entranced by the flashing lights and the noise of levers crashing down and coins dropping into slots. Why hadn't she brought some money with her? She had taken her purse out of her pocket to make room for the sugar. There was a group of boys in their early teens clustered around the fruit machine. Pattie edged closer.

"D'ya want a go?" said one lad.

"Haven't any money," said Pattie. She dug her hands into her pocket to demonstrate and pulled out sugar lumps. The boy laughed.

"How many more of those have you got?"

She turned her pockets inside out to show them. "Not many." She'd eaten more than she thought.

"G'arn, then, here's a penny, have a go."

To Pattie's joy and everyone's surprise three oranges came up at her first attempt and ten pennies tumbled out at the bottom. She had another go, and another, and went on until she had spent all her winnings and was penniless again. The lads wandered off and Pattie realised she was hungry. She'd better get back to the beach.

What with the fruit machine and Woolworths and getting lost and looking into shop windows to see what she might buy her mother as a holiday present, Pattie was a long time getting back and her uncle (long returned from tennis) had alerted the lifeguard to her disappearance. Anxiety followed by relief made them all react in different ways. Irene and Bertrand were angry, Heather tearful and Lesley incredulous. She could not understand how her cousin could be so thoughtless. After the lifeguard had been told that their lost child had returned Irene, taking a deep breath, said "Tell me again why you went off?"

"I wanted to find the donkeys."

"Why?"

"She kicked one of them yesterday," said Lesley.

Pattie hung her head. "I wanted to say sorry. I went to find them."

"Oh, Pattie!" said Irene, softening, and Heather reached over to hug her cousin.

"And to give them some sugar."

"Sugar?"

"I had some in my pocket. But I've eaten it."

"The sugar you took this morning?"

"Yes." Pattie decided she'd better confess. "But there wasn't very much so I took the rest."

"So we'll have Mrs Rix to face when we get back. We'll buy some more. Now Pattie, I want you to promise you won't ever go away like that again without telling anyone. Pattie?"

"Promise," muttered Pattie, fingers crossed behind her back.

"Now we'd better get back. If we hurry we can get to the shops before they close."

2

One wet, drizzly day towards the end of the school holidays Pattie's mother received a letter. Pattie's friends were away and she was bored. She could see the corner of the letter peeping out of the pocket of her mother's overall as Phyllis tidied up the kitchen.

"Who's your letter from?"

"Mind your own business," her mother replied sharply, so that Pattie's curiosity was further whetted and she continued to plague her with questions. Phyllis then denied that there was a letter. When Pattie pointed to the little triangle of blue paper on her mother's hip she pushed it further into her pocket, out of sight, and said that it was a shopping list. Pattie didn't believe her. They had done the shopping the day before. However, she knew from experience that pestering her mother when she was not in a good mood (and she was never in a good mood during school holidays) could lead to banishment to her bedroom, so she allowed herself to be distracted by the arrival of the ice cream van outside the house. When she got back the nylon material covering her mother's hip was smooth and flat, and the mysterious letter had disappeared.

After dinner, Pattie remembered the letter again. Coming up behind her mother as she stood at the sink she affected to give her a big hug, at the same time slipping her hand into the pocket where the letter had been. Phyllis, startled by Pattie's embrace and irritated by the inquisitive little hand, turned round and lashed out at her daughter, catching her on the side of the face with a wet, soapy hand. Pattie, shocked, burst into loud sobs. Phyllis, also shocked, bundled her out of the kitchen and up the stairs to her room, Pattie sobbing and protesting at every step.

"You can just stay there," said Phyllis, guilty and embarrassed.

"Don't let me hear a sound from you. I'll tell you when you can come down."

Pattie stopped crying almost as soon as her mother had left the room. The tears had been the result of surprise rather than real pain or unhappiness. She went to her mirror and fingered the red mark her mother's hand had made. When she pressed it hard it felt sore. Perhaps she would have a bruise tomorrow. Pattie brightened at the thought. She would go and play with Janet who lived round the corner and tell her that her mother had beaten her. She planned how she would tell her story, embroidering as she went on. She wasn't really the child of Allan and Phyllis Mitchell, they had stolen her from a princess and her real home was in a castle. Or else.... Pattie was at the age when fantasies like that no longer satisfied. Perhaps she and Janet would run away. They often thought of doing so and had been building a den in some woods half a mile or so from their houses, where they could hide. They were supposed to be saving money and any food which they were able to smuggle out to the den. The food never lasted very long, as both children were continually hungry, and Pattie in particular was never able to save any pocket money. The little she received was needed for essential items like sweets and comics (and, on one never to be repeated occasion, pink fluorescent socks). There was nothing in the den at present. Pattie wondered about creeping downstairs while her mother was sitting in the lounge with a magazine (her refuge in times of stress), but decided against it. There was no point in upsetting her further. But she did want to know what the letter was about. It had to be important if her mother was keeping it a secret.

Pattie jumped on to her bed and looked out. The surrounding houses had gardens backing on to each other, and the view from Pattie's window was of cultivated greenery. The only exception to this was the garden which backed directly on to theirs, which was neglected and weed-ridden and a constant source of irritation to Pattie's father. From the ground floor the offending garden was mostly hidden from sight by a privet hedge, neatly trimmed on the Mitchell's side, but long and straggly on the other. Although Allan could have reached over and trimmed right across the top, and thus saved himself some aggravation, he refused to do so on the grounds that "he wasn't going to do the lazy blighter's work for him."

Long grass and weeds inevitably held an attraction for Pattie, who found the garden beyond far more interesting than her own. There were a couple of gnarled old apple trees which were excellent for climbing (the lower branches of which could be reached from her fence) and some overgrown bushes which could be converted into a wonderful den. It would be more convenient than the one she and Janet were building in the woods and so overgrown that no-one could see what they were doing.

Pattie wasn't allowed to do anything in her own garden except skip and play hopscotch on the paved area by the back door. She was forever getting into trouble for treading on the flower beds, or leaving her toys on the lawn. Allan liked his garden to be neat and tidy and

23

mowed the lawn at the first sign of a daisy. Pattie thought this was a shame. Her Uncle Bertrand was much more relaxed about gardening, and the Atfields' garden provided plenty of opportunities for making daisy chains, puffing at dandelion clocks, and racing around.

Gazing out at the misty grey-green day, Pattie mused over her life and fate. She longed for adventure. Fingering her bruise, she fell into a day-dream in which she was kidnapped, the bruise being the result of her fight to escape. She was walking along a road and suddenly a big white car stopped and a man jumped out and bundled her in, and there on the back seat was a girl of her own age with auburn hair and green eyes and she was a princess in disguise - or better, she had witnessed the princess being kidnapped and had gone to rescue her and had been kidnapped herself and threatened with death. Pattie, no reader herself, liked the Famous Five and the Secret Seven stories when they were read to her.

But day-dreams gave limited satisfaction and after a while Pattie grew restless again. She wandered disconsolately around her room, which was up in the dormer. Floor and bed were covered with toys and clothes and picture books. Her mother's parting shot before going downstairs had been, "If you want something to do you can tidy your room." If she was very good and did as she was told, perhaps her mother would tell her about the letter. The trouble was she didn't really feel like tidying her room. She picked up an armful of clothes and slung them on the bed, then kicked a teddy bear and a couple of dolls against the wall under the window. She dumped a pile of comics on top of her chest of drawers.

Toys and games were supposed to live in a box in the corner, at the foot of her bed. Sighing heavily, Pattie picked up a jigsaw and some dominoes, and put them in the box. Then she pulled them out again and delved into the box to see if she could find something to amuse herself with. There wasn't much for a child to do on her own. Not for the first time, Pattie wished she had a brother or sister. It was lonely being an only child. She wasn't even allowed a dog. She had a hamster once, but it died. When she was younger she had a pretend dog called Timmy, but she was too old for games like that now. She had made the mistake of telling her cousin Lesley Atfield about Timmy - Lesley had looked at her as if she were mad.

Normally she spent a good deal of time with her cousins, Lesley and her sister Heather, but they were away on holiday, as were most of her friends. Sometimes she went away with them but this week they were visiting some old ladies, aunts of Uncle Bertrand. They must be really old. Pattie wouldn't have wanted to go with them. But she was bored. If only she had a brother, someone who would rescue her when she was kidnapped, or a sister. A little sister would be really nice, because Pattie could pet her and dress her and tell her what to do.

She found a pack of playing cards and decided to play patience. She lay on her tummy on the bed and laid the cards out on the floor. The cards didn't come out (they never did) and she had to resort to cheating. There were degrees of cheating, of course. Picking a card at random from under the pile hardly counted. Going through the pack until you found the card you wanted was a more obvious cheat. Sometimes, though, you had to cheat and cheat before you came out, and somehow winning that way was never entirely satisfactory. Her cousin Heather never cheated. She said it was wrong. Lesley said she didn't cheat but she did slide cards out from underneath sometimes. When challenged, she said it was a new variation of the game which she had just invented. Lesley never got into trouble. Heather did, despite the fact that she didn't cheat. It was funny.

Pattie quickly tired of patience. She went heavily to the door, opened it, and called "Mum-mee! Mum-meeeee!"

Eventually a tired-sounding voice said "What is it?"

"I want to do a wee," hissed Pattie in a penetrating whisper.

"Do you need to tell everyone? Alright, then, you can go."

"Can I come down then?"

"Have you tidied your room?"

"Yes."

"Alright. You can put the kettle on for a cup of tea."

"Goodee." Pattie came tumbling downstairs.

Pattie's father arrived home at half past five. Pattie hoped that her mother would not tell him that she had been sent to her room. She was in trouble anyway because she had failed her 11+ and would be going to the secondary modern school. Her cousins had both passed; Heather already went to the grammar school and Lesley would be starting in the autumn. Pattie didn't mind too much, because Janet and one of her other friends would also be going to the secondary modern. But her father had been angry, accused her of not trying, and sent her to her room, telling her she should be working, not playing out all the time. He hated to see his sister in law's family doing better than his own. Pattie wondered whether to warn her mother not to mention that she had been in trouble, but decided that as her crime had not been very great (in fact she had only a hazy notion of what it had been about) her mother would not trouble her father with it. It was uncomfortable for everyone when Allan was annoyed.

Normally, Allan kissed his wife and then his daughter on returning home from work. Pattie was always disappointed with the way he kissed her, she wanted it to be like it was for her mother - a big hug and then a kiss on the lips, and then his eyes gazing into hers for a few seconds, while all she got was a peck on the cheek. The worst of it was that her mother always laughed and drew back and protested that he was creasing her dress - catch Pattie doing that! She would give as good as she got. Pattie thought that perhaps the kissing had something to do with the fresh powder and lipstick which her mother applied to her face every afternoon at 5pm; she borrowed them one day to see what effect they had, but her mother caught her at it and made her wash it all off again. Phyllis always washed her hands and did her hair and took her overall off before Allan came home.

After tea Phyllis said to Pattie, "You've been in all day. Why don't you go and see if Janet wants to play?"

"It's Thursday." On Thursdays Janet went to Brownies. Pattie used to go, but she thought it was silly and in the end they asked her to leave because she was too disruptive.

"Oh. Well, Sylvia then."

"Sylvia's away. I want to play with Daddy."

"Well, you can't, not tonight. Daddy and I have to talk."

"I can talk too."

"It's not for little girls."

Pattie's face showed what she thought of this. "Mum-my."

"Do what your mother says," barked her father suddenly, from behind the evening paper. He did this sometimes. He'd sit there quietly so that you didn't know what he was thinking, and then he'd suddenly shout at you or cuff your shoulder or send you up to your room. Pattie, who on the whole was good at managing her mother, was constantly being taken by surprise by her father's moods, which she had never learned to recognise, or anticipate.

"Just take yourself off for an hour," said her mother more gently, but with the sharpness of anxiety in her voice. "Don't be too late." Half to herself she added "I do wish Irene and Bertrand were back."

Slouching to the door Pattie stopped. "You're supposed to look after me when they're away," she said. Without looking, she knew that her father's face had darkened. Feeling that she had made her

26

point she hurried out, expecting to feel her father's hand on her shoulder at any minute. Pattie spent a lot of time with her cousins, with a vague understanding that it was because her own parents were unable to cope.

She came home, late, after meeting up with the Simpson twins and a friend of theirs, another boy, from the other end of the estate. The twins were two of the naughtiest boys she knew. They made her exploits seem tame. They put treacle on people's door knobs, they tied cats' tails together, they even set an old barn on fire and the fire brigade had to be called out. Somehow they got away with it, they never got punished like Pattie was punished. Parents and teachers seemed to have given up on them. Sometimes, when Pattie was told that wicked people went to hell, she would look at the twins and find them thriving and know that this couldn't be true. When she was told by her aunt Irene to say her prayers and ask forgiveness for her misdeeds, she thought of the twins again - it was impossible to think of those two on their knees by their beds - and yet they were forgiven over and over again. It was a puzzle. Pattie maintained a healthy disregard for Christian beliefs in sin and retribution.

That evening she came home, tired and dirty from racing down the hillside behind the estate on a tin tray which one of the twins had found in a rubbish tip, and was glad to have her bath then go to bed with her milk and a biscuit. Her father was reading his paper again, and the discussion seemed to be over. Pattie was no longer interested; grown up talk was always boring.

Allan left the house at 7.00 in order to reach work at 7.30. Phyllis got up with him but the routine was that Pattie stayed in bed until she heard him go, when she and her mother had their breakfast. On school days she was expected to get up as soon as he had left the house, but during the holidays she was allowed to stay in bed until 8, if she wished. She rarely did wish, preferring to meet the day head on.

On this occasion she had woken up thinking about the mysterious letter that had arrived the previous day. She was confident that she would tease the secret out of her mother sooner or later. She was up and dressed and ready to fling herself downstairs as soon as she heard the front door bang, but this morning there was a delay while her parents talked on the doorstep. She couldn't quite make out what they were saying. Normally it was a hug and a kiss and a 'be a good girl' and then he was off. It was like last year when they were planning to go away on holiday without her. She knew there was something up then, and she knew now. She remembered how upset she had been when they had finally told her, only a few weeks before they were due to leave, that they were going away on their own. It had been awful when they told her. When it actually happened she hadn't minded too much because she had gone to Whitby with her cousins instead, but she could still remember that awful, empty feeling of being unwanted. It couldn't be that this year because they had had their holidays, but it might be something equally bad. Pattie no longer felt like running downstairs. Instead, she flung herself face down on top of her bed and began to pull the fur out of her teddy bear.

She heard her mother go into the bathroom, and then her bedroom. A few minutes later she came into Pattie's room. "Aren't you up yet? It's a lovely day." She sounded nervous and excited.

"'s'not time yet," Pattie muttered.

"You're usually up and about by now. I hope you're not sickening for something." She gave her forehead an amateurish pat.

"Don't feel very well," said Pattie, brightening. Perhaps if she was ill they wouldn't do the terrible thing they were planning. On the other hand it would mean being confined to bed. Pattie was in a dilemma. So was her mother. She sat on the bed, wrinkling her forehead and casting her eyes about the room. "Oh what have you been doing to your poor bear!" she cried, catching sight of the bald patch and the little pile of fluff on the pillow. "You are a wicked girl. Just look at the poor thing. Why did you do it?"

Pattie looked, and felt terrible. She scorned dolls, but was very fond of her bear. He looked so forlorn. The bald patch started at his left eye and continued over his ear and down towards his shoulder. She didn't know why she had done it.

"You are a destructive child. Whatever makes you do these things? I can't think where you get it from." Phyllis gathered the fluff into a ball. "Now get up and come downstairs. We're going out."

She seemed to have forgotten that Pattie might be ill. Still, the 'we' sounded hopeful. Unless the plan was to leave her somewhere while her mother went off on her own. Well, she wouldn't stay. She'd run away. This time she would really do it. She would take her money box with her just in case.

She trudged downstairs wearing yesterday's crumpled skirt and a stained tee shirt. The table was laid for breakfast and her mother was drinking tea and leafing through a bus timetable.

"I can't make head or tail of this," she said. "We have to go to Bradford anyway. I suppose we can ask when we get there."

Pattie slumped on to a chair. She reached for the packet of Sugar Puffs from her slouched position and clumsily tipped it towards her bowl, in the process spilling some on the table. She heaped sugar on top, added milk, and stirred everything round and round with her spoon.

"Don't mess" Phyllis said automatically.

"I hate them when they go mushy," Pattie growled.

Phyllis looked up from her timetable. "Whatever is the matter with you this morning? I thought you'd like to go out."

Pattie slumped further down in her chair and squashed the remaining Sugar Puffs down with the back of her spoon. "You're going to leave me somewhere."

"Of course I'm not going to leave you," said Phyllis, guiltily aware of the times that she did.

"Now hurry up and eat up those cornflakes."

"They're not cornflakes," her daughter sulked. Then she snivelled

"I thought you were going to leave me behind."

"Don't be silly. Where would I leave you? Everyone's away."

Pattie scrambled down from her chair and flung herself into her mother's arms. Phyllis patted her back. "That letter came and you wouldn't tell me anything about it and you sent me out so you could talk to Daddy."

"Daddy and I have to have grown up talks sometimes. We can't tell you everything."

"Why not?" demanded Pattie, sitting down to her breakfast again. She now spooned Sugar Puffs into her mouth with the determination of someone who had been starved of food for a week.

"You're too young." Pattie pulled a face, but the point had been made so many times that it wasn't worth arguing about.

"Where are we going, then?"

"We're going to see a little girl who's - no, she's younger than you, she must be about seven. She's living with her father and now he's poorly and so we're going to see if we can help. That was the letter that came yesterday."

Pattie thought about this. "Where's her mummy?"

"She doesn't have a mummy. She died a few years ago."

"O-oh." Pattie's heart was wrung by this. It distracted her from reminding her mother that she had lied about the letter. "Can't she come and live with us?"

"Don't be silly," Phyllis said nervously. "Now go and get ready, it's a long way, and for goodness' sake put a clean tee shirt on."

Phyllis, who rarely made journeys on her own, was anxious about this one. Pattie, however, travelled to school every day on the bus and was free with her advice. They caught the bus to Bradford and gradually her mother relaxed and began to tell Pattie more about the people they were going to see, talking absentmindedly, half to herself, a habit she had when she was pre-occupied.

"Your uncle married Fay in London. We didn't go - it was too far and your father never really got on with Hugh. But she wrote and he brought her to see us once - oh, and we all met on holiday one year. Elisabeth was just a baby, it was before the polio, you would have been about three or four. She seemed nice enough, Fay that is. A bit nervy, perhaps. But I don't know." Phyllis shook her head. Pattie had the sense to keep quiet. It would all come out, sooner or later. "It was hard to keep in touch, they were always moving from place to place and Hugh was never much of a letter writer. Marriage didn't seem to make him any more settled.

"They invited us to stay one Christmas, they were living in Manchester and they thought it would be nice for you and Elisabeth - but Allan wasn't keen on driving over the Pennines in winter, and anyway we always spent Christmas with Irene. So we didn't go. I'm sorry, in a way. It was only a year before Fay died. I often wonder - still. What could we have done?

"They got married in 1948, or was it 1949, and the baby was born quite soon after. That makes her - let me see - it's in the letter." She opened her handbag. Pattie knew quite well that her mother had said, at breakfast, that the little girl was seven.

Phyllis searched in her bag for the letter. No hiding it now.

"Seven. She's seven. She's your cousin, Pat."

"My cousin!" said Pattie, marvelling.

"Poor little thing. She can't have had a very happy life. Motherless, and with Hugh for a father. He wouldn't have the first idea about bringing up a child, and then he's always on the move. I suppose he takes her with him."

"Why is he always on the move?"

30

"He's an actor." Pattie's mouth dropped open. "An unsuccessful one. Why he doesn't give it up I'll never know."

"But he might be famous."

"He isn't and he won't be. Don't start thinking about him as if he were a film star."

Pattie, secretly, imagined telling everyone at school that her uncle was a famous actor. Her mother continued to voice her anxieties.

"I wish I could speak to Irene first. She always knows what to do. Although she can sometimes be severe with poor Hugh. Daddy thought we should wait until the weekend, but I can't settle until I've seen him. I wonder if I've done the right thing bringing you, though. You must promise me to behave. Don't say anything until we're on our own again. And don't be surprised - well, he may be living in a poor way. And he sometimes acts a bit oddly."

"What do you mean, oddly?"

"Well - not quite like other people. He's an actor, you see. He, well, he just might have changed. I haven't seen him for a long time. But I wonder if I should have seen him on my own, first."

"But my poor little cousin," Pattie reminded her.

"Yes, of course. You'll be nice to her, won't you, love?"

"Course," said Pattie, hurt.

In the centre of town they had to change buses. Pattie took charge and found an inspector (he was wearing a uniform and peaked cap, so she knew that was who he was) and he told them which bus they needed. Phyllis was nervous so Pattie took her hand and guided her to the right stop, feeling grown up and responsible.

Waiting in the draughty shelter (there was broken glass in the windows and the concrete walls were stained and covered with names and hearts and messages, some quite rude which Pattie hoped her mother wouldn't notice), Phyllis continued to share her thoughts. "We got on well as children, Hugh and I in particular - we were more of an age and Irene was always serious, made us feel silly. She meant well, of course. It's different, being the eldest. Poor Hugh, so much was expected of him, you know, being the only boy. It didn't matter what Irene and I did, we knew we would get married, but Hugh had to have a career, he had to do well, but he just, somehow, couldn't do it. So he tried first one thing, and then another, and each thing he tried he seemed to do just a little bit worse than the last."

31

Their bus arrived at last. Phyllis was concerned to see that the conductor was Pakistani. "What shall we do," she hissed, as he swayed down the aisle towards them, "I don't know where to get off."

"I'll ask him."

"He won't understand."

Pattie shrugged. It didn't embarrass her to try. Phyllis pressed some coins into her hand. "One and a half to Rowlands Road, and ask him to tell us when we get there." Pattie did so and the conductor nodded. Although he had a strange accent he appeared to have no difficulty in understanding them.

"I don't suppose he'll remember," said Phyllis.

The bus took them past row upon row of dreary terraced houses, arranged at right angles to the road. Then they came upon an area of cheap looking shops, some of which were boarded up. The artists who had been at work in the bus shelter had obviously travelled this bus route, and the wooden boarding was covered with writing and pictures. Some of it Pattie couldn't make out and then she decided it was foreign writing - Pakistani, perhaps. It looked exotic and rather wonderful. A bomb site came next, made pretty by wild flowers, and some half derelict houses. It was another world to Pattie, so different from her own neat estate. The bus stopped at a junction, and the conductor came up to them. "Rowlands Road next," he said, and pointed to the left. "We're there, Mummy," said Pattie, digging her mother in the ribs.

They stood on the pavement by the bus stop, taking in their surroundings. Pattie had never seen anywhere like this, and her mother was silent with shock. There was a strange, pungent smell. On the corner three women were talking together, clutching string shopping bags. Their heads were covered and they wore skirts down to the ground, so it was impossible to see how old they were. A couple of men in patched coats sat on a step, smoking. Down an alley, ragged children were playing in the gutter. Two Pakistani men in long coats, with white caps on their heads, waited to cross the road. They also carried string shopping bags. The men on the step looked towards them, and one of them spat.

There was litter everywhere. The few shops were dilapidated, the houses dreary tenements. A few hundred yards down the main road grey smoke and heavy metal gates indicated a factory.

"Well," said Phyllis helplessly.

"We'd better ask."

"Who?"

"Well." Pattie looked around her. "There's a paper shop."

"We'll try there." The shop had yellowing newspapers in the window and a few jars of unappetising looking sweets. Inside were more newspapers and sweets, and packets of cigarettes. There were a couple of shelves of books with the same exotic writing that Pattie had noticed earlier. It was like being in another country. Fancy being in Bradford and not speaking English. However, like the bus conductor the newsagent spoke English, though with a strong accent, and he was able to tell them how to find the street they wanted.

Although far from rich, the Mitchells were able to live in a semi-detached bungalow, with a dormer bedroom and a small garden, in a pleasant estate at the edge of a small country town. Fear of unemployment (it had happened to Allan twice but each time he had managed to find another job within a week) made them careful with money, but they had always been able to afford clothes and shoes for Pattie as she grew up, and a holiday once a year. Allan owned a car. Phyllis worked part-time, partly for interest and partly for the extra money. They put her money in a savings account which they drew on occasionally for things like holidays and Christmas. They had never seen poverty such as they now faced. Even Pattie was quiet, and kept close to her mother.

3

As Pattie and her mother walked away from the main road the sun came out from behind the grey cloud which had hidden it for the last hour or so, their surroundings improved a little, and although the house they were seeking had peeling paintwork and a gate falling off its hinges, the terrace in which it stood looked in reasonably good condition and Pattie felt her mother's hand relax although it retained a hold and Pattie did not try to wriggle free. They pushed open the gate and walked - three steps was all it took - to the front door. Phyllis took a deep breath, and faced her daughter.

"Just be good," she said. She knocked. Nothing happened. After all the build up this was an anti-climax. She knocked again. "I think this is the one," she worried, rummaging in her handbag for the letter. Then they heard shuffling footsteps from inside the house and the door opened. A large woman wearing an overall, down at heel slippers, and rollers in the front of her hair, stood there. She folded her arms and looked at them. "Well?"

"I - we've come to see Mr Lindsey," stammered Phyllis.

"Oh aye?"

"He does live here?"

"If you call it living." The woman continued to stand in the doorway. Pattie lost her fright and stared. She didn't think she'd ever seen anyone so large. Her bust was enormous and she didn't seem to be wearing much underneath because the top buttons of her overall were undone and you could see the cleft between the two mounds of flesh which sagged nearly as far as the middle of her body – you couldn't call it a waist. The woman glared at her and then turned to Phyllis. She said nothing more but held her hand out, palm turned upwards.

"May we come in?" asked Phyllis, puzzled and a little frightened.

"Three weeks."

"What?"

"Three weeks rent he owes me."

"Oh. Well, I'm sure - that is I can't pay you now. I need to talk to him."

"Just give him a message from me," said the woman. "If it's not paid by 5 o'clock tonight he's out. And his daughter. I'm not a charity."

At last she stood aside and let them in. They squeezed past her bulk and into the narrow dingy hall. She jerked her thumb towards a door.

"I'm upstairs," she said, nodding her head towards the stairs. "I'll be waiting." Shocked, Phyllis pushed open the door, forgetting to knock. She stopped short, just inside the room. Pattie pushed her face under her mother's arm, and peered in.

At first she could see nothing. The room was semi-dark, with only a little light filtering through the drawn curtains. There seemed to be a bed, and chairs, and piles of what looked like clothes, and books, and papers. There was a strong smell of food and something else, an odour Pattie didn't recognise. There were other smells, too, of dirt and sweat and unwashed clothes. Pattie gave her mother an imploring look and pulled at her sleeve. She no longer wanted to meet her uncle. She wanted to go home. But her mother ignored her. She closed the door behind her and took a step towards the bed.

"Hugh?" she said, questioningly. The mound on the bed moved. "Hugh, it's Phyllis." The mound sat up and became a body, a man.

"Phyllis?"

"Hugh, oh Hugh, what have you been doing?"

"Oh, you darling girl, you've come! I knew you would!" The voice was thin and cracked. "I can't see you, I think I'm going blind, but I'd know your voice anywhere. I'm ill, you know, Phyllis, quite ill. Thank God you've come. Now, if I can find a cushion I can sit up, I may be able to see you - Lizzie, where are you hiding? I can't see you either. I'm really going blind this time."

"Oh Hugh," said Phyllis, distressed. "It's dark in here, I can't see anything either."

She stepped carefully over to the window, and opened the curtains. "Christ, Phyllis, don't do that! I'm ill I tell you! I can't stand the light."

Phyllis adjusted the curtains so that they were half open. "Shall I get a doctor?"

"No, no," he said. "Don't fuss." Pattie stayed close to the door. Sick people were often irritable, her Auntie Irene had told her that. She had also been told not to stand close to someone who was ill, in case of germs.

The light from the window showed a second mound on the bed, huddled up against Hugh. Pattie, adjusting quickly, said "Is that my cousin?"

The man turned his head and looked at her. Pattie stared back, appraisingly. "Forgive me," (his voice sounded softer now, and less cracked), "my mind's wandering. I'm sorry I didn't see you. You're Phyllis's daughter?"

"Patricia" supplied her mother.

"Of course."

"People call me Pattie."

Her Uncle Hugh looked at her, then smiled. His teeth were brown and discoloured but his lips were red and his eyes very blue. His hair was matted and he had several days stubble on his face, but somehow you forgot all that when he smiled. He reached down and gently shook the small body huddled against his legs. "Lizzie, Lizzie! Your cousin Patricia has come to see you. Darling, say hello to her and then be an angel and fetch me the - the medicine from the cupboard. You know, the bottle with the brown liquid. Come on, darling, Daddy's feeling poorly. He'll be better with the medicine inside him. He needs you to help him."

Elisabeth raised her head from the bed and looked at her visitors. Both Pattie and her mother were shocked by her smallness and fragility. She looked no more than five. She had a pale, thin face, grubby and tear-stained, hazel eyes, and long, matted hair. Pattie did what she was best at. She went up to her cousin and kissed her, germs forgotten. "I've been dying to meet you, ever since Mummy told me," she said. "We've come to spend the day with you. We can play together. What games do you know?" She hesitated before sitting down by her cousin. The smell by the bed was stronger and she wrinkled her nose. Elisabeth drew back a little. Pattie took her hand and bounced it gently up and down, the way she had seen people doing with babies. "We've come all the way from Aireton. We had to get two buses. There was an Indian conductor on the second bus and Mummy didn't think he'd understand but he did. There are a lot of Indians here, aren't there? Have you been on a bus?"

Elisabeth withdrew her hand. Pattie looked accusingly at her uncle. "Why doesn't she say something?"

"She's not used to meeting people. We don't get many visitors."

"I'm not surprised," Pattie said robustly.

"Pattie!" said her mother.

"Well, I can't see anything and it smells. Can't we open a window?"

"Just a little," said her uncle. "Mind you don't open the curtains too wide. My eyes are very weak."

Phyllis, who was nearest, opened the curtains another few inches and with an effort raised the sash window. Hugh lay back and shaded his eyes. The room was revealed as an average sized living room with a bay window at one end and a door at the other. Next to the fireplace was an alcove containing a small table and cupboards. There was a bed and a couple of armchairs. The walls were stained and what they could see of the carpet was threadbare. Pattie couldn't see any toys anywhere.

"Darling," he said to Elisabeth, "my medicine. Hurry, sweetheart." Elisabeth slid off the bed and went out of the door. Hugh sank back on to his pillow. "What a place to come to, hey? Not much, is it. Not much of a welcome for you. I've been down on my luck a bit lately, and then my wretched health, but things will improve. I've just got to get back on my feet."

Elisabeth came back, holding a glass with pale brown liquid in it. "Oh Hugh, do you think you should?" exclaimed Phyllis. "Wouldn't a nice cup of tea be better?"

"It's my medicine, Phyl. It will do me good. Sends the blood circulating around the body. See, I'm perking up already. I'll get up when I've had it and try to clean myself up a bit. If I'd known you were coming..."

"But you asked me."

"I did? Oh, yes, I remember. Had to borrow a stamp from that old battleaxe upstairs. Lizzie took it to the postbox, didn't you darling? Two days ago I thought I was dying. I knew you'd see that I had a decent funeral. Did you tell Allan?"

"Of course I did."

"Irene? I thought she might have come with you."

"They're on holiday."

"So you had to deal with it on your own. Poor Phyl."

"I'm here," interposed Pattie, who felt that she had been out of the conversation for long enough. "Uncle Hugh, what's the matter with Elisabeth's arm?" She had noticed it hanging limply by the little girl's side.

Elisabeth turned and buried her head against her father's shoulder again. He cuddled her to him and gently picked up her wasted left arm. "Polio," he said. "She was only three. We thought she was

37

going to die. It left her with this. But she's learned to cope with it."
Phyllis tutted. "She can do most things except stand on her hands."

"I can stand on my hands," said Pattie. "Against a wall anyway.
I'll show you if you like, only we'll have to go into the garden. There
isn't enough room here."

Hugh smiled. "We don't have a garden here, pet."

Pattie was amazed. She thought everyone had a garden. Theirs was
small but her cousins - her other cousins - had a big one. Her Auntie
Irene was always complaining about the size of it.

"There is a park, though," said Hugh, his voice growing stronger.
He had a nice voice - low and a little husky, with a caressing note in it.
It wasn't like her father who had a strong Yorkshire accent and tended
to speak abruptly, nor like her Uncle Bertrand whose voice was deep
and resonant and followed you around. You somehow wanted to go
on listening to Hugh. "Lizzie, why don't you take your cousin there so
that Phyllis and I can talk."

"Oh, I don't know that we should let them go on their own,"
worried Phyllis. "It's not a very nice neighbourhood."

"They'll be alright. Lizzie knows the way."

"Yes, but - I think I should go with them, Hugh."

Hugh sighed. "If you must. We'll talk when you get back."

Elisabeth didn't want to go.

"Go on," he said, pushing her gently towards the door. "I promise I
won't leave you. I'm going to clean myself up for these nice ladies -
you don't want them to think I can't look any better than this, do you?
Look, if I feel strong enough I might even come to the park to meet
you. Go on, Lizzie." (This last was spoken with a hint of impatience.)

Pattie took her right arm and tugged. "Show me your park,
'lis'beth. I love parks."

"Go on, Lizzie. I'll meet you there."

At last they got her out of the door and on to the street. As they
walked she kept turning around to see if her father was following
them. Once in the park she insisted on remaining in sight of the gate
by which her father would enter. As the park was a small one this was
not difficult. It was a flat rectangle of grass surrounded by a hedge. A
path ran all the way round, and between path and hedge were flower
beds that were littered with fish and chip papers, cigarette cartons and
empty bottles; the few plants were tough and thorny enough to
withstand the attentions of the park's users. There were seats but most
of these were broken and vandalised. In the centre of the grass there

38

was a paddling pool. Pattie ran eagerly towards it but stopped short at the edge. It contained a couple of inches of muddy water, and a quantity of tins, bottles, and broken glass. "Oh – yuk," she said. Ther swings at the far end of the park were being monopolised by a group of teenage boys, and even Pattie was reluctant to join them. Instead the two children and Phyllis sat in a row on one of the few unbroken benches. They were all uncertain what to do next. Phyllis only knew that she had come to see her brother who was in trouble. She had not thought beyond that. But of course it couldn't end there. Something would have to be done. Hugh and Elisabeth couldn't continue living in such squalor. And the rent needed paying.

She tried to find out from Elisabeth how they had been living for the past few years, but Elisabeth was uninformative. She said that they had been living in that house for a few weeks, she thought, and before that in another house not very far away because they had walked with their belongings from one to the other. Before that they had lived a long way away, in another city; they had travelled from there by bus and it had taken all day. She didn't know what it was called. She had a pretty voice, with a touch of her father's huskiness, and no particular accent.

"And do you remember your mummy?" asked Phyllis cautiously. The child screwed up her face into a grimace which indicated that she did not want to talk about this subject. She sat miserably on the edge of the bench, shooting frequent anxious glances at the gate. Phyllis was lost. She had never been very good with children and had no idea how to encourage this one to talk.

Pattie, too, was unusually quiet. Like her mother, she was out of her depth. She had never seen poor people before, not really poor, like her cousin. Elisabeth's coat was too small and her toes poked out of her shoes, where the soles and uppers had parted company. She wore no socks. Her dress was torn and dirty. Pattie didn't like the park where they were sitting. She wasn't sure about her uncle, it was funny talking to a man in bed like that, dirty and unshaven. And he smelt. Mummy had been a bit funny about that, too. But she thought she liked her little cousin, despite the fact that she was so quiet and her face was dirty and her hair needed washing. Oh, and her poor arm. Pattie put her own arms round her and gave her a hug. "Don't worry, we'll look after you," she promised. Elisabeth submitted, but did not respond. Released, she wriggled off the bench. She had seen her father approaching and ran to meet him.

39

Left alone, Pattie and her mother looked at each other. "Well, I don't know," said Phyllis.

"She's ever so pretty," Pattie enthused. "I bet when her hair's washed it will be auburn, like the princess I rescued."

"What princess?" Phyllis asked, mistakenly. Pattie started to tell her.

Hugh came up to them. He had washed and changed, although he hadn't shaved. He wore a pair of clean, worn trousers, a crumpled shirt and threadbare jacket. He waved his hand at the park "Our local beauty spot." He sat down among them on the bench. His eyes were bloodshot. He was very thin. "Don't mind me," he said. "Feeling a little shaky yet. Lightheaded. It may be lack of food. When did we last eat, Lizzie?"

"We had toast last night," Elisabeth said promptly.

"Goodness me," said Phyllis, shocked.

"That's right. We scoffed the last of the sardines, didn't we? Hey ho. Well now, what more can we show our visitors? We can't offer lunch because there's no food in the house. However, I seem to recall a fish and chip shop close by. The only thing is..." he made a pretence of rummaging in his pockets, "I seem to have come out in the wrong jacket. You don't happen to have a few pence, do you Phyl, to buy fish and chips all round? You don't object to fish and chips, I hope? Only the cuisine here is not exactly haute."

He had lost Pattie but she said quickly "I love fish and chips." Phyllis quietly got her purse out of her handbag.

"Well, in that case perhaps you wouldn't mind fetching them," said her uncle, smiling at her. Pattie smiled back. She liked to feel useful.

"Can 'lis'beth come with me?"

"Of course, she can show you the way, can't you my pet?" She tried to cling but he set her down on her feet. After one reproachful look back she walked quietly beside Pattie. Pattie was proud to have been entrusted, not only with the purchase of fish and chips but also with the care of her young cousin. Until now, she had been the youngest in the family and the one everyone else was told to look after. It was nice to be given a responsible role and Pattie took it very seriously, holding on to Elisabeth's hand all the way and taking great care in crossing the road.

There were several people in the shop and they had to wait their turn. Elisabeth stood like a little statue, but Pattie hopped up and down, unable to keep still.

"Your father's funny," she remarked.

Elisabeth's pale face flushed. "No he's not."

"Yes, he is. Why was he in bed when we came? And the room was smelly."

"No it wasn't."

"Yes it was. So are you, though not so bad. I don't s'pose it's your fault. I don't s'pose you can wash yourself very well."

Elisabeth's face grew redder. She began to hit out at Pattie with one fist. "I'm not smelly," she screamed. "Daddy's not funny. I hate you, I hate you, I hate you."

Pattie was amazed. She couldn't think what she had said to upset the child so. She stepped back to avoid the blows and her cousin whirled round and ran out of the shop. The other customers were looking on, amused. Why didn't they stop her? Couldn't they see she was handicapped? For a moment, Pattie was immobilised in a dilemma of responsibilities - food for her uncle or the care of her cousin - before she too ran out of the shop. By this time Elisabeth was several yards ahead of her, running back down the road which led to the park. If she should try to cross the road! Pattie was frightened. She hastened to catch up. Hearing the footsteps behind her, Elisabeth swerved and seemed about to run out into the road. Pattie's knees turned to water and she yelled "Stop! 'Lis'beth, stop!" To her relief a passer-by saw what was happening and caught Elisabeth just as she was about to jump off the pavement. Pattie came panting up. "Oh, thank you, thank you!"

"You want to look after your little sister better than that," said the woman. "Lucky it's not a busy road. Where are you going?" Pattie pointed across the road. ""Mummy's waiting in the park." She picked up the now unresisting Elisabeth and staggered a step or two.

"Don't be silly, you'll both fall over," said the woman. "Just take her hand. What's the matter with her other arm?"

"Polio," said Pattie, on the defensive.

"Oh, the poor little thing." Elisabeth squirmed unhappily.

"I'd better take her back," Pattie said importantly. Clutching Elisabeth's hand, she looked ostentatiously up and down the road before crossing carefully, the woman calling encouragement from the other side.

Safely across, Elisabeth complained "You're hurting," and when Pattie loosened her grip she wrenched herself free and flew into the park to where Phyllis and Hugh were still sitting on the bench, talking.

41

They stopped as the children came running up but looked at them with the funny, distant look which Pattie had often seen in grown ups.

"You've been quick," said her uncle.

Her mother sighed. "These children," she said. "You can never get away from them." Pattie was unruffled, having heard this many times before, but her uncle turned on the charm.

"Joy of our lives, though, Phyl. What would we do without them? Would you rather eat here or take them back to the house?"

"Here, please," said Phyllis quickly.

Pattie stood on one leg. She felt hot inside. During the excitement of the chase, she had forgotten the purpose of the exercise. Now she remembered. She looked imploringly at her mother, who ignored her. She tried to scratch one ankle with her other foot, and nearly over-balanced. Phyllis spread a handkerchief on her knee, and looked expectantly at her daughter. "Well, let's have them."

Pattie hung her head. "Haven't you got them? Was the shop closed?" At this, Pattie raised her head hopefully but in doing so caught Elisabeth's eye and realised that she wouldn't get away with it. "Elisabeth wanted to come back," she said at last. She didn't want to get her cousin into trouble but she really couldn't think of a satisfactory alternative story. Fortunately, her uncle seemed to understand the implications of this. "You didn't run away, did you?" he asked, cuddling her, while she stared at Pattie from within his encircling arm. To Phyllis he said "You see what I mean?" He sounded neither surprised nor angry. Pattie felt relieved, and began to describe their walk and the care she had taken crossing the road.

In the end, they all went to the shop and ate there, standing at a counter, before returning to the house. Pattie and Elisabeth were sent to play in the small back room, so that their parents could talk. "You've been talking all day," protested Pattie, but she was glad of the opportunity to make up the quarrel with her cousin. She chatted non-stop about her school and friends and her cousins. Elisabeth said little, but appeared to be listening from behind the mane of hair which fell in front of her face whenever she bowed her head, which was most of the time.

The back room was sparsely furnished. In amongst her chatter Pattie looked around. Under the window was a sink, and next to it a two-ring gas stove. There was also a cupboard, some shelves, a drop leaf table and two rickety looking chairs. There were some dirty cups and plates on the draining board, but little other sign of food, or food

42

preparation. There was, however, a tall bottle containing a brown liquid which Pattie took to be her uncle's medicine. It certainly seemed to have done him good - he was much brighter than he had been when they first arrived. There were a few books - a couple of Penguins with orange and white covers, and some children's books - proper books, though, not picture books, so of no interest to Pattie. There was a game of Snakes and Ladders, which Elisabeth confided was her father's favourite game. Beyond the kitchen was a lean-to, and beyond that a small square yard. They could have played hop scotch, but Elisabeth didn't think there was any chalk, so they played snakes and ladders instead.

"Where were you when your mummy died?" Pattie asked, running out of talk.

"I don't remember."

"Hm," said Pattie, disbelieving. Elisabeth threw her dice and looked up. She had large, clear, hazel eyes.

"I can remember all sorts of things," Pattie boasted. "I can remember when Daddy had app - append - when he had to go into hospital, and going to Mablethorpe on holiday *and* Whitby and going to Harewood House when I was four and I fell into the water, and I can remember sitting up in my pram when I was one." She looked defiantly at Elisabeth as she said this. Her cousin Heather had said that no-one could remember anything until they were three. "Babies don't have memories," Heather had informed her with the superiority of someone who was 13 and had just started general science at school. "They grow them when they are about 3 or 4. Some people don't grow them until they are six or seven."

Pattie never did find out what Elisabeth's reaction would have been because at this point her mother hurried into the room and told her to hurry and go to the toilet because it was time they left to catch the bus. "I mustn't be late for your father's tea." The toilet was dark and dingy, on a landing up a flight of stairs. Pattie did her business as quickly as she could, hovering above the seat as she had seen her mother do, and wiping herself on the hem of her skirt (which she hadn't seen her mother do) and came down without washing her hands because she couldn't find a wash basin and didn't want to search for one.

They left in a bustle. Phyllis was panicking because she had stayed longer than she had intended. Hugh said he would go with them to the bus stop.

"I'll get something for our tea. And then I suppose I'd better face Mrs Battleaxe. Now, I had a ten bob note yesterday, didn't I? What do you think I've done with it?" Elisabeth stood by, gravely, and said nothing.

"Oh, take this," said Phyllis, fumbling in her bag again. "Come on, do, I'm late enough as it is."

They set off, Elisabeth perched on her father's shoulder. He was relaxed, easy, a different man from the one huddled under the blankets earlier that day. He talked to Pattie, saying that he often thought about her and wondered what she was doing. He asked how old she was and told her that she would be as pretty as her mother when she was a little older. He asked her about her friends and her favourite games and never mentioned school. In short, he charmed her. No grown-up had ever shown such interest in her before.

4

On the bus home she told her mother how much she liked her uncle. "Most people do," said Phyllis. "He was so popular when we were young. A real ladies' man," she said with a laugh.

"What's a ladies' man?"

"Oh - girls liked him a lot. But he could never settle down. Poor Hugh."

"I thought Elisabeth was sweet," enthused Pattie. "I said she could come and play on my swing."

Phyllis fell into a reverie, gazing out of the bus window. Pattie drummed her feet against the seat in front of her until the man sitting there turned and frowned at her. She yawned. She was tired now, and confused. She couldn't understand the family relationships, or why she had only just learned about her uncle and cousin. "I don't understand," she began.

"Mm?"

"I dunno." In her head she planned how she would tell Lesley about her new cousin. This prompted her to ask "Is Elisabeth Lesley's cousin too?"

"Yes, of course. Uncle Hugh is Auntie Irene's brother as well as mine. There are three of us."

"Oh," said Pattie, disappointed. She had hoped that her new cousin would be hers alone. Still, at least she had met her first.

The next day was Saturday. The weather was cloudy and wet, and rain dripped off the gutter and on to the patio below. Pattie remembered that her father had promised to take her swimming the next wet weekend, when he would be unable to garden. She pulled on her shorts and a tee shirt, visited the lavatory and the bathroom, where she splashed a few drops of water on her face and rubbed them off with a towel, then ran into the dining room. Her father was sitting in his armchair, reading the paper and drinking a cup of tea.

"Daddy, it's raining," she announced, having already forgotten his irritability the evening before when she had tried to tell him all about her new uncle and cousin.

"I can see that," he said, uninterested. Phyllis came in from the kitchen, bringing with her the smell of cooking bacon. "Don't worry your father until he's had his breakfast," she warned. Pattie knew that this made sense. On work days he hurried; at the weekends he liked to take his time.

"Do you want a bacon sandwich?" Phyllis asked Pattie.

"Yes, please."

"Sit at the table, then."

Pattie made a superhuman effort to keep quiet all through breakfast. Her mother, sounding nervous, chatted about this and that, and her father made a few brusque comments about the contents of his newspaper and the state of the world. Pattie waited impatiently until he had reached his third and final cup of tea, and then burst out:

"You said you'd take me swimming next time it rained." There was no response. "Daddy! You promised."

"Pattie," her mother said apprehensively. Her father lowered his paper and looked at her.

"Are you shouting at me?"

"No, but Daddy you promised. You said you'd take me swimming. You did, you did."

"Well, now I'm unpromising. I can't take you today. I'm sorry," he said, looking at her stricken face. "I'll take you another time. I've got other things to do today, things I didn't expect to have to do. Let that be an end of it," he warned as Pattie raised her voice again.

"You said," she drooped over the table. "You promised."

"Stop whining."

He was not always irritable - he could be jolly, and play games with her, and make plans. When he was in a good mood he would wink at her and grin and make her feel as if it was the two of them caught up in some big game that only they understood. She liked it best when he treated her and her mother as equals, and would stand with his arms around them both and call them "My girls". Only somehow Pattie always spoiled it by being too noisy or boisterous, or just being where she wasn't wanted. She knew that her mother came first for Allan, and always would. She came next, he was her father, of course he loved her. It was just now that she was growing up he seemed to find her difficult. And failing her 11+ had been stupid – she just hadn't tried. Uncle Bertrand said she wasn't stupid, she could have passed. But somehow she couldn't take school and exams seriously.

Phyllis got up to clear the table. "Give me a hand, love. Daddy and I have to go out this afternoon, that's why he can't take you swimming."

"Oh, can I come?"

Phyllis hesitated. "No, love, not this time. I'll pop across and talk to Mrs Hanson and see if you can play with Janet again. We won't be very long."

Pattie stuck out her lower lip. "Where're you going?"

Phyllis hesitated again. She looked towards the dining room but there was no sound other than the rustle of Allan's newspaper. "Come on, bring those plates through. We're going to see your uncle in Bradford again. But it's all going to be grown-up talk. You wouldn't be interested."

"Yes, I would. I could play with Elis'beth. Let me come, oh please, *please*."

"Daddy thinks it's best for you to stay at home this time. No, don't go and pester him. Don't argue, just do what we want for a change. Now dry those dishes, there's a good girl."

Pattie sulked. As she went into the dining room to collect the tea pot she threw a parting shot:

"I don't see why Daddy can't take me swimming before you go to Bradford."

"What's that?" Allan half rose to his feet. Pattie scurried out of the room.

Pattie sulked and moped around most of the morning and complained that she was bored. Allan escaped by going into the garage and tinkering with the car; by twelve o'clock Phyllis had had enough. She said, "I shall be glad when Irene and family get back. You seem to behave better when you're with them. She knows how to bring up children and I don't, I suppose. She was trained to deal with children. Half the time I just don't know what to do with you."

Pattie had heard this many times before. Much as she loved her parents, somehow things were easier when she was with the Atfields. Her aunt Irene had a way of being firm without getting angry or upset. Pattie needed activity and people, and she longed for a baby sister of her own. As that failed to materialise, she cooed over other people's children, picking them up and lavishing kisses upon them. Once she was caught lifting a baby out of its pram and was surprised and alarmed when told by the distraught mother what a wicked girl she was. She hadn't intended any harm. Her father, out of his depth, spanked her severely and sent her to bed where she spent the night, miserable and bewildered. A couple of days later, however, she was back on form, demanding to know where babies came from and how soon she could have one of her own. Phyllis, in a flap, telephoned her

47

sister for advice. Irene told her to give a simplified version of the truth.

"How simplified?"

"Well," said Irene, slightly embarrassed, "just that babies grow in mummies' tummies - I wouldn't bring fathers into it yet."

"But she's asking when she can have one."

"Well that's easy, just tell her she can't until she's grown up. And you have to be married first."

"She'll want to know why."

"There are all sorts of things she can't do until she's grown up - driving, or voting, for example. Really, Phyl, she's your child, you must be firm with her."

Pattie knew without being able to put it into words that her mother and father had special feelings for each other, and that these feelings left little space for her. Often she came into the room to find her mother sitting on Allan's knee. Phyllis would then get to her feet, smooth down her skirt and get on with something; Allan would go back to his paper. Pattie was left feeling unwanted. Her Uncle Bertrand was also devoted to her aunt, Irene, whom he praised extravagantly as a pearl beyond price, but somehow that didn't mean he didn't have time for his own children. With Uncle Bertie a lot of it was talk, he had the gift of the gab, according to Allan. But it made you feel good.

Pattie was delighted to have found a new cousin. She was so sweet - just like the little sister Pattie had been yearning for. She had liked her new uncle too - quite. He was a bit funny, not like her father or Uncle Bertrand - more like a child, really. You could tell him things and he wouldn't be shocked - he'd just laugh. She wondered what was going on in Bradford. She felt as if she were being left out of everything these days - first the Atfields going off on holiday without her, and now this. If they wouldn't let her play with Elisabeth she'd run away, she really would. Then they'd be sorry.

She went to Janet's, but came back home early because she didn't want to miss her parents when they returned. She moped in her room, scratching away with her nail at a torn bit of wallpaper, knowing that her mother would be angry with her for making it worse, but unable to stop herself. The paper was cream, with pink flowers on it, and Pattie was busily working round one of the flowers. She thought she could paint the wall underneath pink, so that no-one would know the difference.

48

At last they came home. She heard the front door open and close, and her father put the car away. She waited. She heard the door open and her mother's voice. She went to the top of the narrow staircase and looked down. The doors were closed so she couldn't tell which room they were in. There was a suitcase in the hall. That was funny. She hurried down to look at it, forgetting her sulk. It was a battered old brown suitcase, with tape around the handle. She didn't recognise it.

"Mummy," she shouted, trying the handle to the lounge door.

Her mother came out of the kitchen. "Oh, there you are, love." She sounded nervous again. "Why aren't you still at Janet's? Daddy is just putting the car away then he was going round to fetch you." She went to the door and called, "It's alright, Allan, she's here."

"Whose is that case?" enquired Pattie, pushing into the kitchen.

"We're having a visitor to stay for a few days," her mother told her, but it really wasn't necessary because Pattie could see Elisabeth sitting at the kitchen table, sucking her thumb, her hazel eyes big and scared but somehow defiant, like Janet's new little spaniel puppy when he had just arrived and they had all crowded round to look at him. He was in a strange house and there were too many people and he missed his mother. That's what Janet's daddy had said.

All this passed through Pattie's head while she was exclaiming delightedly about Elisabeth's unexpected arrival.

"Will you stay for a really long time? Where's your daddy? Oh I hope you can stay for ages. It'll be like having a little sister. Why don't you stay here always? Gosh, I prayed for a little sister. I promised to go to Sunday School if I got one. Do you go to Sunday School? Lesley and Heather do. Have you met them? No, of course, they're away. They've gone to see their other family. They don't take me when they go there. Mummy, is Elisabeth their cousin too? Or just mine?"

"Theirs too, of course. I told you before."

"Oh. Still, I met you first. She's very quiet, isn't she?"

Elisabeth had been gazing at Pattie. Now she bowed her head and studied the table cloth. "I expect she's tired."

"Where's uncle – where's her daddy?"

"He's gone away for a few days to find a job. It was difficult to do that with Elisabeth – she's too young to be left alone. When he's found one he'll come back for her."

"And take her away again?"

"Yes."

"Aaah. Where's he gone?"

"London, I think."

"London!" Pattie was impressed. Uncle Bertrand was the only other person she knew who had been to London.

"Set the table for me, will you? We're all tired and we shall have to put the folding bed up in your room after tea. I hope I've got enough sheets."

"Ooh, is she going to sleep in my room?"

"There's nowhere else. But you must be good and not keep her awake with your chatter – she's a lot younger than you, don't forget."

"Shall I use the best tea service?" asked Pattie, looking at it longingly. This was made of fluted bone china, with gold handles and a waterlily pattern in green and gold, with blobs of real orange paint for stamens. It had belonged to Allan's grandmother and was kept locked away in the china cabinet in the lounge and only brought out on special occasions.

"Good heavens no. Whatever for?"

"We have a visitor," Pattie reminded her with dignity.

"She's only a little girl. The rosebud set will do."

"What are we having?"

"Fish. We called in at Rawson market on the way home."

Pattie laid the table in her usual haphazard manner, clattering knives and forks onto the table and pushing plates into any available space. Unnoticed at first, Elisabeth straightened those within reach. "Oh, look," said Pattie, seeing. "Gosh, isn't she neat!"

"She's obviously a tidy little girl," said Phyllis, smiling. "Would you straighten the rest for me, please?" Elisabeth stepped cautiously from her chair and moved round the table, smoothing the cloth and setting everything straight. Phyllis, catching Pattie's eye, breathed a sigh of relief. Elisabeth's silence and passivity had been unnerving.

"Where's Daddy?"

"He'll be listening to the football results. Don't disturb him until we're ready."

Pattie could tell from her mother's voice that things were not quite right. She was tempted to disobey and run in, throwing her arms round his neck, but it would be too awful if he shouted at her in front of Elisabeth. She wondered why her father had these times when he was not to be disturbed. Uncle Bertrand never minded children being with him. In fact, he liked them to be there. He often said so.

The kitchen was a good size, and they ate most of their meals there, although there was a dining alcove in the lounge. It was clean and bright, with yellow and white wallpaper and blue painted cupboards. There was a porch by the back door, which prevented draughts coming into the house. Phyllis was a nervous cook. This evening, she was frying in breadcrumbs the fish bought at the market. Her face was pink and spotted with perspiration as she stood over the frying pan. She was used to having three fillets to fry - four was an awkward number and would not fit into the frying pan. She hoped that Elisabeth would not be fussy and refuse to eat.

"Pattie, open the window and let out some of these cooking smells. And then tell Daddy we're ready."

Pattie went dancing in. "Daddy, tea's ready. Daddy!"

"Alright, alright, I'm coming."

"Daddy, Elisabeth's here. Isn't that fun? She's going to sleep in my room. It will be just like having a little sister."

"She might keep you out of mischief," he grudgingly admitted, getting to his feet and switching off the wireless.

"Come on, Daddy."

Pattie laughed and chattered all through the meal. Nobody else had much to say. Allan always ate in silence. Elisabeth pecked at her food. Phyllis worried and when the meal was over she told the two girls to go up to Pattie's room to play quietly while she and Allan finished their meal with a cup of tea in the living room.

Upstairs, Elisabeth sat on the floor against Pattie's bed and sucked her thumb. Her hair, which had been combed, hung over her face. Pattie got out all her toys and games to tempt her cousin, but there was no response. Her resourcefulness failed her and she ran downstairs to the living room for advice. Her mother was sitting on the rug in front of the fire, leaning against her father's knee. He was stroking her hair.

"Pattie, I told you to play upstairs."

"Yes, but she won't. She won't say anything. What'll I do?"

"Oh dear," Phyllis said.

"Just leave her," Allan said. "She'll come round."

"Well," said Phyllis, getting to her feet. Allan picked up his paper. "What is she doing?"

"Just sitting there. What's the matter with her, mummy?"

"She's unhappy because Hugh has gone away. She's not sure when he's coming back."

"She's got us."

51

"It's not the same."

They went upstairs together. Elisabeth was still sitting on the floor, but she had pulled a book towards her and was turning over the pages.

"Oh, it's that boring school story, the one without any pictures in it. She's reading it."

"She can't read, she's too young."

"Yes, I can," said Elisabeth, speaking for the first time. "I can read better than children twice my age. Daddy said so."

"Well, that's good," Phyllis said helplessly. "Well, look, Pattie, just get some books out for her tonight. Put the other things away, and then I'll ask Daddy to put up the spare bed."

Phyllis decided to give Elisabeth a bath while Allan was busy with the bed. It was a long time since it had been used, and she knew he hated being watched when he was unsure of what he was doing. Pattie, torn between the two activities, was persuaded by her mother to accompany her to the bathroom.

Elisabeth did not wish to be given a bath. She fought, silently, as Phyllis undressed her. Pattie tried to help but only made matters worse. She and her mother stood in the doorway and regarded the unhappy child with her dress around her neck and her vest twisted over one arm. Elisabeth stood by the side of the bath with her lips turned in and defiance in every inch of her small body.

"If we take her shoes off she won't kick so hard," advised Pattie. Phyllis had, in fact, received a nasty kick on the shin.

"Or p'raps she'll undress herself."

They stared at her. Elisabeth scowled back.

"P'raps she doesn't like us watching her."

"I'm not leaving her here on her own. It's not safe. If she doesn't hurry up the water will be cold."

"P'raps if I get in she'll join me."

"I doubt it. Well, you might as well have one. I don't want to waste this hot water."

"You mustn't watch," said Pattie, suddenly modest.

"Don't you start! Look, I'm going to leave you for a few minutes to see how Daddy's getting on with the bed. Here's your nightie, and here's one for Elisabeth. See if you can persuade her to wash if she won't bathe. And for heaven's sake keep an eye on her. I'll leave the door ajar."

When she had gone Pattie turned her back on her cousin and wriggled out of her clothes. With much preliminary squealing and squawking she finally sat down in the bath.

"Gosh it's lovely and warm. Why don't you get in, there's lots of room. Oh, I haven't got Horace. Horace is a duck. I always have him in my bath. There'd be three of us then, but I expect there'd be room. This is my flannel. There's another one, I expect Mummy got it out for you. She's nice, my mummy, isn't she? She works, you know. She'll have to go on Monday, she's taken all her holiday. I wonder what we'll do? I usually go to Auntie Irene's but they're on holiday and they're not back yet. We'll go when they get back. It's nice there. They have a swing and a sandpit and a smashing tree, and Uncle Bertrand is going to make us a tree house. Then we can all sit up there and no-one will know where we are. Whee!" Pattie launched herself down the bath, sending water slurping over the side. She then lost her balance and slipped backwards in the water, wetting her hair.

Elisabeth took advantage of Pattie's loss of attention to get out of her remaining clothes and into Pattie's spare nightdress, which swamped her tiny figure. She picked up the face cloth that had been pointed out to her, wet it and soaped it and cleaned her hands and face. She left the bathroom while Pattie was still splashing and spluttering. By the time Pattie was out of the bath and into her nightdress, Elisabeth had climbed into the bed which had been made up for her and was lying, a tight little ball, under the bedclothes. Phyllis sat on Pattie's bed, watching her.

Pattie went downstairs with her mother for some milk and a biscuit. She was not hurt that Elisabeth had rejected her attempts at friendship. She could see that she was unhappy - she was only a baby, after all. And she hadn't like her father going off and leaving her. Pattie was used to spending time in other people's houses but she had been upset when her parents had gone off to Spain last year without her. Not very upset, but a bit. They had never left her for a fortnight before. She had kept hoping that they would cut short their holiday and appear before her on the beach at Whitby. And Elisabeth didn't know when her father was coming back. It wasn't fair. He should have taken her. She was very good when she was with him.

She thought about this as she tried to lap up her milk with her tongue. It ought to be possible, cats and dogs could do it, but although she practised frequently she never succeeded. This time, as usual, she dribbled milk down her dressing gown.

"Oh Pattie," said Phyllis, rubbing her daughter's bony chest with her handkerchief.

"She needs a bib," Allan said.

At last she trailed to bed, under threat of severe punishment if she disturbed Elisabeth by chattering. Once upstairs, her cousin's motionless body did not encourage conversation.

"''Night, 'lisabeth," she said experimentally, but there was no response.

The next day, Sunday, was little better. The whole family, Allan included, put itself out to amuse their visitor. Pattie set out all her toys and games; Phyllis showed her how to make gingerbread men; and Allan took them all for a drive into the countryside in the afternoon. It was no good. Elisabeth remained locked inside herself. She said 'Please' and 'Thank you' politely enough, and spoke when it was necessary, but that was all. By tea time Pattie was bewildered, Phyllis fretful, and Allan annoyed.

5

When Pattie woke next morning to the sound of rain on the dormer window she saw Elisabeth sitting bolt upright in bed, her eyes red and wet. Pattie yawned and stretched and wriggled for a few minutes. "You're awake early," she then said. She tried to remember the sort of thing her mother or Aunt Irene might say. "Did you sleep well?"

"I want to see my daddy," Elisabeth said.

"He's gone to London."

"I'll go to London."

"You can't. It's ever so far. Don't cry, he'll come back for you when he's found a job. You're having a holiday with us." Elisabeth hunched over her knees, her face tight and closed as it had been yesterday.

Pattie lay in bed and thought. This was a real life drama, better than imaginary kidnapped princesses, but more difficult to resolve. If only Elisabeth could see her father, so he could tell her that everything would be all right. It would be difficult not to believe anything Uncle Hugh said, he had such a jolly way of talking and a nice smile. Perhaps he would telephone, but he might not have their number. Then Pattie had her bright idea. If Elisabeth wanted to see her daddy, she would take her there. Elisabeth was too young to go alone, that was clear. But she, Pattie, was older and responsible and could take her. It was easy to go to London - you got a train from Leeds. Uncle Bertrand had been there.

"How much money have you got?"

"I haven't any."

"Oh. I think I've got 3s 6d in my piggy bank."

She pictured the scene as she brought Elisabeth and her father together. They would hug each other and maybe he would swing her round and then they would turn to Pattie and say how wonderful she was, and all the people round about would want to know what had happened and there would be a reporter there from the Telegraph and Argus and the next day there would be headlines: "Father and daughter re-united! 'Pattie saved our lives,' says grateful father." In her rush of sympathy for her little cousin Pattie had forgotten that Hugh had asked her parents to look after Elisabeth.

"D'you want to see your father very much?"

Elisabeth was still hunched over, her good arm hugging her knees, her left arm laid on top

55

"Yes."

"Well, I'll take you," Pattie announced grandly.

"How?"

"We'll get a train. It's easy. But don't say a word to anyone. Do you know where he's gone?"

"No. But I've got Auntie Annie's address. We've stayed with her before."

"You've been to London before?" Pattie was impressed.

"We used to live there. Before Mummy died."

"You can't remember. You were too young."

"I do remember. We went down a lot of steps to our house, and the door was red."

"You went *down* a lot of steps. That sounds funny."

"We did."

Pattie swung her legs out of bed. "Come on, it's time to get up. Mummy's going to work today. Let's hope she hasn't arranged for us to go anywhere this morning. We'll say we're just going to play quietly. She doesn't like leaving me but she does it."

Phyllis was already having her breakfast when they came down, worrying about getting to work on time and fretting about leaving the two girls. "I'd forgotten that Irene and Bertrand wouldn't be home until today. I know I should have spoken to Mrs Hanson yesterday. I haven't got time now. Pattie, go round at about ten and see if she can have you until dinner time. And do take care of Elisabeth. Don't let her out of your sight. Oh dear, I wonder if I should telephone and say I can't come in. I would, only I'm just back from holiday, it doesn't seem right."

"We'll be alright," said Pattie. "Elisabeth's feeling better."

Phyllis still looked uncertain. "Irene's back today but I don't know what time. I'll be back at dinner time and if I can get away earlier I will. I can make up the time later."

"We'll be alright," repeated Pattie. "Honestly, Mummy. You've left me before."

"I don't suppose I should."

"Auntie Irene does."

"Only when Heather is there, and she's older. Oh dear, I'd better go. I could ring to make sure you're alright but they don't like you making personal calls. I'll go in for an hour or so, if I can find someone to cover I'll come right back."

Finally she left. Pattie gave an exaggerated sigh of relief. "Whew! Now we can get going. We'll go to Leeds anyway, I know how to do that. We'll just have to see if we can find a London train - if we can, that's fine, if not we'll come back and try again another time. Maybe Uncle Bertrand will take you. Anyway, we'll have a bash. We'll need some money to get to Leeds. You'd better stay here while I see what I can find." Briefly, it occurred to Pattie that it would be sensible to wait for Uncle Bertrand and ask him to take them to London. But Pattie felt that her cousin was her project, and she wanted to be the one to make Elisabeth happy.

Pattie's piggy bank was in the form of a house made out of cardboard with a slot in one of the chimneys through which you posted money. It was easy to raid by means of a sliding panel underneath. Previous raids had, however, reduced its contents to two shillings and threepence. She then tried her parents' bedroom. Phyllis had taken her purse to work with her (what a pity Pattie hadn't made her plan the day before!) but there was a heap of pennies, eight in all, on the dressing table. And a threepenny piece. Allan hated weighing down his pockets with coins. She then opened the wardrobe and felt in her father's pockets, and was rewarded with one sixpence and one more threepenny bit. That made three and eightpence so far. That ought to be enough to get them to Leeds and back, but she didn't think it would be enough for the train to London. She went back into the kitchen, where Elisabeth had washed up the breakfast things and was putting them away.

"Gosh, that's good," said Pattie. "Mummy will be pleased." She opened the kitchen drawer, so called because it held all the odds and ends - string, rubber bands, notes for the milkman, receipts, shopping lists, pencils, rubbers, etc. Phyllis also kept an old purse with money in it for the milkman and the window cleaner, so that she would not be caught short when they called. Clearly, neither had called for some time, for in the purse Pattie found a ten shilling note, and four half-crowns.

Now they had plenty of money. After some hesitation, Pattie replaced one of the half-crowns, and then a second one. She was guiltily aware that some might call what she was doing stealing. She sent Elisabeth off to get ready

At last they set off. Pattie carried a brown paper bag containing two apples, some biscuits, and a piece of cake in one hand, and her favourite pink plastic handbag in the other. Elisabeth, having with difficulty been persuaded to leave her suitcase behind, had nothing except a scrap of paper with an address on it, stuck in the top of her vest. After some thought, Pattie had decided that they should go to Leeds by train. It was more expensive than the bus, and they would have to walk to the local station, but it would take them into the main railway station at Leeds.

She was taken aback to find that the ticket clerk at the local station was Mr Moffatt, who lived a few doors away from them. He was a small, balding man with a grey moustache, who when he wasn't working was usually to be seen digging his garden or mowing the lawn. In the summer he worked with his sleeves rolled up and a handkerchief, knotted at each corner, keeping the sun off his bald patch. He and Allan were moderately friendly. In his station uniform he looked bigger and more imposing, and Pattie felt a little nervous as he asked her where she was going.

"We're going to Leeds," she said cautiously. "To see my uncle," she added hopefully.

"On your own?" Mr Moffatt frowned at her over his glasses.

"He'll meet us there."

"And who's this?"

"My cousin."

To her relief he accepted this, and issued them with two day return tickets. She felt pleased that she had been able to tell the truth - or a version of it. It seemed to augur well for the rest of the adventure. Not that telling lies troubled Pattie. She couldn't understand why grown ups thought them so important. A lie to Pattie was only a variation of the truth - something that might have been true had other things been different. For example, playing with Janet a couple of weeks ago was something she might have done - in fact, she had planned to do so. But on the way to her friend's house she had met up with Robin and Simon carrying cardboard boxes on which they planned to slide down the steep slope known as the Bank near their home. This seemed more fun, so Pattie had joined them, but somehow it had seemed easier afterwards to tell her parents that she had played with Janet. She couldn't see that it mattered one way or the other. When her father found out, however, he saw it very differently, and she was smacked and sent to bed.

They waited a several minutes on the platform for the train to arrive. Elisabeth was silent, as usual. Pattie shifted and fidgeted and shuffled her sandals on the hot tarmac. She felt as if Mr Moffat were watching everything she did. Working at the railway station he saw everyone's comings and goings, which he passed on to his wife, a woman who liked to know everything that was going on and often stood at her husband's shoulder as he dug his garden, keeping an eye on the estate. Her father called ha busybody.

At last the train arrived, snaking down the track, and pulled up alongside their platform. The two girls scrambled in, and found seats. "Whew," said Pattie, feeling hot and bothered. "Golly gosh. They can't stop us now."

"Why should they?" asked Elisabeth.

"Well - grown ups are funny. They like to stop children doing things."

If Aireton station had been a nerve-wracking experience, Leeds was a thousand times worse. Pattie had been before, but only with a grown-up holding her tightly by the hand. It was big, crowded, dirty and noisy. An engine on a nearby platform let out a loud hiss of steam, and Pattie and Elisabeth nearly jumped out of their skins. They clutched each other's hands. Pattie wished she had never had her bright idea. Everything was black, grimy, and very, very big. The roof, constructed of iron girders and sooty glass, reared up into the skies. The trains were terrifyingly large. Two porters came by, pulling a trolley laden with parcels. The two girls stepped out of their way and collided with an irritable couple struggling with suitcases. Everyone seemed in a hurry, rushing about in all directions.

Pattie was crushed by it all. She wanted to go back home. She saw a man who looked like an official walking down the platform. He wore a peaked cap with gold braid on it, and he looked nicer than Mr Moffat. Still clutching Elisabeth's hand she moved towards him, meaning to ask him how they could get back to Aireton. However, a well dressed lady, in high heels and a little feathered hat, reached him first.

"We want the London train," she said in a clear voice that carried above the general din. "Which platform for the London train?"

"You'll want number 5. Due out at" (he consulted his watch) "ten twenty-five."

"Thank you. Come on, Ted," and a middle aged gentleman in a dark suit moved down the platform with her.

"Come on," hissed Pattie, ready for adventure again, and they followed the couple, walking as close as they dared so that it would look as if they were all one family. They pushed through the barrier with a crowd of other people, and were not stopped. A train was already standing on platform number 5. The well dressed lady checked with a porter that it was the London train, but they could see the stickers on the windows saying LEEDS-WAKEFIELD-DONCASTER-GRANTHAM-PETERBOROUGH-LONDON KING'S CROSS. Pattie felt a real thrill, a mixture of excitement and apprehension. She sniffed the air, and found the metallic, sooty smell of the railway station stimulating. "C'm'on," she said again, and they crowded close to the couple they were following. The gentleman helped his wife up the steps, then noticed the children standing next to him. "Are you getting on? Up you go," and he lifted first Elisabeth and then Pattie on to the train. Pattie was delighted. Anyone watching would think they were all one family. She beamed her thanks, but thought it best to abandon their escorts for the journey itself, as they might start asking awkward questions, so pushed Elisabeth ahead of her down the train in the opposite direction. It was not crowded, and they found an empty compartment. Pattie put her coat on one of the empty seats so that it would look as if someone was sitting there, and she and Elisabeth sat opposite. The trick worked, people glanced at the seats and then moved on. "Phew" said Pattie. A minute or two later they could hear a loud but unclear voice making an announcement, followed by a whistle. There was a hiss, a cloud of steam obscured the platform, then the train jerked forward and pulled out of the station. They were off. Pattie settled back in her seat, feeling pleased with herself and her adventure. She thought she was managing extremely well. The Famous Five would be proud to have her join them.

The first part of the journey was quite interesting as they travelled through the suburbs, past houses and gardens and allotments. They saw playing fields, a school, and an open space with some boys flying a kite. It all looked much more fun than Aireton.

At Wakefield more people got on. Two teenagers sat down opposite the children, tossing the coat onto the seat next to Pattie. The boy had greased back hair with long side burns, and he wore a jacket with a velvet collar and a thin black tie. Pattie guessed he was a teddy boy. His companion had a blonde bouffant hairdo and bright blue eyeshadow. Her eyeliner turned sharply upwards at the corners of her eyes. She wore a sleeveless summer blouse and a full skirt. They both smoked. The two girls shrank back in their seats and were very quiet.

The teenagers got off the train at Doncaster. "Maybe this is London," said Pattie hopefully, but Elisabeth shook her head. A middle-aged couple took the seats opposite before Pattie had a chance to put the coat back. They spent some time arranging themselves and their luggage, the woman directing the man as to which bag was to go under the seat, which on top, and which was to stay with them. Then the sandwiches and the thermos flask had to be extracted, together with the magazines, the newspaper, and the lady's knitting.

"Well, we've got a long journey ahead of us," she said, speaking to her husband but looking round as if to include anyone in the carriage who might be interested. "You might as well be comfortable." Settled, her gaze fell on the two girls. "Are you two travelling alone?" she asked.

"Um - yes," said Pattie, after weighing up several different responses.

"You're very young. Aren't your parents worried about sending you off on your own?"

"Oh, we're being met," Pattie improvised.

"And someone saw you on to the train, I suppose. Well you can't come to much harm on a train like this. The ticket inspectors always keep an eye on things. Are you going all the way?"

"Yes," Pattie said. It seemed safest.

"We're going to visit our daughter," the lady confided. "She and her husband have just bought a house in Kent. It's the first time we've been there, isn't it, Harold? It's a long way to travel, and they're both working so they don't get up to see us so often. It's a shame. I don't know why people have to move away from home. But she met Derek when he was doing his National Service, he's from down there, and he's got a good job. You can't argue with that, can you? Says he wouldn't be able to get the same work up north. Are you going to visit family?"

"Yes," Pattie said again, restraining her normally garrulous tongue. What bad luck, to have such an inquisitive lady sitting opposite. She felt in her bag for the book she had brought with her to keep Elisabeth quiet. "Here, Elisabeth, let's look at this." The lady concentrated on her knitting, the man opened his newspaper, and Pattie breathed again

The countryside became flatter and less interesting - just boring old fields and hedges. Pattie wriggled more and more. Sitting still for hours was agony for her, and not talking even worse. She stood up to stretch and straighten her skirt, and looked around her. Perhaps they could pretend to get off at the next stop and sit somewhere else. Only she'd have to explain to Elisabeth without their companions hearing. And, oh bother, she'd said they were going all the way. To London. She got to her feet and wandered into the corridor to look out of the window. Far down the train she saw a man in a blue uniform with a peaked cap. He seemed to be looking into the compartments and talking to the passengers. Gradually it dawned on her that he was a ticket inspector and he was checking and punching everybody's tickets. Quickly, she tried to think up a convincing story; had it not been for the inquisitive lady sitting opposite she could have said that her parents were further down the train, but she couldn't say that now. She decided upon escape instead. "C'mon, 'lis'beth," she hissed, trying not to attract their neighbours' attention.

"C'mon where?"

"I want to wee."

"I'll stay here."

"No, you come too. Come on!"

Reluctantly, Elisabeth got out of her seat. Pattie wondered if they should take all their belongings with them, but decided against it. Already the talkative lady was looking up from her knitting and smiling at them. "Don't lock yourselves in," she advised.

Pattie smiled, weakly, and hurried down the rocking train, away from the inspector, with her small cousin trailing behind. They walked through the next carriage where they found a lavatory. Pattie opened the door and they squeezed in. There wasn't much room. Two grown-ups would never have fitted. Elisabeth sat on the seat and Pattie squeezed up between the wash basin and the door. Elisabeth began to cry, quietly. "Oh well, I might as well go as I'm here," decided Pattie. "Move over." She changed places with her cousin, pulled down her knickers and squatted on the wc. The train jerked as she stood up again and she fell on top of Elisabeth. "Oh golly, sorry, oh golly, don't cry. How do you pull the chain, there isn't one. D'you want to go?"

Elisabeth sniffed and shook her head. Pattie surveyed the tiny cabin, pressing every knob she could find, until by accident she stood on the knob on the floor which operated the wc. "Golly, that's clever!"

Just as Pattie was thinking that it must be safe to emerge, there was a knock on the door. "Ssh!" she hissed.

There was a second knock, and the handle moved. "Anyone in there?"

"Yes," said Pattie cautiously. "We're children."

"Are you all right? Not locked yourselves in and can't get out?"

"Oh no. We're alright. My sister can't go," said Pattie on a brainwave.

"I'm checking everyone's tickets. Are you travelling with your parents? Have they got your tickets?"

"Yes."

"Whereabouts are they sitting?"

"Um - two carriages away."

"Front or back of the train?"

"Back," lied Pattie.

"I'll look out for them." And the ticket collector departed.

"Oh golly." Pattie was weak with relief. "Just give him a minute and then we'll go."

Elisabeth was still crying when they got back to their seats. "She couldn't go," Pattie explained for the second time.

"Oh, the poor thing. I expect it's the excitement of the journey. I can take her later, if you like."

"Mm," Pattie nodded.

"Did you see the ticket collector?"

"No. Yes."

The lady gave her a quizzical look. "I told him to look out for you."

Pattie felt frightened. They would have to move to another part of the train if they weren't to be found out. She wracked her brain for an excuse for doing so. At the same time she was reluctant to move. The adventure was beginning to frighten her. It was taking too long. This lady and her husband were safe, they had grown up children. Pattie was tempted to tell them everything. But could she protect her from her father's anger when he found out? That was unlikely. Pattie wished fervently that they had never set out, that she was safe at home in her own room with her teddy and her toys. But poor little Elisabeth had been so unhappy, she had been pining because her father had gone away. Pattie had only wanted to help.

"Is London a big place?" she asked.

"Oh yes, enormous. I can never find my way around. The traffic frightens me to death, and my daughter has to hold my hand when we use the underground. People get trapped in the doors unless they're very quick."

Pattie despaired. "Bigger than Leeds?"

63

"Oh yes. Much bigger. Ten times the size. What do you say, Harold?"

"What?"

"London. I say it's ten times the size of Leeds."

"Oh, more. Five million people live there, you know. Let's see, if the population of Leeds is, say,..." He found a pencil and started working it out on the margin of his newspaper. Pattie felt smaller and more frightened. Among five million people, how would they find Elisabeth's father? They could ask a policeman, but then he would start asking them questions, and find out that they had travelled without tickets on the train, and before they knew it they would be in prison. And then her father really would be angry.

"Have you got that address?" she asked Elisabeth. Elisabeth fished around the front of her dress. Then she shook her head. Tears were rolling down her face now.

"Oh, golly, you must have it. Let me feel - oh alright, we'll have to go to the lav again. Maybe you dropped it there. Golly, Elis'beth, don't cry. Can you remember the name?"

"Auntie Annie," sniffed Elisabeth.

"No, her real name, her surname. Like I'm Pattie Mitchell and you're Elisabeth Lindsey."

Her cousin shook her head. Things were getting too difficult, so when the lady sitting opposite announced that the inspector was coming back down the carriage, Pattie felt almost relieved. The adventure was bound to fail, they had taken on too much, it was a question only of when to admit defeat.

"Here we are, inspector," called the lady cheerfully, leaning out of their compartment. Pattie could have strangled her. Rebellious again, she determined to battle on as long as she could. "I told you there were two children travelling alone. Here they are."

The inspector frowned at Pattie. "Are you the two who were in the lavatory a few minutes ago?"

Pattie hesitated. "We might have been."

"You said you were with your parents?"

"Did I?"

"Yes, Miss Clever, you did."

"How do you know it was us?"

"Because I've accounted for everyone else on this train. Come on, now, let's have your tickets."

The moment had come. "I haven't got them," said Pattie.

64

"Well, who has?"

"No-one - I mean, I've lost them."

"Oh come on, don't give me that. Let's have them."

"No, we - Elisabeth dropped them. Down the toilet. She was trying to flush it. She only has one arm you see, one arm that works anyway. She lost her balance. That's why we were such a long time. We tried to get them out, but then we trod on that button thing on the floor, and they were washed away."

It sounded convincing. Elisabeth was by now crying too hard to say whether or not she had dropped the tickets. The train lurched, the ticket inspector nearly lost his balance, and the lady put down her knitting. She tut-tutted and looked as if she would like to pick Elisabeth up. The ticket inspector, who was much sterner looking than Mr Moffatt, scratched his head. He was not used to dealing with children.

"Now let's see, you say you had the tickets but you lost them. Where did you buy them?"

"Mummy bought them in Leeds. She put us on the train and Uncle Hugh is meeting us in London. We're... Only Elisabeth wanted to hold them and then the train jerked and she dropped them."

"Why is she crying so much?" intervened the inquisitive lady. "Come here, little girl, let me pick you up." Elisabeth shrank into her corner.

"Because she dropped the tickets," Pattie answered, brilliantly.

"There's not much we can do until we reach Grantham," said the inspector. "I'll get in touch with the office then. But mind you stay in those seats and don't budge."

"Oh, I'll keep an eye on them," said the busybody lady. Pattie scowled.

It all came to an end in Grantham. The train was halted for 15 minutes while the inspector telephoned his head office, who informed him that a message had been received about two little girls who had disappeared from home, and might be travelling to London. He took the descriptions back into the train, and read them out.

"Well," said the lady, who by now had an unresisting Elisabeth on her knee. "That's you two alright, isn't it?" The accusing look she gave was directed at Pattie.

"The little devils," said her husband.

"Steady, Harold," she said.

Pattie gave up the fight. She was tired, and hungry, and she wanted to go home. She told the inspector how they had managed to get on the train, and why they had done it, and said she was sorry. That sometimes helped when she was in trouble.

"There's not much point in our giving them a telling off," he said to the lady. "They'll get a rollicking when they get home, I shouldn't wonder."

"Children today," said Harold. "They think they can do what they like."

"It's not the little one's fault - she's too young. Didn't your mother suspect what you were planning?" she asked Pattie.

"She was at work," said Pattie, who was trying her best not to cry.

"Leaving the two of you on your own? I don't know," said the lady.

Pattie and Elisabeth were escorted off the train and taken to an office where a policewoman was waiting for them. They were given tea and sandwiches while waiting for a train to take them back to Leeds. Several telephone calls were made. On the return journey they were put into the charge of a guard who was travelling back to Leeds, a young man with neither the ability nor the inclination to amuse children, who made it very clear from the start that he wouldn't be answerable for the consequences if they caused any more trouble. They slept some of the time, but in between Pattie thought with trepidation of her home coming. Maybe they would be so pleased to see her that they wouldn't be cross. This seemed unlikely somehow. All in all, it was a miserable journey.

HEATHER

Pattie's other cousins, Heather and Lesley Atfield, knew about Elisabeth. They sent Christmas cards every year, although they didn't receive any in return. Sending them was always a gamble, as they were never sure if the address to which they wrote was still current. However, their mother said they should make an effort to keep in touch and so they did.

Phyllis, Pattie's mother, had always been closest to her brother Hugh, and remained so despite the fact that she was almost as bad as he at keeping in touch. She was the sister to whom had he turned when he could no longer continue to look after his daughter. It was unfortunate that this had coincided with the Atfields being away on holiday because otherwise Phyllis would at once have gone to her sister for advice. The holiday, a duty visit to relatives of Bertrand who lived near Chester, was not particularly enjoyable. Heather enjoyed it most, as she was the aunts' favourite, but even her statements about the lovely time she was having lacked conviction. It was unusual for Heather to be favoured above Lesley, and she took her role seriously, showing concern in case Lesley felt left out, and making sure that any treats were divided with scrupulous fairness. It never occurred to Lesley to feel left out, however, and all Heather's worrying of the subject did nothing to change this.

The house was as uncomfortable and prickly as were the aunts. Built in the 1920's, it was semi-detached, with bow windows, mock Tudor timbering between the bays, and pebble dashing everywhere else. The windows were rarely opened, and the whole place smelled fustily of old ladies and old furniture. The two aunts gave every appearance of living in genteel poverty. This irritated Bertrand, who knew that in reality they were comfortably off.

Heather was always eager for approval, and flattered when she had it. This led her to spend an afternoon on her own with them while the others went off to see a local beauty spot, and it had been a very long afternoon indeed. She had sat on a stool between the two old ladies and answered their questions (this was not difficult, as the answer was usually suggested with the question: "I suppose you're doing very well at school?" "What are your favourite subjects? I expect you like History and Geography"), receiving approving smiles and clucks of approval when she followed their suggestions, and several pats on her plump pink cheeks. Then they had wanted her to read to them, to play her recorder for them, to show them how neatly she could sew, and knit, and all the time they had leaned over her, and outside the sun was shining and the others were enjoying themselves in the sunshine and she was stuck with two old ladies in a fusty room, dark and sombre with heavy curtains drawn to keep the sun out, and heavy Victorian furniture covered in dark greens, and reds. The chairs were stuffed with horse hair, which tended to poke out and scratch the legs of the person sitting down. Irene always chose to sit on an upright chair in order to protect her nylons. In the evenings the only light came from lamps draped with heavy, fringed shades. The living room carpet was overlaid with rugs which the children were constantly tripping over.

It was a relief when the others returned, happy and relaxed after a day in the fresh air. Lesley described what they had done, and then settled down with paper and crayons to record some of the things they had seen. She never noticed 'difficult' atmospheres. Bertrand sighed and tried not to feel guilty. Irene got out her knitting and counted the remaining hours of the visit into her stitches.

Leaving, they twisted round in the car, waving, smiles glued to their faces, until they had turned the corner on to the main road. Then they sank back, relieved that the visit was over for another couple of years. Bertrand began his usual post-visit discourse about why it was necessary to make these visits, while Irene thought about getting the girls ready for the next school year.

"You'll have to work hard at school this year, Lesley, it's very different being at grammar school."

"I do work hard."

"At everything, not just the things you like. Spelling, for example. I think we'll start doing some practice in the evenings." Irene was always more critical after a visit to the aunts.

"I'll help her," Heather offered, with the easy superiority of someone who was two years older. Meanwhile, Bertrand was telling those who cared to listen about how the aunts had looked after him after his father had died, and helped him through college. "It's no good," he always ended by saying, "I know it's a bore for you but they helped me then, and I must help them now." Irene, proud of her family for getting through yet another difficult time, assured her husband that they understood the situation perfectly well.

"Of course, they're getting a bit past it now," he said, tapping his forehead significantly. "You can't listen to everything they say."

"I don't think you should say things like that about them," Heather pouted, regretting her days of glory now they were over.

"Don't be rude to your father," Irene said automatically.

"I wasn't," Heather protested.

"She said he was," interposed Lesley.

"Stop squabbling," said Bertrand.

They were all feeling edgy. Irene was tired, Bertrand had a headache. It was a long drive home. The last thing they wanted was a distraught Phyllis on their doorstep ten minutes after their arrival. The girls were sent upstairs to unpack, but delayed long enough to hear that a newly found cousin had almost immediately been lost and, as usual, it was all Pattie's fault.

"But where are they now?" asked Irene, trying to clear a mental path through Phyllis's confusion and hysteria.

"Grantham," said Phyllis.

"Grantham! You are surely not asking Bertrand to go there to bring them back."

"No, the man said he would put them on a train. To Leeds. They want us to meet them there. Only I can't remember the time - how long does it take from Grantham to Leeds?"

"A long time," said Bertrand, his head sunk on to his chest.

"I don't know, I can't remember what time he said. Oh what shall I do? Allan will be furious, I think he'll murder her."

"Of course he won't. Stop panicking, Phyl. We can check train times. And of course I can meet the train. But why did they try to get to London? What's Elisabeth doing here? What does Allan say?"

Phyllis wrung her hands. "He doesn't know."

"Doesn't know? Phyllis, for heavens' sake."

"He isn't home yet and it's difficult to ring him at work. Well, I was going to ring, and then I thought - do I need to tell him? I mean, he wasn't too keen on the idea of having Elisabeth to stay - well of course he was sorry for her - but he insisted it should only be for a short time. And of course Hugh said that was all it would be. And he does get angry with Pattie - I know she's naughty, but I can't bear it when he's cross with her. If we get them back I thought perhaps I could say they were playing here and decided to stay the night..."

"No," Irene said firmly. "Don't be silly, it would all come out and then he'd have a right to be angry. You don't imagine Pattie could keep an adventure like this to herself. You must tell him." At this point she noticed her own two children huddled on the staircase,

70

listening to every word. "Have you two finished unpacking?" she enquired. "No? Then off you go and do it. Put the dirty clothes in the basket."

"Who's Hugh?" asked Lesley when she and Heather got upstairs, and then rolled about laughing because it sounded funny. "Who's Hugh? Who-y-oo's H-y-ugh? Who-o-o-.."

"I bet you don't know how to spell it," said Heather.

"H -o-," attempted Lesley. "H -y -."

"H-u-g-h" said Heather.

"Hug," said Lesley. "What a stupid name." She laughed again. Later she asked "Do you think we'll be allowed to go with them?"

"I might," said Heather, without thinking.

"They won't leave me on my own. That means Mummy will have to stay behind."

"I don't suppose either of us will go," said Heather, being honest. "There wouldn't be enough room in the car."

"I wonder if Uncle Allan will go."

"It might be better if he doesn't," said Heather. "You know what he was like when Pattie spilt ink all over the carpet."

"S'pose we'll have to go to bed."

In the morning they were anxious to know what had happened. "After church," said Irene, washing up the breakfast things in her best hat and rubber gloves.

"Oh, now!"

"Then we can pray for her," Heather added, piously. This earned her a frown from her father, who was suspicious of Heather's religious enthusiasm.

"There's little to tell," he said. "I went with Allan and Phyllis to Leeds station. We had to wait about ten minutes for the train to come in. There was a guard with the girls, and he brought them to us."

"What's Elisabeth like?"

"Oh, she's a few years younger than you - six or seven, I'd say. She didn't say very much – didn't say anything, in fact. She's got something the matter with one of her arms - polio, I think your aunt said."

"Poor little girl!" Heather exclaimed.

"Did she cry?" Lesley asked.

"I didn't see her cry. But she was very tired."

"Did Pattie?"

"A little. When she saw us."

71

They had seen her first. Phyllis had clutched her brother in law's arm, she looked so small and frail. She had climbed down from the train, her hand held firmly by the guard, lips squeezed tight together and her fair head held stubbornly high. The sight of her mother had been too much for her, however, and she had wrenched her hand free and hurtled towards them, flinging herself into her mother's arms. Phyllis had been caught off balance and stepped back against Bertrand, treading heavily on his foot. He hopped on the other foot, grimacing with pain, and for a moment or two nobody took any notice of Elisabeth, still held captive by the guard. They were in danger of being separated by the crowds of people pushing their way out of the station. Phyllis hugged her daughter, releasing her as Allan stepped forward and took her by the arm.

Bertrand, recovering, turned his attention to his second niece. "Elisabeth!" he said, holding out his arms. The guard released her but Elisabeth didn't move. She gazed at her uncle with blank dark eyes, so that he had to go to her and take her hand to take her to the car.

Sunday lunch in the Atfield household was normally a relaxed affair, during which the family discussed its own, and other people's, affairs. This day, however, Irene tried to hurry them along.

"Heather, if you don't want the cabbage just leave it. Don't mess," she said.

"What's up?" Lesley asked, getting to the point.

"Nothing's up, Lesley, don't use slang. We're going to your aunt's house this afternoon, and I don't want to be late."

"We'll miss Sunday School," Heather objected.

"Good!" said Lesley.

"Your father and I are going while you are at Sunday School. I'm going to ring Mr Jones the taxi and ask him to take you to Granny's. We'll pick you up from there."

"I don't mind missing Sunday School," offered Lesley. Heather looked tearful. Irene said in her no more arguing voice, "It's all arranged. Heather, give me your plate. I really think you are being slow on purpose. Come and help me with the custard, please."

Heather went reluctantly into the kitchen, worrying in case Lesley extracted more information from her father. She left the door open so that she could hear. But Lesley had lost interest in family secrets, and was talking to her father about the frieze she planned to paint around her bedroom walls.

"Do we tell Granny about Pattie and Elisabeth?" Heather asked later, rather like a soldier asking for battle orders.

Bertrand hesitated. He was opposed in principle to family secrets, or secrets of any sort, but at the same time he knew that matters affecting the children had to be explained carefully to his mother in law. In the end he said "Well, don't make a secret of it. But don't bring it up unnecessarily. I'd rather your mother and I told her ourselves, when we know better what's going to happen."

"What *is* going to happen," asked Lesley, standing by her father's chair.

He pulled her on to his knee and tickled her ribs. She wriggled and said "Stop it, Daddy," turning round to face him. She was his favourite, and she knew it.

"What is going to happen?"

"Heather," called Irene from the kitchen, "come and do some drying for me."

"In a minute, in a minute," shouted Heather in a panic. "Daddy's just telling us..."

"I want you now. We have to be off in ten minutes."

"I *can't*, Mummy," wailed Heather, bouncing about on her chair. Two tears rolled slowly down her cheeks.

Bertrand put Lesley down and stood up. "We'll all give Mummy a hand," he said. He stood in the middle of the kitchen with a tea towel in his hands. "What would you think if your cousin came to stay for a few days?"

"Pattie?"

"No, Elisabeth." They thought about this.

"Oh Bertrand," sighed Irene, pushing past her husband, "couldn't it wait?"

"They have a right to know."

"Yes, but now?"

"We don't know her," suggested Heather.

"No, none of us do, and she's had a funny old life. From what I've seen she's a quiet little thing. Younger than you. And she's disabled - she had polio when she was a baby – that's when the muscles waste away, and it's left her arm very weak."

"Oh, Daddy, she must come," exclaimed Heather. "I can look after her." Heather had dreams of becoming a nurse.

"Which arm?" asked Lesley.

"I don't know."

"I don't mind. Pattie comes often enough. How long for?"

"Oh, a few weeks. Until her father finds a job."

"OK."

Lesley always got on well with her grandmother, whereas Heather was her grandfather's favourite. However, Ernest had had a stroke six months earlier, and although he had recovered quite well he couldn't move about easily, and needed help to get up and downstairs, and into bed. He resented the loss of independence, and had become grumpy and irritable. Irene and Phyllis were trying to persuade the two of them to move to a bungalow, but neither Mary nor Ernest wanted this. They had lived in the same house on the outskirts of Aireton for nearly thirty years. Mary had, however, been persuaded that the dining room should be turned into a bedroom, and Bertrand and Allan had agreed to move the furniture. There was already an old washhouse downstairs, and Bertrand said it would be possible to turn this into a bathroom. It was just a question of persuading Ernest. He had good days and bad days, and on his good days he saw no reason for any change. On bad days he said he wouldn't be around much longer, so why bother?

When Heather and Lesley arrived it appeared that their grandfather was having a bad day, and he was staying in bed. Heather offered to sit with him for a while. "I wouldn't bother," said her grandmother. "He doesn't want anyone today."

"But I must say hello to him, granny," Heather protested. "He'd be so hurt if he knew we'd been here and hadn't been to see him."

"He won't take any notice of you," repeated Mary, "but you can try if you like."

The bedroom was of a reasonable size, but so full of heavy furniture that it looked small - it was not unlike the great-aunts' house in this respect. The bed was large, and had a table at one side and a green wicker linen chest at the other. The table top was covered with bottles and jars, and the linen chest, which had a glass top, held a glass of water. Then there was a wardrobe and a dressing table with three angled mirrors, both in heavy mahogany. There was a tallboy, with photographs on top, a couple of chairs, and a stool at the dressing table. A tiled fireplace was in the wall opposite, but this was never lit. There was an unpleasant smell in the room, a sharp, sour smell that made Heather catch her breath. Lesley retreated to the landing.

"Oh Ernest, why didn't you call me?" muttered his wife, going to the bed and feeling beneath the blankets. "Well, Heather, if you want to be helpful, here's your chance. Help me get him out of bed and into a chair. Pass me his dressing gown first." This was hanging on a hook behind the door. Heather passed it, in a panic. What was she being asked to do? Would she have to take him to the lavatory?

Mrs Lindsey wanted to change her husband's pyjamas, and change the bedding. "Come on, Ernest, you can get out of bed when you want to." She put the dressing gown round his shoulders and showed Heather how to hold him while she swung his legs over the side of the bed. They then put his arms over their shoulders and helped him over to one of the chairs. It was not too difficult, for he had lost weight since his illness. When they moved him he muttered something which Heather couldn't make out although her grandmother said "Alright, Ernest, I'll do it later. Let's get you to the bathroom." She and Heather helped him along the corridor, then Heather was sent to find clean pyjamas and clean sheets. She put the pyjamas outside the bathroom door then made the bed while her grandmother attended to her husband. When it was all over and he was back in bed, he turned his head away and closed his eyes. Heather was upset but managed to hold back the tears. She was fond of her grandfather, and grieved to see him so changed. Pity for him conflicted with a feeling of revulsion; she had wanted to help and yet was frightened of the sick man and sickened by the smell and mess of his room. The things her grandmother had to do! She could never ever do that for anyone. She could never be a nurse.

She made her way downstairs and into the garden, where Lesley had gathered rose petals and was laying them out in shades of pink. "When you get married, my bridesmaid's dress can be pink as long as it's that pink," she pointed to one of the petals. "And p'raps a bit deeper at the waist - that one - and again at the hem. That would be smashing. I'll paint it for you when I get home."

Heather pushed the petals around with her foot. Lesley snatched them out of the way. "Be careful, I want to take them home."

Heather snuffled and said, "Granny said he was having a bad day, he's not always like that."

"I know."

"How do you know? You wouldn't go in."

"I heard what she said."

"You should have helped us. I had to help Granny when she asked."

"She didn't ask me."

"It was horrible. I don't want to be a nurse after all."

"Didn't think you'd like it. Don't cry, Granny's coming with a

75

tray."

Heather brightened and rushed off across the grass to help her grandmother, who avoided a collision by stepping on to a flower bed. She sent Heather off into the kitchen to find another chair. Lesley, unflustered, rose to her feet and helped her grandmother put the tray down.

Mrs Lindsey sat down with a sigh. "I do ask myself sometimes what we've done to deserve all this. Some days he just gives up trying. He's been used to being in charge, it's hard for him."

"Why's it anything to do with what you've done?"

"Don't they teach you that at Sunday School? About the sins of the fathers."

Lesley shook her head. "We had to read this passage from the Bible, something about just desserts." Lesley giggled. "I thought it meant you didn't get any pudding if you were naughty, but Heather told me it meant you got what you deserved."

Mary smiled and patted her head, as Heather came back with the chair.

"Where is Patricia this afternoon?" she asked, handing round cake. Mary's cakes were always excellent and they hoped, selfishly, that Ernest's stroke wouldn't mean she stopped baking.

Lesley and Heather looked at each other. "I think she's in a bit of trouble at home," said Lesley.

"What kind of trouble?"

"Not sure."

"Did she go to Sunday School with you?"

"Um, no," said Heather. "This cake is wonderful, Granny."

"Well, I daresay I'll hear about it sometime. Now tell me about your holiday."

When Bertrand arrived to pick them up he did not want to linger. "Thank you for looking after them, Mother," he said, giving her a peck on the cheek. "We'd better be getting back. Irene will telephone you tomorrow. Come on, girls, get your things. If Grandfather is sleeping I won't disturb him."

"Your mother," he said as they bundled into the car, "is a wonderful woman. A wonderful woman," he repeated, thinking about it. The girls said nothing. They had heard such statements many times before, and were well aware that their mother was a wonderful woman. "How many other women would take in someone else's child?" he demanded.

"Auntie Phyllis?" suggested Heather, taking him literally. Bertrand ignored this. "Truly, girls, if you grow up to be half as good as your mother you will be doing very well."

"Is Elisabeth coming to stay, then?" asked Lesley.

"Yes, she is. For a short time. We must all be very kind to her, I don't need to say this, I know, but she's had a difficult life and she's not easy to get to know – she's very withdrawn. Understandable of course. She doesn't know who to trust."

"What's withdrawn?" Lesley asked.

"I know, I know," Heather boasted. "It's - um -."

"Don't say you know something if you don't," rebuked her father.

"I *do* know only I don't know how to say it. It means, like, shutting yourself away."

"Yes, not bad. She's not talking, not eating much, not saying what's going on inside her head. She's unhappy, of course."

"When is she coming?" asked Lesley

"Tonight."

"Tonight? Golly gosh," she said, using an expression of Pattie's.

"Yes, it's rather sudden. But Phyllis hasn't got very much room, you know - and after last night - we decided it would be better to get her settled down as soon as possible."

"Is Pattie coming?"

"No, Pattie is not coming."

"How's Auntie Phyllis?"

"A bit upset - yes, a bit upset." Phyllis had been distraught.

"Is Uncle Allan angry with Pattie?"

"Well yes, and he thinks it will be more of a punishment for her if Elisabeth leaves. I must say I don't altogether agree with his using Elisabeth as a sort of punishment, but at the same time I can see that it's difficult... They really don't have enough room." Allan and Bertrand in fact disliked each other quite strongly, but Bertrand at least refused to admit this, and always tried to see the positive qualities in his brother in law.

"We start school next week," said Lesley, and as usual her father understood the meaning underlying her words.

"Yes, just as well, we'll all get back to normal then. Your mother will talk to the school on Monday about taking Elisabeth."

"Oh, poor Elisabeth," exclaimed Heather, trying unsuccessfully to imagine what it must be like to be unwanted and unloved. "It sounds as if nobody wants her!"

Bertrand started to deny this but Lesley commented "She sounds like a parcel that hasn't been stamped." In her mind she visualised a cartoon Elisabeth, wrapped up in brown paper and string, waiting forlornly on the post office counter. Bertrand gave his short vigorous laugh.

When they got home, Heather asked her mother "Why have we never seen her before?"

"You have, but it was a few years ago. Do you remember one day at the seaside, a lady and gentleman and a little baby came up to us on the pier, and we all sat on the beach together? That was Hugh and his family. You were about six."

"Oh yes, I remember," said Heather. She did, faintly.

"But why haven't we seen them since?"

Irene hesitated. She didn't want to admit that she had never really forgiven Hugh for quarrelling with their parents and breaking up the family. Mary and Ernest hadn't spoken to him for twelve years. Left to herself, Mary would have forgiven Hugh but Ernest was adamant. His son was irresponsible, a wastrel, a cause of grief to his mother. He would have nothing more to do with him. None of the family had gone to his wedding; Irene felt, now, that she should have made an effort, even at the risk of upsetting her father. Bertrand would have come with her, and they could have taken Mary. The meeting at Cleethorpes had been engineered by Phyllis, and had not really broken the ice. Somehow the years passed, they were all so busy, and then Elisabeth's mother, Fay, had died. Poor Hugh. "He was always bad at keeping in touch. And he changed addresses so frequently - it was impossible to keep up. He knows where we live - he could always get in touch with us." This was beginning to sound as if she were making excuses. She said "I've found some photographs, would you like to see them while I make tea? Daddy will go over about seven to pick her up."

Heather and Lesley pored over the photographs. There they all were, in the old stone house where their grandparents still lived. Grandfather looked so young and Grandmother was pretty. What a hat she was wearing! And Irene as a little girl - oh you couldn't believe she ever looked like that! And that sweet little boy, holding hands with the child who was Auntie Phyllis - it was funny, she hadn't changed much, it was easy to recognise her - that must be their wicked Uncle Hugh. And there was a dog, and a cat - Heather wondered whether to bring up the subject of guinea pigs again. And here they were again, older now. Hugh and Phyllis looked so alike, with their fair, gingery hair. Irene was darker. And one more, a blurry out of focus shot, showing Hugh and a lady and a baby - that must be Elisabeth, and Fay who had died.

The girls studied these photographs, trying to breathe life into them, while Irene made the tea and Bertrand stood on a stool on the landing in order to find the spare sheets in the top of the airing cupboard. He said Elisabeth would sleep in the spare room for the time being, where Pattie slept when she stayed. If the visit lasted longer than a few days he would do something about the attic. It was intended for living in, for there was a staircase going up, it was clean and spacious, and only needed decorating and perhaps some extra power points. "It will be good to use the room," he said. "I'm looking forward to having our little niece to stay."

2

Elisabeth took time to settle down. She had areas of extreme sensitivity: any criticism of her father was fiercely resented, and she loathed attention being drawn to her disability. For the first few days after the London adventure she had hardly spoken, ate very little, and spent most of her time huddled in a chair, retreating to her bed in the spare room whenever she could.

Over time, however, Irene found that Elisabeth responded well to rational argument, which was her own preferred approach, and gradually they reached an understanding. Bertrand, more outgoing, tried to encourage her with stories and games, and was not put off by her lack of response. Lesley accepted the addition to the family in her usual pragmatic way, and Heather fussed about her new little cousin but in such a well meaning way that Elisabeth submitted to her hugs and kisses and, over time, began to look less haunted. Irene was proud of her family.

Nothing was heard from Hugh. Irene said to Bertrand that she was not surprised. When she had agreed to take Elisabeth on (well, what else could she do?) she had known that it was likely to be a long-term commitment. Bertrand said, yet again, what a wonderful woman she was. Phyllis, guilty about giving up her charge so readily, and anxious about her brother, suggested a notice in the newspaper, but they could not agree which paper he would read and anyway, said Bertrand, he knew perfectly well that they would be expecting him to get in touch with them. Mrs Lindsey, the cousins' grandmother, saw no point in pursuing Hugh. "He'll turn up when he's good and ready and not before," she said. Allan's considered opinion was that he had gone for good. "And good riddance," he said, under his breath, but Phyllis heard and was upset. She felt her usual mixture of love, fear and guilt. It seemed impossible to please everyone. She sneaked in to see Pattie (shut in her bedroom in disgrace) when Allan was out, petted her and brought her up to date with family news. Pattie was devastated to learn that Elisabeth would be living with her cousins, and remained subdued for some time, but was never able to understand what she had done wrong, other than board a train without a ticket.

Irene met the head of the primary school that the others had attended and arranged for Elisabeth to go into the first form of the junior school. To Elisabeth, Irene explained that her father was anxious that she should go to school and as he was moving around the country looking for work it was better for her to stay with them for a while. Irene spoke in her usual reasonable, no fuss manner, and spoke at length about the importance of education while Elisabeth hid behind her long auburn hair. However, she seemed to be listening and in the event never argued or tried to avoid school. To start with she came home for dinner, but during some bad weather in November it was decided that she should stay at school, and that continued. It gave Irene a break. She had been feeling a tinge of resentment - never properly admitted - that just as the elder two were becoming more independent, she had to start again with a seven year old.

In the autumn, Elisabeth had a postcard from her father, posted to her at her auntie Phyllis's. Pattie brought it round. Most of the card was taken up with love and kisses, and a promise that he would come and see her just as soon as he could. Meanwhile she was to be a good girl and do what her aunt told her.

Pattie handed over the card then mooched over to the table, where Lesley was doing a jigsaw, and began to annoy her by trying to force pieces into spaces where they didn't fit. Elisabeth read her card carefully. Then she ran across to Pattie, put her good arm around her cousin as high as she could reach, and gave her a kiss before scuttling back to her corner. Pattie went bright pink with pleasure. For once she was at a loss for words. "Golly gosh" she managed, then she gave Lesley a big grin and the two of them settled down to the jigsaw.

Elisabeth was thrilled with her card. She kept it with her at all times, tucking it into her bodice during the day and under her pillow at night. When she saw that it was getting dog eared Irene tactfully suggested that she should have a box to keep it in, along with any other treasured possessions. The two of them explored the dresser in the dining room and found a box which had once held toffees. It had yellow ribbon round one corner, and the lid had a picture of an old-fashioned village in spring, with daffodils round a duck pond. Elisabeth bore it away to her room, and put the card safely inside together with a notebook and pencil, a ribbon and a handkerchief which had belonged to her mother, and a small knitted dog, stuffed with newspaper, which the landlady of one of their lodgings had given her.

Heather had mixed feelings about going back to school. The autumn always aroused in her feelings of sadness and of nostalgia, for summer holidays gone and winter coming and this year, perhaps, of childhood passing. Within a week or two she had normally settled down, and on the whole enjoyed school. She was a conscientious worker, usually among the top half-dozen in her form. She was good at sport, and excelled at swimming. She was reasonably popular with her class mates and with her teachers, although some of the teachers were irritated by her fussy ways.

This year she and the rest of her class were asked to think about the subjects they would take in the GCE examinations, to be taken at the end of the following year. At Christmas they would have preliminary interviews with their teachers. By Easter the girls had to decide on their preferred subjects, focusing on either arts or science. Heather was torn. She had thought she wanted to be a nurse, but in her heart she knew that she was too squeamish. She enjoyed general science but was a little frightened at the thought of specialising in physics, say, or chemistry. They were such big subjects. However, she liked the exactness of science. She also had a slight crush on the science mistress. It was difficult.

She liked history and her father thought she should take arts subjects including French and possibly another language. Heather was not convinced. Her written French was good, but she panicked when spoken to, and her accent was poor.

All this was in the future, and they had been promised plenty of opportunity for discussion but Heather, an inveterate worrier, was thinking about it as she made her way to school on the first morning of the new term. It added to her natural anxiety about being in a new form. There was another concern for her, too, which was that Lesley was starting at the same school that morning. Heather had had two years of being the only Atfield there, and now felt a faint twinge of jealousy at the thought of her younger sister's enviable confidence and ease. Lesley got on with everybody. She was bound to be popular. They travelled on the bus together and Heather showed Lesley where to hang her coat, and took her to the classroom, but there was really no need; Lesley would have found someone to ask and would not have felt awkward about doing so. Heather loved her sister, and was proud of her, but at the same time felt that she was sometimes overshadowed by Lesley and that this wasn't fair. Heather became increasingly anxious to find something which she could excel in - oh, would she be any good at physics?

Heather loved her sister, and would have defended her against the world (not that it would ever be necessary) but she found her a challenge. She loved her cousin Pattie too, although she was shocked at some of the things she did. Pattie was going to a different school, having failed her 11+. She and Lesley sometimes teased Heather, who took her two year seniority very seriously and expected her sister and cousin to do the same. Heather was easily threatened and made to feel insecure and the teasing hurt, although she tried not to show it.

Before the new term was far advanced new grounds were discovered for teasing Heather. She fell in love and, being Heather, found it impossible to hide her feelings. Her moods switched from elation to gloom and back again. She cried easily, she sat dreaming over her homework and became abnormally forgetful. She went to school early, was often late home, and found weekends an ordeal. Sunday evenings found her cutting chrysanthemums and late flowering roses, and persuading Lesley to arrange them artistically in an old vase, which she then smuggled out of the house on Monday morning.

Her parents were at first puzzled by this erratic behaviour. When questioned, Heather either giggled or rushed away to her room. It was left to Lesley to enlighten them.

"She's got a new form mistress, Miss Goodman," she explained. "She's got red hair. The flowers are for her."

Bertrand was amused, Irene irritated. "I never expected to have a silly daughter," she said.

The passion proved most disruptive. Heather's school work suffered. Even English, the subject taught by Miss Goodman, fell a victim to Miss Goodman's Titian hair, the way her lips moved when she spoke, exposing small white teeth and a little pointed tongue, and her thin, freckled, chalk-dusted hand. She particularly liked to see Miss Goodman perched on the edge of her desk swinging her legs, with the afternoon sun turning her hair into a blaze. (Needless to say, Heather was now quite certain that she would join the arts stream the following year).

Miss Goodman gave no sign that she knew of Heather's passion. She was a popular teacher - all the girls liked her and several others had mild crushes on her. She remained cool and detached, and treated everyone equally. Anonymous notes remained unopened; flowers were admired and put in vases and jam jars around the room; she never appeared to see anything unusual in the fact that the blackboard was always spotless and the girls sitting up straight at their desks when she walked into the room. She only had to mention that it was warm and someone was wrestling with the window pole; that she was thirsty, and a glass of water appeared in an instant; and, on one notorious occasion, that she had a particular aversion to the colour pink. "Well, with my hair," she said, patting it. Overnight, the class's wardrobe changed. Out went pink dresses, blouses, ribbons, hair-slides, and in came the greens and browns which the class noted Miss Goodman seemed to favour. Irene was shocked to see a fluffy pink mohair cardigan, once a favourite of Heather's, consigned to the jumble bag.

In class, Heather silently adored her idol. She made excuses to talk to her, before and after school and in the breaks. The teacher dealt with her briskly but it was enough for Heather to have had her undivided attention, if only for a second, and to look into Miss Goodman's pale green eyes.

Towards the end of November Miss Goodman began to talk to her class, as a group and individually, about the subjects they wanted to study for O level. She made out a timetable showing at what time she would be talking to which girl. Heather's interview was fixed for the second week in December.

This prospect put Heather into a great state of excitement. On the evening before the interview she was so agitated that her mother was afraid she would run a temperature. She suggested keeping her at home for a few days which caused Heather to burst into floods of tears and accuse her mother of cruelty.

The interview was at 4.30. Another girl was seeing Miss Goodman at 4, and Heather was told to wait in the library until she was ready. When Sally came to tell her it was her turn she was staring into space, her mind blank. What did she want? what would she say? She could only think of Miss Goodman's eyes, looking into hers. She walked down the corridor, her palms damp and cold and her head hot.

Miss Goodman was as cool and distant as usual. She gave no indication that Heather was in any way special or unusual, nor that she was aware that she was special to Heather. She explained what the meeting was about, and the time scale involved, went through the subject options briskly, and assured Heather that she would not be asked to make a final decision until Easter. She then asked Heather if she had thought about it.

"My parents think I ought to do French," mumbled Heather, too scared to raise her eyes and look into her teacher's sharp freckled face, so close to hers. "And they want me to learn German."

"I see. Well, your written French is quite good, but your teacher thinks you need practice with the spoken language. It will mean going abroad on an exchange. What do you think about that?"

The idea terrified Heather. She stole a glance upwards. "Do I have to go?"

"It's not compulsory. But it would give you more confidence in speaking and give you a better chance of getting your O level - there is an oral part to the exam."

Miss Goodman rested her sharp little chin on her folded hands, elbows on the desk, and looked directly at Heather. She was wearing a cream blouse with a high neck, and a knitted brown and cream waistcoat with a brown skirt. Heather thought she was the most beautiful person she had ever seen. She spoke beautifully, too, a clear unemotional voice with no trace of accent.

"What about science? You seem more comfortable with practical subjects."

Heather shook her head. "Daddy doesn't think I'll be any good at chemistry." Science held no interest for her now.

Miss Goodman looked at her notes. "You could take maths or geography instead of the chemistry. You would of course continue with English, and it would be sensible to do French. But there wouldn't be any time for German."

"Do you do English anyway?"

"Oh yes. Everybody sits English language at O Level, whatever else they are doing. It's so important to every other subject, you see, you have to write essays even if you are studying science, or domestic science. And everyone is encouraged to take maths."

"Oh." So she wouldn't have to give up Miss Goodman. But English was her teacher's chosen subject, and therefore Heather wanted it to be hers. Miss Goodman tapped on her desk with her pen. "This brings me on to something else, Heather. Your school work has not been good this year. I have been looking at last year's reports, and I'm sorry to see that it has deteriorated. Last year you were averaging B+ or A in most subjects, but this year it's B- and C+, and even a C- in French. You'll have to do better than that if you want to have a choice next Easter. You have always been thought of as potential college or University material, but if this year's lack of progress continues we shall have to change our opinion What do you think about that?"

Heather's face was bright red and a tear trickled down one plump cheek. She knew that her work was no longer as good as it had been and it made her unhappy. She didn't like getting low marks. She could no longer concentrate, that was the trouble. It used to be so easy, she used to enjoy working through problems, and she was unhappy that this was no longer the case - well of course she was if Miss Goodman was disappointed. She had other things to think about, and her mind would not stay on her lessons. It simply would not. However hard she tried, very quickly the words became a meaningless jumble, the sums on the blackboard an abstract pattern, and her brain seemed transformed into a floating cloudy substance, a soft amorphous barrier between her and her understanding, which gradually became the Titian hair of Miss Goodman. It was the same at home, although there at least she didn't have the agony of wondering whether the teacher would address her directly, or the exhilaration when she did. But her mind was no clearer - Elisabeth could beat her at almost every game they played and she stumbled over words when reading aloud. She was clumsier than ever and seemed to go out of her way to fall over things or stub her toe. Her legs were covered with bruises. She had dropped so many things that her mother had forbidden her to help any more with the washing up.

Miss Goodman looked at her watch.

"Do stop crying, Heather. You really will have to toughen up if you are to survive in this world. You are the last person I have to see today so get your coat and I'll walk with you as far as the bus stop."

It was now 5 o'clock, and most of the school was in darkness. The main corridor was lit and there were pools of light where the cleaners were working. It gave Heather an odd feeling of intimacy to be walking with her teacher through an almost empty school. It was so quiet, so different from day time, and their footsteps sounded very loud. Instead of the usual muffled roar of scores of school girls arriving, changing classrooms, and tumbling out at the end of the day, the only sounds were the sharp click-click of Miss Goodman's metal heels on the wooden floor, and the squeak of Heather's rubber soles.

Instead of descending the steps to the lower ground floor they turned left along the corridor which led past the headmistress's study to the front door, the entrance used by the teachers. This was also strange and Heather felt a mixture of privilege and nervousness. They walked down the broad stone steps into the dark, chilly December night. A drive bordered with shrubs led to the road; it was lit, but dimly, and Heather instinctively drew closer to her companion. It may or may not have been a response but Miss Goodman spoke again of Heather's need to work harder - "I know you can do it," making Heather glow inside - and to think about what she really wanted to do with her life. "Yes, I will," breathed Heather.

"Languages are always useful, but you need to enjoy speaking them. You shouldn't find it too difficult to get a job in a commercial firm - as a secretary, or possibly on the marketing side. Science - well, not many girls do science, and you'd have to be particularly good in order to compete with men. But there's always teaching, of course, whatever subject you do. You might make a good teacher. Do you like younger children?"

"Oh yes," said Heather, loving her teacher even more deeply for the interest she was showing. "My little cousin is living with us and I'm trying to help her because she's started school a bit late - well, she hasn't really been before. Not regularly. My mother was a teacher," she added.

"Was she?"

"During the war. Then she married Daddy," Heather explained.

"Teaching is a vocation," Miss Goodman continued. "Forming young minds and young characters is a privilege and should never be treated lightly. Too many young people now do teaching because they can't think of anything else to do - that is quite wrong, in my view."

They had to cross a busy main road before they parted company, Heather to catch a bus to Aireton and Miss Goodman to walk through town to her flat. Miss Goodman remarked "Be careful, Heather, it's a busy road," and picked up Heather's woolly mittened hand in her own neat leather covered one. "Come on now." Heather crossed the road in a daze. Her palm tingled and her knees felt wobbly. The warm feeling she had had earlier had returned. If only she wasn't wearing her mittens. She could take them off but if she pulled her hand away Miss Goodman would think she didn't like holding her hand. She would never in her life wear mittens again, just in case.

Safely on the far pavement, Miss Goodman continued to hold her hand. Heather gazed adoringly at her. "Now go home and don't worry. There's plenty of time to decide what you want to do. But please concentrate on your work, and stop having silly crushes." She gripped Heather's hand even harder. The tawny little face framed by a large fur collar, pulled up around the ears, was bent close to Heather. "Don't be so emotional. Don't show your feelings so openly. It is embarrassing. I don't like it. I think you know what I mean. We won't talk about it again, but I want you to think about what I have said and to come back after Christmas in a more sensible frame of mind. If not we may have to think about transferring you to another class. Now here's your bus. On you get." She released Heather's hand in order to flag the bus down, and gave Heather a little push in the small of her back. Heather, too shocked for tears, staggered to a seat and sat down, as Miss Goodman disappeared into the dark. She felt numb. She couldn't quite think about what had happened. She wouldn't think of anything just yet. She couldn't bear it. She gazed out of the window at the dark streets, but could not keep her thoughts at bay. The tingle in her right hand reminded her that Miss Goodman had held it, and then...oh that was the horrid part. She had been so kind, telling Heather not to worry, and then...she had said that Heather was embarrassing. That she didn't like her. That she wanted her to go to another class. She knew that Heather loved her, and she yet she wanted her to go to another class, out of her way, so she wouldn't have to see her. Oh it was cruel. How could she be so cruel? She felt hot and her skin prickled as if it was too tight for her. She caught sight of her woebegone face in the glass and wanted to weep but she couldn't, not on the bus. The conductor was a Polish man, nice and friendly but with hardly a word of English. He always smiled at her. This time she couldn't smile back. She huddled into her seat. Fortunately there were people getting on and off and they distracted him. She stayed in her seat past her normal stop and allowed it to carry her on to the terminus, two stops further on. The conductor gave her a sympathetic look and shook his head as if he knew there was something wrong. Heather felt sick and wretched. Soon everyone would know about her humiliation. She would have to leave school. She could never see her teacher again. Never see her again - oh how could she bear it? But she couldn't face her. And what about her class mates - did they know? Of course they knew she was keen on Miss Goodman, as they put it, but did they know that Miss Goodman hated her?

The bus finally shuddered to a halt at the terminus at the top of the hill, and Heather reluctantly dismounted. She trudged home slowly, deep in her thoughts. That was the end of it all. Her academic career. She would do neither physics nor German nor domestic science. She wondered how old you had to be to work in a factory, or Boots. Perhaps she would go to Australia, or find her uncle Hugh in London. But Pattie had tried that, and failed. And how could she bear it if she never saw Miss Goodman again? Heather began to feel very sorry for herself. She longed to be home but at the same time dreaded it. How could she tell her mother? Reluctantly, she turned into the drive.

As it happened there were distractions. Lesley opened the door to her sister, her head swathed in a towel. "It's hair washing night," she said glumly. From upstairs came the sounds of splashing water and an occasional cry. Hair washing was an activity which all three girls hated. All of them had thick hair which tangled easily. It was one of the few occasions when Elisabeth, normally stoical and silent, cried and protested; in addition to the vigorous combing and the soap in her eyes, her modesty was outraged because Irene insisted on taking off her dress, which meant exposing her withered arm.

"I washed mine last night," Heather said wearily, lifting the satchel off her arm and unfastening her gabardine.

"Because of your interview? What was it like?"

"Alright."

"We did biology today. We cut up a rat. It was yukky. Beth and Maggie fainted and had to go to the sick room. Miss Jones said next time people who were prone to fainting would have to leave the room before she started dissecting. We thought we'd all say we were going to faint, then she wouldn't have anyone to teach. Brenda was cross and said she was going to complain to the RSPCA because she keeps rats as pets. She's creepy. Can you imagine anyone keeping rats as pets?" She chatted on until Irene came downstairs with the damp, resentful bundle that was Elisabeth. She hated hair washing night almost as much as the children.

"Now you two get in front of the fire and dry your hair," she commanded. "Don't scorch yourselves. Lesley, keep an eye on Elisabeth. Heather, help me to set the table. How did you get on?"

"Alright."

"Only alright? What did Miss Goodman have to say?"

"I don't have to decide until Easter." By which time, thought Heather, I shall be safely in Australia.

"We know that. Anything else?"

"If I do languages I'll have to go abroad on exchange."

"Dear me, will you? Well I suppose that can be arranged. Will the school arrange it?"

"Yes. But I don't want to go."

"Well, we'll have to see. Are they talking about this year?"

"I don't know."

"Well, don't worry about it. We can find out more. Any more thoughts about the science?"

"I can do maths or geography as well as arts. No German and no chemistry."

"Can you? You didn't mention that before."

"I didn't know."

They sat down to eat in the kitchen. Heather pushed the food about her plate and ate very little.

"What's the matter, love, aren't you hungry?"

"Not very."

"I hope you're not sickening for something," said Irene. Her mother's words stayed with Heather and in bed that night she decided on a course of action. She would make herself ill for a few days, and then tell her parents that the only cure would be for her to leave school. She lay awake for most of the night, tossing and turning and crying into her pillow, with the result that when she announced the next morning that she felt too ill to go to school, her mother could see that she looked pale and shadowy eyed. It was unusual for Heather to be ill, and she had never cried off school before. It was nearly the end of term, and Irene decided that it would do no harm to keep her at home for a day. She sent Lesley off with a note. Later in the day she took Heather's temperature, but found it normal. Heather however complained of a headache and feeling sick. She had been crying again and her eyes looked red and hot.

"If you're no better tomorrow we're going to the doctor," Irene decreed. Later, she had another idea. "I wonder if your periods are about to start."

The menstrual cycle had been explained to Heather some time ago. Several girls at school had already started, and went about carrying their sanitary pads rather ostentatiously in drawstring bags.

"You say you keep feeling hot?"

"Yes."

"That's probably it, then."

Heather began to pray that her periods would start. They would explain why she had been feeling so peculiar, why she hadn't been able to concentrate, her obsession for Miss Goodman. Once she menstruated she would be grown up, not a little girl any more. She would be different from, superior to, her sister and cousins. She went to the bathroom every half hour, dabbing hopefully between her legs with toilet paper, but came back each time bitterly disappointed because there was no blood.

She continued to complain about feeling ill, and cried and got into a state of panic when her mother tried to make her go to school. The doctor came, but could find nothing wrong with her. He thought she might have been overworking, and suggested that she stay at home for a few more days. Irene did not like this suggestion.

Bertrand thought she should talk to the headmistress of Heather's school. Irene did, with some trepidation, and without telling Heather. It was rather different interviewing a grammar school head from a primary head, but afterwards she was glad she had done so. Mrs Ball was very understanding. She said that she thought Heather was going through an emotional crisis not uncommon among girls of her age. She told Irene that Miss Goodman had taken Heather to task over her school work, which had deteriorated that term, and was now worried that she might have been too hard on her. Mrs Ball assured Irene that Heather was normally a conscientious, hard-working girl, and she was sure that she would return to normal once she had got over her current problems.

"What should I do?" queried Irene, out of her depth. Emotional crises had never occurred in her family, and no-one had ever stayed home from school or work unless they had been really ill. Except Hugh, of course.

"Oh, I should keep her at home until Christmas. There are only another few days of term to go, and a lot of time is taken up with the carol service and the nativity play and various class activities. She usually enjoys these things, but this time I suggest we let her have a good break and she'll be back to normal in the New Year, I'm sure." They talked a little more about school work, and Mrs Ball congratulated Irene on having a second bright daughter. "Lesley has settled down remarkably well. She is a very happy, outgoing girl, very popular. We look forward to seeing her progress through the school."

Irene told Heather where she had been when she got back. Heather turned white with shock.

"Oh Mummy, you haven't!"

"I can't keep you away from school for no apparent reason without talking to them," said Irene. "Mrs Ball was very nice about it. She said that a lot of girls of your age have similar problems, and that you are normally a hard worker. You didn't tell me that Miss Goodman criticised your work when she saw you."

Heather burst into tears and turned her head into the back of the settee, where she had been lying.

"Oh, it was awful! I can't go back, Mummy."

"You don't have to, not until after Christmas. That's what Mrs Ball said."

"Not ever!"

"Don't be silly. You'll feel better in a day or two."

"You don't understand!"

"Not altogether, no," agreed Irene. "Why has your work gone off?"

"I don't know."

"Mrs Ball said that Lesley was doing very well."

Heather burst into tears again.

A few days before Christmas Heather awoke about six with a wet feeling between her legs. At first she thought that in her unhappiness she had wet the bed but when she got up she saw that her nightdress was stained with blood. Panicking, she called for her mother. Her body felt heavy and uncomfortable, and her back ached. Irene rose quickly, as she always did. She took Heather to the bathroom and helped her to clean herself up, at the same time reassuring Heather about the normality of the event.

"Don't treat it like an illness," she said, remembering what she had read, and trying to forget that her own mother had called it 'the curse'. "It's the most natural thing in the world - it happens to every woman."

They went back into the bedroom and examined the sheets, which were lightly soiled. "Now you need to keep a record of when you started," advised Irene, stripping the bed, "so that you'll know when the next period is due, and you can make sure that you've got a supply of sanitary towels. They may be a bit irregular for the first few months, so you ought to make sure you have a towel with you a few days before you think you're going to start."

"It sounds awful," moaned Heather, forgetting her wish to be grown up.

Irene gave her a kiss, and tucked her into bed again. "You're growing up, little girl. It's not so bad, really, but in any case you can't avoid it."

3

Heather loved Christmas. Even this year, despite the awfulness of the last few days, she was unable to resist its allure. Christmas Day itself could be something of a letdown (her mother hot and irritable after battling with the turkey, her father noisy after one drink too many, the neighbours outstaying their welcome) but the preparations were always fun. Cake and puddings had been made in the middle of November, but there were still cards to post, presents to wrap, mince pies to bake and decorations to hang. Lesley and her father made most of their own decorations, but every year they went into town and bought one expensive glass bauble for the tree. Both girls loved the delicacy of the fluted glass shells, white on the surface but glowing with colour at the heart. The colour seemed to intensify the more they gazed. Heather never dared to touch them, knowing that her clumsy hands might crush them into a thousand glittering shreds, so Lesley hung them and then she crouched under the tree and gazed up with wonder and admiration.

The Christmas cards were Heather's responsibility. She had a clear, round hand, and wrote most of the joint family cards. This took some time, as she liked to ask about the people whose names were mentioned only at Christmas time, trying to fit them into the pattern of family life. Some were difficult - it was hard to imagine, for example, that her mother had been a schoolgirl and had had friends just like she did, with whom she was still in touch.

This year, the house was looking particularly festive. They were making a big effort for Elisabeth, and trying to see that she never had time to sit and brood. She was beginning to look hungrily at the piles of post which landed on the doormat, twice a day, but so far there was nothing with her name on it. Her grandparents and aunt, of course, delivered theirs by hand.

Irene was sorry for her. She wrote a strongly worded letter to her brother and persuaded Phyllis to do the same, but had little confidence that the letters would reach him, or that he would respond if they did. The last they had heard was a short note at the beginning of November, saying that he was being auditioned for a leading part in an American musical. Irene didn't believe any of this, although Phyllis did and scoured the newspapers for reviews. She found them, but Hugh wasn't mentioned.

They tried to make it up to Elisabeth in different ways. Heather promised to teach her to swim; Lesley showed her how to make paper decorations; Irene let her spoon mincemeat into the mince pies; and Bertrand took her to Leeds to see Father Christmas. Best of all, Phyllis came over with Pattie and produced tickets for the pantomime. She said that someone at work had arranged a block booking and she had three tickets. Allan didn't want to go, so Elisabeth could come instead. Pattie was already hopping up and down with excitement, although they were not to go until the middle of January and there was Christmas and New Year to get through first. Pattie was now going to a different school and had different friends, so the Atwoods saw less of her, but Irene invited her to stay for a few days during the Christmas holiday, and Pattie was very pleased. Elisabeth had by this time moved into the attic, so Pattie could have the spare room again.

Elisabeth seemed to have trouble understanding what Christmas was all about. She had seen lights and decorations, but the routines and rituals which the others, even Pattie, took for granted, were strange to her, and had to be explained. She had never been to church until she came to the Atfields, and only went under pressure, with a stubborn face. Irene hoped that the good influence would gradually work its way into her small niece's soul. She wondered whether Elisabeth had ever been christened, and determined to have this out with Hugh at the first opportunity.

By ten o'clock on Christmas Eve all the children were in bed. Everything was ready. The lights on the tree were working, and Bertrand's balloons were so firmly attached to the ceiling that there was little chance of them coming down before Boxing Day, at least. Most of the presents were wrapped, the turkey stuffed and the silver polished. At 11pm Heather, restless, heard Irene leave for the midnight service. A little later there was a ring on the doorbell. Her father went to answer it, and she could hear voices in the hall, followed by the sound of the door closing and a car driving away. Then she heard an inner door open, the rustle of clothes, followed by the pad-pad of feet along the landing and down the stairs. Puzzled, and interested, Heather got out of bed, thrust her feet into her slippers, pulled on her dressing gown, and made her way downstairs. The hall was now empty but she could hear voices coming from the sitting room. She pushed the door open. Her father was standing with his back to the fire, smoking his pipe and looking at a man who stood in the middle of the room, Elisabeth in his arms. Her arms were round his neck (the right hand clasping the left wrist so that it wouldn't slip away). Her face was buried in his shoulder, and all Heather could see was tumbled auburn hair and the two arms.

The man turned his head when the door opened and Heather came in. He held out a hand, smiling. "Hello there. Let me see - you must be Heather?"

"Yes," Heather said, wondering. Her father came forward.

"Come in, love, and close the door. Come to the fire. Is Lesley awake?"

"I don't think so." Lesley was always a sound sleeper.

"Meet your Uncle Hugh."

He put his arm round her shoulders, drawing her into the group. Elisabeth raised her head and regarded them dreamily. She hung on to her father's neck and wouldn't let go. Bertrand pulled forward a chair and guided Hugh into it.

"I'm sorry it's so late," Hugh began. "Elisabeth, darling, just let go a little or you'll strangle me - that's better - but we were rehearsing until late and then I went to Phyllis's - Allan brought me round. I didn't realise Elisabeth was here. It's very good of you, Bertrand. What happened with Pattie?"

"I'll tell you another time," Bertrand said hastily. "We did write to you, you know - or at least Irene did."

"I've been moving about."

Bertrand and Heather sat down together on the settee. Heather's eyes were wide. So this was Elisabeth's father - her wicked uncle, the ne'er do well, the black sheep of the family. But her father was talking to him as if he were just a man like any other man, and he didn't look wicked; he looked rather nice, actually, with his moustache and sandy hair and twinkling blue eyes. And yet he went off and abandoned his daughter.

"Well, Heather," said wicked, charming Uncle Hugh, "I can see that you've looked after my little Lizzie really well. She's positively blooming," and indeed her normally pale little face was pink and glowing.

"I'm teaching her to swim," volunteered Heather.

"Are you? Goodness me. How many lengths can you swim, darling?" Elisabeth giggled and hid her face in his shoulder.

"Not lengths," Heather said seriously. "Widths. She can nearly do a width. The shallow end is very shallow," she reassured him, "and I've got my bronze lifesaving medal."

"Oh Heather, what a responsible girl you are." Hugh seemed

suddenly overcome by emotion. He fumbled in his pocket for a handkerchief. Heather was embarrassed and looked away. "Bertrand, Heather, I can see you have done a marvellous job. I can't thank you enough. It was a terrible decision to have to make, to leave my little girl behind, but I knew I couldn't leave her in better hands." Uncle Hugh seemed to have forgotten that he had left Elisabeth in Phyllis's hands. Heather wondered whether to remind him of this, but Hugh continued, "It's paid off, you see. I've got a job and I see no reason why I shouldn't continue to find work. It's the first break that's all important. But I couldn't have done it with Lizzie - all that trailing around to auditions, moving from place to place, and then of course the hours when I am working. You see my problem."

"We must talk about it," Bertrand said, "but not now. It's very nearly Christmas Day, Irene will be back soon. A good time to celebrate. What can I get you to drink, Hugh?"

"A whisky always goes down well."

"Two whiskies." Bertrand went over to the sideboard where the bottles were kept. "Girls? Lemonade, fizzy orange or dandelion and burdock? Are you asleep, Elisabeth?"

Elisabeth opened her eyes and looked defiant. "Dandelion and burdock, please."

"Heather? Would you like to go and see if Lesley is awake?"

"If she was she wouldn't still be upstairs."

"That's true. Well, Hugh, you'd better fill us in on what you've been doing. You're working, you say? Acting? In what?"

"Pantomime," Hugh said, sounding dignified. Bertrand sipped his whisky. "It's not the lead, not yet. They need a name, you know, a big name. But it's only a matter of time. It's the break I needed. My career is definitely on the up and up. And panto is so popular, you're seen by so many people. Agents are always on the look-out for talent."

Heather was impressed. "Pantomime! Elisabeth's going to the pantomime, with Auntie Phyllis and Pattie. Oh, I wonder if I can go too!"

"Are you, Lizzie? What are you going to see?"

"Dick Whittington," she whispered.

"Oh, that's at Bradford. I'm in Puss in Boots at Wakefield. Never mind, darling, you can see that as well. I'll send you a ticket."

"Oh, can I come too?" begged Heather.

96

"Of course you can. You can all come. A family outing. Family! What a wonderful ring that has; something you only really appreciate when you're without."

Heather clapped her hands.

"We'll have to ask your mother first," Bertrand cautioned.

"They're not what they once were, that's true," agreed uncle Hugh. "But pantomime has a long and honourable theatrical tradition. Did you know that there are all sorts of rules governing what you can and can't say on stage, and who must appear with whom, and what colours can be used in the grand finale? Blue and silver, or red and gold - never a mixture."

"Why?" asked Bertrand.

"I don't know," said Hugh.

When Irene's key was heard in the lock, at quarter past midnight, the two men exchanged a glance. "I'll let her in," said Bertrand, going out into the hall, and letting cold air into the warm room. Had Heather been feeling less sleepy she would have pointed out that this was unnecessary, since Irene had her key. Her tummy quivered a little with excitement. What would her mother say? Surely she wouldn't turn Uncle Hugh away, not at this time on Christmas Eve - oh no, of course, it was Christmas Day now.

"Happy Christmas," she said to him.

"Happy Christmas," he responded softly. Elisabeth was now fast asleep in his arms.

Forewarned by Bertrand, Irene came quietly into the room and looked at her brother. "Well, I don't know, Hugh," she said. She had taken off her hat and gloves, but still wore her fur coat. Hugh smiled at her over Elisabeth's head. "My dear Irene, how well you look. The cold weather suits you. You have a kind of glow. Forgive me for not standing up."

"She ought to be in her bed," Irene said. "And Heather. What are the children doing up at this time. They'll be too tired to enjoy Christmas. Whatever made you come so late? And no warning? Couldn't you have telephoned?"

Heather was on the edge of her seat. Her mother didn't understand. Uncle Hugh wasn't wicked after all. He would explain everything, but she must listen.

"Mummy," she began.

97

"Bed," Irene said, rather absently. She was concentrating on her brother. Gosh, thought Heather, he was her brother. Like Lesley was her sister. It was hard to imagine what having a brother would be like.

"Midnight on Christmas Eve seems a funny time to turn up," pursued Irene.

"I came as soon as I could. Well, I called in at Phyllis's first. I thought Elisabeth was there."

"We did write," Irene said sternly.

"I know. Bertrand told me." He gave her an apologetic smile. Heather couldn't understand why her mother sounded annoyed.

"It's the life you see. On the boards. Show biz. You can't have a family life as well. We were rehearsing until 10. Dress rehearsal. We open on Boxing Day. Dick wanted me there tomorrow but I said I couldn't. Simply couldn't. I'm back home for the first time in years, and I must see my family, I said. He agreed in the end."

"Whatever are you appearing in? Theatres aren't open on Boxing Day, surely?"

"Puss in Boots."

"Puss - oh, Hugh, not pantomime!"

"And why not? It's a perfectly respectable form of theatre."

"He's been telling us all about it, Mummy!"

"Bed," Irene said, more forcefully.

"Yes, it's time," said Bertrand. "You can talk to your uncle in the morning. Where is Hugh to sleep, Irene?"

Irene looked at him. Bertrand looked steadily back while Hugh bent down over Elisabeth's sleeping head. Irene looked away first.

"He can have the room Pattie uses. She'll have to go in with Elisabeth if she stays. How long is it for, Hugh, you're not planning on coming back from Wakefield every night?"

"Oh no, no, I've got digs there. But it would be nice to spend Christmas with the family. It's years since I've had a proper family Christmas. Will mother and father be coming over tomorrow?"

"All being well. Father's poorly, you know."

"Yes, Phyllis told me. Oh, it will be wonderful," said Hugh. "We'll make up for all those lost years. Irene, a corner, the settee, which is so comfortable that even Heather is falling asleep on it."

Heather jerked awake. "No, I'm not."

"Bed," Irene said for the third time, and this time there was no doubt that she meant it. Heather trailed up to bed and Hugh relinquished Elisabeth to Bertrand, who carried her upstairs.

In years to come Heather was to remember that Christmas, the Christmas she was fourteen, as somehow encapsulating all the good things about family life. After a difficult start everything turned out well. Everyone got on, there were no family squabbles, Pattie behaved well and didn't upset Allan, which meant that Phyllis was less nervy and even the grandparents seemed pleased to see Hugh again. Mary got a little weepy from time to time; he gave her a hug and teased her about the tears. Ernest seemed to be enjoying himself although it wasn't always easy to tell. He said "So you're back," to Hugh, but very little else, but he wasn't well so it didn't really matter. There was no snow but the weather was crisp and bright which Irene said was the next best thing.

Hugh sensed Heather's new awareness that she was no longer a child, and treated her accordingly, asking her opinion and encouraging her to join in the grown-up talk. Heather was flattered and followed his lead. She chose to sit with her parents and grandparents and listen to the Queen's Christmas Day broadcast rather than play with the younger children. Her presents this year reflected her new status: *Girl* and *Schoolfriend* annuals, as usual but also a framed print, a pretty lace-trimmed slip from her mother, and a lipstick from her Auntie Phyllis. Irene was rather shocked to see this, but it was a soft, young pink, and she supposed it would be suitable for special occasions. When they started playing games, however, Heather forgot her maturity and acted just like the rest. With Hugh there it was inevitable that they should play Charades. He directed them and awarded points and insisted that prizes should be given. Irene proved to be surprisingly good and was given the prize of Best All-Round Performer. Elisabeth was hopeless; she couldn't concentrate; in fact she spent most of Christmas in a happy daze, but her father decided that she could be Most Promising Newcomer. Titles were invented for all of them, and they all got prizes: a spray from the winter flowering honeysuckle for Irene, a chocolate mouse wrapped in many layers of tissue paper for Pattie (Best Comic Actress - she couldn't stop giggling), and a crude but lively sketch of them at play in the living room for Lesley (Best Set Designer). Lesley was interested to see that her uncle was talented, though untrained; why then did he not pursue it, why was he not interested in art? She remained mildly distrustful of him, and the two never became close. The grandparents sat apart, together, enjoying the fun.

The only thing wrong with that Christmas Day was that it was too short.

Hugh had to be at the theatre at Wakefield by lunchtime on Boxing Day. Bertrand drove him there, and took Elisabeth and Lesley with him. Elisabeth was pale and distressed at the thought of losing her father again, but Hugh was clearly looking forward to work. He promised Elisabeth he would come back to see her. Irene raised her eyebrows at this, but said nothing. An unspoken agreement had been reached over the Christmas turkey that Elisabeth would stay with the Atfields until such time as Hugh was able to establish a more settled life style.

Heather had stayed behind to help her mother. She also wanted to talk to her. One of the more positive things that Miss Goodman had said was that she might make a good teacher. She had thought a lot about this. She told her mother. "Oh, it's early days yet," said Irene, still preoccupied with Christmas. "There are still some sprouts left, I expect your father will have those. We can have carrots."

"I thought I might become a Sunday School teacher for now," continued Heather. This was her own idea. "It would be good practice."

"Are you old enough?" frowned Irene, who was not really in the mood for a heart to heart talk with her elder daughter.

"You have to be fourteen. You only teach the little ones."

"You're only just fourteen."

"It doesn't matter, as long as you're fourteen."

"Well, if it's what you want to do... You'd better talk to Mrs Moorhouse." Mrs Moorhouse was the Sunday School superintendent.

So that was settled. Heather was pleased. She sat at the kitchen table and removed the outer leaves from the sprouts. "Cut a little cross in the stalk," Irene reminded her. "They cook quicker if you do."

"I think there ought to be church services on Boxing Day," Heather said piously. "Don't you?"

"It isn't a holy day. I don't think you would get many people turning up."

"I like going to church," announced Heather. She had certainly enjoyed the Christmas Day service, the religious significance of which had deepened for her this year. She wished to be more active in her faith, without quite knowing how to do this. It was not easy to find ways of being good that people would notice; but Sunday School teaching was one way.

She went back to her grammar school in the New Year with some trepidation. She took the opportunity of the new term to move to a desk nearer the back of the classroom, and avoided Miss Goodman as much as possible. Miss Goodman herself was as cool and remote as ever, and treated Heather no differently from anyone else. Nothing was said about her absence from school, and the Christmas interview might never have happened. Heather, embarrassed by her memories, no longer admired her teacher as intensely as she once had. The red hair now looked carroty, and the thin artistic fingers ended in chewed nails. Heather no longer sat in classes and gazed at her idol instead of her books, she no longer followed her about the school, she no longer brought her name into conversation at every conceivable opportunity. She was a sadder but wiser Heather, who kept her head down and tried to make up for the poor work she had done the previous term.

That same year Lesley joined the Guides. She was neat and disciplined, enjoyed team events, and passed most of her badges with ease. She was also popular, and quickly became a leader. Her enthusiasm infected Pattie, who attended a few meetings, but she could not take it seriously, laughed when told of the Guide promises, and so disrupted the activities that she was asked not to come again.

The greatest surprise was when Elisabeth joined the Brownies. The Brown Owl was an intelligent girl who realised that Elisabeth knew better than anyone what she could and could not do, and she encouraged her to try anything which she felt capable of doing. Together, they found alternative ways of doing certain things to accommodate her handicap, such as knitting with one needle tucked firmly under her arm. She was able to take part in most games and sports; she could already swim, thanks to Heather, could catch a ball well enough in one hand, and could even do a somersault. Brownie activities helped to fill the gap after Hugh returned to London. While he was appearing in pantomime he had come over almost every Sunday to see her, but now he was back in London looking for work, and communications were once more erratic. But the Christmas visit had persuaded Elisabeth that he had not abandoned her, and although she never lost her wistful look she settled down into her new life and made a few friends. She remained loyal to Pattie. Pattie was the first cousin she had met, Pattie had tried to help her in the summer, and although it had been a misguided attempt, Elisabeth appreciated the motive behind it, and perhaps, too, Pattie was a little bit of an outsider, as Elisabeth herself was and would remain.

4

When she was 15, Heather fell in love again. Cynthia Theakstone was a tall, quiet girl, two years older than Heather, who had passed through the same school quietly and competently, attracting little attention until the day she jumped into the canal at Saltaire to save a little boy from drowning, and became famous overnight. Her photograph appeared in the local paper, and girls at school went out of their way to talk to her and sit next to her at dinner time or walk with her in the breaks. Girls who barely knew her boasted of their friendship with her, and how they had always known she would do something heroic one day.

There was a ceremony at school at which Cynthia was presented with a medal. The mayor was there wearing his gold chain of office, and he gave a speech and the headmistress gave a speech and Cynthia replied with a brief and modest statement. Then the whole school sang *O God Our Help in Ages Past.* Heather was overcome with emotion. She wept as the headmistress read a prayer of thanks, and as Cynthia stepped down from the platform, a little flushed but otherwise calm and modest, she longed to put her arms round her and become really close to her. She absolutely had to become Cynthia's friend. She tried to talk to her afterwards but Cynthia was surrounded by girls of her own age, most of whom had taken little or no notice of her before that day but all of whom now felt they had a right to touch her and talk to her and describe themselves as being her friend. Heather, watching this from her place among the younger girls, considered the situation. She was anxious to make friends with this brave and exciting person, but she didn't want to be one of the multitude. In any case, being younger meant that she would be looked down upon by Cynthia's contemporaries – but not, she was certain, by Cynthia herself. Instead of trying to get Cynthia's attention at school, she found out where she lived, which to her delight was not too far from her own home, and went to see her one Saturday afternoon, a bunch of late roses from her mother's garden in her hand.

The Theakstones lived in a semi-detached house half-way down the hill on which their town was built. Steps ran down the side of the neat front garden to the house, which had pebble-dashed walls that Heather thought were very smart. Cynthia's father opened the door to Heather. He was older than her own father, tall and thin, with glasses. Heather made the speech she had been rehearsing as she walked along the road.

Her heart was beating and nervousness made her voice higher than usual, but the little speech came out almost as planned:

"I'm Heather Atfield, I live on Sycamore Avenue, and I go to the same school as Cynthia. I just wanted to tell her I think she's so brave, I wasn't able to speak to her at school, I'd just like her to know, and to thank her for what she did..."

Mr Theakstone looked startled but not displeased. "I'll tell her you're here," he said, disappearing into the house. Heather waited. Cynthia then drifted gracefully down the narrow staircase and smiled vaguely at Heather. Heather made her speech again. "I'm Heather Atfield and I live on Sycamore Avenue and I'm in the Upper Fifth at the Grammar School and I just wanted to say how brave you were when you rescued that little boy - I didn't get a chance at school, there are always so many people around you. Everyone is so proud of you." Confronted by Cynthia's calm silence, Heather stumbled to a halt, her cheeks pink and her eyes glistening. How lovely Cynthia looked, standing tall and straight in that poky hall, accepting Heather's tribute like a young queen. Heather thought she would never like anyone so much in her life.

"Come in," Cynthia said at last, "I know you by sight. Aren't you in the swimming team?"

"Yes, and I've got my lifesaving medal, and I know how jolly difficult it is," Heather said. "And that was in the pool where it's warm and you're wearing a swimming costume and you know there are people there to fish you out if you get into trouble, not a canal in October with all your clothes on. I couldn't have done that."

"I expect you could," Cynthia said, accepting the flowers and leading the way into the sitting room, which had the cold, unwelcoming tidiness of a room that is hardly ever used. Heather, brought up to notice other people's houses, looked around. There was a small settee and an armchair facing an unlit gas fire set in a buff coloured fireplace. Two upright chairs were pushed against the back wall, one each side of a sideboard. In the bay window was a small table, and the sill held a cut glass flower vase. Opposite the window was a small glass fronted cabinet, with a tea service and some glasses inside, and a kidney-shaped table that looked rather unstable. The carpet was patterned, and looked worn. Heather, without being able to explain it, could see that the shabbiness was of a different order to the shabbiness of her own home. Cynthia waved her on to the settee.

103

"You don't think about it, you just do it. That's not really being brave. I didn't even notice how cold the water was until after I got out again. Does that sound silly? When I did remember I started to shiver and couldn't stop. I seemed to go on shivering for the rest of the day." She bent her long back to the gas fire, and switched it on.

"Oh, Cynthia! You might have caught pneumonia!"

"Just a slight cold, and I'm nearly over that. Just the odd sniffle."

"Oh, you shouldn't have come to school!" exclaimed Heather, trying to sound mature. "You should have stayed in bed and kept warm."

"It really wasn't necessary. I didn't want to make a fuss," said Cynthia.

Heather liked her more and more. Cynthia talked to her as if she were her equal, not two years younger. They discussed school. They discussed religion. Cynthia said that although she had taken Religious Instruction at O level she had decided against continuing to A level. "Sadly, it isn't taken seriously as an academic option. It should be. OK, on the surface it's not too difficult to understand, and we all know something about it. But if you go into it in depth, and try to understand, why it's one of the most difficult subjects - and one of the most rewarding. Religion - our religion (you're not a Catholic, are you?) is just the most important thing in life. Well, it is life. And death. All the important things. Don't you agree?"

"Oh yes," breathed Heather.

"It's what life is about. It is life."

"Oh yes."

"For century upon century, gaining strength," said Cynthia. "I think it's so wonderful."

"Oh, so do I!"

"We did comparative religion too." Heather did not know what this was. "Looking at different religions, not just Christianity." It had not occurred to Heather that any other religion was worthy of study.

"Isn't that a bit dangerous?" she queried.

"Oh no, it strengthens my belief, to see how misguided other people are. Sometimes with the best of intentions," she added, impressing Heather with her fairness. "It's truly amazing what some people believe. Did you know that Buddhists believe in reincarnation? That means that one person can be born over and over again. Can you imagine?"

Heather tried, but failed.

104

"They take it all so seriously. Well, I suppose it's better than having no religion at all. It must be easier to believe in Jesus if you already believe in something, don't you think?"

"Oh no," said Heather, eager to be involved and used to family debate. "I should think it would be easier if you didn't believe in anything - you'd be sort of empty, and then you could be taught anything."

"Anything - precisely," said Cynthia, who did not care to be contradicted. "Shallow people who don't believe in anything are open to any influence. They might accept Christianity for a while, and then a - a Hindu might come along, and bang, they become Hindus."

"You did say 'easier'," began Heather, but just then the telephone rang.

"I expect that's for me," said Cynthia, sitting calm and upright in her chair, and sure enough, a minute or so later, her mother tapped on the living room door and looked in. "A telephone call for you, dear."

Cynthia rose gracefully, saying "Excuse me" to Heather, and went into the hall. Mrs Theakstone stood aside to let her pass.

There was an awkward pause. Heather could not decide whether she should leave or wait for Cynthia to return. However, after hesitating in the doorway, Mrs Theakstone came into the room and sat on the edge of the chair nearest the door, looking ready to fly off the minute she felt her presence was unwanted. She was a small, plain woman, with iron grey hair and unexpectedly beautiful grey eyes behind horn-rimmed spectacles. "It's always nice to meet Cynthia's friends," she said, blinking nervously. Heather felt bound to explain that she wasn't really a friend, not yet, she was two years below her at school, but she had just discovered that they lived quite close by, and she had wanted to tell her how much she admired her bravery.

"Where do you live?" asked Mrs Theakstone.

"Sycamore Avenue," Heather said for the third time.

"Oh, very nice," said Mrs Theakstone, sounding more nervous than ever.

"Well, I think I should be going," Heather said at last.

"Oh, no, you must wait until Cynthia comes back. There's always someone ringing her up these days, her father says he wishes we'd never had the telephone put in (he's joking, of course)," she added, worried that Heather might take her seriously, "and you should see the letters she's had. Would you like to see some of them?"

"Oh yes, please."

Mrs Theakstone opened the front of the sideboard, which came down to form a desk top. She then pulled open a small drawer, and took out a brown paper parcel, tied with string. She untied this, and gestured towards the letters inside. "Come and look at them here, you can spread them out. You will be careful with them, won't you, we want to keep them. I thought that wrapping them up would stop them fading, what do you think?"

"Daddy might know," Heather said helpfully. Mrs Theakstone seemed to accept this. "The newspaper cuttings are the real problem. They do go brown so quickly." She took the letters out, one by one, and spread them on the desk for Heather to read. They were mostly simple letters of praise, many of them written by children.

"We had one or two funny ones," Mrs Theakstone said. "I threw those away. And some asking for money. I think they thought Cynthia was given a reward but she wasn't - just the medal."

The medal was kept in a separate drawer on its own, wrapped in cotton wool. Mrs Theakstone handled it reverently, and they both gazed at it with pride.

In a little while Cynthia came back from the telephone. "What about a cup of tea, Mother?" she said. "I'll finish showing Heather these."

Mrs Theakstone took the hint and disappeared. Heather wondered if she should offer to help, but was distracted by Cynthia.

"Here's one from the headmistress of my primary school. Isn't that amazing? And one from the minister - which church do you go to?"

"St. Mary's."

"Oh. We're Baptist."

"Oh," Heather said, startled. She hadn't met any Baptists before.

"You sound surprised. There aren't many of us, I agree and the church is at the far side of town, and it's dreadfully poor. We don't have money for fancy services, like you Anglicans do. But we're all terribly committed and enthusiastic. You don't get any half-hearted Baptists. We support a missionary in Brazil. The trouble with the established church is that people go for all the wrong reasons - because it's the thing to do, that sort of thing. And it's got this sort of upper class feel about it."

"We're not upper class," objected Heather.

"Upper middle, then. Your father's a professional, isn't he?"

"He's an architect," Heather said proudly.

"Well then. We've been doing sociology at school," Cynthia explained.

Mrs Theakstone came in with the tea tray, which she placed on the kidney shaped table. It wobbled a little and Cynthia said, "Mother, is that quite safe?"

"Perhaps if I pour it in the kitchen," worried Mrs Theakstone, and went away with the tray. She came back to ask Heather if she took milk and sugar. She then returned with two cups of tea, this time accompanied by her husband, who held out a biscuit tin. The cups and saucers were decorated with small pink rosebuds.

"Oh, Auntie Phyllis has cups and saucers like these!"

"I expect your own parents have something rather better," smiled Cynthia. "You'd better sit down to drink it." Her mother folded the letters and wrapped them in the brown paper. "If your father can suggest a way of protecting these papers, I'd be glad to hear of it," she said.

"I'll ask him," Heather promised, glad that it would give her an excuse to make a return visit.

"Thank you for the tea, Mother," said Cynthia. Her parents disappeared.

The two girls settled down on the settee. Heather forgot her surroundings and her initial awkwardness in the warmth of their conversation. She felt happy and contented and could have stayed all afternoon but was anxious not to outstay her welcome on her first visit, so after a while she said she supposed she had better go and do some homework. She was a little disappointed that Cynthia made no effort to stop her although she accompanied her to the front door very graciously, and told her that she must call again soon. The hall was so narrow that there was barely enough room for Heather and Cynthia to stand together, and when Cynthia opened the front door Heather had to step back into the living room.

This was the start of a close friendship between the two girls. At first, Heather kept her distance at school, but memories are short and Cynthia's star quickly waned. Her act of heroism was overshadowed by the threat of mock O and A levels, the inter-schools hockey match, Buddy Holly's death, and the reason behind the headmistress's banning of black stockings. Cynthia, never an enthusiastic group member, was more often to be seen on her own. Some of the girls in the sixth form had boyfriends, but Cynthia explained that boys would be a distraction at this stage of her career. She had had a very close relationship with another girl when she was Heather's age and doing O levels, but something had gone wrong (Cynthia was a little mysterious here) and they were no longer friends.

Despite these strictures about mixing work and pleasure, Heather and Cynthia met regularly. When the weather was fine they would go for a walk round the hockey pitch and through the little copse of trees at the end of the school grounds. Cynthia professed to love nature, and believed that it was important to get fresh air and exercise no matter how much work you had to do. She said the brain didn't function properly if the body was sick. Heather was not too sure about this, pointing to her cousin Elisabeth who had a polio-withered arm but who was already showing signs of being extremely bright. Cynthia said that that sort of thing was quite different.

Heather by this time was fascinated by her new friend. Cynthia had such new and original ideas. Her own family quickly grew tired of hearing of Cynthia's latest ideas and, for her part, Cynthia seemed indifferent to Heather's stories of her family. It was the only disappointment in an otherwise rewarding friendship.

One day in November when the trees were putting on their last show of colour for the year, they met as usual by the changing rooms and set out down the cinder track between the tennis courts, and along the side of the hockey pitch. The sun was unseasonably warm and the trees very beautiful.

"Season of mists and mellow fruitfulness," Cynthia said with emotion. "Oh, to live forever surrounded by trees like this. Can you imagine anything more beautiful?"

"My sister Lesley thinks that trees are most beautiful in the winter," said Heather, who at this early stage in the friendship frequently forgot that Cynthia did not like to be contradicted, especially when she was in a lyrical mood.

"Oh, surely not," Cynthia said, sounding shocked. "Why, everything's so bare and drab. Early spring, yes, when everything is so softly coming into green leaf." She paused, wishing she had brought a notebook with her to record this pretty thought.

"It's because you can see their forms," Heather explained. "Lesley draws, you see, and she prefers drawing trees in winter because you can see them better. She says you can't really draw trees with leaves on and you can only paint them in a splotchy sort of a way."

"Other artists have managed," said Cynthia, a trifle huffily, but without giving an example. Art was not one of her subjects. "You seem to set a lot of store by your sister."

"Well, she is good at drawing. I expect she'll be an artist when she grows up, although Daddy would like her to become an architect."

"It's hardly a suitable occupation for a girl, I shouldn't have thought."

"Daddy thinks it would be OK."

Cynthia was always slightly irritated by Heather's frequent references to her father, who was clearly a rival for her heart and soul. "Oh well, of course, your father is a socialist, isn't he?"

Heather blushed. This was a source of some embarrassment to her. Bertrand had always professed to be a Labour Party supporter, voting for them after the war and being generally in favour of Hugh Gaitskell. His political beliefs were shared by some of his colleagues at work but not on the whole by his family and friends. Despite this, he had joined the Labour Party, and was threatening to stand as a local councillor. His wife and children were not enthusiastic.

Having made her point, Cynthia became more gracious. "The trees can look pretty in the winter when there's been a frost and the snow stays on the branches. I expect that's what your sister means."

Heather knew that this was not what Lesley meant, but this time she held her tongue. They walked on, scuffing their feet in the leaves. A little later Cynthia said "You and your family are all very close, aren't you?"

"I suppose so." Heather couldn't think of any other way of life.

"I haven't got much family," said Cynthia. "I've no brothers and sisters, and no cousins - well, one step-cousin, but he doesn't really count. I knew my grandfather - my mother's father - a little, but he died when I was ten."

"Oh Cynthia," Heather said, sad for her friend, and at the same time wondering what a step-cousin could be.

"I'm not looking for sympathy," Cynthia said, smiling bravely. "On the whole I think I prefer it my way. You can sort your life out better if you're on your own. I wouldn't like to be at everybody's beck and call. And my parents realise that I am likely to do better in life than they have, and don't get in my way. I'm just trying to explain how different it is."

"Yes, I can see that," said Heather, who had indeed been aware of the difference the very first time she had set foot in Cynthia's house.

Everything was somehow smaller and tighter - everything except Cynthia herself, of course. Her own house was quite shabby but it was shabby in a comfortable way, there was space for everyone and never any stinting on things like food and heat and trips to different parts of the country. There was even talk of going abroad on holiday next year. Irene sometimes talked of the hard time they had had when first married but the girls found it difficult to imagine that things could ever have been different.

"We do get on each other's nerves sometimes," she said, doubtfully. "But when we do, somehow there's always someone else to turn to. And quarrels never last very long. Not that we quarrel much. Lesley just doesn't and Elisabeth goes quiet and Pattie - well, she doesn't quarrel either, really, now I come to think of it. She just goes a bit wild if she's upset. I suppose I'm the only one..." She paused to think about this. Cynthia was still admiring the trees and not taking much notice of what Heather was saying.

"What do Baptists do for Christmas?" Heather asked as they walked back to school.

"We celebrate like everyone else. Perhaps more quietly than some. We go to church. There's an old lady who used to live next door to us - she's in a home now, but she usually comes to us on Christmas Day. But that's how it ought to be, don't you think? If you can see a chance of doing good to someone, do it, but otherwise spend the holy day quietly with your close family. It was never intended that we should give each other expensive presents and have wild parties."

"I suppose not," said Heather, thinking of their noisy family parties. She wondered if Uncle Hugh would come again this year.

"Christmas is becoming too commercialised."

Heather had heard the same complaint from her mother, her uncle Allan and her grandmother. What they meant was carol singers who never sang beyond 'We wish you a Merry Christmas' before asking for money and Father Christmas and Christmas goods in shops before the end of November. But Cynthia meant something deeper than this, and Heather was afraid that if they pursued the subject her own enjoyment of Christmas would be spoiled.

Fortunately, by this time they had reached the tennis courts in front of the school building where they separated, Cynthia to go round by the front door, which only the staff and the sixth form could use, and Heather to use the back stairs. At school they were discreet about their friendship, finding other ways to meet: in the public library when they

110

wanted to change their books, and going for walks together at weekends when the weather was fine. Now and again they visited each other's homes, but both were ill at ease on these occasions; Heather because of the Theakstones' nervousness and anxiety to please, and Cynthia because she never felt she was being taken quite seriously enough by Heather's family.

Towards the beginning of December Heather began to talk of having the Theakstones to the house on Christmas Day. Her parents tried to dissuade her. "Darling, you haven't known her for long and we don't know her parents at all."

Heather tried to explain the importance of her friendship with Cynthia. "And they have such dreadful Christmases, just an old lady in a home, and you say Christmas is a time for goodwill and friendship and all that."

"Yes, I know, but they probably enjoy their Christmas in their own home, just like we enjoy ours," but Heather was not to be persuaded. She took the problem to Lesley. Lesley sometimes came up with good, practical solutions to problems which had been puzzling everybody else for ages.

"Have them round for drinks before lunch, with the Murrays," advised Lesley. "That way they won't have to stay too long."

"Ye-es," Heather said doubtfully. What she really wanted was for Cynthia to participate in her Christmas as if she were one of the family, but of course she could not ask her without her family's agreement, and she had to admit that although she was sure that Cynthia would quickly fit into the Atfield family life, Mr and Mrs Theakstone were more of a problem. Then another thought struck her. "I don't think they drink."

"I expect Daddy can give them orange juice."

"Yes, but they might not like the idea of a drinks party."

Lesley shrugged, losing interest.

Heather told her father that she thought it would be nice if she could invite the Theakstones to the house on Christmas morning. He thought that this was a reasonable compromise. Other neighbours called in, and he liked to have his house full of people. "I've found a super recipe for a Christmas punch," he told her. "It should put a bit of the old Christmas spirit into people if it's not already there. It's a hot drink, too, should warm everyone up. What do you think? Where's the recipe, let me show you. You need rum and..."

Heather listened politely. Then she said "I don't think they drink."

111

"Who don't?"

"The Theakstones."

"Not even at Christmas? Not even a sherry?"

Heather shook her head.

"What are they, Methodists?"

"No, Baptists."

"It doesn't seem very hospitable to offer people orange juice, but I suppose you girls will be drinking it. I hope they're not going to look disapprovingly at my punch."

"Oh no, Daddy," Heather reassured him. "It's only that they don't like it themselves."

The Theakstones' debut in the Atfield home went reasonably well. They stayed for just over half an hour, between church and collecting their old lady, sitting stiffly on the settee in the living room, sipping the fruit punch which Bertrand had made in addition to the alcoholic punch. Heather knelt by the settee, and talked to them. The other guests were neighbours, friends from church and from Bertrand's office. Irene's parents, Ernest and Mary Lindsey, were there, sitting quietly in the breakfast room with Phyllis and Allan, and a couple of older guests. Cynthia was mingling with the other guests in a mature, confident manner. Heather was impressed and faintly jealous. She had never really seen Cynthia in company before. She herself had discovered that the art of conversation with the elder Theakstones was to talk about their daughter. Then they grew animated, their eyes brightened, and they conversed happily about their favourite subject. She was Heather's favourite subject too, so this was no problem.

"She looks well in company," admitted her mother.

"She's looking lovely," Heather enthused.

Cynthia's long straight ash blonde hair, normally fastened in a plait, was loose, held back from her face by an Alice band, and she wore a dark green wool dress. She was tall and slender, a silver and green goddess, making everyone else in the room seem dull in comparison. The dress was short on her long legs, and the collar and cuffs a little worn. Heather knew that the Theakstones could not afford a new dress every Christmas, such as she and Lesley had, and she longed to buy one for Cynthia. She wondered if her father would give her the money if she asked. And would Cynthia accept such a gift? She thought perhaps she might. Oh, if only she had thought about it earlier, she could have given Cynthia her own new dress, she herself could easily wear last year's.

She was proud to see such a mix of people enjoying themselves. It gave her a nice warm feeling of contentment. All that hard work had been worthwhile.

After half an hour the Theakstones were ready to leave. They were beginning to fret about the time, about collecting the old lady and basting the turkey and putting the potatoes on. They wished to say goodbye to their host and hostess but were nervous about interrupting them. Bertrand was in the midst of an animated talk, so Heather went in search of her mother. Irene was also anxious about her turkey. She was in the kitchen, struggling to take it far enough out of the oven so that she could spoon hot fat over it. She looked up in relief as Heather put her head round the door. "Thank goodness you've come! Put an apron on quickly and give me a hand. Quickly, please, this is heavy. Take the spoon and see if you can get up enough fat to spread over the bird. I don't want to have to take it right out of the oven if I can help it."

"Yes but Mummy the Theakstones are going. They want to say goodbye to you."

"Oh, Heather, I can't possibly come now. Where's your father?"

"Talking. It won't take a minute, Mummy. They'll be terribly hurt if you don't come."

Irene was hot and flustered. "They'll just have to wait a minute. Are you going to give me a hand or not? I can't stay here all day holding this. Spoon the fat over the bird - tie a tea towel round your waist, don't splash your new dress - then I can come. For goodness sake, Heather! They can surely look after themselves for five minutes."

Biting her lip, Heather did as she was bid, but her hand was shaking and some of the hot fat splashed on to her mother's wrist. Irene gave a yelp of pain. "Oh you clumsy girl. I shall have a blister there. Quick, turn on the cold tap." She pushed the turkey back into the oven and held her wrist under the cold water, grimacing at the pain. "Now a clean tea towel." She patted her wrist dry, and examined it.

"You must be more careful."

"Shall I tell them you're too busy to come?" asked Heather stubbornly.

"Tell who? Oh, good heavens - alright, I'll come." They went out together and found the Theakstones standing alone in the hall. Cynthia was in the doorway between the hall and the living room, bending down gracefully in order to talk to small Elisabeth, who was wriggling, anxious to get away. Mrs Theakstone explained yet again about the old lady and the turkey, and the time it would take them to walk home. Still they stood there. Irene suddenly realised that they were waiting for their coats, which had been put away in the cloakroom under the stairs. She sent Elisabeth to fetch them. Elisabeth, released, scurried away with speed. She came back with an armful, and the Theakstones extracted their shabby raincoats from amongst the furs and camel hair coats of the Atfields' other guests. As they were saying goodbye, Cynthia and Heather pressed gifts into each other's hands.

"Merry Christmas," said Heather, glistening. She wished that Cynthia could stay all day. Cynthia took Heather's hands in her mittens. "God bless you," she said, and kissed her. Heather's stomach did funny things, and her face burned. Oh, if only Cynthia could stay all day - could stay with them over the Christmas holiday, in fact. Perhaps she could come and stay - just one night. She would ask her mother. Cynthia turned and followed her parents down the drive. It was a cold day with a hint of snow in the air. Heather stood at the open door watching them until they were quite out of sight.

"Close the door, love, you're letting in all the cold. Unless you'd like to cut some more holly. I need it for the dining room. Take Elisabeth with you, I think she's had enough of the party."

Elisabeth materialised beside her dressed in her duffle coat and woolly hat and carrying a pair of scissors. Heather didn't feel like going back into the party just yet. She didn't really want to talk to anyone. Elisabeth was an ideal companion, being silent. She just wanted to walk and think of Cynthia. She was warm and glowing inside, and felt in no need of a coat. Cynthia had kissed her. Of course it was Christmas, her own family kissed everyone, but she had never seen Cynthia kiss anyone before, not even her parents. And she had done it so beautifully, cool and dry, on the lips. Heather had been so surprised that she had just stood there and let herself be kissed. Now she began to worry that Cynthia might feel hurt because she hadn't kissed her back.

The ground was hard and dry, with a dusting of frost. Elisabeth darted about the garden, looking for holly. The cold air made her cheeks glow and her brown eyes sparkle, and the dark blue velvet dress given to her by her aunt and uncle suited her well. She retained her extreme reticence but had lost the haunted look she had worn during the first few months of her stay at Sycamore Road. She no longer doubted that her father would return for her one day. Meanwhile the postcards and occasional visits gave her hope. He had sent her a Christmas card, and there was a letter inside explaining that he couldn't join her that year as he was appearing in a pantomime in Glasgow, but he would come and see her in the spring. Elisabeth accepted this.

Heather, overflowing with emotion, watched her and was filled with a great love for her courageous little cousin. She put her arms round her and gave her a big hug before they walked back to the house together. Elisabeth wriggled, then gave her a shy smile, before darting into the house. At the door Heather was filled with such an intense feeling of joy and love that she felt impelled to stay outside a few minutes longer. She leaned against the doorpost, looking over the lovely wintry garden. Any more beauty and she felt as if she would burst. If only Cynthia had been able to stay a little longer, to share this feeling with her. She tried to hold it in her mind, to capture it in order to describe it to her friend. All at once, she knew what it was. It was the Christmas spirit, filling her to overflowing with the love of God and man. Heather felt uplifted, utterly convinced of the reality of God. His son's love for the world was all round her and tangible that Christmas Day. She had always believed in God but now she really knew it for herself. She knew then that her life's work had to be to convince other people of her belief and to show them that Christ's message was a joyful one. Transformed, Heather lingered in the cold before turning into the house to face that other reality, family life.

The party was breaking up. Watching everyone depart, she pondered on the difference that money made to family life. She was standing in the hall, knowing that there was room for her and a coat rail and the departing guests, compared with the narrow little space that counted as a hall in Cynthia's home. The really poor were different, she couldn't imagine what it must be like. But genteel poverty was something she could see for herself. The Theakstones wanted the same things as the Atfields, they had the same aspirations, she and Cynthia went to the same school, but she and Lesley had new clothes and toys and books and games and they left rooms heated even when they weren't in them and they could afford to go on holiday. She wasn't sure what Mr Theakstone did for a living but knew that it was unlikely to be a well paid job. She thought again of her new dress, and Cynthia's well worn one. It seemed unfair. Her father earned well and they were never short of anything. From time to time

Bertrand claimed to be a socialist, although his beliefs had not so far been put to the test. He thought the Conservatives were out of date, privileged, ridden with scandal. She wondered what he would have to say about her views on poverty and social inequality. In communist Russia, she had heard, everyone earned exactly the same amount so everyone was equal. She would tackle him later on, after they had pulled the crackers.

5

When they met in the New Year Heather told Cynthia how much she had enjoyed Christmas, and then, shyly, tried to describe the joy she had experienced in the garden. Cynthia said "It was very kind of your parents to invite us," to the first statement, and "How nice," to the second, responses that Heather found a little disappointing. She had noticed, however, that her friend liked to introduce ideas and revelations herself. She tried to think of a topic on which Cynthia would have an opinion, in order to encourage her to talk, after which she could return to the topic she wished to discuss. She told Cynthia that the boy next door had asked Lesley to go to the pictures with her. Her mother had said she could only go if she went with a group.

"How old is she?"

"Thirteen," said Heather.

"Dear me!" said Cynthia.

"But what age do you think - I mean if a boy were to ask me to the cinema, should I go?"

"Has anyone?"

"Well, no. But if."

"That would be up to you and your mother."

"Would it be alright for you?" Heather was in need of advice from her clear thinking friend about the significance of boys in one's life. Girls of her own age were going to mixed parties and dances and a few of them had boy friends with whom they claimed to be going steady. Heather did not have a boyfriend, nor did she have any desire for one, but she thought that sooner or later she would have to have one although she wasn't sure that she really saw the point.

Under pressure Cynthia gave her opinion. She said that just at present her work came first. She didn't rule out friendship with a boy, but it would have to be a very special kind of boy, not one of the silly rough schoolboys who fooled around on the buses and embarrassed the girls by their wolf whistles and personal comments and were clumsy and rushed down the stairs first and bumped into you with their duffle bags and satchels. For this reason she thought that her first special male friend was likely to be a few years older than she was, someone with whom she could have a serious, spiritual relationship. "I'm not interested in the physical side, not at the moment. I'm sure I shall be, in time. I shall need to be awoken, gently and with sensitivity. A young boy wouldn't understand my needs. Women mature much

117

earlier than men, you know. I'm 17, and in order to be equally mature a man would have to be - oh, 21 or 22. But I have always been drawn to even older men - like Mr Maddox, for example."

Mr Maddox was the vicar, an austere-looking man, balding, and given to wearing half moon spectacles. He taught the classes in Religious Instruction that Cynthia had attended.

"But he's old!"

"Not very. About 35 or so, I'd say. He may look older because of his baldness - that's often a sign of great spirituality, you know."

"Is it?"

"Think of all the bald men you know."

Heather couldn't think of any except the butcher. "Oh, and your father."

"He's thinning rather than balding. But yes, he is quite a spiritual man in his way. However, I'm sure that if you looked at a selection of ministers - men of the church - you would find that a large proportion of them were bald."

"And he's married." Mrs Maddox was small, dark, and jolly, and very unlike her husband. Heather had heard her father say that it was a pity that she was not the vicar instead, but decided not to pass this comment on to her friend.

"I wasn't speaking literally. I was putting forward Mr Maddox as an example of the sort of man I admire."

"I think I prefer women," said Heather, who was sitting on the floor in the Theakstone's lounge, leaning against her friend's legs.

"You can't do that," Cynthia said. "There's a word for women who like other women - and it's not a very nice word."

"What is it?" Heather asked anxiously.

"Lesbian," Cynthia said softly, "it comes from the island of Lesbos where the poet Sappho used to live. Sappho was a lesbian." Her fingers played with the lobe of Heather's ear. Heather found this very pleasant.

She had never heard of Sappho. "What a lot you know," she sighed. But "I don't see what's wrong with it. Why, I like you and my mother and Lesley better than anyone I know - except perhaps Daddy."

"Family's all right," said Cynthia judiciously. "But close friendships between women have always been frowned upon. I'm not sure why," she admitted. "I think perhaps it's because you can't have babies."

118

"But I don't want babies," exclaimed Heather, sitting upright. This was something of a preoccupation for Heather at present; she spent time worrying about how she was to avoid having the babies that seemed to be an essential part of a grown up woman's life. Cynthia pulled her back and her soothing fingers stroked the soft flesh beneath Heather's chin.

"You're a baby yourself. You don't have to have babies. But that's what sexual relationships are supposed to be for. The church certainly believes that."

"But - that's men and women," said Heather. "Like they say in the marriage service. And biology lessons. That's what sex is."

"Not always," said Cynthia, fingers stroking.

"You mean - women and women?"

"And men and men. It's illegal of course."

"Ugh," said Heather. In fact, she said "Ugh" mentally whenever she thought of sex. Cynthia's fingers were still for a moment. "It happens a lot in boarding schools," she said. "You can understand it. Girls living close together, separated from home and family, often lonely. Friendships can become - well - intimate. It's understandable. However, it is considered to be wrong. Our parents would be shocked if they knew that we were talking about it." It made Heather feel very grown up to think that she and Cynthia were discussing topics which would shock their parents. At the same time "Lesley and I can talk about anything we like at home," she said, proudly and foolishly.

"How fortunate you are," said Cynthia. "Now get off my foot would you, dear, you've given me cramp."

That night, Heather found herself thinking about their conversation. She understood the basic principles of human reproduction, at least as far as its biology was concerned, and its various elements, though untidy, connected logically. From novels and discussions with friends she knew something of the complexities of the sexual relations which might exist between men and women. One biology lesson had been given over to this, and they were told that men had this highly sensitive thing (they were given the proper name but she was uncomfortable using it even in her thoughts) which was likely to get them and their girlfriends into all kinds of trouble, and it was up to girls to take care not to let passions get too heated.

Sex between man and wife in order to have children was clearly alright, thought Heather, if that was the only way; after all the Church said so, but until you were ready for that it was better just to have friendships, and it was probably better to keep those friendships to members of your own sex, given that men had this sensitive and volatile thing attached to them. She didn't believe what Cynthia had said about lesbians. Well, they existed, Cynthia was right about that, she had looked the word up in the dictionary when she got home but all the dictionary said was "Homosexuality in women", and when she looked up homosexual, the entry read "(Person) who is sexually attracted only by persons of his or her own sex; relating to the same sex", which wasn't very helpful either. It seemed to Heather that women couldn't be sexually attracted to each other because they didn't have the thing that men had, that seemed to be the key to it all, and there was nothing wrong with the sort of warm friendship that she enjoyed with Cynthia. So that was that. And yet it wasn't. Cynthia had said that the Bible had said it was wrong to be attracted to the same sex, but surely friendships were all about being attracted to some people and not others, otherwise you'd have to be friends with the whole world and that clearly wasn't possible. She decided to ask her parents about it.

Heather waited until they were all sitting down to lunch on Sunday, which was always a leisurely affair. "Daddy, what's a lesbian?" she enquired. The others stopped eating, forks half way to their mouths. Lesley sniggered.

"What on earth made you think of that?" demanded Bertrand, playing for time.

"Oh, Cynthia and I were talking yesterday. Well, I know what it is, sort of, but I don't understand. Cynthia says the Bible says it's wrong."

"It probably does."

"Because you can't have babies that way?"

"Um - yes."

"But what I can't understand is what they can do that is so wrong." Heather noticed Elisabeth at the end of the table, and refrained from mentioning men's things. "And if they do why they want to."

"I really don't think this is a suitable time for a discussion of this sort," said Irene, who was less enthusiastic than Bertrand for talking everything out en famille.

"They want to because they like it," said Lesley.

"But why do they like it?" persisted Heather.

"Heather, really," said her mother.

"Why does anyone like anything?" queried her father. "It's a physical pleasure like - like running into the sea on a hot day or coming down a helter skelter or riding on the big wheel. You know how exciting that is."

"I shouldn't like to do that all the time," said Heather.

"Nobody does. That's just a kind of analogy - you know what an analogy is? A very crude one, leaving love out of it altogether. But you see, most grown up people get that sort of excitement from being with someone of the opposite sex. But just a few people get it when they are with the same sex. It's not exactly wrong..."

"Oh, Bertrand!" interposed Irene.

"...but it's not to be recommended for various reasons. People who feel like that are not quite normal, they are out of step with the rest of society."

"And they can't have babies."

"Er - no."

"So if you don't want babies, ever, it might be alright."

Bertrand frowned. Irene interrupted. "How much time do you and Cynthia spend discussing this sort of thing? I thought you were supposed to be studying together?"

"Oh we are, only afterwards we sometimes talk."

"I don't know that Cynthia is a very suitable friend for you," continued Irene, who was feeling a little out of sorts. "She's too old for you. Why can't you make friends with girls of your own age?"

Heather pouted. "Cynthia's very suitable. She knows a lot."

"And I don't see how you can work together when you are two years behind her."

"We just like being together. I can concentrate better when I'm with Cynthia. She says she forgets how young I am."

"Well, perhaps she should remember."

Heather was upset. "You're always getting at me," she accused. "You don't complain about Lesley's friends. Why don't you like Cynthia?"

"We didn't say we didn't like her."

"You don't, I know you don't. You always say I should talk to you about everything and then you complain when I do. I shall never tell you anything again!" Heather said dramatically.

Cynthia, the next weekend, was not surprised at this outcome, and was kind. "I told you they'd be shocked. You say you can tell your parents everything, and I'm sure they do their best, but they are a different generation, and however hard they try they will never quite

121

be able to understand. That generation hates talk about homosexuality especially, they see it as something quite wrong. It's because it frightens them. Have you ever thought that so many of the things which are said to be bad or wrong are only so because people are frightened of them? But our generation takes a more liberal view."

Both girls had examinations in preparation for their GCEs in February, and the real examinations in June, and were working hard so meetings were limited. One beautiful day during the Easter holidays, however, they decided to go out for the whole day. They would walk over the moors to Ilkley, rest for an hour or so, and then get the bus back. Irene made sandwiches, and put them with two thick slices of fruit cake and two apples into Heather's haversack. Her father gave her some money to buy tea in Ilkley, and lent her his compass and a map. At the last minute Lesley and Pattie nearly spoiled everything by deciding that they wanted to come too, but Heather kept her head and told them how far it was (treacherously adding on an extra two miles) and they lost interest and decided to take Elisabeth swimming instead.

Cynthia was ready and waiting, bearing patiently Mrs Theakstone's concern in case they got lost/wet/tired/cold. As soon as Heather appeared she gave her mother a cheery goodbye and they set off.

"I'm afraid she'll worry like that all day until I get back but what can I do?" she said casually. "It's likely that I shall be leaving home in the autumn, and she'll have to get used to that."

They followed the road past the golf club and then cut across the fields towards the hikers' pub, a place well known to walkers. The April sun was warm and the day was soft and balmy. A gentle breeze fanned their faces, and sent soft white clouds drifting across the sky. Larks were singing, newly born lambs were staggering on bowed little legs, and the hedgerows were misty green with new leaves. Winter lay behind them; summer was ahead. All was here and now. The two girls were overwhelmed with the beauty of the countryside. "It's heavenly!" they kept saying to each other. Cynthia perched on top of a stile and gazed at the moors all around her. "It smells different up here," she said. "Sweet. I expect that's the gorse, it's just coming out. On a day like this I wonder why I ever think of going away."

"Why must you go away?" Heather asked, sadly.

"I can't stay here for ever. There's so much more world out there."

"I don't think I want to go away," said Heather.

"It's different for you. You're younger and your parents are more - well - more worldly than mine. They have a broader experience of

122

life, and you can talk to them about life. Mine are very caring, very loving, but they don't see how trapped I feel. I need to spread my wings before it's too late."

Heather was impressed with Cynthia's reasoning, but she protested "But you already have a broad understanding of things. That's what I admire so much about you. You know so much about so many things."

"It's nearly all from books," said Cynthia. "I do try not to be narrow. But it's not easy. Still, on a day like this I wouldn't be anywhere else but here, with you. Come on." She jumped off the stile and allowed Heather to climb over, less gracefully. They walked across a rough field, marked with thistles and cow dung, keeping a wary eye on the herd of brown and white cows at the far end.

"I'm not scared of cows," said Cynthia.

"Neither am I," agreed Heather.

"But you can never be quite sure that there aren't any bullocks among them. And they're so big. If they come galloping up to you, even in a friendly way, they could easily knock you over."

"And then trample on you."

"So it's best to be safe. Don't run or laugh or wave anything at them. It might startle them."

"Daddy says it doesn't have to be red," Heather said as they approached the gate.

"What doesn't?"

"The rag you wave at a bull. Any bright colour will do. It's just something to catch its attention."

"I shan't put it to the test, I assure you," Cynthia said. "Actually, you know, I don't think farmers keep bulls with cows. They just put them together occasionally, when they want the cows to become pregnant."

"I don't think they even do that," said Heather. "They do this thing - what's it called - artificial something."

"Insemination. Artificial insemination."

"Yes, that's it. I don't think the bull ever gets to see a cow."

"I wonder how they do it," said Cynthia.

Heather shuddered. "I can't think."

Twenty minutes or so later they reached the pub. It nestled in a hollow under the road.

"In two months time I could go in there," said Cynthia. "As it is we shall have to sit on the wall and swing our legs on the side away from

123

the pub. D'you think we would get arrested if we sat with our legs the other way?"

"I shouldn't think so," said Heather. "I think you've got to go inside, to the bar. And anyway we wouldn't be arrested, the publican would."

Cynthia burst into a peal of laughter. "Heather, you take everything so seriously!" They drank some orange juice and had a sandwich each.

"I shall need to go to the toilet soon," said Heather, who had a weak bladder.

"No problem, you can go up there." Cynthia indicated the brownish-green moors which stretched in front of them, bare and bleak even on a day like this.

"Can't I go in the pub?"

"You're not allowed."

"No, but there's a ladies just outside, look."

"Oh alright, I'll come too."

"I would worry otherwise," confided Heather as they came out.

"You worry too much."

"You do too."

"Only about important things."

They crossed the road and walked alongside the dry stone wall until they found another stile. They climbed over, then followed another stone wall up a steeply sloping field, rough with clumps of thistles, the wiry stems of heather, and gorse. Above this field the moors proper started, and they paused for breath, looking back over the little moorland settlements in the valley below. To their left a reservoir sparkled in the sun. Heather had a sudden yearning that her life would always be peaceful and secure, as it was today. Then they turned their faces to the moor again.

A broad track led up through the heather and gorse. Half a mile away they could see two dark figures silhouetted against the clear sky. The gorse was indeed flowering, filling the air with its sweet, smoky scent, but it was too early in the year for the other moorland flowers. In the late summer the hills would be transformed by the purple heather. Birds were singing, higher, wilder songs than their fellows in the suburbs.

A little further on Cynthia consulted Bertrand's map and said that there were some tumuli on their right. "Shall we go and look?"

They ventured off the track and through the heather, looking for tumuli, though neither of them were sure what they were looking for. A little cloud came from nowhere and momentarily blocked out the sun, making the moors instantly dark and foreboding.

"Oh look," said Cynthia, pointing up the hill to where there was a movement in the long grass, moving towards them and slightly to the left.

"Is it a snake?" asked Heather, nervous.

"A snake wouldn't move the grass like that. It's more like wind."

"But there's no wind anywhere else." A swathe of grass a foot or so wide bent and swayed. Everywhere else was quite still, and silent. Even the birds were hushed. Without the sun, the day seemed suddenly cold. Heather shivered, but neither girl moved until the swathe of moving grass had veered away from them, and down the hill.

"Is it still there?" whispered Heather, peering.

"I can't see."

"It must have been an animal."

"Then surely we would have seen it, and it us. It wouldn't have run in such a straight line. It was like a sort of mini-whirlwind. It's the weirdest thing I've ever seen."

Heather felt proud to have witnessed with Cynthia the weirdest thing her friend had ever seen. They were both rather subdued by the experience, which seemed to carry some meaning beyond the purely physical. They suspected some extra-terrestrial force, although neither cared to admit this. Tumuli were forgotten. They made their way back to the track, keeping a careful watch for further signs and portents among the grass. Once back on the comparative safety of the track, they reconsidered what they had seen.

"We must have been near the tumuli," Cynthia mused. "Maybe what we saw were the spirits of the ancient dead, coming with a message for us."

Coming from Cynthia, this did not sound fanciful.

"What message?"

"Warning of danger, perhaps, or bidding us to follow it. Did you see where it went?"

"It just seemed to disappear in the grass, somewhere over there." Heather pointed down the hill.

"Do you want to investigate?"

"No."

"I shouldn't think we would find anything. We weren't quick

enough to pick up the message. Next time we'll follow."

At the top of the next hill they stopped for a rest. From here they could see nothing but the moors stretching all around - heather, bracken, gorse and springy tussocks of grass, with occasional outcrops of grey rock. Looking back the way they had come, road and pub and fields and cottages had all disappeared.

Cynthia found a clearing in the bracken and sat down. "If we lie down we shall be completely hidden from view," she said. She lay on her back, her long fair hair spread over the turf. Heather put out her hand and touched it.

"Your hair is so fine and pretty," she said, admiring too her friend's pale oval face. Cynthia smiled, though her eyes remained cool and watchful. "Silly," she said. "Lie down and look up at the sky." Heather did so, and they gazed up into the great bowl of blue, and at the larks and linnets wheeling and calling. Around them the young bracken was unfurling delicate green fronds. All was utterly peaceful and they lay side by side, holding hands, for some time.

"It would be nice," Cynthia mused," if this peace could be enjoyed by everyone."

"It would get very busy," Heather objected.

"I don't mean here, I mean peace like this. If people could find peace in their hearts, they would put down their weapons and live in harmony with their neighbours."

"Oh, yes!" Heather thought that sounded wonderful.

"And how will they do that?"

"Well…" It was difficult when Cynthia asked questions. Too often Heather gave the wrong response. She had found that hesitation led Cynthia to provide the right one, as she did this time.

"Through finding God. It's the only way. We should go out, among the troubled peoples of the world, and try to bring them peace."

"How will we do that?"

"We're too young now. But when we finish our studies, we should go abroad, go to Africa, and bring people there to God."

"Like missionaries?"

"Perhaps. When the time is right we'll find a way. Meanwhile we must seek to influence, as best we can." She sat up. "Time to move on."

Comfortable rocks presented themselves at the highest point of the moors, before the path descended, gently at first, and then more steeply. In the distance they could see a clump of fir trees and some white cottages, and beyond that houses and a glimpse of river. Ilkley was in sight. They relaxed and settled down to eat the rest of their sandwiches, and the apples. The fresh air had given both girls healthy appetites, and they ate quickly. Heather had brought her camera, and she took several photographs of Cynthia among the rocks. Cynthia obligingly took one of Heather. Then they continued on their way, down a path that became rocky and wound steeply downhill among austere grey rocks. A few straggly trees appeared, and then a clump of firs and pines which the path skirted. On the far side of this their way became very steep, and stony, leading to the cottages covering the site of the old Roman baths. Now they could see the town quite clearly, and the river Wharfe winding through the valley. They staggered the last quarter of a mile on weak legs and collapsed on a bench outside the semi-derelict cottages. Below them was the children's paddling pool and play area, and beyond that the road leading into the town. There were a number of parked cars and people sitting on benches. They were back in civilisation.

"This is as far as most visitors come," said Cynthia with scorn. "They think they've seen the moors when they come this far."

It was painful walking on tired legs down the steep hill that led into town, past the guesthouses and small hotels, all built in the local grey stone. They were tired and hot, but satisfied. Bertrand had provided money for tea, and Heather automatically led the way to Betty's, which was where her parents came. Betty's had tasteful plastic flowers on the tables and waitresses dressed in black with little white aprons and the tea came in a silver pot with a separate jug of hot water. There was a menu and a trolley of cakes and gateaux. They walked in without thinking, but were quickly aware that their youth and untidiness made them conspicuous among the well dressed and middle aged clientele. They sat down at a corner table, and after some considerable time were approached by a waitress with neat brown waves in her hair, who asked them rather coldly what they wanted to order. Heather asked for tea and a toasted teacake, which was what her mother normally had. An elegant lady a few tables away nodded and smiled at her and Heather, recognising the wife of one of her father's partners, smiled back. The waitress, noticing, became friendlier. Cynthia, ill at ease, refused a cake.

"What about walking back over the moors?" she asked, turning her back to the room.

"Alright," said Heather gamely, but Cynthia laughed and said that she had only been joking. "Would you do anything I asked?"

"Yes," said Heather staunchly.

"To the moon? Round the world on a bicycle?"

"Yes."

"What if it were morally wrong?"

"You wouldn't ask me."

"But if I did."

"You wouldn't."

"But *say*."

"Well - I suppose I'd try to argue, persuade you that it was wrong," said Heather, nervously biting into her tea cake.

"But if I knew that and still wanted you to do it?"

"Well then, I suppose - I don't know. Why do you ask me?" Heather's appetite for her tea was diminishing.

Cynthia sat back, dabbing her mouth with her serviette.

"Hmm," she said. "I don't think I could ever be so much under someone else's influence."

Heather felt miserable. She could not understand Cynthia's motives. She pushed away the remains of her bun.

"Don't you want that?"

"No."

Cynthia picked it up with the corner of her serviette and transferred it to her own plate. "The walk has given me such an appetite," she announced. She looked from under her lashes at Heather's downcast face.

"Oh cheer up," she said. "I was only teasing you. Sometimes you act just like a child. I don't want to walk back. We catch the bus."

Heather had never been able to distinguish between teasing and more deliberate cruelty. However, when Cynthia told her she was teasing she knew how to react. She blinked the tears from her eyes and said in a wavering voice, "That's a relief. I don't think I could make it all the way back over the moors."

"I know I couldn't!"

Heather felt better, and her appetite returned. She looked down for her tea cake, but of course Cynthia had taken it. It was unlike Cynthia to display an appetite, the walk must have done her good. Normally she pecked at her food.

Cynthia's teasing had been the one flaw in an otherwise idyllic day. Although at the time she told herself it meant nothing, in bed that night she brooded on what Cynthia might possibly expect her to do that was wrong. Stealing books from the library, perhaps. Heather knew that the Theakstones had little spare money, and it could be that Cynthia desperately needed the books for her A Levels. Well, in that case she would buy the books herself, her father would always give her the money. She tried to think of some other crime. Telling lies? Cynthia had done something wrong (what that could be Heather could not imagine) and asked Heather to cover up for her. Well, yes, she would do that. Lying was wrong, but it didn't hurt anyone. She would do that for her friend. She would do almost anything if she felt that Cynthia really needed her help. She would lie down and die, if necessary. Heather fell asleep trying to think of circumstances in which she might be expected to lie down and die, for Cynthia's sake.

After Easter they were both too busy to see much of each other. Cynthia needed to study with her own age group. Heather understood. She realised that the two year difference in their ages was a barrier at this particular time. She missed her friend and was envious of those girls who because of an accident of birth could be closer to Cynthia than she could. She had, however, persuaded her friend to join a school trip to France in the summer, knowing that once Cynthia was at university they would inevitably be less close. It would be different when she too was at university, and after that, perhaps they would go out to Africa together. Heather's imagination had been caught by Cynthia's vision of bringing people to God, and by doing so bringing peace to the world. She lay in bed, imagining them together, in a little white church among small thatched huts, surrounded by jungle where antelopes and giraffes and zebra roamed. There would be lions and tigers too, which worried her a bit, but someone would tell her how to deal with them when the time came. As Cynthia said, at the moment they were both far too young.

6

After the exams the Atfields went on holiday, first to the aunts near Chester, and then to the Lake District. Later in the summer there would be the school trip to France, where they would be staying with French families. Heather, already nervous about this, needed to talk to her friend and on her return from the Lakes she cycled round to the Theakstones only to find that Cynthia was out, a meeting at the Church, her mother said, although she was unclear what the meeting was about. However, she was sure Cynthia would soon be home. She stood back to let Heather into the house and indicated that she should go into the front room. She was no longer shy when speaking to Heather (indeed, she sometimes seemed more at ease with her than she was with her own daughter) but she had never yet invited her into the back room, where the family lived. Heather politely discussed holidays and exams, before explaining that she wanted to meet her friend in order to talk about France.

"France?"

"We're going in just over two weeks and there's masses to do."

Mrs Theakstone looked puzzled. "Cynthia hasn't said anything about going to France. She did mention Scarborough."

"Oh no, we're going to France!"

"I don't think…" Mrs Theakstone's voice trailed into silence. "I don't think France…" her voice trailed away again. Heather was embarrassed. Surely Cynthia had told her parents. She often tried to protect them, saying that they worried about her. But it was only two weeks off, she would need money, and a passport - goodness. She got to her feet. "I'll see if I can find her at the Church. We need to talk."

Mrs Theakstone looked doubtful, but Heather, forgetting that her friend was not keen on surprises, could see no reason why she shouldn't go in search of her.

So she cycled off to the far side of town and the Baptist church hall. She always felt a nervous excitement about going into a place of religion different from her own. The Baptist Church wasn't so different, not like Catholicism which felt so foreign, but still it wasn't her own.

The hall, however, was locked and there was no sign of any activity. The church also seemed deserted. Perhaps the meeting was a big one and they were using the Anglican church hall which held more people. She cycled back to the vicarage which was next to the church, half way up the hill. As she hesitated at the gate, unsure whether to go in, Mrs Maddox, the Vicar's wife, came up behind her, pushing her bicycle.

"Heather, my dear," she puffed. "Whew, let me get my breath back. There are days when I think walking would be better than the bike. Except once I stop using it I might never start again. Now, how can I help? Were you looking for me, or Jim?"

"Well, actually I was looking for my friend Cynthia. Cynthia Theakstone. You won't know her, she goes to the Baptist Church. But there's no-one there and I thought she might be here, her mother just said she was at a church meeting."

"I think she may be with Jim now," Mrs Maddox said. "They've been a while, I expect they've nearly finished, come in and have a cup of tea and we can wait for them."

"That would be lovely," Heather said politely.

Inside, Brenda Maddox led her down the hall and into the kitchen.

"Jim uses the front room for seeing people so if we stay here and leave the door open we can hear them come out. Now, tea or a cold drink? I've made some fresh lemonade."

"Lemonade sounds lovely, if it isn't any trouble," said Heather.

"No trouble, it's nice to see you. Sit down and tell me how you all are. How's that quiet little cousin of yours?"

"Elisabeth is fine," said Heather, trying to put concerns about Cynthia out of her mind. "She's doing very well at school. Mummy says she needs to find her own level - I'm not sure what she means but basically we just treat her like one of the family - well, she is of course - and kind of encourage her to do things but don't push her too hard. She can be terribly stubborn."

"Sounds like a good rule for life," said Brenda Maddox, taking a glass jug out of the fridge and pouring the contents into two glasses. "Encourage but don't push, I mean. Pull up a chair and sit down."

Heather hesitated, "If you're busy I won't stay long - I can ring Cynthia from home."

"Oh, I'm sure they'll be finished soon and then Jim will come straight through for a cup of tea."

Brenda Maddox kept Heather talking about her family for a little while until the sitting room door opened and voices could be heard in the hall.

"Why, there she is," exclaimed Heather, recognising Cynthia's voice, and hurried into the hall where the Vicar was shaking Cynthia's hand. At the sound of her voice they turned. Cynthia looked taken aback, and frowned. Brenda came out to stand next to Heather.

"Heather is looking for her friend, Jim," she said quietly. "She thought she might be here."

"Your mother said you were here, Cynthia," Heather said helplessly, knowing she had made a terrible mistake. "Well, she just said Church and I assumed the Baptist hall but there was nobody there so I thought I'd try here. Then I bumped into Mrs Maddox and she invited me...." her voice trailed away. Cynthia said nothing. Jim Maddox coughed and looked towards his wife.

"Why don't you two walk home together," Mrs Maddox said. "Jim, I've put the kettle on for tea."

"Thank you, dear," said the Vicar, edging round the girls.

Cynthia pulled herself together. "Yes of course," she said, smiling at the Vicar and his wife. "Thank you so much, Mr Maddox. I find our discussions quite stimulating."

"Thank you for the lemonade," Heather added.

They left the vicarage, and walked down the road, Heather pushing her bicycle. There were so many things she wanted to tell Cynthia, but Cynthia was not encouraging.

"We had a smashing holiday," she began. It was easier than talking about France. "I've got a present for you. Shall I bring it round to your house?"

It was a white china horse. She hadn't wanted to bring it on her bicycle in case it broke.

"If you like."

"And I really wanted - we need to talk about France."

There was a short cut through some houses which brought them out close to where Cynthia lived. The swing gate was only wide enough to take one person at a time. Cynthia went through, and then turned back to Heather, looking lost on the far side.

"I'm not going to France." Her face was expressionless. Heather was shocked. Her voice trembled.

"You're not coming?"

"No. It seems silly, going with a school group now I've left school. And I need to work, to earn some money."

"If money's a problem..." Heather started nervously.

"Money is always an issue, something people with your advantages cannot appreciate."

"But it's only two weeks..."

"It doesn't stop you going."

"We were going together…" Tears gathered in Heather's eyes.

"There'll be other girls. Girls your age. And do you know, I think it will be good for you to go on your own. I can't always be there for you. In the autumn I'm going to university, you'll be on your own then."

"Why didn't you tell me before?"

"You've been away. And I didn't want to trouble you during the exams."

"You could have written." This was the closest Heather had ever come to quarrelling with her friend. Cynthia reached through the gate and patted Heather's arm. "Dear, I knew it would upset you and I didn't want you to back out. I'm sure it's for the best. I've been offered a job, you see, I couldn't turn it down. You wouldn't understand."

Heather did her best to do so. She sniffed and rubbed her wet cheeks. Of course Cynthia didn't have the money for trips to France. But if she'd only known! They could have found a way. "What's the job?"

"I'm going to be a kind of social secretary at a hotel run by the church. Mr Maddox arranged it. The person who was going to do the job dropped out at the last minute, and the manager told Mr Maddox and he thought I might be interested. I have to act as a sort of courier, arrange trips, make sure everybody is happy. "

"Where is it?"

"Scarborough. I go next week." Cynthia leaned her arms on the gate and studied Heather's face. "And I should tell you I'm going to join the Church of England. That's why I'm talking to the Vicar; he's been telling me about confirmation. I haven't told my parents yet. So please don't say anything to them meanwhile."

Heather was astounded. She and Cynthia had often agreed that the best thing about their friendship was their willingness to talk everything out, and religion was something they frequently discussed. And yet Cynthia had kept this from Heather, her best friend. And had changed her mind about France.

Cynthia stood away from the gate to allow Heather to push her bicycle through. "Cheer up," she said, touching her shoulder again. "I really think it's for the best. I need a job, and you need to become more independent."

"I think it's awfully brave of you to get a job," Heather said gloomily. "Perhaps Daddy will take us to Scarborough for the day," she said, brightening.

Cynthia frowned. "Well, let me know first if you do. Don't just turn up like you did today. I might be busy. I shall be working, don't forget."

Heather agreed, meekly. "And will you come round to our house? For your present?"

Cynthia considered this. "I have my packing to do, and other things, but alright. As I shan't be seeing you for some time."

And so, to Heather's great relief, they parted friends. The cloud of Cynthia's disapproval passed over. She wondered if Cynthia had ever intended to go to France; it didn't appear that she had said anything about it to her parents. Perhaps this was one of the tests of their friendship that Cynthia had talked about after their walk to Ilkley during the Easter holiday.

LESLEY AND PATTIE

1

It was the autumn of the following year. Lesley and Pattie were in the ladies' cloakroom in the church hall. They had been there for more than ten minutes, preening themselves in front of the mirror, which was spotted and so small that they had to take it in turns to look at themselves.

Lesley was concerned about her eyebrows. As they were thick she had begun to pluck them, and was now worried that her work had left them uneven. She studied her face and tried to measure the distance between eye and brow at various points.

"D'you think this one goes down too much? It's impossible to see in this awful mirror."

"They look alright to me," said Pattie, uninterested. Her own brows were fair and delicately arched. "Lemme in, I want to put some more eye shadow on." Pattie's eyes were outlined heavily in blue. Lesley turned to look at her.

"You've got enough on already. Any more will make you look cheap."

"No it won't. You remember what that article in *Date* said, you have to wear bright make-up if you're going to be under electric lights. So." She thickened the blue around her eyes and regarded the result with satisfaction. Then she frowned. "Oh shit."

"Don't say that here."

"Why not?"

"It's church."

"So what?"

Lesley shrugged. She wasn't really concerned. "What's the matter anyway?"

"I've got a mark on my dress."

"Let's see. Oh Pattie, you messy thing. What is it?"

"Lipstick, I think."

"Don't try to wash it off, it might make it worse."

"What am I going to do? It looks terrible."

They studied the pink smudge on Pattie's left breast for a minute or two. "How on earth did you get it there?" They sniggered.

"Try dabbing it with the towel."

Pattie pulled at the roller towel and rubbed at the mark. "I think it's worse."

"Where's your eye shadow?" asked Lesley suddenly.

"Why?"

"It's nearly the same colour as your dress." She found a handkerchief and dipped the corner into Pattie's powder eye shadow, then patted gently at the mark. She did this a few times, and then stood back to admire her handiwork. "Not bad."

"Great, thanks Les, let's go now," Pattie was impatient.

"Just a minute, I haven't finished yet." Lesley was meticulous about details. She continued to work at the mark while her cousin yawned and wriggled and chewed her nails. "There," she said at last, "as long as you don't have a bright light shining directly on it, nobody will notice."

"Gee," sighed Pattie, who affected Americanisms from time to time, "I thought you were never going to finish."

Lesley folded the soiled handkerchief and returned it to her bag. Pattie scuffed her feet on the floor. "Come on. It will all be over by the time we get there."

"You're the one who wanted to do your face," Lesley pointed out. "Just see if my seams are straight, will you?"

"Gee, my seams, I'd forgotten them!" They were 14 (Lesley a few months older than her cousin), and this was the first time that either of them had worn stockings. The occasion was a dance organised by the church youth club.

The cousins were less close since both now went to different schools, and were finding new interests with new friends. On this occasion Pattie was staying with the Atfields as her parents had gone away for a few days on holiday. Bertrand and Irene felt a continuing responsibility for Pattie given that, in their view, Allan and Phyllis were incapable of supervising her or giving her proper support. It was a great pity she had failed her 11 plus and had had to go to the secondary modern school, where she made the sort of friends that Irene would be reluctant to invite into her own home. It was particularly worrying now that Pattie was showing an interest in boys. Every so often Irene took her sister to task, but Phyllis just looked upset and said "What can I do?" So Irene felt compelled to continue to have Pattie to stay and hope that the positive moral influence of the combined Atfield family would counteract any negative influences that Pattie was subject to from her crowd of friends.

The girls took it in turns to stand on the toilet, precariously balanced, one foot on either side of the white ceramic bowl, while the other checked her legs. Lesley, well trained by her mother, lifted the wooden seat first. "Do you wear your knickers outside or inside your suspender belt?" asked Pattie, casting a cursory glance over Lesley's legs. "They're alright."

"Are you sure?" asked Lesley, jumping down and peering round to look. "Outside."

"Why?"

"How would you go to the toilet otherwise?"

"Oh." Pattie thought about this. "I'd better change."

"Not now, Pat! We'll never get to the dance. Wait until you want to go."

"OK. Just check my seams again."

She climbed on to the wc. As she did so the door opened and Mavis Thornton came in.

Mavis Thornton helped to run the youth club. She was efficient and although probably less than 30 seemed middle-aged to the two teenagers. She had not approved of the plan to hold a dance, but the decision having been made, felt it her duty to 'keep an eye on things', as she put it. She stopped short when she saw the two girls.

"Well, I don't know," she said, and stood long enough for her disapproval to be felt before going to the wash basin and washing her hands vigorously. Pattie giggled. Her foot slipped on the shiny surface and she nearly lost her balance. She landed heavily on the floor. "Ow!"

They hurried out in to the corridor, Pattie limping ostentatiously for a few minutes until she forgot.

"Well I don't know!" mimicked Pattie, giggling.

"Silly old stick," Lesley said tolerantly. "Daddy says she's like that because she's not married. He says single ladies get like that."

"Why isn't she married?"

"Who'd have her?"

"I nearly fell in," said Pattie. "Just think, if I'd fallen in. Yuk!"

"I'd have pulled the chain and flushed you away."

"I wouldn't have gone."

"Yes, you would. The water is terribly strong. You'd have been swept away, down the drains and out to sea."

"Don't be daft."

They stood together, just inside the door, uncertain. They had only recently joined the youth club and didn't know many people. The hall was crowded. Besides the St Mary's people, youth clubs from the other churches in the neighbourhood had been invited. There was a big group of Methodists, and they had been told that the new minister would be there.

The hall, with its balloons and paper decorations, and lights covered in coloured paper, looked very different from the way they normally saw it, at Guides and Sunday School and Bring and Buy sales. There were clusters of tables and chairs which would be pushed aside when the dancing started. The small stage at one end of the hall was decorated with streamers and a big poster saying *CHURCHES GET TOGETHER*. There was a table with a gramophone and loud speakers, and a 'hailer' standing on its end at the side of the table.

"Is Heather here?" asked Pattie.

"No, she's in mourning. Cynthia's gone back to college."

"That's funny, I thought I saw her."

"No, she's at home."

"Not Heather, Cynthia."

"You can't have, she's in Durham."

"I did," insisted Pattie. "She was with the vicar."

"I don't believe you."

They were interrupted by the curate, John Murray, a cheerful man with curly fair hair and protruberant pale blue eyes, whose unflagging enthusiasm and unremitting cheerfulness attracted some mockery from the more cynical members of his flock. The younger people found him embarrassing. He was responsible for the youth club and the dance had been his idea.

"Well, well, well, here you are! Where have you been hiding? You mustn't be shy, everyone's having a wonderful time. Doesn't the hall look super? D'you see the sign? Clever, isn't it? You see it has two meanings, not everyone sees that at first, but if you read the 'get' as a verb first, and then as part of 'get-together' which is a noun, a bit slangy of course, but there it is. D'you see? Good, good. Your father helped us with the lighting, Lesley, I've thanked him myself but do tell him how good it looks, won't you? Now let me find some people for you to talk to."

"We're alright here, thank you," said Lesley, who hated to be pushed into anything.

"We were looking for the vicar," put in Pattie naughtily.

"He came for a few minutes at the start but he's a busy man, you know. Busy man." Pattie smirked at Lesley. "Now here's someone you might not know," and he put out his arm in order to restrain a man who was making his way through the crowd. "Alec Davies, the new minister of the Methodist church, and his sons, um, Christopher, isn't it? And Colin. Yes, yes. Alec is the one who is getting all the churches together - good idea, isn't it? Now this is Lesley Atfield, you may know her father, the architect, and er..."

"This is my cousin Pattie," put in Lesley, who realised that the curate might not recognise Pattie from her rare visits to church. She could feel Pattie shaking beside her and realised that she was getting one of her fits of giggles. She tried to think of something else to say. The older boy saved the situation by saying: "It's Chris, actually. We were just going to find the food before it disappears. Have you eaten yet?"

"No," said Lesley, "that's where we're going. C'mon, Pattie."

"I haven't danced yet," Pattie complained, but not too seriously. She was never averse to food.

"I shall insist on a dance with you the minute you are ready," the curate promised gallantly. Lesley pulled her cousin away before she developed further giggles. They made their way to the kitchen, where they found soft drinks, sausage rolls, cheese on sticks, sandwiches, bowls of tinned fruit and jugs of cream, cakes (two baked by Irene) and biscuits, arranged on two long trestle tables. Pattie continued to giggle, exasperating Lesley. She saw some girls from her school, and moved away to talk to them. The boys turned to the food and busied themselves with plates. More people came into the room and stood between them. Pattie started to feel neglected. She elbowed her way through and took some sandwiches, first opening them to see what was inside. She helped herself to three sausage rolls then changed her mind and put one back, taking some cheese instead. The drinks were at the other side of the table and she hesitated, as there was now quite a crowd. Chris, now standing at the far side near the drinks, caught her eye. She mimed her need for a drink. He pointed to the glasses and raised a quizzical eyebrow. She nodded vigorously. He pointed to Lesley, and raised his eyebrows again. Pattie, miffed at Lesley's neglect, shook her head. He reached for a glass of orange juice, turned to work his way through the crowd, and then changed his mind. He pushed the juice across the table as far as he could. Pattie leaned across but couldn't reach it. Chris took a plate and used it to push the glass further across. Pattie's fingers missed it by an inch. It was now out of the reach of both of them. Pattie started to giggle again, and this time Chris joined in. They laughed helplessly, moving from foot to foot, bending down, holding their sides, until people started to look at them.

There were a few sympathetic laughs from people who didn't know what the joke was. Lesley, distracted from her friends, swung round.

"Pattie, do shut up! You've gone mad!"

Pattie held on to her cousin's arm. Her eyes were watering and the blue shadow was smudged. "My - my orange juice. He pushed it - and I couldn't reach it, and just look - it's in the middle of the table and nobody can reach it! Oh, oh! I think I want to wee!"

Lesley glared at her cousin and looked at the table and then across at Chris, who was sobering up, although there was still a glint in his eye. Pattie disappeared with an exaggerated hobble to the toilet, abandoning food and drink. Lesley turned back to her friends.

When Pattie returned people were sitting down with plates balanced on their knees. She recovered her food and looked for a seat. Alec Davies got up and brought another chair to the table where he and his younger son were sitting with the curate. Pattie, subdued at finding herself sitting with such heavyweights as the Methodist minister and the curate, kept quiet and concentrated on eating. Colin, who had red hair and freckles, asked her about Aireton, and what it was like living there, and she said 'alright', never having thought about it before. She told him that she and Lesley were cousins. He was very young, very polite, and a bit dull. Pattie finished her sausage roll and ran her tongue around her lips to make sure there weren't any crumbs. That was the trouble with lipstick, she'd found, things tended to stick to it. And it disappeared when you were kissed so you had to put it on again, which was really boring. Colin said that his family had recently moved to Aireton, and he was going to the local grammar school, Chris had just started university and was home that weekend because a friend had given him a lift. They had a sister, Jenny, who worked as a secretary. Pattie nodded and smiled and ate her sandwiches and wondered when the dancing would start.

Before the dancing there were games. The curate was Master of Ceremonies. He said that after such a wonderful feast people needed to sit down and digest their food (the older people nodded in agreement, the younger ones looked impatient) but there would be dancing, and lots of it, very shortly.

The games included Beetle, and a quiz, and competitions with prizes for people in possession of such things as the shiniest shoes, the longest hair, the smallest feet. Pattie won a hair ribbon as the prize for the person with the blondest hair. Both she and Lesley forgot their attempts to be grown up and got absorbed in the games like the

141

children they almost were.

At 9 o'clock the tables were moved to the sides of the room, the record player was set up, and dancing started. True to his promise, the curate danced with both cousins. His style was energetic, enthusiastic and unco-ordinated and he kept up a steady stream of conversation so that Pattie nearly got the giggles again. The organisers had arranged a mixed programme of dances, waltzes and foxtrots for the older people interspersed with rock 'n' roll. Towards the end of the evening they had a ladies' excuse me.

"Don't be shy, ladies," called out the curate, as nobody moved.

"I'm going to," declared Pattie, and marched straight up to Chris. "This is to thank you for helping me with the orange juice," she said pertly. He stood up, trying not to look self-conscious. He gave a sort of half bow, took her hand, and they hesitated together at the edge of the dance floor, he tall and fair, with grave good looks, and Pattie, cheeks flushed with excitement, vivacious and pretty. She flourished on occasions like this. Her blonde hair, caught up in a pony tail, gleamed under the lights. Lesley was pleased to see that the mark on her dress did not show. The curate put a waltz on the gramophone, and gradually a few more people joined in - engaged couples, first of all, and then sisters asked their brothers' friends, and the brother of one of Lesley's guiding friends said he wouldn't say no if she asked him. Soon they were all waltzing around the floor, and the curate beamed with delight. Pattie was a natural dancer, but hadn't bothered to learn the proper steps despite Lesley's offer to help her that afternoon. She and Chris stumbled around together at first, but by the time the dance ended they had found a rhythm.

"I prefer jiving," she said at the end of the dance.

"I'm afraid I'm not very good at that," he said.

"I keep forgetting what I'm supposed to be doing. You don't have to think when you're jiving, you just do what you feel like doing."

"You're lucky, then," he said.

"What d'ya mean?"

"To be able to do just what you feel like doing."

"It's easy," said Pattie, puzzled.

"I don't find it so."

Pattie regarded him with scorn. "You're daft," she said.

After this there was a conga, led by the curate, some jiving, and finally the evening ended with the Dashing White Sergeant. Most of the older people had left by then, but Pattie and Lesley and the

142

younger crowd stayed until the end, when Bertrand arrived to take them home. The church and chapel people busied themselves clearing up, the men moving the furniture, the women in the kitchen. Lesley helped Mr Davies to roll up the paper streamers. She was aware that Mavis Thornton and some other women were in the kitchen, clearing away the food and washing the cups, but she decided that it was not necessary to offer to help. Pattie didn't give it a thought. She was content to sprawl against the piano, watching everyone else.

Chris sat on the piano stool and picked out some tunes with one hand. Pattie helped him to find the notes by humming the tunes. She had a good ear and could pick up a tune with ease, but this accomplishment was disregarded by everyone who knew her, including Pattie herself. If she thought about it at all it was as a skill she thought everybody had.

Chris said, to nobody in particular, that members of the Methodist youth club went walking on Sunday afternoons, when the weather was fine. The next day they were planning to walk to Hawksmoor. Anyone who wanted to join them was welcome.

"Try 'Blue Suede Shoes'," demanded Pattie.

"It's good fun," said Colin, who was trying hard not to appear tired.

Chris tried a few notes. "Can't do that. What about this?"

"Walkin' back to happiness," sang Pattie. "That's good."

"I wondered if you and Lesley would like to join us. Only if it's fine."

"Sounds a long way."

"It doesn't seem far when you're part of a group and talking and all that."

Lesley finished folding her streamer and said that she would like to come. Pattie pulled a face, but thought she might. If she woke up in time.

"2.30 by the stone trough. Or I could call in for you a bit before then."

Lesley shrugged. "Whatever you like. Don't go out of your way."

"It's not a problem."

"See you, then, 12 Sycamore Avenue."

When Chris arrived at Sycamore Avenue the household was in disarray. Pattie was nowhere to be seen. She had already incurred her aunt's displeasure by failing to get up in time for church that morning. Then she had gone to change for the walk in a summer skirt and flimsy sandals, and had been sent off to try again.

Lesley answered the door and brought Chris into the kitchen where her mother and sister were still washing up the lunch dishes. After greeting him, Irene said "Lesley, why don't you take Chris into the garden and wait for Pattie? If she's not down in five minutes I suggest you go without her. Heather, just finish these dishes for me, would you?"

"I'm supposed to be writing an essay," complained Heather, but turned back to the sink. Lesley led Chris into the garden where her father was teaching her young cousin Elisabeth to catch a ball with her left hand.

Bertrand Atfield greeted Chris with his usual warmth. He was always enthusiastic about new acquaintances. He was looking forward to meeting Chris's father.

"Yes, sir, my father asked me to tell you that he's thinking of setting up some sort of discussion groups - all denominations - to discuss sort of general issues. Social things, issues I mean. He wants to get a few people together, and he asked me to ask you - hello," he said to Elisabeth, who was hiding behind her uncle. Elisabeth was introduced. She blushed and ran into the house. Chris looked startled.

"I hope I didn't frighten her."

"She's very shy. We're trying to bring her out but it's a slow process. Yes, I'd be delighted to be involved in your father's group - an excellent idea. Can't think why nobody's thought of it before. We all believe in the same God after all. Will the Catholics be involved?"

"I think so."

"Hm. Well, the priest there is getting on and set in his ways. But new brooms, you know, new brooms. Your father might get somewhere. We'll see. Now, what he needs to do first..." and Bertrand started to explain how he thought the thing could be arranged.

Lesley idly bounced the ball. She knew they would be late for the walk, but did not let it upset her. She was ready, sensibly dressed in corduroy trousers, walking shoes, a shirt and thin waterproof jacket. From a distance she looked like a boy with her short curly hair and slim figure.

At last Pattie appeared, wearing a pair of Lesley's trousers which were too big for her, an anorak and her own school shoes. She was pulling a face and saying that she wouldn't get as far as the moors, let alone walk across them.

"Then you'd better stay at home," her aunt said, tartly.

Pattie tossed her pony tail and said, "Aren't we going, then?"

When they reached the old market square there was no sign of the people they had arranged to meet.

"I told them to set off if we were late," Chris said. "They can't have gone far. We'll soon catch them up." They set off up the road leading to the moors. Pattie lagged behind and claimed that her shoes hurt. Chris was concerned but Lesley told her cousin not to fuss.

"You wear them every day to school."

"Only since September. And they hurt every day."

Once on the moors, she sat on a rock and took them off, running in her socks across the tussocky grass. Heather would have fussed about wet feet and broken ankles. Lesley merely picked up her cousin's shoes and continued at her own steady pace. Chris gave her an amused look but Lesley did not notice. She was simply doing what she always did, getting on with her own life and allowing everyone else to get on with theirs. She knew that if she didn't pick up Pattie's shoes someone would have to turn back for them and the walk would be delayed even more. It was far simpler to carry them than remonstrate with her.

"They'll be even more uncomfortable when she puts them on again. The ground is quite wet."

Lesley shrugged. "That's her problem."

"It doesn't concern you?"

Lesley looked at him in surprise. "Why should it?"

"Well - kind of responsible?"

"Pattie does her own thing. She always bounces back."

He smiled. "You and she are very different. All of you, I imagine, but I don't know the others."

"You don't really know any of us."

"No, but we get to know people pretty quickly, with Dad's work. We move around so often, you learn to adapt. This is a real bonus, though, living here. We were in Doncaster before."

"Why do you have to move around so much?"

"The Wesleys were itinerant preachers, and there's always been that tradition. Of not becoming too settled and comfortable."

"I don't think I'd like that."

"I'm not sure that I do."

They reached the highest point of the moors, where the air was fresh and clear. There was a breeze, but the autumn sunshine was warm on their bare heads. The hills were brown and purple with

145

bracken and late heather, and blue haze softened the bleak outlines of the distant hills. They walked along the top of the valley and looked down at the little row of cottages and then across to the far slopes with their pattern of fields bounded by dry stone walls.

"Funny how it's all moorland this side and farmland over there," commented Chris.

"It's the sun. That side of the valley will be south facing."

"Oh, I see."

"That's what I think."

Pattie came running up to them. "I've trodden in some sheep muck, yuk!"

"It will be worse down there." Chris pointed out their route, a footpath which led across fields towards the woods in the valley bottom, half a mile or so away. At the far end of the path they could see a group of people. Chris stood on a rock and waved vigorously. One of the group waved back, and then they all turned and waved.

"Come on, they're waiting for us."

"Pattie, put your shoes on," said Lesley, sounding like her mother, and Pattie obeyed, sitting on the rock which Chris had vacated and rubbing her feet vigorously on the tufts of grass growing at its base. Chris, showing signs of impatience at last, set off before she was quite ready, and the two girls hurried down the hill to catch him up at the gate leading into the field, Pattie hobbling with her shoes half tied.

They crossed another field and then walked down a lightly wooded slope to the stream. The rest of the group were standing at the far side. There were six of them: Chris's brother Colin, at 13 the youngest, two girls of Lesley's age, and a girl and two boys a year or two older, about Chris's age, Lesley thought, though she was not sure how old that was – about eighteen perhaps. Colin had said he was at university.

Large flat stones straddled the clear brown stream, and it was not difficult to get across. Chris went over lightly and easily, and Lesley followed, but Pattie danced about at the far side and said she daredn't, she'd fall in, she knew it. Lesley turned round to help her cousin. "Put your right foot on that stone - oh Pattie, it's perfectly safe. Look, I'll come back and you can follow me."

But Pattie couldn't. She was working herself up into a panic. Lesley looked at Chris. "I shall have to go back."

"No, you stay here, I'll help her across."

"OK." Lesley waited on the bank. Chris went back. He faced Pattie, with a stone between them. He put one foot on it, and held out his hands.

"Put one foot on that stone - come on, I'll hold you, I won't let you go. Now transfer your weight on to that foot - that's right. Now bring your other foot to join it - good girl. You see, it's quite flat." The water, only seven or eight inches deep, gurgled unconcernedly around their feet. By holding on to her hands, and stepping backwards himself, Chris managed to get Pattie across half a dozen stones. They stood close together on a large flat central stone, while Chris looked behind him at the four remaining stones and tried to work out the best way of stepping on them. The next one was small and uneven, and there was only room for one foot. Beyond that was a larger, flatter rock.

"Pattie, I can't hold your hands across this one, there isn't room. Watch what I do and do exactly the same. Put one foot on this one and then go straight across - like this. Don't hesitate or you'll wobble. I'll be ready to hold you again."

Pattie, shivering and sniffing, tried to do what he said. She stretched out one leg and put her foot on the small stone, and then lost her nerve, straddled between the two. "I'm falling, I'm falling!" Chris leaned forward to try to reach her. At the same time Pattie gathered her courage and sprang forward, landing on the same stone as Chris and knocking him off balance. He was forced to step off the stone and into the stream. The stones in the water were uneven and for a moment it looked as if he was going to lose his balance altogether and sit down in the water, but he managed to stay upright. Pattie began to giggle hysterically. Lesley, safe on the bank, giggled herself and then felt remorseful and annoyed with her cousin. Why was Pattie always so stupid? You never really knew if she was putting it on or not. Surely she'd been across those stepping stones before. Chris looked furious and for a brief moment as if he would like to pull Pattie into the stream too, but then he said, "It's easy from here, if you're scared just get into the water with me. You can see how shallow it is. Your feet are already wet." Lesley came back to help her cousin and Pattie negotiated the remaining stones without incident. At the top of the bank the rest of the group watched, bemused.

"You stupid dolt," Lesley said to her cousin, by way of an apology to Chris. He emptied the water out of his shoes and squeezed what he could out of his trousers. "Let's get a move on," he said curtly.

147

"You're wet," Lesley pointed out needlessly.

"You don't need to tell me that," he retorted and marched off up the footpath to join his friends. Lesley and Pattie followed.

Lesley was briefly annoyed with her cousin for creating so many difficulties on what should have been a straightforward Sunday afternoon hike. However, the incident was over and there was the rest of the walk to look forward to. Chris would be uncomfortable with wet feet but unless somebody had a spare pair of socks there was nothing anybody could do. If he chose to be angry, that was his choice. Lesley understood that Chris might be annoyed with Pattie, but there was no reason why she, who had no connection with the accident, should feel responsible. (The fact that Chris might be angry because she had witnessed the accident was a subtlety beyond her experience). So she followed his squelching footsteps among the trees, leaving Pattie to trail several paces behind, complaining every so often that her feet hurt. She was ignored.

They all paused in a clearing. Chris sat on a log and squeezed out his trousers again. He rubbed his ankle. Pattie also sat down, and eased off her shoes, sighing loudly. The others gazed at the autumn beauty surrounding them. At the top of the clearing stood a magnificent beech tree, its grey bark setting off to perfection the rich russet of its leaves. Lesley was awed by its beauty and size. She forgot about Pattie and Chris and lost herself in contemplation of its colours: pale grey, russet and gold, with red hawthorn berries behind. When she got home the pattern of colours would remain, clear in her mind. When she was ready, she would try to translate what she had seen on to paper.

Somewhat mundanely, she thought it would make a good colour scheme for her bedroom at home. What would it be like, though, to be surrounded by autumn beauty in the spring? To have grey and red and brown when outside all was fresh pale green and yellow. Perhaps she could have two schemes, green and yellow in the spring and summer, and warm, tawny shades for autumn and winter. The walls could stay a very pale grey. Her mother was good at finding materials, she would have to bring her here to see the tree.

So absorbed was Lesley that she failed to notice the others moving off. Chris touched her arm. "Wake up."

Lesley was startled to find that they were alone in the clearing, although she could hear voices echoing back through the trees. "It's so beautiful."

"Yes, isn't it. You don't get this sort of thing in Doncaster."

"I could come back with my paints," said Lesley, still under the spell of the tree.

"You like painting?"

It was rarely that Lesley was asked that question. Everyone who knew her knew she was good at art - it was as much a part of Lesley as her square jaw or hazel eyes.

"Yes," she said, glancing at him, wondering whether to say more, unsure about how he would respond. She decided to try.

"I can paint trees, but somehow what I paint misses something. It looks like a tree - everyone else thinks it looks right but I know it isn't - quite. It's not this tree."

Chris said "I write a bit - that's the thing I'm best at. When I was younger and saw something that excited me I used to rush home and write a poem about it. But, like you, it never really described what I had experienced. It didn't go deep enough, and left me feeling dissatisfied. Perhaps for you it's not enough to describe the tree, the way it looks, branches, leaves, etc., - you want to get beneath that."

Lesley walked along beside him, thinking hard. "I hadn't really thought about it like that. To me it's just a question of feeling right." Like the pattern of leaves, she wanted to reflect on these new ideas, over time.

"You know, when it does?"

"Oh yes."

She was aware that the others were some way ahead of them. "Do you still write poetry?" she asked, turning to follow them.

"No. A level English put an end to that. You study Shakespeare and Wordsworth and Shelley and your efforts become so pathetic."

"But," said Lesley, trying to imagine not painting, "you're not trying to write like Shelley and Wordsworth. I mean, it's something you're doing for yourself. Like me painting."

He shook his head. "I can't do it any more." He looked at her. "Don't you worry that you're not good enough?"

She shook her head. "I don't think that way. Like I said I don't always get it right, but usually that means that what I'm trying to do is wrong, or needs approaching differently, or something. Or I need more time."

"You don't see it as failure if you don't get it right?"

"Oh, no. You just end up with something different, that's all. And then you try again."

They caught up with the others and Lesley moved forward to walk with her cousin. The sun was gradually dropping below the trees, and the sky was changing from a clear light blue to hazy blue and pink. A drift of mist was rising from the ground. At the edge of the woods a wooden bridge crossed the stream, running faster and deeper here than it had been further down the valley, and then the path divided. One footpath led them to the road which took them back over the moors to the town. The other continued up the far side of the valley to a village from which, one of the boys assured everyone, they could catch a bus back to Aireton.

"On a Sunday?"

"There's a cafe, we can get a drink."

"On a Sunday?"

Chris looked at his watch. "Bus or not, I'll have to go straight back home. I'm going back to London this evening."

"You're not giving yourself much time."

"I'm all ready. My friend's picking me up at half six and I don't want to keep him waiting."

"I'll come with you," said Lesley, who was eager to paint the tree.

"I don't want to go back yet," pouted Pattie.

"I thought your shoes were hurting."

"We-ell.."

"If there isn't a bus we can always walk back by the road. It's only three or four miles," said Dave, the boy who wanted to walk further. That decided Pattie. "Oh, I'll come back with you two." The group divided, two or three going with Dave and the rest heading for home.

"What are you doing at university?" asked Lesley.

"Law. Dull and respectable," he added, with a look at Pattie. Her expression showed that she thought so too. She trailed along, kicking up the gravel, then dropped back to chat to the others.

Lesley continued to walk with Chris, hands thrust into her pockets, thinking about the tree. She was startled when he said, "I'm afraid this has been boring for you."

"Oh no," she said. "Why do you say that?"

"You've hardly spoken for the last half hour."

"I was thinking."

"What about?"

"Oh, just things."

"I was afraid you weren't enjoying yourself."

"I always enjoy myself."

150

"Lucky girl."

"Don't you?"

"About half and half. Do you never feel fed up?"

Lesley considered this.

"Well, last year I had flu and felt really tired, and had to miss school and some things I wanted to do. I couldn't even paint, I felt so low. Oh, and then Daddy got flu, and that was worse, because he's never been ill before, not that I remember."

"You're very fond of your father?"

"Oh yes," Lesley said, as if this were a self-evident truth.

"And what about the rest of your family - are they all like you?"

"Well Pattie, you know, you've seen what she's like, she complains but it never lasts very long. You just have to distract her and then she's off again. My sister Heather - she worries about things."

"And the little one? Is she your sister too?"

"Elisabeth? No, she's our cousin. She lives with us. I think Elisabeth is unhappy most of the time." She had never realised this before. She had never thought about her family in this way before.

"You're making me think things I've never thought before," she said in her usual direct way, stating a fact.

He smiled, and continued to ask questions. "Why do you say Elisabeth is unhappy most of the time?"

"She misses her father. She's only staying with us, you see, while her father finds a job, but it's been two years now and although he comes to see her sometimes he's never suggested taking her back. Mummy says he never will, but she can't accept it."

"It can't be the same, not living with your own family."

"We are her family. We treat her just the same as if she were our sister."

"The same as if, but not the same."

By this time they had reached the market place where they were to go their separate ways. Chris was getting anxious about the time, and did not linger. He said, "Well, it's been a great weekend. Sorry I've got to dash. Might see you around at Christmas?"

Pattie called after him, "Sorry I got your feet wet!"

He raised his arm in a half salute, but didn't stop. Pattie giggled. She and Lesley said goodbye to the others, then turned to walk home.

"Golly, my feet really hurt now," muttered Pattie. "D'you think your father will come out looking for us?"

"No."

"Oh. Are you in love with Chris?"

"'course not, I've only just met him. Are you?"

"I might be," mused Pattie. "Only I don't want to get in your way. I feel kind of sad that he's gone. Do you think we'll ever see him again?"

"Maybe at Christmas."

"D'you want to?"

"I liked him. He's interesting."

"You're in love with him, you are, you are, you are."

"Don't be stupid," said Lesley, unaroused but unamused.

"Well, I am," announced Pattie. "I've decided."

"You'd better be extra nice to him to make up for getting his feet wet."

"Nar," said Pattie, who had her own guides to social behaviour. "If you're too nice to them they take you for granted. You've got to tease them. It was nice holding his hands," she added. "I wonder if he's a good kisser."

"Are you still letting that Brian Barnes kiss you?"

"Yeah, but I think I'm going to stop. He's giving me French kisses now and I don't like them."

"Pattie, you are awful."

"And he wanted to take me behind the toilets and put his hand up my skirt. The teacher came and we had to go in."

"You'll get into trouble," Lesley warned.

"No, I won't. That Dave was nice, too. I wish I'd gone to Hawksmoor with him. We could have sat on the back seat of the bus."

"He goes to your school, doesn't he?"

"Yeah, he's in Mr Jonathan's class. He's always getting into trouble. I didn't know he went to church. Well I don't think he does, he said he only goes to the youth club to play table tennis. They were going to a pub in Hawksmoor, all that talk about a cafe was a lie. They didn't want to tell Chris 'cos they knew he wouldn't approve."

"Why not?"

"He's a Methodist, stupid."

"So they all are."

"Yes, but he takes it seriously. He's a tee - what do you call it?"

"Teetotaller."

"Yeah. He doesn't drink. I dunno whether I want to be in love with a teetotaller."

"You couldn't have gone into the pub anyway. You're too young."

"We-ell," said Pattie. "I like the way his hair curls into the back of his neck, don't you? I could see quite clearly when he helped me across the river."

Lesley felt a faint twinge of jealousy. "Yes, his hands are nice, too."

"Oh yes?"

"To look at, idiot."

"Oh yes?"

"Oh yes. What colour were his eyes?"

"Blue."

"I thought they were grey."

The conversation continued, intermittently, until they reached home.

2

The cousins continued to see the boys from the Manse among their other friends. The sister, Jennifer, was two years' older than Chris and moving in different circles and they rarely saw her. Chris made himself at home in Sycamore Avenue, flirted with Pattie, talked seriously to Lesley, was polite to Heather and kind to Elisabeth. Colin, younger and shyer, attached himself to Elisabeth. The parents came to know each other well, primarily through Church-related activities. The Reverend Davies was keen to bring the churches together to work on social issues and this appealed to Bertrand, who was sympathetic towards socialism, and had even voted Labour after the war. He was relieved, however, that Chris, who had passed his A levels and got a place to study law in London, was training for a respectable profession; it was early days of course but if he were sweet on Lesley, which Bertrand thought might be the case, then the legal profession offered financial and social stability. He would have been concerned had Chris decided to follow his father into the Church.

A year after they had all met at the Church social, Irene's father, Ernest Lindsey, had another stroke, and three weeks before Christmas he died. Although he had been ill for a number of years, he and everyone else had adjusted to his disability, and the second stroke came as a surprise. Bertrand told them that it was a blessing, really, but failed to convince anyone. Ernest and Mary had been married for nearly 50 years and she missed him greatly. She had always seemed self sufficient, but now she found it hard to be alone, and became depressed. Irene spent a lot of time with her.

They all went to the funeral. Bertrand suggested that the women should stay at home, but Irene said this was old-fashioned. "Then let Heather and Elisabeth stay at home," protested Bertrand. "Elisabeth is too young, and Heather will cry." But Heather wanted to go, never having been to a funeral before, and feeling that it was the proper thing to do, and then it seemed unreasonable to leave Elisabeth out, so in the end the whole family attended. The girls had to get special permission to be away from school.

Mary and Ernest were well known local figures, and the church was full. The family sat near the front, and the girls turned round from time to time to see who else was there, though Irene frowned when she saw them doing it; there were people from church, work people from the mill Ernest used to manage, retired colleagues, two or three of

Mary's close friends, a couple of men Ernest had played cricket with in his younger days, friends of Irene and Phyllis, and those townspeople who turned up to any event. Ernest's younger brother and his wife were there, and Mary's sister. Hugh was not. Irene had written, but she didn't know if he had received the letter. He had found some work with a repertory company and moved about the country which made it difficult to keep in touch, and it was several months since they had seen him. Just as the service started Elisabeth turned her head to gaze once more around the church, and Lesley, noticing, guessed that she had been hoping that he would appear. Irene, also understanding, gave her hand a little squeeze, and Elisabeth settled back in her pew.

Lesley stood between her father and sister. Heather began to cry as soon as the coffin was brought in and continued throughout the service. Occasionally she tried to join in the hymns and prayers, her voice wavering and squeaking. Lesley was not easily embarrassed but she was afraid that Pattie, on Heather's other side, would giggle, so she nudged her sister and said "Ssh." Heather looked at her sister with hurt wet eyes. "Don't sing like that," hissed Lesley. Heather sniffed.

After the service the family greeted the people they knew before moving out to the graveyard for the burial. The day was cold and wet, and Irene stood close to her mother. Heather put her arm round Elisabeth. Elisabeth submitted, thinking this would comfort her weeping cousin. Pattie and Lesley stood together, subdued by the finality of the earth falling on the coffin. It was strange to think that they would never see their grandfather again. They were all glad when it was over and they could go home.

Christmas, inevitably, was a quieter affair than usual that year. Mrs Lindsey stayed for a few days, sleeping in the room that Pattie usually had. Bertrand talked about putting in a bathroom downstairs, and turning the small sitting room which the children used as a playroom into a bedroom, for his mother in law's use. Their usual Christmas morning party was cancelled. The weather was bitterly cold, with a strong wind and driving sleet. Irene had caught a cold at the funeral and was off-colour. The coalman failed to deliver, and Bertrand and the girls had to scour the woods for logs to put on the fire, but the ones they found were wet and didn't burn, so on Christmas Eve they went into Bradford to buy two electric fires. The shops were crowded and the selection was poor and Bertrand was unhappy with what they eventually bought. He said that in the spring he would install central heating.

The girls were preoccupied with work that year. Lesley was working for her O levels; Heather had A levels in June; even Pattie had some tests to take in the new term. Elisabeth was in her first year at grammar school. Bertrand was busy; his firm had tendered successfully to build some high-rise flats in Leeds, and there was a great deal of public discussion. Irene listened to his concerns and worried about her mother.

Easter was early, while the weather was still very cold, and the cousins spent most of the holiday indoors. One Saturday at the end of March the four girls were in the sitting room while the afternoon grew dark. The trees in the garden bent and swayed in the wind, and from time to time bursts of rain came scudding against the window. Heather sat in an upright chair, knitting, with a book on her knee; Lesley and Pattie were at the table, Lesley idly sketching and Pattie shuffling playing cards, and Elisabeth was curled up in a chair by the fire, reading.

They heard the front door bell ring, but none of them could raise the enthusiasm to see who it was. They knew that Irene was in the hall, polishing the big oak chest. Without being able to hear it they sensed her sigh, and then heard the door open. There was the sound of young male voices. After a minute or so she came into the room with Chris and Colin. "Here are some visitors to cheer you up. Whatever are you sitting in the dark for? Put some lights on." She flicked the switch by the door as she spoke. The girls winced in the sudden harsh light.

"Ow, Mummy," Heather said. "It's too bright."

"You can't sit in the dark. No wonder you're feeling miserable."

"I'll put the lamp on," said Lesley, going over to the bookcase. "That's better," she said, turning off the main light.

"Up to you," Irene said. "Go in, boys, find somewhere to sit. Though with an atmosphere as gloomy as this I shouldn't think you'll want to stay long."

Heather roused herself. "I'll go and make some coffee. Why don't you sit by the fire, it's warmer. I'm sorry we're not very welcoming, we're not being rude, we're just..."

"Fed up," Pattie said, still shuffling cards.

"Mm."

"It's pretty miserable outside," Chris said, probing.

"It's not just that," said Heather. "It's been a horrid year."

"Why? Tell me."

"Well - grandad died..."

"Yes, I know that, I'm sorry."

"..and granny is - oh, she's so sad. She's really gone to pieces."

"It's early days. They lived together for a long time. She's got a lifetime's habits to change."

"I suppose so."

"She used to be so organised," explained Lesley. "You could rely on her for anything."

"And the house was spotless and now Mummy has to go and clean up for her. She just doesn't notice anything any more."

"She gets our names mixed up," said Elisabeth, who had been very hurt one day to see her grandmother struggling to remember who she was.

"Mummy thinks she ought to come and live with us," Lesley said. "She doesn't want to now, but she might. And - oh I know it's selfish, but we don't really want that. She was never very easy, but you knew where you were with her. Now she's kind of all over the place and keeps changing her mind and you just don't know how to talk to her. It would mean giving her this room, and Daddy would build a little bathroom for her out the back - he's applied for planning permission just in case. But we had thought we might have a conservatory one day."

"If she wants to come she must, of course," Heather said. "She doesn't really want to. But now Daddy is on the case, and he's been reading books on the modern family and thinks society is going to pieces because we don't have extended families any more. Oh well. I'll go and make the coffee."

The others continued to discuss Mrs Lindsey's problems. Colin was emboldened to tell them about a friend of his, whose mother had died and whose father had then had a kind of mental breakdown, locking himself into his house and speaking to no-one. Pattie burst into tears.

"He's alright now," said Colin, alarmed at the effect of his words. His freckled face was bright red. Elisabeth ran up to her cousin and put her arm around her. "She'll be alright, don't cry Pattie!"

Heather came back, carrying a tray with steaming mugs of coffee. She stopped in the doorway, seeing Pattie in tears.

"What have you been saying? Pattie, don't cry, oh don't!" She sniffed loudly and the cups rattled on the tray. Chris stood up quickly and took the tray from her. Lesley cleared a space on the table.

Heather sat down heavily and buried her face in her hands.

Lesley made room on the table for the tray. "It's Auntie Phyllis," she explained above Pattie's wails. "She's not well and she's had to go into hospital for some tests. That's the other awful thing that's happened. They don't know what's wrong. Pattie's staying with us for a few days."

Lesley didn't say that Allan had accused Pattie of upsetting her mother and making her ill. Heather knew what Lesley had chosen not to say. She brushed away her tears and put on her social voice. "Sugar?"

Colin looked to his elder brother for guidance. "Two for Colin and one for me, please," Chris said.

Colin was at an awkward age. Nearly 15, he had ginger hair and freckles, which he was self-conscious about. He was jerky and uncertain in his movements. In a strange house he kept unnaturally still out of fear of knocking things over, or tripping over his own feet. He was uncomfortable with girls, despite having a sister of his own. Jennifer was a very pretty 21 year old, who led a hectic social life, and whose future career seemed set far from the Methodist manse. Colin found the stream of young men and girls in and out of the manse disturbing. He spent a lot of time in the room which he had to himself when Chris was at university, where he made model cars and followed the exploits of his Leeds United heroes, and sometimes, guiltily and unhappily, studied the pin-ups which were regularly passed round his class at school. But he found it hard to accept that these sophisticated, near naked women, with their gleaming breasts and thighs and buttocks, belonged to the same species as his sister and her friends, with their high heels and pretty dresses and layers of petticoat. He felt relatively comfortable with the Lindsey girls, although Pattie disturbed him with her teasing. He liked Elisabeth best, although (or perhaps because) she was so much younger. She was quiet and he could relax when he was with her. And she was clever, too, and read a lot, and he could discuss books with her. Colin took his coffee and went to sit by the fire, hoping that she would join him.

"But there's more to come," Heather said as Pattie stopped crying. Elisabeth lifted her head. "At least, it's bad for us." Elisabeth gave Pattie's hair one last stroke and went back to the fire where she curled up on the floor near Colin and gazed into the flames. "Elisabeth's father is getting married again and they want her to go and live with them. I don't know what we shall do!"

The two boys were shocked. It had never occurred to them that Elisabeth might go away. "Does she want to go?"

"She's delighted," Pattie sniffed. "She can't wait."

Elisabeth kept her head down. They all turned to look at the small curled figure with its mass of beautiful hair outlined against the fire. The shape pleased Lesley, and she began to draw again. Heather went forward and spoiled the pattern by putting more coal on the fire, dulling the flames. She spilt coal dust on the hearth and fussed about with the brush and pan until she had cleared up the mess. The others waited patiently for her to finish.

"When are you going?" Chris asked over Heather's humped back.

"In the summer," murmured Elisabeth. "Auntie Irene thinks I ought to finish this year at school."

"Will you be going right away, away from Aireton?"

"Mm, I think so." She looked into his concerned face with her big hazel eyes.

"Oh Lizzie, Lizzie, I can't bear it," exclaimed Heather, dropping the brush and putting sooty hands around her cousin. "You can't go. Your father will have to come and live with us instead."

"What about Granny?" Lesley said.

"He's getting married again," Elisabeth explained. "So I shall have a new mother and we can have a proper home. He was always living in rooms before and moving about and thought it wouldn't be good for me to live like that. So that's why I couldn't live with him."

"What's she like?" asked Colin. "Your - the lady your father's marrying."

"Very nice," said Elisabeth, biting her lip.

"They came to see us last week," said Heather, tears streaking her face again. "They're not inviting anyone to the wedding. She's religious and has persuaded Uncle Hugh to go to church again. So that must be good."

"I thought she was horrid," said Pattie at the table.

Elisabeth turned round, her face bright with anger. "She's not, she's nice. She's going to be my mother."

"She made us say grace before meals. She's no right to do that in somebody else's house."

"He's given up being an actor," Lesley said. "She thinks the theatre is a wicked place. He's going to take up preaching instead."

"I don't think the Bible says anything specifically against theatres," Heather said judiciously, "although St Paul may have had something to say about idle entertainment. But I'm sure a more stable life will be better for Uncle Hugh."

"I didn't know your father was an actor," Chris said to Elisabeth.

"Was he famous?" Colin asked.

Elisabeth hesitated.

"I don't think he was very good," Lesley said objectively. "He never had any big parts."

"He was useless," Pattie said crossly.

"He was not! Don't you say such things!"

"Oh, let's stop talking about it." Lesley hated conflict.

"We always end up quarrelling. Let's do something instead."

"I'll play the piano if you like," Heather offered.

"OK. Only not hymn tunes."

"Play some pop songs, play 'Love me do', I know you've got the music," pleaded Pattie.

"I like hymn tunes," said Heather, but she rummaged in the piano stool for the song sheet.

She put the music on the stand and played diligently all the way through. They listened in silence.

"It didn't sound right," Pattie complained.

"I played what it says here."

"It's not like the Beatles."

"Of course it's not, they play guitars."

"I wish I could play the guitar," mourned Pattie.

"Perhaps the rhythm wasn't quite right," suggested Chris.

"The notes were all there, but the beat wasn't, quite."

"Perhaps you can do better," Heather said huffily, vacating the piano stool.

"No, no, I can't play half as well as you," Chris said hastily, but he sat down nonetheless.

"I'll just try it with one hand," he said, picking out the notes and exaggerating the rhythm. Pattie started to sing the words and Lesley joined in. Elisabeth beat time with the hearth brush. Colin smiled and nodded his head, although he did not dare trust his voice. Heather, aggrieved, went out.

"That was great," cried Pattie. "Play it again." Chris obeyed. This time he added a few left hand chords. "I'm not really a pianist," he apologised. "I do better on the guitar."

"You play the guitar?" asked Lesley, impressed.

"We both do. We prefer traditional folk music to pop, though.

160

Colin's good."

Pattie wrinkled up her nose, but Lesley said that she liked traditional songs.

"I'm only learning," Colin said hastily.

"You're doing alright. He won't play on his own in public, but he will with me. Oh, only at church and youth fellowship, that sort of thing." Colin freckled face reddened.

"Is it difficult to learn?"

"No, not really. Easier than the piano."

"Oh, will you teach me? Please, please," begged Pattie.

"Well, I suppose I could try," Chris said. "You'd have to have your own guitars, though."

"Are they expensive?"

"Good ones are, but you should be able to get one to practise on cheaply. Try Woods in Darley Street."

"Goodee," said Pattie. "We can go next week. I'm glad you came." She was looking happier. She pressed him to tell her about the clubs and coffee bars and parties which she was sure were a permanent feature of London life.

"I can't really tell you very much - there's usually a disco on a Saturday night at the college, and the odd party. I'm afraid I lead a rather dull life," he said apologetically. Pattie's expression showed that she thought so too.

"And what about the shops, surely you go to the shops, the boutiques and Selfridges and places. And see all those famous people, telly people and film stars and stuff."

Chris smiled and shook his head.

"You might as well be in Leeds." Abandoning Chris she went to the fire, gave Elisabeth a hug and sat down on the arm of Colin's chair.

"Has Heather abandoned us altogether?" asked Chris, still at the piano.

"She's a bit sensitive at present," Lesley said.

"I didn't mean to hurt her feelings," Chris said, remorseful. "I mean, she plays very well, but she somehow didn't get the beat."

"Oh, she prefers hymns, she's always playing hymns. She's gone all religious. I suppose you play a lot of hymns at your house," she added, remembering that his father was a minister.

"Not specially. I'm sorry if I upset her. I think we'd better be going before we upset your mother by staying too long."

"Oh, she'll tell you if she thinks it's time you went," Lesley assured

161

him.

The families continued their friendship. Chris kept his promise to teach Lesley and Pattie the guitar although they made slow progress. Pattie had a better ear than Lesley, but she was lazy and didn't practise. She sang instead, and as she had a good voice the lessons usually ended with her singing to the two boys' playing, with Lesley either beating time or playing the two or three chords she had mastered. Lesley persevered for a while before deciding that her fingers were getting sore and this was interfering with her painting.

In the summer Chris was home again from university with a vacation job which meant that he was free only in the evenings and weekends. Things were still difficult for the cousins. Phyllis was out of hospital, paler and thinner after an operation, and Pattie was living at home again, supposedly looking for a summer job. She was forever in conflict with her father, who told her that if she couldn't get a job she should do more to help her mother; the conflict inevitably upset Phyllis. Heather was becoming increasingly absorbed in religion, encouraged by Cynthia. Elisabeth had left Aireton at the beginning of August to live with her father. Work started on a new downstairs bathroom to make it possible for Mrs Lindsey to come and live with them while at the same time Bertrand drew up plans for a conservatory at the back of the house. This took their minds off their young cousin although they all missed her, in their different ways.

Lesley found Chris easy to talk to and liked the way he encouraged her to think independently. She was so used to discussing art and other topics with her father; they knew each other inside out and she loved talking to him but it was good to be with someone whose reactions she could not anticipate. She found this stimulating. She did not regard him as her boyfriend, more as an older brother, and there was no romantic talk between them. She understood that he had friendships with other girls at university. She spent time at the manse, sometimes alone with him, sometimes with his family. She confided less in her father and other members of her own family, and hardly ever in Pattie, who had a different set of friends and was getting a reputation as a flirt. The conflict between Pattie and her parents continued, and Irene was concerned, partly for Pattie's own sake, but more because of the effect on her sister. Lesley talked to Chris about this.

"She's going around with a bunch of people - they're a bit rough. Oh, that makes me sound like my mother, but I don't know how else to describe them. They just hang around. They don't actually do anything wrong, but you feel they might do. They're none of them interested in training for anything, and some of them aren't even bothering to find jobs and well, Pattie's so easily influenced. They spend all their time in coffee bars or at the youth club at Morton or playing music. And Uncle Allan gets angry when Pattie's out so much, because he thinks she ought to stay at home and help her mother, but when she's in they quarrel, and Auntie Phyllis gets upset and then Uncle Allan gets even more angry, and then my mother gets upset and starts to ask me about my friends. It's like they suddenly don't trust us any more. And she ties herself up in knots trying to keep it all from Granny. Fortunately she likes you," said Lesley. Then she added, "I don't suppose you could talk to her, could you?"

"Who, your mother?"

"No, Pattie."

Chris was doubtful. "Why would she listen to me?"

"She might. She likes you."

"I seem to have made a hit with your family," said Chris. Lesley took this at face value.

"Yes," she confirmed, "that's why it's so nice talking to you."

"Pattie probably wouldn't see it that way."

"I can see you can't just go and start lecturing her," Lesley said. "I just thought sometime you might find the opportunity to take her for a coffee or something."

"Maybe," said Chris, unconvinced.

A few weeks later Pattie surprised everyone by passing the two O levels she had taken. She was trying to decide between a hairdressing course or a catering one. Hairdressing was more glamorous but the training was longer and you earned a pittance. She liked cooking and was praised by her aunt for her light touch with pastry, but she couldn't imagine spending her life in a kitchen. So it would probably be hairdressing. Up to this point Pattie had not given much thought to jobs and careers, but had discovered that nearly everyone else she knew was either staying on at school or going to college to do some sort of training, and she felt left out. She had also discovered that working in a factory or a shop, the only alternatives open to someone without qualifications, was a lot harder than going to school. The hours were so much longer for a start. And the pay wasn't as good as she had been led to believe. No-one had told her about tax and national insurance. She had a temporary job in a shoe shop and didn't

163

enjoy it one little bit. If it hadn't been for the money she would have chucked it in the day after she started, but she did want a new pair of boots for the winter and there was no chance of getting any money out of her father. That was another thing, leave school and everyone thought you were a wage earner. The fact that your wages were barely enough to pay the bus fare to town and back didn't count. Since she left school she had to pay for her own stockings, shampoo and entertainment, and most of her own clothes, although her mother said she would help her with essentials. But boots weren't essential, not in August anyway.

Phyllis was taking time to get over her operation and had given up her job. Pattie was upset, though she didn't show it. She had found the best way of getting over problems was to ignore them. If she pretended that everything was alright then everything was alright.

Had Irene been less preoccupied with her own family, she might have recognised this. Allan, however, only saw that Pattie was selfish and uncaring. When he told Pattie to do the housework, Pattie grew hysterical and said how could she, she didn't get home from work until half past six, she was exhausted, how could she do the housework as well? Why couldn't her father do it? He was home before she was. Phyllis got upset and this made Allan angry. Phyllis said she would be bored to tears with nothing to do. Pattie could help her at weekends. Pattie continued to protest vigorously. She couldn't be tied in at the weekends. Was she to have no life of her own? Phyllis said, weakly, that all she wanted was a little help. Allan was furious. One day he raised his hand to hit Pattie. Pattie dodged, and ran out of the house. She went first to find her friend, Janet, but Janet was out, so Pattie caught the bus to town, and went into her favourite coffee bar. The man behind the counter, an Italian, started to chat her up. Pattie answered back smartly and felt better. She perched on a stool swinging her legs and watched him pour steaming coffee into big white cups with a graceful Italian nonchalance. If she chatted him up right she'd get a free coffee. Waiters were safe, they couldn't leave their cafes to follow her home. Then a group of young men and girls came in, talking noisily. She eyed them up to see if she knew anyone and to her delight saw that Chris was among them. She slipped off her stool and ran up to him. "Hiya, Chris!"

"Oh, hi Pattie! What are you doing here?"

"I've run away from home," Pattie said gloomily, remembering. She sat down with Chris and his friends at a formica topped table, poured sugar out of the container into a small heap on the table and stirred it with her little finger.

"Why's that?"

Pattie licked her finger. "They're horrible to me. My father hit me today."

"Oh, Pattie, no. Why? Did he hurt you?"

Pattie toyed with the idea of claiming a broken arm, or ribs, but realised that the evidence was lacking. "Well, not quite. I dodged and he missed. So I came here." She poured out her troubles to Chris, ignoring the other two, who after giving him an amused glance moved away to another table. He accepted the inevitable - somehow along with his friendship with Lesley he had picked up some of the family responsibility for her wayward cousin. Pattie tried to pick up the sugar in her fingers and pour it back down the metal funnel into the container. A few grains went in and the rest fell back on to the table. Pattie stirred it again. Chris listened patiently, then tried to get her to see the other point of view.

"Your mother's been ill, she has to take things easy."

"But I can't do it all!"

"I don't suppose they're asking you to do it all."

"I've got to cook the dinner on Sunday."

"Well, that's not so hard, is it? In my family we all take it in turns. I was told you were a good cook."

"Why can't Dad do it? All he ever does is shout at me."

"I expect he has other things to do."

"And the shopping and the hoovering and the washing up as well. I already do that."

"Pattie, I'm sure it won't be as bad as all that. You must be pleased to have your mother out of hospital. And it's good to feel you're needed, isn't it?"

"I'm fed up," she grumbled.

"Here, have another coffee and cheer up." Pattie accepted the coffee and hunched over it, still gloomy. Chris went over to the juke box and studied the list, then chose the Rolling Stones. Pattie perked up.

"I'm fed up with work," she offered.

"Why, what are you doing?"

"Working in a shoe shop. It's murder. Up and down ladders all day, watching fat old women trying to stuff their feet into shoes two sizes too small for them. They pong, too. I got told off the other day for being rude to a customer. And another day, I got the shoes all mixed up. This woman had about eight pairs out, and it was busy, and I just shoved them all back into the boxes, and then another woman came and wanted to try a pair on, and she said 'That's funny,' (Pattie mimicked a posh voice) 'the right foot fits perfectly but I can't get the left one on at all', and the supervisor was telling her that everyone has one foot bigger than the other and she said 'no, no, it's no good' and then," Pattie drew breath, "they found out that she had a size 6 on her right foot and was trying to get a size five *and another right shoe* on her other foot." Pattie laughed loudly at the memory. Chris's friends listened in and laughed too. Pattie felt better. She was tired of all this talk about A levels and qualifications.

"But you'll get a better job at the end," Chris explained patiently. "It must be better to work in an office than a shop. Fred and Jim are working but they're on trainee schemes. They're all getting trained."

Pattie pulled a face. "Boring."

"There are all kinds of courses. They can't all be boring."

"We-ell. I might do this hairdressing course. I can't stand the shoe shop much longer. Then I'll be a student too, like everyone else."

"That's right. You'll have fun."

His two friends went to the juke box and stood jingling coins and considering the titles. Pattie jumped up and joined them. She insisted that they played the Beatles. She was crazy about the Beatles. She hummed and danced her way back to the table.

"You dance with me, darleeng," said the Italian behind the counter.

"Alright," said Pattie.

"We go back here," he said, lifting the counter flap and indicating the kitchen.

"Not on your life," she retorted, and sat down.

Pattie looked as if she intended to stay in the coffee bar until it closed. Chris, with an early morning start in the factory where he had a summer job, thought otherwise. He also felt a responsibility for Pattie. She wasn't safe to be out alone at night.

"C'mon, kid, time to be going home."

"What, already? We've only just got here."

"Yes, but we've both got to go to work in the morning. I've borrowed Dad's car, you won't have to get the bus."

The car persuaded her. Pattie loved driving. She said goodbye enthusiastically to Chris's friends, who were staying, and more coolly to the Italian waiter, before turning at the door and blowing him a kiss.

166

In the car, Pattie wanted to drive fast. She thought Chris a real stick in the mud for keeping to the 30 mile an hour limit. She also thought the car, a Morris Minor, was disappointing. "You should have a sports car."

"Yes, Pattie."

"No, really. It would suit you. I can see you and me in a sports car, with the top down, zooming down the M1. We could go to France in it."

"You buy me one, I'll be happy to drive you."

"Money's a drag," said Pattie.

The bus took twenty minutes or more, travelling round various housing estates. By car it was little more than ten. "Here you are," said Chris, pulling up outside Pattie's house. "Be nice to them."

"Thanks a million," said Pattie, who had forgotten all about the row with her parents. She scrabbled around on the floor of the car for her bag. Then she flung her arms round Chris's neck and kissed him on the mouth. "Come dancing with me sometime, will yah?"

Taken aback, he laughed and said nothing. She opened the car door.

"Didn't you like that?" she enquired naughtily. He tried to pass it off as a joke.

"You'd better watch your step, young Pattie. You might get yourself into trouble one of these days."

"Nar," she retorted, and ran off into the dark.

Chris later told Lesley something of this, omitting the kiss. Lesley shrugged. She and Pattie were growing apart. Pattie did her own thing, she always had.

LESLEY

1

The summer was an unsettled time until the GCE results came out. Lesley, unusually, was in disagreement with her parents about her wish to leave school and go to art college. She was committed to a future as an artist and could not see the point in doing anything other than art. Pattie, less surprisingly, was also in conflict with her parents. Phyllis was still unwell, Elisabeth had left for London, their grandfather had died and Mrs Lindsey, the girls' grandmother might be coming to live with them.

"Everything's upset," Heather said. "Everything's changed, nothing's the same."

Bertrand agreed. "If there's one thing you can be sure of it's that there will be change. But it seems to be happening faster these days."

His firm had a major new building project, for a ten story block of flats, which involved meetings with planners and community groups, often in the evenings. He complained that he spent all his time talking to people and filling in forms and never had time for drawing.

The Atfields and the Davies's met from time to time, although Chris was working in order to earn money to see him through the next year and had little free time, and with Elisabeth's departure Colin had retreated into his earlier shyness. Lesley, who shared the general feeling of restlessness and uncertainty, discovered that it was helpful to talk to someone outside her own family, and that someone was often Chris. She wasn't sure what the problem was with her own family, she loved them as much as ever but somehow they were too close. She could anticipate their reactions. And she knew that they were disappointed that she didn't want to stay on at school, and this was the first time she had disappointed them in this way. She called in at the Manse one evening and found Chris alone, doing some college work. He put it aside when Lesley arrived and made some coffee.

When she explained how things were, his comments were flattering, but not particularly helpful.

"Knowing you, you'll make the most of whatever you do, and get a lot out of it."

"That doesn't really help."

"Is there anything other than art that really interests you?"

"No. I mean, not in terms of what I want to do with my life."

"Well, you're old enough and intelligent enough to know what you want to do. Of course you listen to what your parents say, but you make your own decisions."

"They are trying to be helpful."

"Yes of course. And I should also say that time passes incredibly quickly. I'll be in my second year at uni next year."

"So if I did two years in the sixth form you'd have finished university and I wouldn't have started."

"That's life. You can't change the age you are."

"Thanks, Chris."

"Any time. More coffee?"

Time passed, however, and by the end of August the results were out and both Lesley and Heather knew what they would be doing the following year. Heather had a place at Durham, studying history, and after much discussion it had been agreed that Lesley would stay on at school for one more year during which she would study A level art, together with other non-examination subjects. If she passed the following summer she could leave school and do a pre-diploma course at the local art college. It was a good compromise, not least because she had discovered that many art schools now expected students to have at least one A level. She would be one of only a handful of girls taking art at this level (and the only one trying to achieve it in one year), and history of art classes would be held at the boys' grammar school, with a joint project with the boys in the Easter term. After five years at a girls' school Lesley looked forward to this. She didn't know many young men, apart from Chris, and John next door, and her cousin Stuart, Bertrand's sister's son, but he lived in Bath and she hardly ever saw him. It would be nice to meet new people, especially as both Heather and Chris were away, and Pattie was doing her own thing with her own friends.

In December her father took Lesley and her mother to London for three days to see the art galleries and do some Christmas shopping. They were unable to meet Hugh and Elisabeth, who were doing a course related to their Church; it was hard to imagine Elisabeth agreeing to this without protest. They did, however, meet up with Chris, who showed them around the University. Pattie pleaded to come with them, but neither Bertrand nor Irene wanted to have the responsibility of looking after her in London. All Pattie was interested in was boys and music and clothes; art galleries would have bored her to tears. She spent a lot of time at home hanging out in pubs and coffee bars with her friends.

Despite their various preoccupations they all missed Elisabeth. She had been a quiet presence, but when she had gone they noticed the gap. Heather and Pattie both wept. Pattie felt that Elisabeth had been her find, and that they had had a special relationship. Heather was equally sure that she had been closest to Elisabeth. "I helped her with her ll plus, and I was teaching her to knit. And I used to bathe her and put her to bed when she was little. She was like my own child," she said dramatically.

Of them all, Lesley had been least close to Elisabeth. She considered this, then put it to one side. It was one of those things. Elisabeth had needed so much drawing out and somehow Lesley had failed to do this. She had now moved away, and her grandmother was moving in; that was just the way things were. She pointed out to her more emotional sister that Elisabeth had never been a permanent member of the family; right from the start it was said that she would return to her father when he was able to look after her. Heather accused her of being unfeeling, but Lesley knew it wasn't that; she might be unsentimental, but it didn't mean she didn't care. If there was nothing to be done, however, she could see no point in worrying or crying.

Bertrand had always been a little nervous of Elisabeth, though he would never have admitted it - nervous of her smallness and fragility, and secretly afraid of damaging her with his large, expansive personality. She was so unlike his own strong, healthy daughters. Yet she had been intelligent, as clever academically as Heather (he would never admit that she might be even cleverer) and he was disappointed that he wouldn't be able to guide her through school to college or even university. After all, he had developed her, he and his family had encouraged her intelligence to flourish. Had she stayed with her father she would have done no better than Pattie. He could only hope that what they had given her would have become part of her, and would not be dispersed by new influences.

After a speech to this effect, made at breakfast time on Sunday, he gathered his reduced family around him in order to attend morning service together, at which the curate made a brief, cryptic reference to "One of our flock who has now left us to enter a new life" after which there was a brief silence during which they all thought of Elisabeth. It felt a bit funereal and brought tears once more to Heather's eyes.

Bertrand had arranged this. Lesley remembered that Elisabeth had only attended church under sufferance. She wondered how she would cope with her new life, and a stepmother who was far more rigorous in her religious observance than any of the Atfields, even Heather. Heather herself was planning to write to her cousin that afternoon to tell her about the curate's words. She was sure that Elisabeth would be pleased to know that she had been remembered in this way.

Irene, who was tired and worried about her sister and her mother, wondered how much Elisabeth would miss them. She had been tearful on leaving, but at the same time her cheeks were pink with excitement. There were times when it seemed as if the four years she had spent living with them had been an interlude for Elisabeth, something to be endured until her father was ready for her. How much would she really miss them? She spoke of her doubts to Bertrand that Sunday night as they were getting ready for bed.

Bertrand was shocked. "Well, of course she was torn, poor little mite. She hero-worships her father, the Lord knows why. She's spent the last four years waiting for him to come back for her."

"Well exactly," said Irene. "You would think that after four years she would have settled down more happily with us."

"She's a one-man girl," said Bertrand. "No-one will ever take the place of her father. I wonder how it will be when she starts having boyfriends. I hope she finds someone good and kind."

"For heavens' sake, Bertrand, she's eleven."

"Well, alright. But don't think she didn't love us all, she did. Why, she said to me, if only Daddy could live here too, she would be perfectly happy. It was a wrench for her to leave this house, she loved it. I expect they'll live in a poky little terraced house somewhere in the fringes of London. She'll miss us."

Sitting at her dressing table, Irene said "You've been a better father to her than Hugh could ever be."

"That's how it is," said Bertrand, not denying it. "You can't change your nature."

"She never let me treat her like one of my own. She was never open with me."

"But she wasn't one of your own, and you both knew it. And I respect her not wanting a big emotional farewell. It wasn't in her nature. Funny that her father should be an actor."

"Not a very good one," said Irene, rubbing cream vigorously into her skin.

173

Bertrand went over to his wife and took her in his arms, ignoring the cream. "Irene, Irene, you are wonderful. You are everything I ever hoped for. You've created this wonderful home, you've brought up our two amazing daughters, you've made me utterly happy, and you can find the time to take little fledglings into your nest, and the only time I ever hear you complain is about once every five years in the privacy of our bedroom. I can't believe my luck in finding you."

Irene's last words that night were, "I wonder how long it will be before she comes running back."

Lesley took her A level the following June, and passed. It felt odd to be leaving school and with it many of her friends. Once again, she felt unsettled. She hadn't been able to think about the future until she had the exam results, and now art school was only a few weeks' away. She didn't know what it would be like. She didn't know anyone else who would be going. It was another long, uncertain summer.

She found an outlet for her energies in sport; she played tennis, swam, and went for long walks. There were parties, but her heart wasn't really in them. She saw Chris from time to time. He was working hard, at a job in order to earn money and also academically. Although he had little free time he sometimes cycled round to Sycamore Avenue in the long summer evenings. Lesley enjoyed his company, and found him easy to talk to. He never put pressure on her. When she was quiet he let her be. He said once "everyone develops at their own pace," which she thought was very wise of him, not realising that he was quoting his own father. She was still concerned that she was disappointing her parents by not following their wishes. One Sunday evening they were sitting in the garden at Sycamore Avenue, Lesley with a pad on her knee, sketching the trees.

"Have they said they're disappointed?" asked Chris.

"Oh, no, they'd never say that."

"You said the foundation year is an opportunity to try out different things and decide which you really want to pursue."

"Yes."

"So what's the problem?"

"I suppose I've never really disagreed with them before."

"It's called growing up. When you go to art school proper you'll need to live away from home. You need some distance so that you can think your own thoughts."

"Mm. Do you have that distance from your parents?"

174

"Yes. It was even more important - well, you know the church and welfare stuff can be quite over powering. They just live it. I admire them, but it's not for me. Colin will follow in their footsteps, he's even talking about becoming a local preacher. Mum and Dad didn't expect me to do law, but they tried very hard to understand, and when they realised I was serious they kind of assumed that it would be family law. And I'm not, I want to work in commerce. You get paid more. I am so tired of being poor."

Lesley sat up and looked at his clean English profile. "I hadn't thought of you as poor. I mean – you just seem like us."

"That's class. We're all middle class. But Methodist ministers don't get paid much, and then my parents have an unfortunate habit of giving things away. I've got a few more years to go, but then I'm really going to make up for the hard times." Chris ran his fingers through his fair hair, and laughed at her.

"You are serious," said Lesley. She turned over a page and started to draw him.

"Oh yes. Don't worry, I shall be an honest lawyer. But a rich one too, I hope."

"Don't move, I'm drawing you."

When it grew cold they went indoors. Heather and her friend Cynthia, also home from university, were in the kitchen, cooking spaghetti Bolognese with mince and onions and tomatoes. They said it would easily stretch to six, so Chris stayed for supper. He set the kitchen table, while Lesley found thyme and marjoram and mint in the garden, which she chopped and sprinkled on top of the spaghetti once it was on their plates; it pleased her to see the fresh green against the brown of the meat and the red of the tomatoes, on a bed of cream coloured pasta.

Bertrand came in from a meeting he had been having with a local environmental group, who were unhappy about the height of the block of flats that Bertrand was working on. "Democracy, you see," he said, "it's not as straightforward as you might think. People need to have a say, of course they do, but then they can't possibly know as much as the professionals; architects spend seven years training, they understand the technicalities and they also have a better design sense. It's just a fact. I wouldn't try to tell a, a grocer how to run his shop, or a teacher how to teach five year olds. But you have to do it. This could add months to the project."

Heather helped him to spaghetti. "There were some awful pictures on television, Daddy," she said. "These poor little Vietnamese children, and this stuff the Americans use to burn the forests, napalm, well it burns children too. It was awful. You just want to do something to help."

"You should turn it off if it upsets you," said Irene, who had been visiting her mother.

"But it's happening, Mummy. Every day."

"There's nothing we can do about it, these pictures just upset everyone."

"I do understand, Mrs Atfield," said Cynthia, "but I don't think we can ignore what is going on in the world."

"I'm not ignoring it," Irene said, a little sharply, "but I will deal with it in my own way."

"We could all pray," Heather said, "or give money to the Red Cross. I really don't see why the Americans are interfering. They should mind their own business and let other countries mind theirs." She tried to wind her spaghetti round her fork, but it kept slipping off. Cynthia (who cut her pasta neatly before eating it) said, "Well, dear, it's upsetting but we can't have the communists taking over the world, can we? They believe in anarchy, you know, and revolution, and killing everyone who doesn't agree with them. It really wouldn't do."

Chris said quietly, "In Indo-China I believe the people have chosen communism as a reaction to many years of French colonial rule. It's hard for us to imagine what it must be like, being treated like second class citizens in your own country. And it's not quite true to say communists are anarchists, on the contrary they have very strict rules for society. At least that is my understanding," he said, giving Cynthia a not quite sincere smile.

She backed down gracefully, "It is complicated, and you clearly know a great deal more about communism than I do."

Lesley, who disliked Cynthia, listened and said little. She had no strong political views of her own and was disinclined to join the discussion. Instead, she reflected on the fact that she felt so easy with Chris, but actually knew him so little. This was the first time he had spoken of being frustrated at home. He had plenty of friends but as far as she knew he didn't have any really close ones. It was possible that one of the girls he knew at university was more special than the others, but if so he didn't speak of it, and it did not occur to Lesley to question him. If he wanted to tell her, he would. He also seemed to be content

176

with their friendship. As far as she could tell he regarded her as one of the family, but would he always want to be just a friend? She certainly didn't want anything else, not for years and years. She was wary about their being seen as a couple; she didn't want that and she didn't think he did either. Not yet. She had other friends, so did he. He was older than her, he was about to start a professional law course and she had just finished school. She found reasons, once or twice, not to see him, and then discovered that she missed his company. She felt in a state of limbo, somewhere between childhood and womanhood. She thought that she would be glad when they were both at college. It suited her to see him during vacations. It was good to know he was around. Once or twice she sent him a sketch of something she thought he would like, and in return he sent her a postcard from an exhibition he had visited. He was a good friend. She liked him, very much, but not exclusively.

College was very different from school, but once she had got over the strangeness of the first few weeks Lesley enjoyed the freedom to experiment and find her own way, with teachers around to help and advise rather than telling her what to do. She had expected life at college to be more competitive than school had been, and it was. It took her time to adjust and to get used to the group critiques that formed a major part of the teaching. There were some formal lectures, but for much of the time students were expected to learn for themselves; for example they learned about the differences between stone and wood by touch and smell and taste, as well as sight. Then they worked the material, using different tools, so that they could really understand its properties. There again there were frustrations, because some people took longer than others and when you found something you wanted to do you sometimes had to do something else instead because another student had got there first. There was a limited number of lathes, and wheels for pottery. Then they were told to think of some bizarre things, some of them nothing to do with art at all, or so it seemed. You just had to go along with it and hope it would eventually make sense. There was a lot of emphasis on creativity. Lesley found creative thinking difficult to do in the abstract. Still, it was fun trying.

By the second term she had settled down and was growing in confidence. She and her friends wandered round the city, sketching anything that took their fancy. Soon she was sure enough of herself to

177

invite them to her house, where they spent Sunday afternoons arguing aesthetics and building fantastic structures out of paper and string, or designing colourful and impractical clothes for themselves. Once Irene found them studying the contents of her dustbin, looking for ideas. One of their projects was to make a three-dimensional model of the town hall, working in groups. They came to Sycamore Avenue to discuss structures with Bertrand, who was delighted to help.

Bertrand loved to have his house full of young people. He often joined them to listen to the sort of talk which he remembered from his student days, 30 years ago. They tolerated him good-humouredly. Irene took it all rather more phlegmatically, but quietly she was proud of her daughter and found opportunities to boast about her in an off - hand way, to her sister, or friends. "These art students," she would say, "you never know what bright idea they will come up with next," and, "She's not content with decorating her bedroom (she chose grey and gold, and we found some nice red and gold curtains in Brown Muffs) but now she wants to re-do the living room. I don't know what Heather will think."

Heather was not impressed. "She's taken over the whole house," she complained, after arriving home unexpectedly one weekend from Durham, and finding the house full of art students.

"You've got your own room," her mother pointed out. "And you can use the dining room until I need it for tea."

But Heather felt that her sister had taken more than her fair share. "The piano's in the sitting room."

"Nobody's stopping you from playing."

"I can't play with them in there."

"Then you'll have to wait for them to go."

The current fashion was for long straight hair, and every so often Lesley attempted to straighten hers. Heather caught her one day standing in front of the bathroom mirror, pulling at the curls with a wet comb.

"Just because you're an art student it doesn't mean you have to grow your hair long," she said.

"I saw an advert the other day. It said you could have your hair professionally straightened at a hairdressers'."

"I wouldn't waste your money," advised Heather. She took another look at her sister. Lesley was wearing a large red pullover, reaching half way down her thighs, with a wide leather belt, and a pair of black tights. "Are you wearing anything under that?"

Lesley lifted the hem of her sweater to reveal a brief grey mini-skirt.

Heather tut-tutted. "Did mother allow you to buy a thing like that?"

"Nobody allowed me. I made the skirt. Anyway, I've got an allowance, same as you."

"Well, at least I spend mine on sensible things."

"Like going to missionary weekends with Cynthia?"

Heather went pink. She hadn't told anyone about the weekend.

"Who told you that?"

"Carol's sister is at University with Cynthia. She told her. She doesn't keep everything to herself, like you."

"I didn't want to tell people in case they worried."

"Why should they worry? You're not planning to become a missionary, are you?"

"No," Heather said uncertainly. "Cynthia was going and I thought I'd go too."

"You chase after her too much. I bet you're here this weekend because she is."

"What do you mean? She wanted me to come."

"I bet you suggested it. I bet she didn't ask you."

"Yes, she did," blustered Heather, pink again, but she was lying and Lesley knew it. She and her sister would never agree about Cynthia. She thought that the older girl was a hypocrite, the worst kind of showy Christian, and she was unkind to Heather. She thought that Cynthia now simply tolerated Heather, playing with her affections, picking her up when she needed flattery or was short of companions, but dropping her as soon as someone more interesting came along. Lesley did not believe in fighting other people's battles for them, but Cynthia brought out all her affection for her sister. She took a closer look at her.

"Honestly, you talk about my clothes but you look drab. Anyone would think you were thirty. You shouldn't wear all those browns and greens, they don't suit you. You need good, clear colours, blues and bright greens."

"Oh clothes," Heather said dismissively.

"They are important," Lesley insisted. "If you wear nice clothes you look better and you feel better and people feel better for seeing you. If you wear dull drab clothes people think you're a dull drab person."

"I prefer to spend my money on books," Heather said.

179

"Not all of it."

"I just don't have time to think about clothes," said Heather, sitting on the edge of the bath.

"It needn't take long. Let's go out now and buy you something nice. Some material. We'll make you a couple of new dresses."

"There isn't time this weekend. Another time perhaps."

"There is time if you want it."

"Les, you don't realise, I find that sort of thing - clothes, even food - so unimportant these days compared with the real things of life."

"What d'you mean, the real things?"

"Well, love, and suffering and - Jesus. Lesley, I feel so close to Him sometimes I can't begin to describe how wonderful it is. And then there are other times when He seems to retreat and all I can think about is how to get close to Him again. Cynthia understands all this, you see. That's why we're friends."

"Cynthia makes you think all this," Lesley said, unwisely. She attended church out of habit and was content to go along with the formalities, but had no strong religious belief. Heather stumped off, saying that she might have known better than to tell her sister anything. Lesley was concerned, but it was not in her nature to interfere in other people's lives. She decided to buy Heather something bright for her birthday.

2

The art students scattered at the end of the foundation year in order to follow their special interests. Lesley, who after some initial problems had enjoyed the freedom to experiment, was sorry when the year was over and began to see why her parents had advised her to delay studying for the diploma. She wanted to do art because she loved art, and she was confident that painting was her first love; on the other hand she had enjoyed ceramics, and textiles, and print making, and she wasn't sure that she was quite ready to specialise and think about her long term career aims. She would have liked another year of experimentation, free from the pressures of diplomas and careers. However, she had made her decision and after looking at a number of options she decided to apply to the art college in Leicester, where the curriculum was flexible, encouraging experimentation and the breaking down of disciplinary barriers, so that students could continue working with various media and materials and in two and three dimensional art. Bertrand was not impressed with the current approach to art training, which emphasised creativity over technique, and thought she ought to go to a school that taught formal drawing and painting techniques, but this meant the older schools based in the big cities and Lesley didn't feel she was ready for London yet. So, with her new friend Carol, she applied for a place at Leicester and was accepted.

She could, of course, have stayed at Bradford but Leicester was a two hour train journey or a three hour drive from Aireton, just far enough for her to feel independent; she had been persuaded by her pre-diploma year that this was necessary in order to be truly creative. At Leicester she would spend the first year in student accommodation, and then find a flat. She would go home for holidays and occasional weekends, but other than that she would be on her own, making her own decisions, living her own life. She was not a rebel but during her year at college she had mixed with a wider range of people, and had become aware of the importance of thinking independently, and developing her own approach to things.

Lesley's world had already expanded; now she felt on the edge of a great adventure. Her friend Chris had seemed disappointed when she told him she was going to Leicester, as he would be living at home in Aireton while he did his professional training, but then he was one of the people who had told her she needed to leave home. He understood. Anyway, he wasn't her boyfriend, so it really didn't affect him.

Things were very different at Leicester from the foundation course. There was a greater mix of people, including beatniks who seemed left over from the nineteen-fifties with their long hair and black clothes, the women and even some of the men with white faces and heavy black eye make up. They were slightly older than the rest of the students, smoked heavily, and openly took drugs. Their work was dark and disturbing. They liked to use art to represent or interpret their own dreams or hallucinations, introducing jagged shapes and discordant colours into their work. In contrast the course included younger better-off students who copied Carnaby Street clothes and were studying fashion; and others who anticipated the flower power movement of the later sixties by exchanging their mini-skirts and collarless jackets for long flowery dresses and tie and dye shirts. They produced paintings in bright swirling colours that they liked to link to current popular music. It was through that group that Lesley first heard the term 'psychedelic'. And then there were students like Lesley, middle class and relatively conventional, wary of the beatniks and envious of the Carnaby Street group, loving art in an instinctive, unanalytical way. The culture of the sixties, and particularly the music, brought the groups together. They had their favourites but they all listened to the Beatles, the Stones, the Hollies, the Animals. Lesley found herself plunged into a world of new experiences, of sounds, sights, smells, swirling around in an almost hallucinatory way. So many of the students smoked marijuana that it was probably in the air they breathed. It was stimulating, and just a bit scary.

Amidst all these distractions they were expected to work. In an introductory session at the start of the year, the students were told that the diploma equated with a degree and that they would find the work demanding. They would have to think and research and write as well as produce art. They would analyse their work in terms of colour, form, and meaning. They must defend and explain their work to their teachers, their peers, and occasionally visiting lecturers who were practising artists. They would study sociology, psychology, communication, as well as techniques of their chosen medium. They were expected to become familiar with cubism, expressionism, constructivism, surrealism, pop art and kinetic art, and any other movement that came along while they were studying. It was a demanding syllabus. Above all they would be creative and find their own voices. One of the strongest criticisms that could be made was that their work was derivative.

Lesley had been introduced to some of these ideas during the pre-diploma year, so the emphasis on imagination and creativity was not a surprise, although the introduction of topics like sociology and psychology was. She enjoyed learning about painting techniques; she was fascinated to learn about colour, and relationships between colours, and how paints were developed, and the different effects of watercolour on paper and oils on canvas or board, and fresco and batik and many other approaches to painting that she had never fully been aware of. She experimented with brushes and knives and her own fingers. She loved hearing established artists talk about, and sometimes demonstrate, their work, and give critiques. The critiques could be alarming, led by an established artist in front of a student group of ten or twelve, and students got very anxious beforehand and depressed afterwards.

Lesley was an intuitive painter, who, if she had thought about it at all, believed that the purpose of art was to represent real life as accurately as possible. She had expected to spend time drawing models and painting from real life, but found that the old approach to art training, copying models and statues, being true to nature, was no longer relevant in the modern world. The craft skills served creativity, rather than directing it. She was told that her technical skills were excellent, but in themselves they were not art. She was criticised for being too practical, too down to earth. An artist had to see beyond the immediate, to search for meaning, to convey a personal vision. It was simply not possible to depict something real and three dimensional through paint and canvas; the apple was no longer an apple, it was a two dimensional portrayal in pastel on paper. Therefore the only point in painting it was to convey your own vision. But in what way was her personal viewpoint of any particular value to the world? She was only 19, she didn't have the experience to ascribe meaning to the life she knew.

She knew that colours could bring objects forward, or create the impression of distance, but she had not thought about colour and emotion. She read up on Kandinsky, Klee and Miro, and grasped what they were trying to achieve although she could look at a painting by Kandinsky and feel no emotion other than aesthetic pleasure at the unusual juxtapositions of shapes and colours. She struggled to understand some of the lectures on art and meaning, and art and society. She had always understood herself to be creative, in that she could paint a tree that looked like a tree, had ideas for Christmas cards that nobody had ever thought of, and could make clothes that were fashionable but different from anything you might find in the shops. This was no longer good enough.

"The key to being an artist," said one of her tutors, John Standing, "is when your vision excites or inspires or has meaning or resonance for other people. An artist has particular, special insights into the nature of things. This course will help you to see, see with all your senses, but the vision, that special insight into reality, has to come from you. If you can't do that you're a craftsman, not an artist."

It was both exciting, and depressing. The students discussed these issues over and over, in the student bar, in their rooms late at night, walking around town. They agonised over vision, what it meant and how to acquire it. They went through periods of depression. A few left the course. Some created works which confused the other students, but which they claimed demonstrated a unique way of looking at the world. There was a strong emphasis on abstract, as opposed to figurative, art. Abstract paintings could be whatever the creator said they were, a claim that was difficult to dispute. Lesley was happy experimenting with colours and shapes, but every so often someone would ask "Where's the meaning? What's the vision?" and she couldn't answer. She understood that the tutors were trying to break down the students' preconceptions and encourage them to be original. She was fortunate that she was confident in her ability and articulate in her defence of this but even so there were times when she felt depressed and wondered what on earth they were trying to do.

Although sociology was interesting in a general sense, she really could not see the point of it for her art. At a later tutorial she showed John Standing a watercolour she had done of a corner of her parents' garden. It was simple, but she was pleased with the way she had caught the light coming through the trees. She said this, when asked for her comments.

"How do you think a stranger would view it?"

Lesley hadn't thought. "I hope they'd find it attractive."

"What would attract them?"

"Well - colour, light, the fact that it conveys an impression of a garden at a particular time of year."

"Is that enough? Wouldn't you want a stronger reaction? Something that will make people look out for your work?"

"I suppose so."

"People who are interested in art don't just want a pretty picture, they want something that has meaning for them. So what is behind this picture? What did you have in mind when you painted it?"

"I just wanted to capture it. The trees, the light."

"Fair enough, from a technical point of view. Light is extremely important and I'll be saying more about that next term. But let's try to view it differently. It looks like a corner of a big garden, a well tended garden. Is the house large?"

"Reasonably."

"It's your parents' house?"

"Yes."

"So they're middle class?"

"Ye-es."

"So this could be symbolic of middle class ease. It's pleasant, undemanding, but beneath that corner of the garden lies a whole heap of assumptions. Who made the garden, who built the house, how did they make their money? How did they see the world? How do you think someone from the working class would see it?"

"Um – privilege, I suppose. But also somewhere they might like to be?"

"Yes, yes. Social aspirations. Perhaps. The point is that someone from a working class part of a large city might see it differently from the way you and your family see it. Something they might aspire to, something they might resent. I don't know. I'm middle class too. Now do you see what I mean about meaning?"

"Mmm."

"It may be that if you do it again on a dull day you'll find another message there. Perhaps the middle class world is not as comfortable as it appears to be. Try turning the whole thing on its head. Put the garden inside the house and the house outside. Turn the trees upside down. Find the essence of the garden and then challenge it; solid shapes become fluid, soft petals become hard spikes, and so on. Try it and see."

"OK." She did paint the scene again, two or three times, but out of interest in the different effects of light, rather than anything more abstract or surreal. John was one of the more reasonable teachers, someone she could talk to; there were others who tore students' work to pieces with their criticism, made the boys angry and reduced some of the girls to tears. Although Lesley was robust, the critical

185

atmosphere affected her and she worried about whether she was, or could become, an artist, or be satisfied with being a good technician. She went to one or two pottery classes and began to wonder if she would be better doing pottery, which was more practical than painting. She liked the feel of wet clay in her hands. But she didn't want to give up her dream. She could always come back to pottery.

At the start of the second year she was still trying to find a way of painting that conveyed her own particular way of seeing things. She had always loved nature, and over the summer experimented with flowers and plants, trying to create abstract patterns rather than straightforward representations. She incorporated leaves and petals into some of her work, and liked the effect. Back at college, she remembered the beech tree in the woods at home that had impressed her during her first walk with Chris and his friends, so at half term she brought her friend Carol to stay at Sycamore Avenue, and the two of them went to look at the tree again, taking sketch books and pastels. Unlike four years ago the weather was grey and windy, but the rich and varied colour of the leaves was still impressive.

"I've tried to paint it lots of times," said Lesley. "I just can't get it. I'm beginning to think that perhaps it – the tree – is too strong, or dominant – trying to paint it as it is just won't work. Anyway, John Standing would say there isn't any is, there's just what I see. Help me!"

"OK," said Carol, understanding Lesley's difficulty, and going through a routine they had done in class, "focus on the tree. Don't look at anything else, don't think about anything else. Really concentrate. Now, what do you see? What is significant? What is its essence?" At college they talked a lot about essence.

"Well, size. Prominence, being on top of a slope – I suppose that isn't the tree. OK, massivity. Solidity. Grandeur. All those three dimensional things that are difficult to paint."

"You're thinking too much. There'll be a way but first you need to be clear about the essence. Try half closing your eyes. What else do you see?"

"Colour. I guess that's what I notice first. That's why I like to come at this time of year. Years ago I tried to copy the colours for my bedroom - it seems childish now, but anyway I tried. You know, grey walls and russet and gold curtains. My mother and I searched around for ages, and it didn't really work. They're nice colours, but they're not tree colours."

"You're thinking again."

Together they studied the tree. "You know," said Carol, perched on a log, "You'd need a massive canvas to convey the grandeur, if that is the essence. It's just so big, and some of it is hidden by the other trees. Or maybe that's it, the tree dominating other trees. P'raps you can scale it down, just show the effect of that tree dominating the woods."

"The other way would be to take it to pieces and look at its parts," said Lesley, "you know, the bark, the leaves, the branches. Then find some way to combine them, kind of abstract but not entirely. Hey, I like that, I think I'm on to something. I'm so glad you came with me, you've helped me see how I could do it. D'you mind if we stay here so that I can try this out?" She went up to the tree and put her hand on the trunk. "When you look at the bark, just look, it's not really grey, well it is in parts, but there's brown and then the green moss, and even the grey, there are so many different shades. And just look at these leaves. You think they're brown, and then you see that lots of them are still green, then when you pick them up you see that some are pure nutmeg, some gold, but lots are yellow with green streaks, or brown with yellow. Each individual leaf is different. They're miraculous." She picked up some of the fallen leaves, tossed them up and watched them fall to the ground. Then she set to work, while Carol wandered off with her sketch pad.

Back at home Lesley continued to work on her picture, incorporating some of the beech leaves that she had gathered. She built up layers of paint for the bark, until the result looked like low relief rather than a flat painting. She was pleased with it. She realised that by concentrating on elements she could create something more interesting than a conventional depiction of a beech tree.

At college she presented her painting for critique, nervous but underneath the nerves confident that she had done something different and optimistic that the feedback from the tutor would be positive. There was the usual silence as everyone studied it, the students trying to gauge the likely reaction of the tutor before commenting themselves.

"I love it," Carol said loyally. "I was with Lesley when she started it and I know what she was trying to do and I think it's really worked out."

"Hm," was all the tutor said.

"What was she trying to do?" asked someone helpfully.

"Lesley?" They all looked at her.

187

"Well – taking the tree apart. Looking at the different elements. Then re-assembling it." There was some further discussion, mostly critical, the students understanding that the tutor was not over-impressed. At the end he told her that she had made a good start but she needed to take it further.

"You're too cautious. Your subjects are too conventional. Let your imagination soar." It was really impossible. She was fed up. They were given these instructions and then left to struggle with their application. Some of the teaching was actually contradictory; for example they were told to think for themselves, but were then criticised if that thinking wasn't what the tutors thought they should be thinking. Some of the students couldn't cope with the pressures and left. By now, however, Lesley was beginning to think that her own judgement had some validity. She liked what she had produced and she was less inclined to be influenced by her tutor's views.

On the other hand she had to pass her diploma. Lesley went into a local park and studied the trees but couldn't get beyond shape and colour and, closer up, texture. What more did they want? Meaning, essence, words that became less meaningful the more she thought about them. She let her flat mates go off to a party without her one evening and sat on her bed with her legs crossed and her eyes closed, and thought trees. The big beech tree in Spring Wood came to mind almost immediately, and then the walk with Chris and his friends when she really noticed it for the first time, and then she thought about her relationship with him. He and the tree were both significant in her life. But she didn't want to think about Chris right now. She had tried to capture the tree and bring it home, through a colour scheme for her bedroom, but that hadn't really worked, pretty though it was. The essence was missing, the thing that she and Carol had discussed. Colour was significant, changing from season to season. A tree was kind of symbolic of the seasons, you knew what time of year it was by looking at trees. They somehow rooted you to the earth, the seasons. And they had deep roots, trees like that beech must have roots going deep into the earth. And at the other extreme, if you sat on the ground and looked up at the tree it seemed to soar into the sky. Heaven and earth. The enormity of nature, the smallness of people. How to convey it, though. Leave people out of it, they just confused matters, focus on trees, the link between heaven and earth. Lesley slowly got to her feet and found some pastels. She sketched a few ideas, trying to let them come into her imagination and out through her fingers without letting her thoughts intervene. If it wasn't exactly soaring she was working directly from her imagination and found it an exhilarating, though challenging, experience. Later she went to the studio and started to work up some of her sketches. It wasn't easy, in fact it was enormously difficult, but she felt she now had some ideas worthy of the name art.

She told one of her classmates about the instruction to let her imagination soar as they sat in the refectory drinking coffee. She treated it as a bit of a joke, but he took her seriously and said she needed to let herself go. "Try sex," he said.

"What, as an experiment?"

"Go with the flow, let it happen, love the experience. Do it now, come with me, let's fly."

When she declined he said that some people preferred pot. "Or both. Look at Paul Bates, the stuff he produces. How do you think he does that?" Lesley thought of the extraordinary swirls of colour on large canvases that their fellow student painted. She shook her head. "I like them," she said. "They're exhilarating. I don't know how he does it."

"Go to his room and watch him at work and you'll soon know. He's stoned most of the time. There are always girls there. What a genius!"

A lot of imaginations were soaring that year. The students were young, free, irresponsible. Life was for living, and living could be enhanced in so many different ways. Music for everyone, art for everyone, poetry, clothes, sex, drugs. It was a time for experimenting. There were no inhibitions any more, anything went, 'do your own thing' became a mantra. Lesley tried a joint at a party, which made her feel nauseous, so she didn't try again. Not smoking pot made her feel strangely sober when she was surrounded by people who were high, so she became choosier about the parties she went to. There was a lot of sexual experimentation, girls with boys, boys with boys, girls with girls, but Lesley, although curious, did not participate.

She was living in a flat with Carol and two other girls who came from a similar background to Lesley and had the same cautious attitude to drugs and drink and sex. It didn't stop them having a good time. They avoided the wilder parties but even so there were plenty to go to, as well as dances at the university. Every so often they threw a party themselves. They all dated. The others fell for boys from time to time, but Lesley did not. She was still relatively immature.

Something held her back from experimenting with sex, something fastidious in her, that made her reluctant to have physical intimacy unless she was also emotionally close. She disliked the idea of sex without love, and she didn't fall in love.

She continued to be friends with Chris. Once, under pressure at college, she hinted that he was her boyfriend, and found this a useful fiction. He was living at home because the salary he was paid as a trainee solicitor was very low, and itching to get away. He told her that his parents had had some idea that he would be able to work with Colin, who was training to become a social worker and were disappointed when he told them that this was not his intention. "The family firm," he said, wryly. She told him that her parents had come to terms with the fact that she wouldn't become an architect, or a designer, but now they thought she would become a teacher. Lesley knew that she didn't want to teach. But what, in fact, would she do with her diploma in fine art? Sooner or later she would have to earn a living. Chris told her what she wanted to hear:

"If painting's what you want to do you'd better paint," he said. "You'll find some way of earning enough to pay the rent."

He told her he was hoping to move to London when he had finished all his training. "You have to get some big city experience, especially if you're wanting to work in business and commerce."

"Oh, I'll miss you."

"It's not so far from Leicester."

"I suppose not."

"You might want to live in London too, when you've finished your course. Everyone needs to spend some time in London, you can't spend your life in the provinces."

"I'd like that," said Lesley.

"It would be good to have you there."

She looked at him, a little surprised that Chris should be so explicit about wanting a future that included her. It made her think that her fiction about him being her boyfriend wasn't fiction. She was flattered, although for the time being she was comfortable with the way things were. She wanted to concentrate on her work without personal distractions. There was no going back; she had made a commitment to a career in art and she was determined to succeed. Her look must have conveyed some of this, because he gave her a hug and kissed the top of her head, and said no more about it.

Lesley was sociable and she liked to have both men and women friends. She loved Chris, without being in love, and occasionally imagined that her first sexual experience would be with him; but then her mind would skitter away from the thought. It wasn't what she wanted, not yet. For now, he was a friend. The two of them had great affinity - they were easy together, they discussed everything (everything except perhaps their relationship), they found each other helpful and supportive - but she was beginning to think that he wanted the relationship to progress, he wanted them to be adults together, not just girl and boy. She thought he might suggest they had sex together; he had mentioned a friend with a flat in London that they might stay in. She didn't want to sleep with him, she wasn't ready; not, in his case, because she didn't care for him but because she did. Sleeping with Chris would mean a major shift in their relationship. What if it didn't work out? Then she would have lost both friend and lover. She knew he wouldn't press her but it would be awkward to spend a weekend together when he wanted sex and she didn't. She didn't want it to become an issue between them. Lesley would prefer things to remain as they were: she enjoyed his friendship but she had other friends; before tying herself to one person she wanted to explore the world and to measure herself against other people. She wanted to map out her world for herself, to make her own decisions, to live as she wanted to. This future might include Chris - she rather hoped it would - but she was not certain. And she didn't want to be tied, not now, not when the art world was opening up for her.

3

Chris had been working in Leeds and living at home for nearly two years; he had one more set of exams to take and then he would be professionally qualified. Money was tight and he was frustrated with living at home, even though his parents were so preoccupied with church and social work that they took little notice of his comings and goings. Occasionally he enquired about renting a flat in Leeds but he did not want to share and a place on his own would have been more than he could afford. Better to hang on a bit longer and then make his move. Assuming he passed his exams, he could decide whether to spend another year in Leeds, earning some real money and building up his experience, or aim for a London practice. It was his intention to spend a few years in London, it was just a question of timing. The Leeds firm had a head office in London, and he thought he stood a chance of being accepted by them. He was keen to know what Lesley's plans were, once she had finished college. He hoped to persuade her to join him in London. She needed the experience of living in London, and they would be able to get their relationship on to a better footing.

He had made friends through work, and there were still some of the old chapel crowd in Aireton, so he had a reasonable social life, although one that tended to be limited to coffee bars and cinemas and the occasional dance. After London it was dull. Sometimes he met Pattie and her crowd, although they really were not his scene. They spent a lot of time in pubs and he didn't drink. He missed Lesley and looked forward to relaxing with her that summer. It was time to move their relationship forward.

The news that she was planning a holiday in Italy with friends from art school came as a blow. He had daydreamed about spending time with her and maybe going away together for a few days. This daydream had gradually become fixed in his mind until it reached the stage of a positive plan - but one that he had never mentioned to Lesley. Now it was too late. Lesley was intending to spend a month or more abroad - her father had contacts and she might stay on after the rest of the group had left. Bertrand was keen that she should experience classical art for herself, and take classes in drawing. For once in his life, Chris sulked. He was fed up with waiting for Lesley. He was also fed up with being poor, fed up with the lack of sex, fed up with having to live at home again and fit in with his family. His religious belief was weakening, and he had never felt comfortable with his parents' social welfare activities. Christmas after Christmas he and his siblings had been asked to give up their presents for the needy; birthdays were subdued affairs; the house was cold and untidy and meals were hurried, half cooked affairs because both parents were too busy looking after other people. The house was frequently full of strangers. Colin thrived in that atmosphere but their elder sister shared Chris's feelings and had left home at the first opportunity. Chris couldn't wait to get back to London. After years of hard work and study he wanted some fun. He began to study job advertisements.

The day Lesley left for Italy Chris felt like drinking for the first time in his life. Instead he took himself for a long, tiring walk and then telephoned Pattie and took her to a film where they cuddled and kissed so energetically that an usherette shone a disapproving torch on them.

In three weeks' time Lesley's friends came back, but Lesley did not. She had fallen in love with Siena, they said, and decided to stay. One of the friends, however, told Pattie that it was not so much Siena as a Sienese she had fallen in love with, and they couldn't see enough of each other. Pattie, never able to keep a secret, told Chris, and then felt remorse when she saw that the news disturbed him. She thought he was daft, anyway, hankering after Lesley when there were so many other girls to go out with. One of her friends was crazy about him, she had started going to the Methodist chapel just in order to see him. To make up for her tactlessness, she asked him to the party she was arranging while her parents were away on holiday.

Chris went reluctantly, intending to leave early. He knew what Pattie's friends were like and the party was quite as bad as he had expected. The music was too loud, the food consisted of crisps and salted peanuts, the boys kept their leather motorcycle jackets on throughout, and the girls, with mini-skirts, bouffant hair styles and heavy eye shadow, were absolutely not his type. He had brought his guitar but nobody took any notice of him except Pattie and her lovesick girlfriend, who giggled and wriggled and nearly drove him out of the house within half an hour of his arrival. But the friend ate too many peanuts and was sick, and Pattie wanted him to stay, and he felt a kind of duty to protect her from her friends and make sure that the party didn't get out of hand. And he had enjoyed kissing her in the cinema. She gave him some orange juice, which tasted sour. He drank it anyway, before telling Pattie it tasted off. She looked guilty.

"Golly, I'm sorry, I gave you the wrong one."

"The wrong one?"

"That one has gin in it."

What the hell. Did he really intend to stay teetotal the rest of his life? A lawyer who never drank? Ridiculous. Anyway he liked the effect it was having, his mental pictures of Lesley drinking vino with her Sienese lover began to fade, and he saw that Pattie was really far prettier than her cousin. Although her eyeshadow was too bright, her hair had been cut into a neat blonde bob, and the short, tight mini dress showed off her neat figure and slim legs. He had more of the bitter tasting orange juice. The lads were drinking beer and the girls had cider or Babycham, so Chris and Pattie made free with the gin bottle. The rest of the evening was hazy, and he woke up the next morning with a major hangover in Pattie's bed with Pattie's naked leg stretched over his. As he shifted away from her memories of the party returned. Chris's headache thundered in his head, making thought impossible, except the need to escape. He retrieved his clothes without disturbing Pattie and went first to the bathroom, where he was sick, and then through the messy, smelly living room, peopled with the sleeping shapes of Pattie's remaining guests, before making it out into the fresh air, where he was sick again.

Lesley came home from Siena three weeks later, feeling that she had got her life sorted out. She had loved everything about Italy. She had spent hours in the museums and churches, dwelling on every beautiful detail of the early Renaissance paintings, which she preferred to the better known works of the high Renaissance and later Baroque. She adored the formal, formulaic design, the glorious colours (still glorious centuries after they had been painted) and the exquisite, lifelike faces of the saints and donors.

At first she and her friends were overwhelmed by the great art that surrounded them in Rome and in Florence. There was so much, and so much more than they could ever aspire to. Just looking at it was a problem; faced with so much that was good art, how could you know what was great art? Just because it hung in a church and was painted in the Renaissance didn't make it so. And what about copies? Which of the Davids in Florence was the real one? Gradually, however, most of them were able to refine their judgements and accept that that what they saw was awe-inspiring, inspirational, spiritually uplifting, but was also of its time and place. Their own art had to be their own, of their own time and place, and coming out of their own experiences. Lesley herself was inspired. Her subject matter would be very different but there was something about the way the early artists used colour and pattern and built up detail that appealed to her. She felt at home among these pictures.

She loved the painters and she had also fallen in love with Italy itself; the sunshine and colour and warmth in such contrast to the chill greyness of her Yorkshire home. She and Carol decided to stay on, meeting up with an amateur painting group who had just come out from England. The group was staying in dormitory accommodation in an old monastery just outside Siena, and there was room for two more. They changed their flights, and sent cables home to say that they were staying on. They felt very grown up, as if they had gone beyond tourism to travelling.

Lesley attended some of the group's classes; she enjoyed the experience of being with enthusiastic amateurs, all older than her, some quite elderly, who had a straightforward and unanalytical attitude to the art surrounding them. This group set itself limited goals - to capture the blue of the sky, and the green of the olives, to show warmth in stone, to represent the church as a solid object. Lesley, too, gave herself limited goals. She set aside her attempts to find a voice, to have vision, to explore meaning. She chose to look at the detail - a rock half hidden in the grass, with lichen growing over it; the hinges on the door of an old church; some graffiti on a wall; a flower. She worked quickly, sometimes in crayon, sometimes in water colour, exploring colours, textures, and shapes - the bark of a tree, the different grasses - coarse, soft, feathery - dark cedars punctuating the blue Italian sky.

The Italian teacher, a Sienese, was interested in her. Lesley was relaxed about this. Whereas in England she would have been resistant, in Italy she responded to his interest while trying to keep everything low key. He wanted her to sleep with him but she refused. She felt she was ready, now, for sex but although it was tempting, the first time, to have a lover who was attractive, experienced, and Italian, whenever she thought about it Chris came into her mind. It was odd. Perhaps she was in love with him. She didn't actually wish he was with her, but she looked forward to sharing her experiences with him. And the old, cautious Lesley hadn't quite disappeared. What about contraception in a Catholic country? What if she liked it (and him) too much? Or disliked it? How would she face him the next day? Lesley was incapable of flirting and responded to his overtures out of a strong attraction, and because she enjoyed him detailing the kissable nature of her mouth and the beautiful shape of her breasts. She thought she was being honest with him, telling him there were limits beyond which he should not go, and expected him to understand this – as Chris would have. It wasn't easy to say no, when they had been drinking wine and the warm Italian night was all around them. He would take her for a walk round the village and they would sit by the fountain and talk, and on the way back he would pull her into the shadows and kiss her neck and face, while his thumb felt for her nipples through her thin dress. She leaned against him and felt herself softening and wanting his exploring hands to explore further. But still she held back. When he grew more persistent she told him that she had a fiance in England. He gave her a tragic look straight out of opera and complained about English women coming to Italy for romance and then going home to marry Englishmen, which disturbed her until she reminded herself that he was the one who pursued her. She had come for the art. She said this. He shrugged. "So, we will concentrate on art." The next day he was sulky with her, and made a fuss of some of the other women in the group, but after that he was back to his normal, flirtatious self. She felt that now they understood each other. He had made her feel good about herself and although not yet liberated from her middle class inhibitions, she was on the way to becoming so. And he had made her sexually aware, so that she felt ready to lose her virginity.

When she got home she was tempted to tell Pattie about Francesco, but Pattie was in trouble yet again.   She had had a party while Allan and Phyllis were away and a neighbour had complained about the noise; Allan had once more threatened to turn Pattie out of the house. It all seemed a long way from Italy.

Lesley did not see Chris for two or three days after she got back home. She knew he was working, and she too was busy sorting out the things she had brought back from Italy, updating her portfolio, and adjusting to being back in Aireton after six weeks away. She felt much more confident about her art, there was something about formal composition, clever draughtsmanship and exquisite colour that really appealed to her. She wasn't quite sure yet, but she felt that there was something in that for her. The problem was going to be keeping her tutors happy, while continuing to work on the things that really interested her.

By the third day, which was a Saturday, she began to wonder why she hadn't heard from Chris. He must know she was back. Was he annoyed that she had gone away? He had looked put out when she told him but that was weeks ago and it was unlike him to bear a grudge. Or perhaps he had thought that she might want a few days alone with her family. She had faith in his constancy. She had known him for over five years, and he had never wavered in his friendship. So, a little surprised at his silence, she called round at the manse. Everyone was out except Mrs Davies, who explained that Chris and Colin and their father were busy building a 'drop-in parlour' alongside the Sunday School room adjacent to the chapel.

"And when I say building I mean building," she said. "With their own bare hands. They got plans drawn up, and Jowetts are coming in to do the more specialised work, but basically they've organised a team of lads, and girls, to do the routine work. Alec and Chris are supposed to be supervising, but most of the time they muck in with the others. Your father has promised to drop in and see how they are doing." She led Lesley into the kitchen, where she was ironing, and asked her to make coffee for them both. Lesley was familiar with the manse. It was bleak modern house, which had been lived in by two families before the Davies's, none of whom had succeeded in making it homely. Its utilitarian nature resisted all attempts at softening; bookcases and pictures had a temporary look about them as if someone had just moved in and was trying things out. She went to the cupboard on the wall and took out a jar of instant coffee.

"I'm afraid you'll have to wash some mugs," Mrs Davies said. There was a large pile of dirty dishes by the sink. Lesley ran some water into the bowl and started to work through the pile.

"Oh, dear, you shouldn't be doing that," said her hostess. Lesley smiled and continued until she had cleared enough space to take the kettle to the tap and fill it with water. Then she found a space on the work surface, cleared a few papers out of the way, and plugged it in.

"How you do get on with things! Now, tell me about your holiday. How long were you away? It seems a long time since we saw you. I should warn you that I'm expecting the Robertsons to call in, they're having such a problem with their eldest, I said I'd talk to him but I don't know what good that will do. I do sometimes wonder if some children are just born difficult, though I shouldn't say so. Now, your holiday."

"I had a marvellous time."

"Oh, good. You know, I always say it's as well Alec isn't an Anglican. Just think of having surplices to iron!"

The kettle was boiling, steaming up the window. Lesley turned it off and poured the water into the mugs. She looked for milk in the fridge. "I knew there was something we needed. I gave our last pint to the men to take to the building site. I must remember to buy some. Can you drink it without?"

"Yes, of course," said Lesley.

"I'd like to go to Italy," mused Chris's mother. "All that warmth and sunshine. It must make the people happier, even the poor ones. But Alec's no traveller. He thinks that this country has everything anyone could want. We usually go to the Lake District for our holidays. I love it, of course, but sometimes I'd like to go just a bit further afield. Did you take many photographs?"

"Masses," Lesley said, laughing. "I've brought a few to show you." She took a packet out of her bag and laid it on the table. Mrs Davies glanced at the pile of clothes.

"Well, it's time I had a break," she said, turning off the iron and standing it on its end. "Let's have our coffee and look at them." Mrs Davies had heard the rumours of Lesley's Sienese affair. If she had fallen in love, she was hiding it very well - no blushes or embarrassment. But then Lesley never blushed or looked embarrassed. And she was certainly blooming with health - her hair glossy and springy, cheeks rosy and hazel eyes glowing.

"I'm not pushing you out," she said after a while, "but I very much doubt if the men will be back soon. Why don't you go down to the site and see what they're doing?"

Lesley put her photographs back in the envelope. "I'll see," she said. "I've got one or two chores to do. Would you tell Chris I'll be in this evening, if he wants to call round."

He telephoned that evening. He sounded tired. He apologised for this, saying he had just got back from work. He said he hoped she had had a nice holiday. She suggested they went for a walk together the following afternoon, and he agreed, before apologising again for his tiredness and ending the call, leaving Lesley feeling dissatisfied. Was he really too tired to talk to her? Was he feeling aggrieved because she had gone off on holiday without him? She had always believed that he was above such pettiness. That was one of the things she liked so much about him; that he accepted that she had a life of her own to lead which might interest but not involve him.

She was not, however, given to analysing other people's motives. Instead, she began to think about what to do with the evening. She had assumed that Chris would come round so hadn't made any other plans. Heather and her parents were out.

She went to sit with her grandmother, who was staying with the Atfields for a few days. After Ernest died she had sold the house and bought a flat in Aireton, insisting that she needed her independence, but in reality spent a good deal of time with the family. Lesley took her photographs with her, but Mrs Lindsey seemed more interested in watching television than looking at them. Lesley watched the news with her for a while, then made her a cup of tea. When she brought it in her grandmother was absorbed in Coronation Street, so Lesley wandered out again. She decided to telephone her cousin.

Pattie was getting ready to go out. Her voice sounded indistinct and at times faded altogether, because she was trying to put her make up on at the same time as talk to Lesley.

"Oh, hi! I heard you'd had a good time. Hang on while I just – that's better. What was he like? All Italians are dead sexy, aren't they, y'know, like a thingummy in the desert, wandering palms ... did they pinch your bottom a lot? Look I gotta go, I'm meeting Dave and he can get really mean - he hates to be kept waiting. He's a drummer with this group, did I tell you, it's really fab, they do discos and things, they need a singer, we could come to Leicester if you like. It's been really quiet without you, why don't we have a party?"

Lesley put the telephone down and wandered into the kitchen. She felt uncharacteristically restless. Her college friends were all scattered and she had lost touch with people at home. Her best friend from school, Maureen, was engaged and had become coy and silly and quoted her boyfriend's opinion on everything. How could she have changed so? John from next door, who had been quite keen on Lesley a year or two ago, had a steady girlfriend now. She didn't feel inclined to get in touch with anyone else. This part of Yorkshire suddenly seemed very poor and second rate, compared with the splendours of Tuscany. There you would never be stuck for something to do. She might think about going to London, if she could switch courses. She wasn't really enjoying Leicester. She didn't imagine that her new enthusiasm for medieval art would go down well there. They would say it was too controlled. Maybe it was. Maybe all this talk about letting go wasn't for her. Maybe she would find her voice within a framework of order and control.

She took an apple from the fruit bowl, and began to munch it. The telephone rang, and she answered it. It was Pattie again.

"Have you seen Chris?" she wanted to know.

"Seeing him tomorrow."

"Not tonight?"

"No, he's tired, he's been working."

"Oh."

"Why?"

"Just wondered."

"Have you seen him?"

"Um - once or twice. I had a party when Mum and Dad were away and he came."

"Was it a good party?"

"Uh-huh. Some things got smashed."

"What did your father say?"

"I replaced most of them. Well - Chris lent me the money."

"Pattie, he can't afford it any more than you can. How much?"

"£5."

"Look, I'll ask Daddy to repay Chris and you can pay Daddy back bit by bit. It'll be better that way."

"No, I don't want to involve anyone else. I'll pay Chris back. I'm saving up."

"Is Chris angry with you?"

"Dunno."

"I'll find out tomorrow."

"Oh no, don't - not specially. I mean, don't ask him. But if he says something - oh no, Les, don't mention it. Please. Promise you won't. You don't know anything about it, you haven't spoken to me, OK?"

"OK," said Lesley, thinking that the whole world seemed screwed up. "You don't need to make such a fuss. He's never angry for long."

"No, but don't say anything. I wish I hadn't told you, only I thought he might have said something. I must go. D'ya want to meet me dinner time on Wednesday and we can go shopping, I get a long break on Wednesdays. I'll give you a ring. 'Bye."

"'Bye."

Pattie was really crazy. Lesley wandered upstairs with her apple. As usual, her room gave her great pleasure. She had two windows, facing south and west, so from mid-morning until evening it was bright and sunny. It was decorated in cool, subtle colours - pale grey walls, pale wooden furniture, grey and gold and a little red in the furnishings. It had taken her and her mother ages to find what she wanted. She had been inspired by the beech tree, that time she and Pattie had walked in the woods with Chris and his friends. It seemed a long time ago now, but the decoration still gave her pleasure. She sat down at the dressing table, fingering the familiar objects - a china mouse, a tile, some photographs, her hair brush and comb, and a leather wallet with jewellery in it. Her mother would be cross with her for leaving it out. Lesley studied the photographs on her dressing table. Stuck in the side of her dressing table mirror was one of Chris, one of the family at her sister's 21st birthday party, one of her friends at college, and another of her class that had been taken on her last day at school. Lesley pulled a face at that. It could go. And there was one of the whole family one Christmas. It must have been taken by someone from outside the family - Chris, perhaps, or John from next door, - because they were all there, even Elisabeth. And Uncle Hugh. That meant it must be at least three years old. Thinking of her cousin, Lesley felt a pang of guilt. She had never even asked whether anyone had heard from her.

She had been so wrapped up in her own experiences that she had forgotten all about her little cousin. She decided to remedy this by writing to her. Letter writing was not Lesley's favourite occupation, but she could pad the letter out with sketches. And she would send it with a small gift she had bought in Italy. She felt like writing to someone, someone like Elisabeth whom she probably wouldn't see for ages. When, later, she told her parents what she had been doing, her mother said, "Oh yes, poor Elisabeth, I forgot to tell you. We had a telephone call from her while you were away."

"I didn't think they had a phone."

"She used a public telephone box, and reversed the charges. She was very apologetic."

"Well, what did she say?"

Irene brooded, gazing into the empty fire place. Her face looked heavy. It was a look Lesley knew well, and usually meant that Irene was having an internal argument with herself. Bertrand came in with a tray of tea while she was still thinking. "I was just about to tell Lesley about Elisabeth," said Irene, sitting back in her chair.

"Poor little Elisabeth. Yes, tell Lesley, I'd almost forgotten."

"Well, you remember that we had a letter from her in the spring, sounding rather unhappy, saying that her stepmother wanted her to leave school and get a job. Daddy thought we should have a word with Hugh, but I didn't want to interfere. In the end we wrote back and suggested she had a talk with her headmaster."

"She ought to stay on, she's cleverer than any of us," said Lesley.

"No, you can't say that," said Irene, who sincerely believed that no-one could outdo her children. "She works hard and she enjoys studying, but so does Heather. And you work hard."

"Not in the same way."

"Well, anyway, on the telephone she sounded very upset. As far as Hugh and Rhoda are concerned she has left school and has a job at a local factory, making clothes I think. Her headmaster had told her that a place could be found for her in the sixth form but obviously she would have to have permission from her parents to stay on."

"A job in a factory!" Lesley was shocked.

"What could I say? I don't know what she wanted me to do. I don't know what their situation is, they may not be able to afford to keep Elisabeth on at school. I told her that if Uncle Hugh wanted to discuss it with me I'd be pleased to do so, but the initiative would have to come from him. I can't tell other people what to do with their own children." Irene had clearly worried about this. "Then Bertrand talked to her, and told her that she could always study for her A levels at night school. She said she didn't think she'd be allowed to do that. She sounded very moody and stubborn - you remember how she used to get."

"She probably hated asking you for help. What's Uncle Hugh doing now?"

"Preaching," said Bertrand, helping himself to more tea. "You know he's given up the stage for the pulpit. He discovered a natural talent for sermonising and preaching. He's been received into the strange church that Rhoda belongs to, and by all accounts is a born again Christian."

"Good heavens," said Lesley.

"It is a most peculiar sect," said Irene, "an offshoot of the Plymouth Brethren, I think. They believe in the second coming of Christ and have to be constantly prepared for that. They keep themselves very much to themselves. The factory Elisabeth is to work in is run by the church, any profits it makes are ploughed into the church, and members are expected to give a percentage of their salary to the church."

"It's years since we've seen her," said Lesley. "It's funny, first we hardly knew she existed, then she became one of the family, and now she's disappeared again. Why don't we ask her to stay?"

"We have done, but she won't come."

"Or can't," said the more tolerant Bertrand.

"I could add a ps to my letter," offered Lesley.

"Well, you can try."

"What does Heather think?"

"Heather was away."

"A church holiday camp," Bertrand said, with a small frown.

Heather, when told, reacted as anticipated, weeping for the fate of her little cousin, and accusing her parents of hardheartedness. "Heather, don't be silly," said her father. "We can't start interfering in other people's lives. We would be very annoyed if people tried to tell us how to bring up our children."

"I should think so!" said Irene.

"No, I think you should, if you think they are harming their children. And Elisabeth lived with us, she was more like a sister than a cousin. You discuss Pattie with Auntie Phyllis, don't you?"

"Only when she asks me."

"Oh, there must be something we could do. Why don't I go to see her? Cynthia and I were thinking of spending a few days in London. She'd get on with them well, she'd know what to say."

"Heather, be sensible."

"I am being."

"They don't like people who don't belong to their church," put in Lesley.

"Yes, but Cynthia…"

"Even Cynthia."

"What sort of a life is that for her?" Heather demanded.

"We can't judge them, we never see them. Your father and I have talked of visiting, but somehow… We don't know what problems they might have. They can't have much money, they probably need Elisabeth's earnings."

"People get grants to go to college."

"We're not talking about college, we're talking about school."

The discussion continued. Heather remained convinced that something could and should be done to help Elisabeth, and in the end it was agreed that Lesley would add a note to her letter to say that she and Heather would try to arrange a few days in London in order to see their cousin.

Later that evening, still feeling restless, Lesley padded into her sister's bedroom for a chat. Heather was sitting up in bed, her face pink and shiny with cream, with two large rollers in her hair. "What are you doing with your hair?"

"I thought if I used big rollers it might make the fringe less frizzy."

Lesley shook her own curly head. "You haven't a hope. A girl at college irons hers, but it's much longer. We'd burn our heads."

They both laughed, resignedly. Curly hair was a handicap they shared.

"How was Cynthia?" asked Lesley.

"Alright," Heather said a little gloomily. "Well, I think so. She seemed to have something on her mind, but she wouldn't tell me what. I felt we weren't really communicating, so I didn't stay late. She's fed up with living at home, she can't wait to start her new job."

"I like living at home," Lesley said. "That's part of the trouble. I mean, I feel I ought to leave home, but I don't really want to. The best is being a student, half at home and half away. But it won't last for ever. Next year's my last year."

"Of course, we're fortunate, we've got plenty of space, even when Granny's here, and Mummy and Daddy don't mind what we do. Cynthia's house always seems so small and poky, and her parents are terribly fussy, they lie awake at night if she's out, worrying about her. It's such a responsibility for her. She says she's outgrown them."

"That doesn't sound very nice."

"It's not their fault, she says, but she's moved out of their experience of life. She's been to university, after all."

"Your ideas certainly do change as you grow up," said Lesley, rolling on to her stomach. "The same things no longer satisfy. I suppose we've all got to do our bit of exploring."

"I don't like change. I'd like everything to stay the same for ever."

"That would be boring."

"Not if you were enjoying it."

"You couldn't go on enjoying the same thing for ever."

"Some things never change," Heather said portentously.

Lesley heaved a sigh. "Everybody's been acting strange since I came back. I keep feeling as if something's going to happen."

"I thought it just had. You've only just got back from holiday."

"I suppose I'm restless. I'll be better when I get back to college. I think. I'm not sure if I'm going to enjoy next year, I'm not keen on the tutor. And I don't seem to be able to settle to any work at home. P'raps we'll go to London at Christmas, look at the shops." Heather opened her mouth. "You can look at the churches." Lesley rolled back. "Have you seen anything of Chris while I've been away?"

"I've been away too, you know," said Heather.

"I know, I know. But you were around for the first week or two."

"I saw him just before I went away. I asked him to keep an eye on Pattie. Everyone was away, even Mummy and Daddy went away for a long weekend, and Auntie Phyllis and Uncle Allan. We hadn't realised it would be like that. We thought you'd be back, of course."

"Did she do anything terrible?"

"Not that I know of. But I was away."

"She said something about a party." Lesley stopped, remembering the money. She wondered whether to tell her sister, but knew that Heather would think that her father should be told. She decided to wait until she had seen Chris. If he said anything, then perhaps she would. But she had promised Pattie not to say anything.

"You and Chris have a funny kind of relationship. Didn't you miss him when you were away?"

"In a way. I miss him more now I'm back. He's acting strange."

"I expect he missed you. Didn't you wish he'd gone with you?"

"Oh no, it was something I needed to do on my own. But I want to see him now."

4

The next day was wet, so instead of going for a walk Chris came to Sycamore Avenue. Heather was there, and Cynthia, Heather's friend. Bertrand, frustrated because he had planned to mow the lawn, bustled in and out. Irene was with her mother. An argument over politics started between Chris and Cynthia, which made Heather anxious. To ease things Lesley asked Chris about his job, to which he replied politely, but briefly. Lesley began to talk about what she had seen in Italy even though Heather and Cynthia had heard it before, until the silence around her made her feel that nobody was really interested. Even her father was preoccupied with his lawn. It was like speaking to an empty room. So she stopped, and let the others continue with their casual talk and occasional bickering.

She was happy to see Chris, she had found herself smiling with pleasure as he came into the house, and she was surer of his importance in her life. But today he was tense and uncommunicative. It was impossible to ignore. She hoped he would tell her why, but it was difficult with the others there. She wanted to find an opportunity to tell him that her holiday had made her see things more clearly and that she felt more confident and positive about their relationship. She was glad that her Italian diversion had been a diversion and that she hadn't given in to temptation; she knew that casual sex would never be her scene. If she had slept with Francesco things between her and Chris would be even more tense and awkward. As it was there was something wrong and she needed to talk to him alone. She disliked ambiguity and uncertainty and decided that it was time to discuss their feelings and their relationship, if she could find the right time. Chris tended to approach things indirectly, avoiding confrontation and backing off if people appeared to be uncomfortable. This was not Lesley's way. Temperamentally they were very different, and also he was older, more experienced, and had spent the last few years learning to think like a lawyer. Until now they had complemented each other. Now she was becoming aware that the differences between them could cause problems.

She wanted to tell him that she now felt ready to have a more intimate relationship with him but although she knew that was what she wanted to do, finding the opportunity and the words was difficult. She still had a few days' holiday left. Her original plan had been to go straight to Leicester, but she decided instead to stay at home and try to talk to Chris again. Because he was working she suggested they had lunch together.

They went to one of the old-established stores in the town, where her mother had an account. Irene said she would pay, as a treat before Lesley went back to college. In the restaurant there were table cloths and plastic flowers on the tables, with heavy, old-fashioned cutlery. It was very quiet. Most of the customers ate in silence, a silence broken only by the clatter of knives and forks on china, the rustle of paper serviettes, and an occasional cough. It was the sort of place to which a maiden aunt might have brought them and as soon as they sat down Lesley realised that it was the wrong environment for the conversation she wanted. However, she was determined to try.

"You seem very thoughtful," she challenged him, after their ham salads had been placed on the table in front of them.

"There's this case I'm working on," he said vaguely, "but I can't really talk about it."

Lesley found that unsatisfactory. She ploughed on.

"I showed your mother my photos of Italy," she began again.

"She told me."

"It was a wonderful experience, seeing all that art. I'm clearer now, in my own mind, about what I want to do."

"That's good."

"It may not be what my tutors want me to do."

"That's tough."

"I hadn't intended to be away all summer. It's just the way it happened - there was the opportunity." It sounded as if she was making excuses, which she had no need to do. She had never before felt awkward with Chris. She didn't like the feeling. She was aware that eating meant that he had a reason not to look at her.

"You told me."

"I kind of get the feeling you're annoyed. Because I went away."

"It was your decision, you're a free agent."

"But if I hadn't gone, we might have seen something of each other?"

"We might. But I've been busy."

"Of course. So - it's alright? We're still friends?"

"Of course." Lesley could only accept what he said.

"Good, maybe we can meet again before I go back to Leicester. I've decided to stay at home until term starts."

"Don't forget I'm working."

"I know."

Over coffee she remembered Pattie.

"I was talking to Pattie at the weekend and she said she'd had a party. She said there'd been some trouble."

He looked into his cup so that she couldn't see his face properly. "Did you go to the party?"

"Yes, I don't know about trouble, it was noisy and chaotic."

"It was nice of you, I wouldn't go to one of her parties. She has some wild friends."

"Pattie invited me, and Heather had asked me to keep an eye on her, God knows why."

"I know she's in trouble with her parents over it but she was vague about what went on. You know how she is. She did ask me not to say anything, but - well, you understand how things are, we all try to help her, and we can't unless - I gather something was broken and you gave her some money." Chris was silent.

"Well, did you? There's no reason why you should, she's our responsibility. Daddy can give you it back." Silence. "Don't you want to talk about it?"

"Pattie had no right to tell you."

"She did ask me not to say anything to you, but she'll have forgotten. You know what she's like," Lesley said again. "When she does stupid things we all bail her out. We're used to it. There's no reason why you should get involved."

"The money is something for Pattie and me to sort out. We're only talking about five quid for heaven's sake. Do you think your father is the only one who can be generous?"

"You're shouting at me," said Lesley, shocked. She couldn't remember another occasion when Chris had been angry with her. She was conscious of the other diners looking up from their food. "I'm only saying, we all get involved with Pattie whatever she does. OK, you too if you like. When she's stupid it affects us all."

"Pattie isn't stupid. She doesn't think, much, but she isn't stupid. But when you all try to make out that she is, she acts up to it."

Lesley could not understand why he still sounded angry. "If it was for me," she hazarded.

"If what was for you?"

"Helping Pattie out."

"Oh, Lesley, drop it. It was nothing to do with you. Just drop it. Please."

208

"OK," said Lesley, still puzzled. She started to get her things together, ready to leave.

"What else did she say?" Chris asked.

"Who, Pattie? About what?"

"The party of course."

"Nothing much. She was vague, the way she always is when she's in trouble."

After a while Chris said:

"I'm sorry."

"What for?"

"For shouting at you."

"Don't worry, I'm tough," Lesley said, lightly. Then she added, "You never have before."

"Never?"

"Never."

"Sorry."

"It's just – we're worried about her. She stayed out all night last week - she's driving Uncle Allan barmy."

"Why on earth can't they stop her? Who was she with?"

"She says she missed the last bus so she stayed the night with someone. If you ask who she just says 'a mate'. Some of them are into music, and they're talking about forming a group and playing in clubs in Leeds and trying to get a recording contract. She's crazy about music, she's getting into trouble at work for being late. Auntie Phyl is in a state, and Mummy's getting fussed about it, too, but nobody seems to have any influence on her any more. She's slippery, she wriggles out of everything."

"There's nothing I can do."

"I thought maybe…"

"No. Nothing. Please don't ask me."

"OK."

"I have to get back to work."

"OK." They parted. It was still unsatisfactory.

The next day Lesley met Pattie to go shopping, the problem of Chris still on her mind.

"Don't you miss your sexy Italian?" asked Pattie as they moved along the rail of dresses.

"That's history."

"God, you're so cool. I like this one". This was a frilly, lime green dance frock. Lesley pulled a disapproving face. "Well, I do." Pattie inspected the label. "Three pounds seven and sixpence, golly. Were you in love with him?"

Lesley gave an Italian-looking shrug. "No. I thought he was attractive though."

"You must have been a bit. Did your heart leap when he entered the room, did other men fade into insignificance, did you want to wet your knickers when he kissed you?"

"Don't be crude," said Lesley. "I found him attractive. I wasn't in love with him."

"Because of Chris?"

"Mmm. Maybe." Lesley held a dark green tartan dress against herself.

"Was he jealous?"

"Who, Chris?"

"He was really fed up, having to work and you going off to Italy for six weeks."

"We're not engaged or anything, we're not even going out together. Not really."

"P'raps you should."

"Mm."

They took a selection of clothes into the fitting room. They squeezed into a cubicle together and continued talking.

"Does Chris want to sleep with you?"

"He's said he does. But he's been strange since I came back. I think he's working too hard. Have you seen much of him?"

Pattie pulled a dress over her head. Her voice came out muffled

"A bit, parties and stuff. I told you, he was fed up."

"That's OK."

"Is he in love with you?"

"I don't know."

Pattie turned away to deal with a zip. "Bugger, it won't fasten. 'Course he is. He doesn't know what you've been up to, he can't handle it. Go to bed with him, that'll sort everything out."

Lesley replaced the clothes she had tried on neatly on the hangers. She could do without Pattie's advice.

"If I needed it, could you lend me some money?" continued Pattie.

"How much?"

"Dunno. I mean if I need it would you?"

"Depends how much. Are you still paying for the party?"

"We-ell…" Pattie's head was hidden in her jumper.

There was a cough outside and a shop assistant put her head round the curtain: "You girls have been in there a long time, do you need any help?"

"No, thank you, we're just coming. Come on, Pat, we can't stay here." They returned the clothes to the assistant and wandered back through the store. Pattie trailed her fingers along the rows of dresses. Lesley thought about Chris. Was he in love with her? Was she in love with him? It wasn't bells and heart thumping and feeling faint, she knew him too well for that. She just felt that he was part of her life. She didn't like the fact that, right now, he seemed to be somewhere else.

"I gotta get back," said Pattie. "I'm going out tonight. I've met a smashing new bloke."

"Where?"

"Youth club. He's dead sexy."

"Don't you ever worry - you don't know anything about these men you meet."

"It's fun that way."

"They could be married, or escaped prisoners, or anything."

"At the youth club?'"

"Well, maybe not so much there. But at the Mecca dance hall."

"Yeah, you get all types there," Pattie agreed.

Chris could not swim. He was athletic, good at cricket and tennis, and keen on walking and rock climbing, but he couldn't swim. He was actually afraid of the water. He had never been out of his depth and could not bring himself to put his head under water. The cousins found this extraordinary.

Lesley had therefore undertaken to teach him to swim. She had been promising to do this for some time. The September weather was warm and balmy and she thought it would be nice to go to the outdoor pool before she had to return to Leicester, and make one more effort to see if she and he could regain their old easy friendship. She, like the rest of the family, was at home in the water. She loved entering it, feeling the water closing over her body, taking the first strokes, elated by her buoyancy. She swam neatly and cleanly. She liked to dive, not spectacularly, but from the side or the first board, plunging through the water and then up again, into the air. She found it difficult to empathise with someone who not only could not swim, but was actually afraid to try, and Chris, knowing this, did not like putting himself in her hands. He was also self-conscious about his body, which was white and out of condition after a summer spent working. It was not possible to explain any of this to Lesley. She was patient, but he was restive, especially when some friends of hers came to see what was going on, and each added their own piece of advice.

"Hold onto the side and let your legs float in the water," advised one.

"Do the breast stroke with your arms while walking through the water," said another.

"Try floating."

In the end, Chris told them that he would prefer to practise alone. They were concerned.

"Are you sure?"

"Look, if two of us hold you up and Lesley can swim backwards in front of you."

"No, thank you."

In the end they agreed to leave him alone and swam off to the deep end of the pool, taking Lesley with them, while Chris tried a few half-hearted strokes, then climbed out of the pool and went to lie in the sun.

When, twenty minutes or so later, Lesley came to find him he had buried his head in his arms and didn't look up until she put a gentle hand on his shoulder.

"Have I been a long time? It took me a while to find you."

He grunted and rolled over onto his back. Lesley gazed down at him, admiring the clean shape of his nose and jaw, and the long, lean line of his body. Water dripped off her wet hair on to his chest.

"Sorry." She rubbed the water away but left her hand where it was. Her skin was a few shades darker than his.

He sat up and handed her a towel. He was not happy and she did not know why. Her usual tactic of ignoring moods was not working. Her puzzlement was turning into mild irritation. She knelt up and rubbed vigorously at her hair, then at her neck and shoulders.

Wrapping the towel around her she gazed across the blue of the pool. A small distant figure was climbing towards the highest diving board. He paused, arms raised, then bent forward, pulling his arms back, then forward as he flew off the board and plunged down into the water. There was some thin clapping.

"That was Barry," said Lesley, recognising one of her friends. "I didn't know he was such a good diver."

"I don't think I shall come swimming again," said Chris.

"That's up to you."

212

"Don't you care?"

Lesley rarely got annoyed, but he was beginning to needle her. "Don't try to box me in. I like swimming, you don't. That's OK. I'm sorry I suggested it."

"It's not OK. We need to sort things out."

"What things?"

"Just things."

"If you say so." Lesley no longer felt like sorting things out. She stood up and threw the towel at Chris.

"Let's go and get dressed. You look cold." She picked up her bag and waited for him to get to his feet, which he did slowly and with bad grace. They made their way in silence to the changing rooms, where they separated.

Lesley, always a quick dresser, was out again in ten minutes. She sat on a bench in the sun, waiting for Chris, still feeling ruffled. She also felt cold. The September sun didn't have much strength after all. She thought again about Italy. If one could combine all the nice things - the colour and warmth of Italy with the good, honest, practical things of England. Francesco and Chris. She thought that sex might be the issue, maybe he was fed up because she hadn't been willing to sleep with him. She thought that now she was ready. But you couldn't just do it, cold, at least she didn't think you could. You had to build up to it, go for walks in picturesque Italian villages in the warm twilight. You had to really want it. Good, honest, practical wasn't very sexy. Perhaps she and Chris should go to Italy, but Chris didn't have any money, and she had to go back to Leicester.

While she waited two young men, dripping with water, came towards her. One of them was Barry, whom she had recognised diving off the top board.

"Oh Barry, was that you diving? I thought I recognised you. You were very good."

"It's not difficult," said Barry modestly. He was a tall young man with curly dark hair. "It's a question of nerve. If you think you can do it, you can."

"Oh come on," said his friend. "You've been practising for weeks."

Lesley laughed.

"You doing anything tonight?" asked Barry.

"What's on?"

"Just a party. At Tony Webber's. Come along if you feel like it - girls don't have to bring anything - or anyone. But you can if you like," he added, as Chris emerged from the changing rooms and came to stand by them. Lesley introduced them.

"We've been invited to a party," she said.

"OK," he said non-committally.

"Do you want to go?" he asked as they walked towards the turnstile.

"Yes, if you do. They're a nice crowd. We can take some coke for you."

"I don't bother about that now," Chris said.

Lesley, through the turnstile, turned and stared through the bars at him.

"What do you mean? You're not teetotal any more?"

"No."

She stood back and he pushed his way through. "Why not? What happened? Why didn't you tell me?"

"I had a drink - inadvertently, at a party. And having had the one there didn't seem much point in not having another."

"But I thought you didn't believe in it."

Chris shrugged. "It seems one of the less important beliefs."

"You don't have to stop being teetotal just because of one slip."

"There didn't seem to be any point in it any more."

"Hm. Which party was it? Oh, not Pattie's."

Chris hesitated. "Yes."

"I knew it. Did she pretend it was a soft drink?'

"No, no, it was an accident."

When they got back to Sycamore Avenue they found Pattie in the kitchen, kicking her heels.

"What are you doing here?" asked Lesley, surprised and not altogether pleased.

"Heather let me in. She's playing the piano in there," Pattie indicated the sitting room.

"We can hear her." Heather had taken to playing hymn tunes and other religious music with passion and much use of the loud pedal.

"Hiya, Chris."

"Hi, Pat."

"Where've you been?'

"Swimming."

"Why didn't you tell me you were going?'

"Didn't think. Didn't think you'd want to come."

"Well. I'd have mussed my hair. I'm going out later."

"I'll make some coffee," said Lesley, moving towards the kettle.

Chris said, "I've got things to do at home, I'd better go."

"You won't stay for coffee?"

"No, thanks."

"Will I see you later?"

"Do you want to go to this party?"

"Yes."

"OK, then, I'll call for you about 9?"

"Fine." He left the house. Lesley frowned, still puzzled by his strange mood.

Pattie straddled a chair and said that she had come to wait for someone to pick her up. They couldn't meet at her house because her father had told her not to see him again. Heather, who had heard the voices and come to join them in the kitchen, was aghast.

"Then you shouldn't arrange to meet him here."

"I knew you wouldn't mind."

"Mummy would."

"She's out."

"She'll be back soon," Heather threatened inaccurately.

"What's he like?" Lesley asked.

"Oh, smashing," Pattie said vaguely. "He plays drums."

"Is he serious?"

Pattie looked worried. "What do you mean?"

"She means have you been out with him more than twice?"

"Yeah, mind you, this isn't really a date, we're rehearsing. I think this is him now. I told him to come round the back. I'll go get him." She went out of the back door, while the others waited with varying degrees of interest and concern.

She reappeared with a short, dark lad of about 19 with slicked back hair who had his hand on Pattie's neck. He wore a black leather jacket covered in metal studs. Pattie's tastes in music had changed, from the Beatles to the Rolling Stones, and her boyfriends reflected this.

"He hasn't got a motor bike!" Heather exclaimed in horror as they came in. "Pattie, you aren't going to ride on a motor bike are you? It's not safe. You must wear a helmet, at least."

"Don't fuss, Heather," Pattie said, running in to find her jacket.

"It's alright, Mrs Atfield," said the youth, lounging against the door. "I never go over a ton."

Heather flushed, aware that she was being made fun of. "I'm not Mrs Atfield, I'm Pattie's cousin."

"Sorry. With all the fuss I thought you was 'er mother. Fancy a spin round the block?" he addressed Lesley, who was looking at his posture and his thin, sharp face with an artist's interest. "Go on, Les, it's fantastic," Pattie urged, but Lesley shook her head.

After they had gone on their noisy way, Heather turned to her sister with a serious face.

"I don't like it. She has no right to use our house as a place to meet friends her own parents disapprove of."

"She's trying to avoid rows at home."

"She doesn't think about staying at home more?"

"Oh, Pattie doesn't think."

The thought came to Lesley that there had been a time when Chris might well have become Pattie's boyfriend. They had met him together at the church dance, and for a time he had been equally friendly with them both. Over the last few years, however, the friendship between Chris and Lesley had deepened, while that between Chris and Pattie remained what it had always been - light-hearted, affectionate, but without depth. Lesley didn't think that either of them wanted things to be different.

As parties went, Tony's was nothing special. There was a lot of drinking and talking, music, some dancing, and at about half past eleven lights were turned down and those lucky enough to have come with or found partners disappeared into different corners of the house in order to indulge in an hour or two's snogging. It was all fairly innocent. Below the waist was still taboo for most of the girls, and muffled exclamations of "Stop it!", the rustling of clothes and the impact of hand on hand were frequently heard. The rest stayed in the dining room with the records and the beer.

Neither Chris nor Lesley wanted to stay once the lights went down. She didn't like the idea of making love in public – she liked him too much for that, and he didn't try to persuade her. In fact, he had barely touched her all evening. They walked home, still feeling awkward with each other. As they neared the end of her road, Lesley turned to put a hand on his arm, and said, "I didn't enjoy that very much. And there's something – I don't know what – but somehow we're not so easy together as we were. Maybe it's to do with my going away, I don't know."

"I said it wasn't."

"Well, there's something wrong. You said earlier we needed to sort things out. I think we need time together, go away somewhere. Spend a weekend together." In the dark she was blushing, she wanted to be clear about what she envisaged but it was too difficult. Surely he understood.

Last year he would have hugged her and then kissed her, kissed her like a lover. This time he said, "Yeah, great idea."

"We'll arrange something?"

"I've got a few things on. I'll call you."

"So – you'll let me know what you can manage?" Lesley knew it was what he wanted, he had asked her more than once. But this time he hadn't responded as she had expected. She was annoyed with herself for handling it badly. Other girls would have been more physical, cuddled up to him, made it sound fun. She had never before felt so ill at ease with Chris. She supposed he would get over whatever it was that was troubling him. If the time wasn't right for him, she could wait. She was confident that he would come back to her from wherever he had gone.

In bed that night she began to picture how things might be, long term. Next year they would both be looking for jobs. He should earn well once he had a proper job and she would find something that would pay the bills and enable her to paint. She knew how frustrated Chris was with being poor, and how tactful she had to be about money. That could be a problem with going away, she hadn't thought of that. Never mind, they would work something out. The Italian interlude had been just that, an interlude. Francesco was probably already flirting with the next impressionable young English woman. In a year or two he would marry an Italian girl approved of by his family. And she would marry Chris. Perhaps. Because she couldn't imagine ever marrying anyone else.

5

But Chris did not telephone and Lesley returned to college without seeing him again. It was a sign of how things had changed between them that she did not try calling him. Shortly after her return, however, there was a crisis that over-shadowed everything else. Irene telephoned her at college, which she had never done before, to say that Pattie had left home and they didn't know where she was. She was telephoning to see if she had been in touch with Lesley; they were contacting everyone they knew.

"Something always happens when we're away."

"I haven't heard from her. What happened?"

"She said she had given up her job and was going to Liverpool to try her luck in the clubs – singing, she meant. You knew she wanted to be a singer?"

"Well, yes. But I didn't take it very seriously."

"It seems she did. She told her mother she had set her heart on it, there was no future in Bradford, she was going to Liverpool with some friends. Phyllis was distraught, you can imagine, it took me a long time to get the facts out of her, not that there were many. Pattie just kept saying it was going to be fab, we'd be seeing her on television before long (of course she said telly, not television). Allan, of course, was furious, and said if she went she wasn't coming back. Things have been difficult all summer, you missed most of that, this was just the last straw. So Pattie went upstairs, packed a bag and left. They thought she would be back the next day but she wasn't. That was last Tuesday and we've heard nothing from her. We've had to tell the police but they are not much help."

"I haven't heard a thing. Of course I'll tell you if I do." Lesley hung up and explained to the secretary, whose telephone she was using, that her cousin had gone missing.

A couple of weeks later Bertrand came to Leicester on his way to a meeting in Birmingham. He met Lesley in the station buffet while he waited for his train. He told her that he had taken a day off work to go round some of the Liverpool clubs with Phyllis, to see if they could find the missing teenagers, but it was difficult with so little information. He and Lesley sat by the window, drinking mugs of strong tea, watching the window steam up.

"'A pretty blonde girl, about 5'4", with three or four boys, one called Dave, dark haired and wears a leather jacket' – that was as

218

much as I could tell them," said Bertrand. "Phyllis had a photograph but it wasn't a very good one. It was hopeless. I can't believe that Phyllis knows so little about her daughter's friends. And these club people are very cagy, they didn't know who we were, they weren't giving anything away. We ran out of time, of course there was no-one much around in the day time, these places only come to life at night. Phyllis talks of going back and staying overnight, but if so she'll have to take Allan. I've done as much as I can. Pattie's 19, after all, she's not a child. Although she behaves like one."

Lesley felt that her father was consulting her as an equal.

"She could go with Mummy, two women might be less threatening."

"And more vulnerable. I'm not having Irene wandering about clubs and bars."

She said "I don't know her friends. I met Dave, but I didn't really know him. I don't think I ever knew his surname. She used to talk about 'this bloke' or 'my mates', you never quite knew if it was the same one or different. I didn't much like them so I didn't get to know them. They were a different set, Bradford types, you know, a bit rough."

"That's what Phyllis thinks."

"Is Uncle Allan still angry?"

"Yes, but now he's worried as well. I don't imagine he'd shut the door in Pattie's face if she did show up. Well, he knows how upset Phyllis is."

"I think that's what will happen. She'll have a go at the singing and it won't work out and then she'll want to come back home. She'll have forgotten the row. She'll turn up again."

But by Christmas Pattie had not come back. She sent a card to her mother, and another to the Atfields, sending lots of love to everyone and saying the group was going to get a recording contract any day now, they'd soon be making lots of money. The postmarks were smudged, Lesley thought hers said London but she wasn't sure. In any case they failed to arrive until after Christmas which meant that the day itself was gloomy, with everyone worried and upset. Phyllis, who had persuaded herself that her daughter would come home for the holiday, was in a desperate state. She would not leave the bungalow in case there was a message, so the Atfields went there, taking the turkey and pudding and all the other Christmas essentials which Phyllis did not have the energy to shop for. She told her grandmother what had happened and was upset when the old lady told her she should take better care of her daughter. Allan had hardly a word to say to anyone. Heather prayed frequently, and consulted the Bible, and talked to Cynthia, passing on to her family Cynthia's kind thoughts and words of wisdom.

Chris and Colin were helping their parents run a temporary shelter for homeless people in Leeds that Christmas. They called in briefly with cards and messages. Lesley, with a portfolio to complete, occupied herself with work and did not speak to Chris on his own. She would have responded if he had made an effort, but he did not, so she let the opportunity go and kept her hurt to herself. The Christmas message rang a little false that year.

By Easter there was still no news. A card had arrived for Phyllis's birthday, in February, but there was no message other than 'lots of love from Pattie'.

Work helped Lesley to put family problems to one side, but she worried about Pattie and talked about her to her friends. She also thought about Chris, although all she said to her friends was that they had drifted apart; it was true that he had somehow always been separate from her college life. In reality she was both annoyed and upset. She felt he had treated her badly. They were friends, after all, and you didn't just drop friends. And she had thought they were more than friends, and she had decided that she wanted him to be her lover. And having made that (to her) momentous decision, and more or less told him, it was very hard to find herself out in the cold. It was frustrating that they hadn't ever properly discussed their relationship; there was just an assumption, which she had been sure Chris shared, that they were special friends. She tried to think back over everything they had said, but it was difficult; Lesley was not naturally reflective. Surely she couldn't have been mistaken, surely she was special to Chris. She couldn't get away from the word 'special'; she couldn't think of any better way of putting it. Maybe she had been wrong. And if she had been wrong about that, what else was she wrong about? There had been no talk of love, she had to admit. He had sought her company, he had wanted to spend a weekend with her, he had wanted her to move to London, he had said something about wanting them to be adults together. She had assumed he meant sex. She couldn't understand what had happened in the summer to bring about his coolness. Because he had been cool, not just busy, not just tired, but definitely cool. She had been hurt that he hadn't contacted her to follow up her suggestion of a weekend away; it was a rebuff, and she decided she would no longer send the little notes and sketches by which they had kept in touch in previous years. She had had one card from him at the start of the term wishing her well, but even that seemed, not exactly cool, but perfunctory. Dutiful, not loving. He had said nothing about seeing her. She hated ambivalence and wanted to sort matters out, but Christmas was the only real opportunity and the crisis over Pattie's disappearance made it impossible.

She was upset, though she didn't show it. She didn't want to think of her life without Chris; he had been a part of it for so long and already she missed him. She knew now that she loved him. She had taken him for granted, she could see that. She wished she could tell him so. She didn't want to go home to Aireton for the Easter holiday, and not see him. For the first time ever she was reluctant to face her parents, because of the inevitable questions. She thought of staying in Leicester but knew that her family would miss her, and she felt she had a duty to be with them. Of course it wasn't duty, she loved them and wanted to be with them, it was just going to be difficult. Without Chris.

In the end she travelled down on Easter Saturday. She had warned her parents that she would only stay for a few days, making out that she needed to use the college's studio facilities during the vacation. While she was unpacking Irene gave her a letter that had arrived a few days earlier. Lesley recognised Chris's writing at once. She was aware that her mother was watching her, so she shrugged and put it on her dressing table, saying she would read it later. Irene then said she would leave her to read it in peace. Her parents were dears, they must realise there was a problem, but they didn't ask questions. As soon as her mother had gone downstairs she tore open the envelope. Then she took a deep breath before unfolding the letter, not sure what to expect, except it was likely to be upsetting. The letter was short, and it was difficult to judge the tone. Chris apologised for having been out of touch. He hoped she had had a good term. He was sorry to hear about her missing cousin and wondered if there was any further news. He wanted to talk to her and wondered if they could meet.

The temptation was to telephone him straightaway. But she held back. She was struggling with a number of emotions, conflicting, unfamiliar emotions. She wanted to sort them out, as far as she could, before speaking to him. She wanted to be prepared. She wished he had said more. Surely if their friendship was at an end he would have made that clear? Equally, if he wanted it to continue he would have said so. Lesley read the letter two or three times trying to see if there was more to it than she had first thought, but if there was she couldn't find it. He signed it 'C' which was how he always signed his cards and casual notes to her. It was unhelpful of him to send such an uninformative letter, after such a long silence. All she knew was that he wanted to talk to her. Well, they could talk on the telephone. When she was ready. She wouldn't put herself out for him. She was only here for a few days, she wanted to spend the time with her parents and her sister, as well as her aunt and uncle. She would meet him for coffee, just once, and that would be it. And she wouldn't contact him, not for days, not until the day before she left for Leicester.

In the end she did telephone him later that evening, thinking that he would be out so that she could tell herself she had tried and would not try again. But he wasn't out, he answered the phone at the second ring, and her heart gave a kind of lurch at the sound of his voice.

"Lesley! How good to hear from you. Sorry about the note but I wasn't sure what you'd be doing. How's the course?"

"Busy, I have to complete my portfolio by the beginning of June. How's your job?"

"Fine, I'm learning a lot."

"That's good."

"Any news of Pattie?"

"No."

"Oh." There was a pause, before he said, more hesitantly, "look, I'm sorry I haven't been in touch, I've been busy, and I know you have too. There've been things on my mind. I'd really like to see you, I'd like to talk to you. I expect you want to be with your family, but I'm having an extra day off on Tuesday, do you think we could meet then?"

"Well, Tuesday, I suppose - OK. What sort of thing do you want to talk about?"

"Oh just, you know, I'll tell you when I see you."

She really didn't know what to expect. An apology - but for what? There was no commitment, they were just friends, he had said he was sorry he hadn't been in touch. What could she say? They had both been busy, they both had exams and she had been caught up with the family drama. Being out of touch with Chris was no big deal. But she knew something was wrong, and as soon as she saw him she was sure of it. He looked tired. Their usual coffee bar had closed down so they had agreed to meet in Lister Park, where there was a small cafe. He had offered to pick her up but she said she would catch the bus and he didn't argue. He was waiting when she arrived, and they went inside together. The tea came out of a large urn, in a dark brown stream, which splashed over the thick white cups and into the saucers, leaving little room for milk. Chris raised his eyebrows as they carried their cups carefully across the café, which smelt of food and stale cigarette smoke.

"Outside?"

"Yes." There were a couple of empty tables and chairs outside.

"You'll be warm enough?" The day was bright but there was a cool breeze. Lesley was dressed in a short green kilt and cream polo-necked jumper, with a duffle coat on top. Chris was in corduroy trousers and a red pullover, with an old tweed coat which Lesley thought she had seen his father wearing. He looked as if he had lost weight.

"All the coffee bars in town are turning into Wimpys or twee little places with lace curtains and plastic flowers," he said, his gaze sliding past hers. "How is it in Leicester?"

"We usually go to student bars," said Lesley. She wasn't interested in friendly chat if there was something more serious to discuss.

When they were settled at a table he said, stirring his tea, "I wanted to talk to you about Pattie."

"Pattie!" That was not what she had expected. She stared at him but he was looking away from her, towards the trees.

"It's just I've been worried - I feel a kind of responsibility. I don't know - I don't know whether I had anything to do with it. It's difficult to talk about, to you of all people, but you were close to her and anyway it's only fair to you. It's getting in the way. I don't know who else to talk to." He met her eyes at last. She noticed that his hair needed cutting, it was hanging over his collar.

"Have you heard from her? Do you know where she is?"

"Oh, no, nothing like that. It's just - you know I saw her a bit last summer. When you were away."

"Ye-es."

"It started with that dreadful party - God, Lesley, this is so difficult to say." He looked down and then up, over her head. "I have to tell you - I went to bed with her. At least - I found myself there in the morning. I truly don't remember what happened – I mean I have a hazy memory – but, well, I made - we had sex together. I think we

223

did. Well, I'm sure we did. In the morning I had a terrible hangover, and the party had left an awful mess. I just went home. Left her to it. Oh, God."

"A hangover? You mean you'd been drinking?" Initially, that was the most shocking thing.

"Yes. I'd never had any alcohol before. It's not an excuse but – it was a factor."

She remembered now, he had told her at the swimming pool. She knew that he had been seeing Pattie, there was no reason why he shouldn't. Pattie was family, they were all friends. She tried to understand what he was telling her.

"Why didn't you tell me before?"

"I didn't want you to know."

"But now you do?"

"Yes."

"Why?"

"Oh…"

"Was that why you were kind of off in the summer? After I got back?"

"Partly. Pattie was still - well I still thought about her. But she was seeing other men. I didn't know what to do. And you'd been having an affair. The whole thing was a mess. I just couldn't handle it."

"I wasn't."

"What?"

"Having an affair."

"Oh. I thought you were."

"You could have said something."

"Yeah. I didn't know what to say. I was fed up. Mixed up. Cheesed off with my job. Fed up with being penniless. You name it."

Lesley was still trying to make sense of what Chris was saying. She was beginning to feel angry. He should have been open with her, not left her to guess.

"Did you see her again? After that time you truly don't remember?" How could he claim that he didn't remember!

"Yes, I felt kind of - responsible isn't quite the right word, but we'd been intimate - oh hell, I hate these words, they don't express what I mean but they're the best I can do. I think I felt I owed it to her to have some kind of relationship with her. I mean not just a one night stand. Well, I'd been out and about with her a bit before, it wasn't … We didn't sleep together again. There's nowhere to go, and I didn't

224

want to just - well, if we were going to do it I wanted to do it properly. Then you came back and I…" He stopped.

"But you would have if you could."

"What?"

"Slept with her again."

"Well… It didn't happen."

"Because there was nowhere to go."

"Well - it wasn't a crime! I'm telling you because…"

"Were you in love with her?"

"Love… in love… I don't know. I fancied her. I like her. She's fun but really crazy - it couldn't last."

"Were you still seeing her when I got back?"

"I'd stopped phoning her. She wasn't in love with me, there were always other men around, she couldn't stop herself from flirting. I couldn't keep up with all the friends, all the parties. But then when she left home I did feel a kind of responsibility."

"Did she tell you she was leaving?"

"Of course not. I mean she grumbled about home, but I never thought she'd leave. I just hope her going wasn't anything to do with me."

"Why should it? She said she'd joined a group, was going to be a singer. That's why she left."

Lesley knew, she'd always known, that Chris might start going out with someone else. Might fall in love with someone else. But that had been in her head, now she was facing the reality. She gazed down into her tea, which had developed a milky scum on top. Part of her brain considered how she might paint it.

"I know. And I know her father told her not to come back. But I still worry - oh, Lesley, don't you see? What if she's pregnant? What if I made her pregnant?"

She hadn't expected this.

"You didn't use…?"

"No."

"She would have told me," she said doubtfully.

"You were in Leicester. And anyway, if it was me - would she tell you?"

Lesley was silent. The anger had been building slowly and now she felt it strongly. She had heard what he had said about waking up in Pattie's bed, but now the reality of what they had been doing there came home to her. She pictured them, naked together, her cousin and

225

the man she had thought was her man. How naïve and stupid she had been. What a child she was! She felt a kind of revulsion, and then anger, and her head felt hot and tight. She wasn't used to strong emotions, she didn't know how to cope with them. She didn't know who she was angry with, Chris or Pattie. Or herself for saying no to Francesco. And then she'd virtually offered herself to Chris and he'd turned her down. More or less.

"She might need money," said Chris.

"Then let her ask for it," said Lesley, remembering and then pushing to one side the fact that Pattie had asked her for money. "Why are you telling me all this? Why do I have to know? She's gone, she's disappeared, we couldn't do anything if we wanted to." She missed Pattie, who had been like a sister, and would miss Chris if she lost him. Bugger everything! She picked up her cup, found her hand shaking, and put it down again. It rattled in the saucer.

"I feel responsible."

"That's not my problem!"

"I'm sorry. I thought - you and she were close. I don't know what to do."

"So you keep saying." Chris was silent.

"I thought you and I were close," Lesley continued. "But you did this - kept it from me - dropped me."

"I didn't drop you!"

"That's what it felt like."

"Oh, Lesley, I didn't mean - only time went on and the whole thing got harder and harder."

Lesley looked at his pale, tired face. A good face, a face to draw. Briefly, she wished she had her sketch pad with her. How attractive he was. And to think she could have had him, years ago, and had chosen not to. And now it was too late. Because he'd become Pattie's man. Except that Pattie had gone. If she could just forget, put that scene of the two of them in bed out of her mind.

Chris said, "I just feel sorry…"

"She's a monster!" said Lesley. "She always has been, she just goes her own sweet way, doesn't give a damn about anyone. My aunt's going out of her mind with worry. I don't want to talk about her any more. She's taken over too much of my life already." She felt jealousy, for the first time in her life. It was because her cousin had been more intimate with Chris than she had. Had 'known him', as the Bible phrased it. What she and he might have done, he'd wanted it,

226

she knew that, but she'd put him off, and then Pattie, messy amoral Pattie, had done it instead. Her mind was going round in circles. "If that's all you want to talk about I'm leaving." She pushed back her chair.

"Lesley, please…"

"I don't want to talk about it!" They were silent. Lesley stared into her cup. Her mind continued to pick away at the pain.

"Are you sure you didn't sleep with her again?"

"Of course I'm sure."

"You said you hardly remembered the first time."

"I'm sure."

"What did you do, then?"

"Lesley…"

"OK. Have there been others?"

"Others?"

"That you've slept with."

Chris hesitated. "One or two. At University. You know how it is... I wasn't in love with them."

"They didn't get pregnant."

"No, they... No. I'm not trying to excuse myself but I was drunk. I didn't know what I was doing."

"I can't believe that. Anyway, Pattie did."

"She'd had a fair bit to drink too."

"She's such a mess!"

Chris was looking rattled. "Look, I've told you because I thought you ought to know, if we are to have any kind of relationship. But you're acting like I've committed a crime! What did you get up to in Italy anyway?"

"Nothing, I've told you. Nothing like you, anyway."

"So you say."

"You don't believe me."

"Something happened. You'd changed. What the fuck was I to think?"

Lesley started to speak, then stopped. Now wasn't the time to talk about Italy. Her anger was beginning to subside.

"Are you saying that's why you went with Pattie? Because you thought I was having an affair with someone?"

"It wasn't like that. But I missed you. And yes, of course, I wondered what sort of a good time you were having. Oh, why did you

227

have to go away? I'd thought - I'd hoped we could have had a summer together."

They were silent. Lesley was calmer. It was only sex, after all. Everyone did it, no-one thought very much about it. Only she was prudish. And a virgin. At 20.

"When I got back I suggested that we might - I suggested a weekend together. I meant together. And you didn't take me up on it."

"Oh God, Lesley. If there's one thing that makes me feel like a shit - I wasn't sure what you meant. I mean - separate rooms or what. And the Pattie thing was still worrying me, you're right, it wasn't quite over. I felt it was unresolved. And I thought you'd been sleeping with someone in Italy. People said..."

"People? You believed them? You didn't ask me?"

Chris ran his fingers through his hair. "No. It seemed so probable. You came back looking transformed." He put his elbows on the table and rested his head on his hands

She was almost calm, and thinking rationally again.

"Would you marry her, if she were pregnant, if she came back?"

"No, no, I couldn't do that." Chris lifted his head and she could see his face again. He was pale but his eyes were blue and clear and looked straight into hers. "I'd help her all I could but not marriage. I mean she's fun, I like her, but it's not a life thing. I suppose - oh God, I suppose that's at the back of all this. If I have – it's what I should do. But I don't want to and anyway I can't, she's gone. And besides – oh, Lesley, you must know, you're the one I want. Really, deep down. If I flirted with her that's all it was. I've told you about this because I couldn't not. I couldn't hide this from you. Not any longer. I realised how much I missed you. You are so clear, so straight, so sure. You would never get yourself into a mess like this." He put his head on his hands again.

It was true, Lesley didn't get into messes, at least not ones of her making. But she hadn't thought Chris was someone who would get himself into a mess. This wasn't the Chris she had known, or perhaps she had never really known him. She put this on one side to think about later. But what he said made her realise that of the three of them she was the clearest and most rational, and her anger disappeared.

"I don't see there's anything we can do, if we don't know where she is. You know Auntie Phyl's tried the Sally Army, she reads the music papers, there's no sign of her. She thought she spotted her once, in the audience of Ready Steady Go, but when she telephoned Granada they didn't know anything."

"Have they tried the police?"

"Yes, but they're no help, particularly as we do get postcards from her." She thought again. "We don't know she's pregnant, you may be worrying about nothing. Were you the first?"

"What? Oh, um, I don't think so."

Lesley was calmer but she couldn't clear her mind of pictures of Pattie and Chris in bed together. She thought of Francesco. How stupid and puritanical she had been.

She got to her feet. "I need to go."

Chris put his hand on her arm. "Do you forgive me?"

"I don't know. I don't know what to think. I think I'm glad you told me, I can't bear secrets."

"Are we still friends?"

"Is that what you want?"

"Oh yes. Absolutely. More than friends is what I'd like."

"Well, friends, yes, I think so." What she wanted more than anything else was for him to put his arms round her. He stood up, looking concerned. The table remained between them.

"You're looking upset, what have I done to you? I'm so sorry."

"I suppose it wasn't such a terrible thing," said Lesley. "I just wish it hadn't been Pattie."

"Shall I see you again?"

"I need to think." If he wasn't going to put his arm round her the next best thing was to go home and do some painting to straighten her mind out.

Thinking it through in her head was too difficult. When she got home she pulled out some of the drawings she'd done before she went to Leicester, drawings she wasn't going to use in her portfolio. There were a number of the family which she had done as they sat around or cooked or set the table or played in the garden. Some she had coloured in with crayons, but mostly they were simple sketches. Pattie had been the most difficult to capture, never still, pulling silly faces or giggling when she knew she was being watched. The pictures of Chris were better. She picked up one of him in the garden one summer, sitting in a deckchair, long legs stretched out in front of him. She had caught him at his most relaxed, his eyes half closed against the sun, a small quizzical smile on his face. There was another of him leaning forward, talking to Elisabeth. That must have been some time ago. She had always thought he was the one in control, the one who knew his way about the world. She wasn't sure what to make of this confused, uncertain Chris. She thought she still loved him. It wasn't bells and heart pounding and legs going weak; it was just the rightness of him and her together, sharing their lives. Perhaps it would be even better, knowing the weakness in him, it somehow made her feel they were equals. There would be a huge gap in her life if he wasn't there. If he disappeared, like Pattie. Oh bother Pattie. She would not let Pattie interfere with her own desires. She picked up her pad and a soft pencil, thought for a minute, then drew Chris from memory. She portrayed him sitting on a chair, with his elbows on the table and his head in his hands, as he had been during their talk. She was pleased with the way she'd drawn the hair trailing over his fingers. She puzzled about where to put herself, and while she was pondering found herself sketching, very lightly, her cousin disappearing out of a doorway, her pretty, naughty, smiling face turned towards Chris. Oh bother Pattie, I can't get rid of you. She took a harder pencil and drew herself, kneeling at Chris's side, her arm on his knee but looking straight out at the world. Confident, clear, true. Sharing Chris's world. That was how she wanted it. That was how it would be.

She took another sheet of paper and started to doodle with her pastels, and then an idea came to her for a picture, abstract, just like her tutor wanted. It was something to do with clarity coming out of confusion, a way through the fog, light coming through a dense forest, clear water trickling from muddy pools. She closed her eyes, and visualised it; dense grey fog, lighter grey mist trailing through a greeny brown landscape, trees, mud, water, light - that would be white with a touch of yellow. In the distance, something to reach for. Maybe she would use a white ground, and just let the white show through. She began to feel very excited about the idea. It could replace one of the paintings in her portfolio, one she wasn't quite satisfied with. Could she do it in time? Yes, probably, but she'd need to focus, really focus, let nothing get in the way. She could begin to see it, she didn't want to lose it, she'd sketch something tonight and then spend all tomorrow working on it.

Before she went back to Leicester she saw Chris again. It seemed important to have clarity in her life before she could complete her painting. She telephoned, suggesting a meeting, thinking 'if he hesitates, if he hesitates at all, that's it, it's over, I won't see him again.' But he said immediately, "Oh yes, let's do that, let's talk again."

They met again after he finished work, while it was still light, and walked along the top of the hill known as the Bank that gave Aireton its special character. He said immediately, "Is it alright? You and me? We can look forward a bit?" and she said yes, but it would have to wait until she had finished her course.

"I'm doing a new painting for my portfolio, it's crazy starting something now but I think I can do it quickly, now I know what I want to do. I'm really excited about it. So next term I'll just be working solidly, don't expect to hear anything from me until the middle of June."

"I'm looking for jobs, I'd like to work in London, what do you think, would you come too?"

"I'd like to live in London."

He put his arm round her and she leaned into him. "I'm so pleased."

They looked out across the little town of Aireton, and beyond that to Bradford and the Pennine hills. It was time to move on, there were worlds beyond Yorkshire.

"You are so clear. You know what you want and you know how to get it."

That word clear again. "I don't always know. Right now I don't know how I'm going to earn my living without being a teacher, which I don't want to do."

"You'll paint and become famous."

"Even if that happens it won't be straightaway. Anyway, you're going to become a world-famous lawyer."

He smiled and shook his head. "It will do as well as any other as a career, but it's not a vocation, not like art is for you and the ministry for my father."

She couldn't think of anything to say in response to this. She pondered this stranger who was her good friend Chris.

"What do you want?" she asked finally. "I mean - what do you really want out of life?"

"I want you to love me," he said simply. There was a silence. Lesley looked at him and his gaze was steady, and held hers.

"Just that?"

"It's the most important thing right now."

"I think I do," she said.

231

Chris ran his fingers through his too long hair. "I've been wanting to say something like this for months - years, really, and I've held off, thinking you were too young, you didn't want to be tied. Yes, there've been other girls but nothing serious, no-one else I wanted to spend my life with. I love you, there, I've said it, I can't imagine a future for me that doesn't include you. I just can't. The world becomes empty and utterly meaningless. Those are just words, they don't really convey the utter nothingness of a future without you."

"Chris," she said. "I said I love you."

"Jesus, Lesley, you said you thought you did."

Lesley said carefully, "I also find it hard to imagine a future without you." To her surprise, she was close to tears. "Oh please, do something, hold me, kiss me!"

"Lesley, my love." He pulled her into his arms and she relaxed into his embrace and knew that that was where she wanted to be. He told her how much he loved her and how sorry he was and what a mess he'd got himself into and if only she would stand by him he'd do everything in his power to make her happy. He couldn't imagine a world that didn't have her in it; he couldn't explain, it would just be nothingness. Lesley reached up to kiss him. It was better to forgive and forget than feel that terrible anger. She felt, not exactly in control, but as if her life was sorting itself out. She knew that it was going to be alright. He was still her Chris, they would be together. Pattie was just a distraction. Now she could concentrate on her painting, and she knew it would be good.

The visit by Heather and Lesley to Elisabeth and her parents finally took place that summer. Lesley, exams over, her relationship with Chris restored, wanted to look for jobs and flats in London, and Heather had a friend in Wimbledon where they could stay. After much discussion it was agreed that they could make a proposal to Elisabeth. Bertrand warned them, however, not to mention it until they had assessed how things were.

"You're going to re-establish contact," he cautioned them. "That's the main thing. If there's an opportunity to help Elisabeth we'll do it, but you'll have to see how things are."

"Don't say anything if things are at all difficult," said their mother firmly. "Just concentrate on making a friendly social call."

"If in doubt, say nowt. Heather, I'm really talking to you. Better to keep your mouth shut and let Lesley do the talking." Heather looked hurt and started to protest, but her father bundled them out of the house and into the car to take them to the station.

They arrived at King's Cross in the early afternoon, and took the underground to Old Street, from where they walked, as they were not sure where the buses would take them. Old Street station itself was utterly confusing, but eventually they found the right exit and started walking, first of all along a busy main road, then down a smaller, quieter road, past a row of shops followed by a patch of waste land. At the next corner there was a small block of recently built flats, and beyond that an earlier development of buildings around a courtyard. It was crazy, mixed up, and all so unlike Aireton.

"There must have been a lot of bombing round here, in the War," Heather said. "The new buildings will be where the old ones were destroyed."

They took yet another turn to walk past a run-down looking pub, and a terrace of houses, some of which had boarded up windows. There were graffiti on walls and road signs. The few people they saw looked depressed. The whole area had a downtrodden feel to it, a place where life remained a struggle.

They reached a T-junction, and Heather consulted her A-Z while Lesley waited patiently.

"Down to the right, then across the road. Then it's number 68. We're here."

"Oh help," said Lesley.

"Are you nervous?"

"Yes."

"So am I," Heather admitted. "What shall we say?"

"I expect we'll think of something. Uncle Hugh will be friendly, he always is. Come on."

ELISABETH

1

From her bedroom window Elisabeth watched her cousins walking down the road, ostentatiously (it seemed to her) studying a map and peering at house numbers. She felt the mix of excitement and resentment that she always felt when thinking about her wider family. Resenting the present protected her from grieving for the past. She concentrated on those aspects of her cousins that made them seem like the equivalent of Victorian ladies who visited the poor with soup and kind words. Why had they come now? It was because of the telephone call she made, all those months ago, in a moment of weakness, when she knew she would have to leave school. But that had been a waste of time, her aunt had said she couldn't interfere. She had accepted that there was to be no help for her and, she thought, had grown stronger as a result. She was coping, she had her plans, she didn't want her life disrupted by reminders of what might have been. Her aunt should have realised that her cousins' visit, coming now, when it was too late to change anything, would upset her. But why should she think that? What did any of them really know about her? She was 11 when she left Aireton, an ignorant child, full of excitement about being with her father again after all the long years apart, and too innocent to imagine what the reality might be like.

Because it wasn't like her dreams. In those, he had either come to live at Sycamore Avenue, or they had found a house of their own nearby; the miles which were to divide the families had been a disappointment. She had some memories of the time she and her father had lived in London before, when she was very small, and they were not happy ones. And she had never anticipated a stepmother.

She had been disappointed by the reality, but not crushed. She had begun to make mental stories about how the families would interact, spending holidays together, sometimes in London, sometimes in Yorkshire. But even here she was disappointed. She felt that she had been written out of the Atfields' lives.

And now she was 16. Living with a father she adored and a stepmother she hated and who disliked her. Over the years Rhoda had tried to eradicate the badness she saw in Elisabeth, and mould her into a better person, but Elisabeth had resisted the moulding, resisted the religion which was Rhoda's life blood, and persisted in thinking her own thoughts. They had now reached an uneasy truce but the plans Elisabeth had for her own future would cause further conflict, she was

236

sure. She hadn't yet said anything about them but she couldn't wait much longer.

There were two cousins walking down the road, not three. She knew that Pattie no longer lived in Aireton; there had been letters between the families and she understood that she had run away to join a pop group. Nobody had seen her since, although Pattie's mother, her aunt Phyllis, had received an occasional card. Elisabeth was sad for her cousin. She felt that Pattie, like herself, was an outsider, never quite one of the family, in Pattie's case constantly put down, although never showing any resentment. Pattie had got into trouble for being too loving, too impetuous, too free. She had tried to help Elisabeth as a child, when they had caught the train to London to find her father Hugh, and had been made to suffer for what had been an act of kindness. Elisabeth never knew the details of her punishment, but she knew that it was days before her cousin was back to her normal sunny self. And yet she never showed any bad feeling, not towards her parents, who had punished her, nor to Elisabeth, the innocent cause. Elisabeth loved Pattie and thought that Pattie loved her; how could she go away without a word?

The knocker on the front door rapped, three times. Elisabeth remained where she was. Her stepmother was suspicious of all strangers, even members of her husband's family, and she wanted to avoid the risk of the visit being forbidden even now. Elisabeth knew Rhoda felt 'put out' by the girls' visit, which had been presented as a fait accompli ('they are spending a few days in London and are so looking forward to seeing you, Hugh and Elisabeth again'). This meant that she would be prickly and ill at ease.

She heard Rhoda open the door. In that thin-walled terraced house sound travelled easily, and she could hear Heather's excited, rather high pitched voice offering greetings, apologies, explanations. They seemed to stand on the doorstep for ages before they were led into the house; Elisabeth was beginning to worry that they would be turned away after all.

At last they were in. She got off her bed and smoothed her hair, which was tied into a tight plait at the back of her head. She hoped she would not have to put on the head scarf that she wore whenever she left the house. She put a smear of Vaseline on her lips and eyebrows, and dusted a tiny amount of talcum powder over her nose and chin. This was her nearest approach to make-up. Rhoda thought the use of cosmetics was sinful, and in any case Elisabeth did not have money with which to buy them. Since she had started work she handed over her wages every Friday night and in return was given enough pocket money to cover her bus fare, lunches, and church collection. After some argument this had been increased to allow for the purchase of sanitary towels and other essential small items. Over this, Elisabeth practised one of the many small deceptions that had become second nature to her over the past four years. She had discovered a stall on the local street market which sold tights and other underwear, as well as some toiletries, cheaper even than Woolworths. So, while telling Rhoda that the tights had cost her 5/6d, she actually paid 4/9d. She would have done the same thing with purchases that she made on her stepmother's behalf, but Rhoda always insisted on seeing the receipts. There were other small savings to be made, such as walking a couple of stops to get a 10d bus ticket instead of a 1s. one, or doing without lunch once or twice a week. This little hoard, plus the odd shilling which her father managed to slip into her pocket, now amounted to nearly ten shillings, enough to buy lipstick and face powder, and for the last few lunch hours she had been haunting the make-up counter at Woolworths, trying to decide which shades to buy. It was all nonsense, of course, because she would never be able to wear it, but the money in her pocket gave her a sense of freedom.

Essential larger purchases were made for her. After one or two disasters involving shoes that didn't fit, she was now allowed to accompany her stepmother on shopping expeditions. She had become expert at pretending that something didn't fit when in fact she didn't like the style, or the colour. Not that shopping happened very often. Elisabeth's wardrobe consisted of an anorak, a thick skirt, a school pullover, a blouse and two summer dresses, (one of which was three years old and really too small to be decent), one pair of shoes, and a pair of Wellington boots which were just about big enough if she didn't wear socks.

Well, they were poor. She knew that. She hated it, but she had known little else. Even when she was living with the Atfields, who had money, she had known that she was an additional expense, and had tried to live as cheaply as possible. Poverty made her withdraw into herself, and increased her natural reserve. She didn't make friends with girls at school or at work because she knew that friendship would inevitably lead to invitations, and invitations cost money. Even a visit to someone's home meant another bus fare and, what was worse, expectations of a return visit.

At last she was called downstairs. She knew that the long delay was to emphasise that her cousins' visit was to the whole family, not just Elisabeth. She entered the front room and stood between the door and the bookcase, unable to hide her shyness behind her long red hair as it was tied into a plait. Quickly she glanced round the room, seeing it as strangers might, the untidiness, the discomfort, cheap furniture, worn carpet, ugly wallpaper. At least there was a shade over the light in this room. Rhoda had no interest in domestic comforts, and Elisabeth, who had, cleaned and tidied as best she could.

But she barely had time to take in the room, and her two cousins, before Heather cried "Oh, Lizzie, we've missed you!" and came heavily across the room, knocking into a chair and narrowly missing Rhoda's foot as she came. She flung her arms around Elisabeth who, most unusually (for she hated physical contact) returned the embrace, hot tears starting to her eyes, causing her to drop her head even more once she was released. It was a long time since anyone had hugged her quite like that. She allowed herself to be pulled across the room to the settee where Lesley was standing. Lesley also hugged her, and the three cousins sat down together facing Rhoda, who seated herself on an upright chair.

They were the same, and yet so different. Elisabeth could not work it out, it confused her. She would have known them anywhere, and yet they were strangers. She supposed she had expected them to remain as they had been, five years ago. Why hadn't they come before? She had been here, waiting for them to release her – didn't they know that? But how awful it was that they had come - oh, they should have stayed away. These conflicting emotions rendered Elisabeth almost speechless while her cousins talked about their journey, and how they had chosen to travel by Underground rather than bus, "because you know where you are, even if it's wrong," as Lesley said.

She and Heather tried to involve Rhoda in their conversation, but she was stiff and unresponsive and they lapsed more and more into a private conversation about their activities and their parents, and how distraught Auntie Phyllis was about Pattie's disappearance.

"She sent Auntie Phyl a card on her birthday," Lesley said, "but we couldn't read the postmark."

Elisabeth longed to know more, but not in front of her disapproving stepmother. Her cousins were irresistible, though, and her shyness evaporated and she joined in the talk with increasing eagerness and animation. After a while Heather, aware of a lapse of manners, said

239

eagerly to Rhoda, "Where is Uncle Hugh? I do hope we shall see him."

"He teaches a Bible class on Saturday afternoons. He should be home shortly." Lesley's eyes opened wide, but she kept quiet. Heather had always had an affection for her uncle, who had once charmed her out of her teenage unhappiness, and she was delighted to hear about the Bible class, asking questions with a genuine interest that caused Rhoda to unbend a little. No-one else in the family shared Heather's enthusiasm for religion.

"Elisabeth will make the tea," Rhoda announced a little while later. It had been established that the girls would stay for tea.

"Oh, we'll help," offered Heather, leaning forward on her seat. Lesley frowned at her sister; how awful to be left alone with Rhoda. But they couldn't all rush off into the kitchen. However, Rhoda said, stiffly: "Thank you, but we don't ask our guests to do our work for us. Elisabeth can manage perfectly well."

To forestall further arguments, Elisabeth slipped out from between her cousins and went into the kitchen, a narrow, dark room overlooking the yard at the back of the house. The meal had been prepared that morning, and there was only the bread to slice and spread with margarine, the biscuits to put on a plate, and the kettle to fill with water and put to boil. She coped with chores like this by using her good hand to raise her bad one and place it on the bread to steady it, before using her good hand to pick up the knife and cut the bread. As she was performing this last task she heard the gate to the yard open and close, and footsteps come up to the house.

She opened the door and looked out. "Hello, Daddy!"

"Hello, my precious Mrs Fox." He had always called her fox or foxy, because of her red hair. Over the years she had progressed from Little Fox to Mrs Fox.

"A perfect housewife," he said, admiring the neatly sliced bread and butter. "Shall I put it on the table for you? Have our guests arrived?"

"Yes, about an hour ago."

"And how are they?"

"Not much changed. Not really."

"Is Rhoda coping?"

"You'd better go and see."

He laughed and kissed her. "Alright, fox cub. Shall I say that tea is ready?"

"You can do."

She watched him swing out of the kitchen. If that gloomy little house could be brightened, he would do it. But there were times when even Hugh seemed to lose heart and become despondent. She wondered how her cousins would see him now. To her he had never changed. Trying to see him with other eyes she thought that perhaps his reddish brown hair was a little less springy, and there were definite touches of grey about his temples. The laughter lines around his eyes were etched more deeply, but he was as slim and sprightly as he had ever been, and his voice was pliant and musical.

He trotted into the living room. Elisabeth hesitated before following him, hovering in the doorway, ready to retreat or advance.

Hugh pulled a stool up to the settee and sat facing his nieces. Heather was laughing merrily in the way she had, eyes and mouth wide open. Elisabeth could not see her stepmother's face, but she could sense that it was anxious and disturbed. "We kept your chair for you, Hugh," she said in her sharp London voice.

"I'm quite comfortable here, thank you my love. I chose my seat carefully, so as to be equally divided between the two of them. Aren't they grown up, Rhoda? Don't you remember, they were mere children when we last saw them? Why has it been so long? How is my dear Irene? And Phyllis? Where is Lizzie?"

Elisabeth stepped forward, reluctantly. Her father put his arm round her waist. "Even my little fox is quite grown up. Don't you think so, Heather? 16 years old, and a working woman. What do you think of that?"

Heather opened her mouth as Lesley said quickly, "Mummy and Daddy sent their love to you both, and so did Auntie Phyllis."

"Four girls," mused Hugh. "Why no boys? Do you realise, Rhoda, I'm the only man in our family. I wonder why that is."

"We've got some boy cousins," objected Heather.

"Yes, but that's on the other side, your father's side. I was talking about our family."

"Your mother's side," interposed Rhoda.

"I suppose we are a bit female dominated," Heather admitted. "I think I prefer it that way. I shouldn't have liked a brother much."

"Oh, I should," said Lesley. "Boys are more adventurous - more fun."

"How is Chris?" asked Elisabeth suddenly.

"Who is Chris?" asked Rhoda.

"A friend – his family lives nearby. We've known him for years. He's very well," replied Lesley.

"He and Lesley are engaged," Heather teased.

"No, we're not."

"Well, sort of."

"No, we've got a kind of – understanding," said Lesley, calm where other girls would have been flushed and coy.

"Oh, you modern girls," said Hugh. "In my day you either asked someone to marry you or you didn't. She accepted you or she didn't. Understandings are a modern luxury."

Lesley laughed. "I'm sure it was never that simple, Uncle Hugh."

Elisabeth gazed at her cousin. Lesley was still boyish, with her short, thick hair, square jaw and straight nose, but there was a softer look about her now. She was dressed simply but well, as usual, and Elisabeth could see that it would be impossible for Chris not to love her.

"He sent his love," she added.

"So did Colin," Heather reminded her.

"Who is Colin?"

"Chris's younger brother. He was very friendly with Elisabeth when she lived with us."

Elisabeth tossed her head. "I don't remember."

"You were only children. But he still remembers you. He's going to college this autumn."

"Elisabeth," said her stepmother. "Is the tea ready yet?"

She got up, not sorry to end the conversation. "I'll just mash it."

"Brew, Elisabeth."

"Oh no, with Yorkshire visitors we can talk Yorkshire," Hugh said, putting on an exaggerated accent. "We'll mash the tea and put t'wood in t'ole, and what else? We should be eating fish and chips out of newspaper."

"Fish and chips out of newspaper! Are you trying to make out that we don't use plates in this house? I always use the best I have when we have visitors."

"Oh, you shouldn't have bothered," interrupted Heather. "You shouldn't make a fuss, we're not really visitors."

"I may not entertain as much as your mother, but we don't eat out of newspaper in our house."

Hugh winked at Lesley. He swivelled round to face his wife. "Rhoda, it was a joke. Never mind. Rhoda is not very good at jokes,"

242

he explained, swivelling back. "Let us go and see what kind of splendid feast has been laid next door. I can tell you one thing," he whispered to Lesley, "it won't be fish and chips. More likely to be a takeaway curry in this part of London."

"Don't make fun of me," warned Rhoda. "I don't pretend to have provided a feast. We don't have the money to do so, and I'm not ashamed to admit it. What we are rich in is faith in the Lord - that keeps us from hunger."

Tea was a difficult meal. Rhoda looked both aggrieved and self-conscious, so that the girls felt compelled to praise everything they ate, at the same time acknowledging the sacrifice which Rhoda implied had been made in providing it. Lesley lost interest after a time. Elisabeth was also quiet, and it was left to Hugh and Heather to keep the conversation going. Grace had been said at the start of the meal, and this led Hugh to a discussion of how religion had transformed his life.

"I blame the Anglican church for failing in its evangelical duty. It could have brought me to the fold years ago had it set about it in the right way. It was there, you see, my belief, lying dormant, like seed under the earth, waiting for the right combination of rain and sun to bring it to life. The rain perhaps being the trials of my life and the sun, my dear wife. The Anglican climate was too dry, there was a lack of nourishment, and I was a delicate seed. But, just in time, I lifted my head, broke through all my worldliness and prejudice, and came out into the light. Girls, my life has been transformed. Tell your father that."

Heather blinked and her face turned pink. "Oh, I will."

"He should hear me preach. I think he would be impressed. You see, I don't think my earlier life was entirely wasted. I respond to a congregation as I responded to theatre audiences - it lifts me to greater heights. I know how to make people listen to me. The technique is the same, but now there is a higher cause. Now I can do what I haven't done before - use my own words, say what I want to say –"

"It's very different, Hugh," his wife interrupted. "You shouldn't compare the House of God with a theatre. The words may come from your mouth, but they are inspired by God."

"Of course. I am only the medium. But I do feel I have a talent - a God-given talent - to turn God's inspiration into words to address to the people. Yes. That is what I do."

243

"It sounds wonderful," observed Heather. "I have a friend like that, who can inspire people. Cynthia."

"My wife's gift is also one of inspiration," Hugh continued. "Not so much by use of language, as by actions. Her whole life is an inspiration. She lives her religion and makes other people long to do the same. I used to wonder, when I first knew her, what is her secret? How does she live such a rich and satisfying life? What is the source of her knowledge? Her energy? Without her my words would have no effect. Without her, I would have no words. She gave me my life."

"God gave me my work to do," Rhoda said complacently.

Both Heather and Lesley were feeling very uncomfortable by this time. God, although very much present in their daily lives (or at least in Heather's) was rarely mentioned by name, and certainly never at tea time on Saturday. Elisabeth was also silent. She hated it when her father spoke like this. It made her feel so alienated from him. He knew she didn't share his beliefs - if beliefs they were. Sometimes she saw it as just another part in another, longer running play. 1500 performances and as popular as ever! 4th magnificent year! She also felt that speech was, for Hugh, a way of disguising uncomfortable truths - the more he spoke, and the more fluently he spoke, the greater the internal conflict of values and loyalties. As they squeezed around the cheap trestle table she supposed he was comparing her cousins' home, and his old life, with the present. Perhaps he was wondering what Irene and Phyllis would think of Rhoda, or how quickly Bertrand would be able to see through his religious protestations. Elisabeth could not believe they were genuine; she was less unhappy to think that he was a hypocrite. Well, he always had been. He was an actor, this time in a major role. He believed that he believed in what he said; but one day he would realise that he did not.

As they were finishing, Rhoda handed them some tracts. She told them that the church to which she and Hugh belonged believed that the Church of England had become weak and apathetic, and had lost influence over people. People had lost sight of the fundamental Christian beliefs: the reality of heaven and hell, and the need to be forever vigilant against the forces of evil. One day soon Christ would descend to earth once more, and they must be prepared. Those who were unprepared would be cast into everlasting darkness. Ignorance and sin was everywhere, and the small community of believers had to be forever watchful lest they become contaminated.

"Goodness," said Heather. Elisabeth saw Lesley nudge her sister, but Heather was undeterred. "But how did Uncle Hugh come to join your Church?"

"God sent him to share my work and my passion, and to save our community at a time of crisis. Our pastor had died, and we were without leadership."

"I was lost, and am found," said Hugh. "Rhoda is my guide and my salvation. Through her I found my life's work."

"Goodness," Heather said again.

Elisabeth nibbled at her bread and margarine. She had long ago learned the art of eating slowly, giving the impression of eating as much as everyone else but in effect having only half as much. She had done this ever since she could remember, knowing only poverty, or other people's charity. She thought it her duty to be as small an expense as possible. She ate - she had no intention of starving - but she ate only what she thought to be necessary for her health. She ate to live. Indeed, of late, it had become quite an effort to eat at all. Meat, in particular, made her feel nauseous, although she had no moral qualms.

She wondered what Heather and Lesley were thinking as they listened to her father talking about religion. They must wonder, as she did, how deep his new found belief was. From pantomime to the pulpit! They must wonder, too, about Rhoda and his relationship with her. Rhoda was narrow, uneducated, and rigid in her views. Her father was broadminded and notoriously flexible. Elisabeth did not like to think about what had attracted them to each other, except that it had to be the attraction of opposites.

What would they report back to her uncle and aunt? She could imagine Lesley describing the scene. Her aunt would be disapproving, her uncle humorous. Then Heather would look tearful and talk about 'poor little Lizzie' and Lesley would shrug and go to see Chris and she – her life would remain as dull and depressing as ever. Chris – she had loved him as a child, in a childish way, and somehow he had remained in her dreams as a symbol of better, happier times. He had always been Lesley's special friend and Elisabeth was surprised to realise how much the fact that they had an 'understanding' hurt. Another dream to lie shattered at her feet.

2

After tea there was an argument about washing up. To Elisabeth's surprise Heather held back while Lesley offered to help and in the end it was agreed that Rhoda would wash, Lesley dry, and Elisabeth put things away. She could do that without difficulty, commented Rhoda, reminding everyone of the things that Elisabeth's polio-wasted left arm prevented her from doing. This was not the first reference to her disability that afternoon. The Atfields and Mitchells had had a policy of ignoring it, and indeed hardly noticed it after a while. They never drew attention to it.

As Heather and her uncle retired to the lounge Elisabeth noticed a look exchanged between her cousins, and was suspicious. This had been planned. She wondered what she was going to say to her father. It was likely to be about school. Elisabeth regretted the telephone call she had made to her aunt, which she had never told her father and stepmother about. Please God, please don't let her stir things up but please God, get me out of all this. Folding her lips together, Elisabeth stacked the clean plates as Lesley dried them and tried not to let herself entertain ridiculous hopes. And anyway, if they did offer her a way of going back to school - and if her parents agreed - could she really accept such charity? Elisabeth, always proud and prickly, had become prouder. Rather than have friends see the eccentricity of her home life, she preferred not to have friends. She had not looked forward to her cousins' visit, for this reason. Although they were family she was concerned about the reports they would take back to Aireton. At least Rhoda was behaving in a reasonably normal way, they wouldn't know the real peculiarity of her personality and religious convictions, which Elisabeth sometimes thought bordered on madness. If she were offered an escape from it all - what should she say? What should she do? What were they talking about?

She learned, a few minutes later, taking crockery into the lounge to put away in the cupboard.   Heather, pink and glistening-eyed, was sitting forward on the settee; her father was leaning against the mantelpiece, lighting his pipe.

"Here she is!" exclaimed Heather. "Now let's ask her what she thinks. I know she'll say yes, and then we must work out how it can be done."

Elisabeth's pride stiffened at this speech. How could Heather possibly know what she thought? This visit had nothing to do with her welfare, it was to do with their guilt. They had given little enough thought to her over the past few years. Thus Elisabeth controlled her emotions and prevented herself from becoming too hopeful. Silently, she knelt on the carpet and placed the plates, cups and saucers inside the cupboard. She could feel the others watching her and made quite a clatter putting it away.

"Lizzie," said her father at last, "come here a minute."

"There are some more things to bring in."

"They can wait."

Elisabeth remained on her knees, head bowed.

"Your kind cousins, darling, want to be kind to you again. They think you are so clever, nothing will satisfy them except that you go back to school. Back to school, my grown up Mrs Fox! They will look after you and pay for you, and send you on to University. If I hesitate, if my voice trembles, it is because I am being asked to make a sacrifice. I am being asked to give you up again." Heather squawked, but her uncle swept on: "It will be very hard to lose my little Lizzie after all those years when we were forced to live apart. We've been together now, as a family, for five years, but I am being asked to give her up again. For her own good, oh certainly for her own good," as Heather tried to interrupt again. "What are my selfish wishes – a father's longing for his daughter – his only child - compared with that daughter's needs." Hugh was getting into his stride. Elisabeth, with greater experience than Heather, knew better than to try to interrupt. It would be like trying to plug a burst water main with plasticine. She wanted to die.

"We know she's clever," said Heather, tearful. "It's such a waste for her to work in a factory."

"You hear that, Lizzie? Our school teacher thinks you are clever. Of course, we know that, my dear niece. Look at the way she discusses theology with her stepmother and me. She goes way over our heads – we're just simple believers." Elisabeth hung her head in shame. How could he? What if Rhoda should come in? He wouldn't stop until he'd finished. "And she helps me with my sermons. Puts them into good English. And writes letters for us, and does our household accounts - why, the household would collapse without Lizzie - will do so. For of course she is going. If that's what she really wants to do. You must, my darling. You'll go on to University, you'll get qualifications, you'll spend your life reading, and studying, you'll become rich and famous - only, Lizzie - you won't forget us,

247

will you? You'll spare a thought between the balls and the punting for your poor old father?" It was excruciating. Elisabeth muttered "Please stop."

Hugh swept on. "It's so kind of them. Lizzie, they are so kind. They see that we are not rich and that we need your earnings to support our household. They see that, and they want to help. They are very kind, darling." Elisabeth shook her bowed head from side to side. Tears rolled down Heather's cheeks. Hugh was working himself up into a climax, standing tall, holding up his arms, his pipe forgotten. His little moustache quivered with emotion.

"Who can say which has priority - the ambition of the young, or the needs of the old and poor? You are young, oh so young!, you are clever, the world opens up in front of you, what a bright vista you are shown! Today's world has been created for the young, we are told this on every poster, at every street corner. The world is for the young, and the young no longer care for religion, for family values, for those who are no longer young. And that's how it is, we can't alter things by clinging on to old values of integrity and responsibility and care. The world belongs to the swingers, and we don't swing. All we ask is to be allowed to live quietly with our memories. So go, my Lizzie, fulfil your ambitions, fly to the heights of academic success, gather prizes and praise and glory - all I ask is that sometimes, just sometimes, you remember your poor old father."

"She can come back for holidays," sobbed Heather.

"What do you say?" Hugh asked his daughter. Elisabeth's face was white and pinched, and her eyes looked almost black.

"How can I?" she asked.

Hugh looked more relaxed. He rubbed his head. "It will be difficult. We know it will be difficult. But..."

"Please stop."

"Well, well," said her father. "No need to be hasty. I'm sure Heather didn't expect us to make a decision right away. We'll think about it over the next few days. May we do that, Heather?"

"Oh yes," sniffed Heather. "I didn't mean to upset you so."

"And I think," he said, moving closer to her, "we won't say anything to Rhoda until we've thought about it a bit more. No point in upsetting her if it's not necessary - and it would upset her to think that Lizzie wants to leave home. She didn't have a family to care for her or send her to college. It would hurt her to think that she had failed to provide Elisabeth with a happy home. So we'll keep it as a little secret between the three of us, just for the time being."

"We don't wish to break up your family," said Heather, very anxious. "We only want to help."

They all sat up as the door opened and Rhoda came in, followed by Lesley, who raised her eyebrows and gave her sister a resigned little shrug. Rhoda's steelier and far less resigned look took in the three of them: Hugh by the fireplace, Heather on the edge of the settee, and Elisabeth kneeling by the cupboard.

"We had expected Elisabeth to come back to help us finish," she said with a tight little smile which seemed to pull down the corners of her mouth. "What have you been talking about?"

Lesley went to sit by Heather, whose pinkness had increased. Elisabeth studied the holes in the carpet. Hugh said smoothly:

"We were talking about Aireton, my dear. It doesn't seem to have changed much over the years. We must pay it another visit one of these days; apparently we have an invitation."

"It's too far."

"We came here," murmured Lesley, whose patience had been sorely tried in the kitchen, but nobody took this up.

"Perhaps next summer," said Heather, who could not bring herself to suggest Christmas. Christmas with Rhoda was unthinkable.

"In the summer, yes, that does sound a good idea," said Hugh. "We could spend our summer holidays in sunny Aireton."

Rhoda said nothing, but made a business out of putting away the remaining dishes. She ignored Elisabeth, who moved out of her way but continued to kneel on the carpet. Despite her pride, her imagination had been caught by Heather's hasty offer of bed and board at Sycamore Avenue while she did her A levels at a local college. Briefly, pictures had raced through her mind of her little bedroom in the eaves, filled with books and opportunities for learning, with trees and lawn outside, and the space and time for the development of her intellect. And then University, maybe, and even greater opportunities for learning and friendship. She would meet people with similar interests to her, she would no longer be isolated, and considered cranky or even wicked because she loved reading. And she would have profound thoughts, and discuss them with her friends, and no-one would ever notice her arm.

But before her father was a quarter of the way through his speech she knew that the dream was impossible. It was impossible for a number of reasons. Her parents could not afford to let her study. Already they were relying on her income to supplement their own. And she could not accept any more charity from the Atfields. She had lived with them for four years; this was something over which she had been too young to have any control. Now it was different; now she was capable of earning her own living. She had to work. But she could study in her spare time and eventually she would go to University. She would get there. She had heard that it was possible to get a grant from the local education authority based on your own earnings, if you had been at work for a number of years. She would get there in the end.

And, though it had confused Heather, she knew what her father's speech had meant. He had thrown everything into this woman Rhoda and her church. He had responded to something dark in her nature, which Elisabeth did not care to think about, and to her passion for the church, which had given him a role denied him by the theatre all these years. He was, however, no longer his own man. He was, deep down, unhappy, Elisabeth thought. It was difficult for him, and he relied on Elisabeth to see him through. He needed her support, her unswerving devotion, her willingness to stand by him, no matter what. He needed her and she could not abandon him. And Rhoda knew that and knew that Elisabeth was necessary to Hugh's stability. So they maintained an uneasy truce.

The last year at school had been difficult and her general unhappiness had led to a drop in the quality of her work. She had got her six O levels, but it had been a struggle. Her confidence in her academic ability had been shaken, but she had thought that the smaller numbers in the sixth form, and better teaching, would help her back to a higher standard. Her disappointment in learning that she would not be allowed to stay on was bitter, and deep; but she had come to terms with it. It was too cruel to have her hopes raised and then dashed again. She felt resentful towards Heather for even suggesting such an impossible thing.

At the same time she felt aggrieved towards her father. He could help her more. She silently promised him, "You can have me for another five years. But when I'm 21 I'm leaving, no matter what. When I'm 21 I shall have my A levels, please God, and I can get a grant on my own account. When I'm 21 nothing will stop me. Not even you."

Five years sounded like an eternity. But of course, Heather and Lesley were 23 and 21, she only had to catch up with them. Anything was possible. She would earn a wage for the family but her stepmother would find out that she could not be taken over, body and soul. She would accept the dreary restrictions on her life, but not on her thoughts. She would read and study as she liked. Books were free, from the library, evening classes were cheap, and examination fees - well, she would worry about those later.

After Heather and Lesley had gone, Rhoda looked hard at her stepdaughter and said: "You forgot your duties very readily this afternoon. Why was that? Were you so busy talking? What were you talking about?"

On occasions like this Hugh and his daughter looked after each other's interests. He said, "We got to talking about the Church again, Heather seemed quite interested.

"She's very religious," Elisabeth confirmed.

"It's never any good talking to Anglicans. It's all formula and ritual with them. Why they don't all go over to Rome I can't imagine. However, I suppose it's better than having no interest at all, like the other one. I simply couldn't get on with her at all. I don't know why everyone thinks she's so special."

Nothing more was said by either Elisabeth or Hugh about Heather's offer. Elisabeth, knowing her father so well, understood that the episode had not entirely left his mind. He was more protective, taking care not to leave her and her stepmother alone for long. He refrained from asking her for money for several days. He tried to think up little treats for her, such as meeting her off the bus after work, or plucking a flower from the gardens in the municipal park to pin to her coat. He even offered to accompany her when she went to enrol for her evening classes, but she preferred to go alone. She told him, more frankly than usual, that the place he could serve her best was at home. Rhoda was not in favour of the evening class project. She was always suspicious of potentially disruptive outside influences upon the family. Neither did she approve of books, other than religious books. But Elisabeth impressed upon her father how important the study was for her, and he protected her as best he could from her stepmother's disapproval. Even so, she knew that she would have to fight for the right to study.

In bed the night following her cousins' visit she tried to take her mind off the bumps and creaks and groans that she could hear from her parents' bedroom (her father's way of making up to his wife for his teasing earlier) by allowing herself the indulgence of thinking back over her life in Aireton. She didn't romanticise it. She told herself how impossible it would be to go back to live with the Atfields - things had changed, life had moved on, there was no going back. She had never really fitted in. She remained an outsider, on the edge of the family group. Elisabeth was aware that people found it difficult to be intimate with her. She preferred it that way, believing that her isolation gave her a measure of protection. Pattie, also an outsider, had none of Elisabeth's doubts about whether or not she belonged. Pattie had no doubts or inhibitions. Where she was was where she belonged. Elisabeth wondered what she was doing now, and hoped that she was happy.

The whole of Sunday was taken up with church activities. The Church was going through one of its regular crises, with arguments over the interpretation of some aspects of scripture, and there was a split between the more and the less liberal elements. One of the problems for Rhoda was that she was naturally authoritarian, while Hugh, inevitably, was a liberal. Hugh could never be a fanatic. He had taken to religion like a new toy. It offered an escape from the constant searching for work, and scope for his oratorical and acting skills. His sermons were mostly declamatory, evangelising. He liked to rouse people. He liked the idea of relinquishing personal responsibility into the hands of a higher authority. He saw his role as interpreting what that higher authority demanded. He relied on Rhoda to help with the interpretation; she was an unquestioning believer, and was always absolutely clear about what was needed. She was strong, and Hugh would always need strong women. Elisabeth knew this; she knew that she too had to be strong, to survive her father. She also sensed, though was too young to understand, that Hugh was both attracted to and alarmed by Rhoda's passionate nature. He needed Elisabeth with her cool and rational attitude as a counter-balance.

He enjoyed the work he did. He was paid a pittance, but the work was easy and money had never been important to Hugh. It paid for the necessities of life and they lived rent free, Rhoda acting as unpaid administrator for the Church. She also worked three days a week at the local factory, where Elisabeth was now employed.

The relationship between Elisabeth and her stepmother, never good, had deteriorated since Elisabeth knew that she would not be allowed to stay on at school. There were times when she believed that her stepmother thought her a positive force for evil. In the early days

252

Elisabeth, used to free discussion of all kinds of subjects at the Atfields' dining table had voiced her religious scepticism, angering her stepmother to such an extent that she had never dared to voice it again. She succumbed to intense pressure to attend church where she sat, sullen and mute, and she wrote letters on behalf of Rhoda, whose writing was poor. But she would not be hypocritical, she refused to enthuse or evangelise. She let her stepmother know that her submission was all on the surface; Elisabeth's soul remained, stubbornly, her own.

Rhoda had been conscious of Elisabeth's malevolent spirit from the beginning. She was so silent (when she wasn't arguing), she was thin, she had red hair, and that wizened left arm could only be the work of the devil. She had a habit of turning in her lips and lowering her eyes when she was forced to do something she didn't want to do, and days went by when she seemed to wear no other expression. At first she had seen her stepdaughter as a challenge, work sent by God, a recalcitrant lamb to bring to the fold. Pride, and a feeling that failure could be seriously under-mining, kept Rhoda battling on. She was a strong woman and on several occasions had been tempted to use physical force on her stepdaughter, but the worst she had done was push her upstairs and into her room. She didn't dare do more. She had no subtlety, and by the time Elisabeth was 16 she had almost exhausted her resources, to little effect. Elisabeth was now too old to be sent to bed without any food and, besides, she ate little enough anyway and was so thin, Rhoda was scared that she would become ill and even die. Her books could be locked away, friends forbidden, but now she went to work social contacts could not be denied, and the books had to be returned to the library. She nagged at Hugh to do something about his daughter, but his efforts were limited to suggestions for compromise aimed at holding the peace.

Hugh was getting tired of the fanaticism and fighting. Life should be more fun. He was sorry for his daughter, but he needed her with him. He still admired and desired his wife but her intensity was draining and he needed some relief. Elisabeth could be equally intense, but loving him as sensitively as she did, she could anticipate his moods and his needs and respond to them, far better than his wife. But Rhoda had given Hugh something which Elisabeth could not supply - she had given him back his belief in himself.

One day, a few weeks after the cousins' visit, Elisabeth and Rhoda came close to physical violence. Elisabeth told her that she had a new job, in the local library, and was leaving the factory. Rhoda was furious. The factory was owned by one of the Church elders, profits went back into the church, and she could be sure that the workers were right thinking people. In the library Elisabeth could find herself talking to anyone and besides, there were books, and Rhoda, a poor reader, was suspicious of books. Fiction, in fact, was banned by the Church.

Elisabeth chose the wrong time to announce her news. One of the elders had, for the first time, criticised Hugh for his liberal views. Rhoda was in an uncomfortable position, torn between her passion for the Church, and her passion for her husband. When she was unhappy her face took on a darkness and a heaviness that warned of trouble. But Elisabeth was less concerned these days about upsetting her stepmother. Rhoda, looking at Elisabeth's shoulder, told her that she could not change her job. Elisabeth said that she could and would. Rhoda said that she would tell the library that her stepdaughter had made a mistake. Elisabeth said that in that case she wouldn't work at all. She would never go back to the factory.

Rhoda saw malevolence in Elisabeth, the devil disguised as a small red haired crippled girl. She felt that this was a battle she had to win, once and for all. She banged her hand down on the table (they were in the kitchen). She accused Elisabeth of wickedness, of having an evil spirit within her that would not be satisfied until the church was demolished and Hugh and she were reduced to beggars. She said that if Elisabeth continued she would be consumed by demons. She went on like this. She seemed to grow in size as she spoke and looked more than ever like a dangerous animal, a panther perhaps but without a panther's grace. Her anger was extreme, and Elisabeth was frightened. She would have escaped but Rhoda was between her and the door. She denied being evil, denied there was any such thing as the devil. She heard her voice quivering.

"Evil," screamed Rhoda, now in a torrent of rage. Her eyes were black and shining, and there were little flecks of foam on her red lips. "Evil with your stunted form and your red hair. That's devil's work. And your mother, destroying God's gift of life – that was wickedness. That's what she's left you with – an evil nature. Your arm is a clear sign of that. Wicked, wicked, wicked."

Elisabeth now felt a rush of pure anger. There was a red haze in front of her eyes. She reached out her right hand and found a knife on the table. "Don't you dare bring my mother into this!" She would have attacked her stepmother but at that moment Hugh, who had been in the lounge but chose not to intervene, decided that he could ignore the conflict no longer and entered the kitchen. Elisabeth's anger receded, and she was shocked to find herself holding the knife. Both women turned to him for support.

"I think you go too far, my dear," he said mildly to Rhoda, who stood panting, her arms by her side. "Let Lizzie go." Rhoda turned and leaned her forehead against the cupboard. Elisabeth slipped past and up to her room where she spent the rest of the day, in a state of black despair.

The episode took the relationship between Rhoda and Elisabeth below the point where recovery was possible. Elisabeth never forgot what Rhoda had said. A few days later, when she was feeling better, she confronted her father. "Is it true what Rhoda said? About my mother?"

"Darling, your mother was a lovely person. Gentle, and talented - she was too young to die. Poor, poor Fay." His eyes filled with tears.

"Rhoda said she was wicked."

"Rhoda didn't know her. Fay was not wicked."

"Did she kill herself?" The words were hard to say and as she said them she realised that she didn't really want to know.

"You mustn't listen to everything Rhoda says. She gets carried away. A good woman in many ways, oh, a good woman, a strong woman. But she gets carried away sometimes."

"Daddy..."

"Little Fox, it was a long time ago. She is at peace now. And you must find peace, so forgive Rhoda. She speaks from a full, an over full heart. The Church is her life. An attack on the Church is an attack on her. Now, tell me about the job, we'll sort it out. I'm sure my little Fox will be happier working in a library, you can read all day to your heart's content. But first, let's have a look at this sermon of mine. What do you think – is there enough fire and brimstone there?"

Elisabeth had always known there was some mystery about her mother's death. The thought that she might have killed herself had crossed her mind. All her father had ever said was that it had been an accident, that she had drowned, fairly soon after she, Elisabeth, had contracted polio; her aunt Irene had confirmed this, but said, "We never knew the details. We'd lost touch, Phyl and I both had young children and your father was acting, they were always moving around." When she tried to find out more from her father he would shake his head and say "Poor Fay," and if she was lucky tell stories about their early married life. Elisabeth knew her father well enough to suspect that he might be hiding something but if so she wasn't sure that she wanted to know the truth.

So Elisabeth went over it all in her mind. If it had been a simple accident why could nobody give her the details? Perhaps she had committed suicide, and her father was trying to cover it up. Why would her mother want to kill herself? Her father had said that she had died soon after Elisabeth had contracted polio - so perhaps she couldn't face bringing up a handicapped daughter. That was a wicked thing to do. The alternative was that she had killed herself because – what was the legal phrase? – the balance of her mind was upset. Mad, in other words. So her mother was either wicked or mad. Elisabeth brooded.

3

One year later a precarious status quo had been established. Elisabeth had left the factory and was working in the local library. The wages were lower, but she now had prospects, and the promise of financial support with her study programme. Hugh was pleased - if Elisabeth was happy at work he no longer need feel guilty about her leaving school - and he undertook to 'square' Rhoda. Elisabeth told him that as well as classes she would need to study at home, and wanted this to be respected. On her side, she agreed to participate in church activities on Sundays, a hated event ameliorated by her using the time to memorise poems and chunks of Shakespeare which she hid in her hymn book, and to continue with her usual household chores. Rhoda, by now, would have been more than happy for Elisabeth to leave home, despite the extra money, but Elisabeth's salary would not stretch to this and anyway, there was still her father. For the present, there was relative peace.

It was late July. Elisabeth had been working in the library for nine months, and was entitled to a holiday. She felt a great longing to get away from London but she had very little money with which to do it. After thinking it over carefully, she decided to write to her uncle and aunt to see if she could spend a few days with them. This would cost little more than the coach fare, and if she spoke to her father he would persuade Rhoda to allow her enough from her wages to cover that. Her secret little hoard would be used to cover small necessities, and buy presents. Working in the library had given her a sense of independence, and she decided that spending a holiday with family could not be regarded as accepting charity.

When she heard from her aunt that they would be delighted for her to stay with them, for as long as she could, she told her father first of all. He was full of enthusiasm, and said more than once that he should like to come with her. Rhoda, however, did not want to go to Aireton and, reluctantly, he agreed to go instead to a Church-run holiday camp with her. She showed no interest in Elisabeth's plans, but put no obstacles in her way.

Elisabeth had said that she would make her own way to Sycamore Avenue. She remembered the route so well. There were two local buses she could catch; one went straight up the main road, and the other went round by the Green and the new housing estate.

The first to arrive was the one that took the longer route; she was pleased, because it gave her more time to adjust. Sitting on the top deck, she allowed her mind to drift over the four years of her childhood she had spent in Aireton. She forgot the difficult times and remembered how much she had loved her family, and almost more than the family, loving the place, the town, the house, the environment, which once again she experienced with rush of pleasure. After years of squalor, dragging around the country with her father, from one sordid room to another, in noisy back streets of large cities, she had felt a kind of passion for the orderliness and cleanliness of the suburbs. Her room at the Atfields had been the tidiest of any. She had few possessions, but she took great care of those few. Her aunt had often praised her for it, and had held her up to Pattie as a good example: "Look at the way your cousin keeps her room, and she's four years younger than you."

Sitting on the bus, watching the shops give way to terraces of houses, and the terraces to tree lined streets, Elisabeth reflected on Pattie. She felt that Pattie had really loved her, loved her for herself, and had proved her love by taking her to find her father when they were both children. Pattie had suffered for her. And Pattie, without trying, without consulting her conscience or positively seeking to do good, had simply accepted her. She hadn't questioned who or what she was, or in what way she was responsible for her - she was simply her new found cousin Elisabeth, come to live with them. Remembering that her best-loved cousin would not be there, Elisabeth felt suddenly apprehensive about her holiday. No Pattie, Lesley and Heather living away now, and her uncle at work. So she and her aunt would be on their own for much of the time.

Could she cope? Did they really want her to stay, or were they just being polite? In sudden fear she allowed the bus to carry her past the well-remembered stop. Her knees were tight as she alighted further down the road, and started to walk back.

Some of her confidence returned as she saw the house again. It hadn't changed, but continued to stand proudly in its own space, solid, secure, comfortable. She walked up the short gravel drive. The brass letter box and doorknocker shone as brightly as ever, and Irene, when she opened the door, greeted her with more warmth than Elisabeth's memory had allowed for.

"I was watching out for you and saw the bus go by the end of the road, but no Elisabeth, so I decided that you would be on the next one, and left my post. Come right in and put your case down in the hall for a minute - let me look at you. Well, you've grown a bit, but you're never going to be a beanstalk, are you?"

It seemed to Elisabeth that there was a new warmth about Irene, and a less authoritarian manner.

She said: "I was dreaming and I missed the stop. I hadn't forgotten, I just got up too late. I was upstairs."

"You should have banged on the floor. Never mind, it's not too far to walk. Is your case heavy? Why don't you take it upstairs and tidy up, and then we'll have some tea. Bertrand won't be back just yet. Yes, you're in your old bedroom. We've kept it for you."

Elisabeth wanted to hug her aunt. She made her way up the stairs, remembering each one with affection - ten straight, then three to the left, and the steeper flight up to her little room under the roof.

And it was still the same, white walls and white paintwork; it had not been redecorated. Years ago, she had read a story about a girl who lived in a little white-washed room at the top of a very tall house. The girl had been a cripple, unable to walk, but despite this she had had a magical time in her little white room under the stars. Elisabeth had identified strongly with the heroine of this story, so that when the time had come for her bedroom to be re-decorated, and she had been asked to choose a wallpaper, she had said, very firmly, that she would like to have it white. All white. Irene had protested but Bertrand had approved, and said that the existing brightly coloured curtains and bedcover made a good contrast. Elisabeth was secretly hoping for these to fall to pieces so that they too could be changed for white. She experimented with her sheets, liking the effect, but could not ask for a change unless they wore out, which they showed no sign of doing. Indeed, they were in place now. So her room was still white, and the blue and green curtains were still in place. Elisabeth went over and fingered them, smiling. All white would really have been too much. She looked out over the garden – not the bright and sunlit place she remembered, on this dull July day, but green and leafy enough to ease her tired London spirit. She had loved the garden. She had even had a patch of her own, in which she grew candytuft and marigolds and, one memorable summer, sunflowers which grew almost twice as tall as she was. She wandered round the room, touching things - the little chest of drawers and dressing table, also white - Lesley's idea, this. The wardrobe, which Irene had said could not be painted. She slipped off her shoes and lay down on the bed on which she had slept for four years. It was ridiculous that it could remain so unchanged - it might be four years ago, and she just home from school. Feeling tears at the back of her eyes she sat up, refusing to allow sentiment to take over. They were being kind to her, that was all. Well, they were kind, but it was easy for them. They were rich and talented and healthy and good-looking. It was not difficult for such people to be kind.

There was no call to be sentimental. Childhood was over, and it hadn't been unmixed happiness. Looking back, from a time of greater unhappiness, it seemed full of sunshine and laughter and love - but of course it hadn't been like that. Always she had been conscious of not belonging, of being the poor relation, of having a father who was unsatisfactory and a mother who was dead and about whom no-one seemed to know anything. She was lopsided, a limbless sapling.

It was time to go down. She considered how best she should behave. She had no wish to appear ungracious or ungrateful, but she had to maintain some distance between herself and this environment, or she would never be able to return to London. Affectionate, of course, but she must hold something back, keep something in reserve.

Her aunt was waiting with tea in the conservatory that formed part of the extension Bertrand had built after Elisabeth left, for her grandmother. The windows opened on to the garden, but Irene said, in her old decisive way, that it was too chilly to sit out. The forecast was good for the rest of the week, however. She poured the tea and handed Elisabeth a slice of sponge cake.

"The garden looks beautiful," said Elisabeth, for want of something to say.

"It's getting out of hand," said Irene. "Bertrand's busy and I can't do as much as I used to." Elisabeth looked at her in surprise.

"It's true. I'm beginning to feel the years. And your grandmother takes up a lot of time."

"She was going to move here after Grandad died," said Elisabeth.

"She was, but in the end she decided she wanted her independence, although she spends quite a lot of time here. We persuaded her to sell the big house and now she has a nice little flat here in Aireton, where it's easy for Phyl or me to pop in. But she's getting forgetful, and I don't know how much longer we can carry on like this, I worry that she'll do something silly like forget to turn the gas off. Phyl suggested we should look at homes but I don't think I can do it. Not my own mother. So she may end up living here after all. Anyway, I told her

260

you were coming and she'd love to see you, so I thought we would go tomorrow. Just be warned, she is forgetful."

"She was before," Elisabeth said, remembering.

"Was she? Well, it seems to come and go. I think she gets depressed, living on her own. She comes to stay here now and again. Bertrand built the extension for her, after all.

"He'll be back later, he was delighted to know you were coming. He misses the girls. He loved it when the house was full of young people. Having you here will seem like old times."

Elisabeth was alarmed that her aunt thought she could be lively. She began to feel rather strange, as if there were two Elisabeths sitting in the old arm-chair - the shy, awkward, prickly one she had always been, and a new improved model devised by her uncle and aunt. She was also confused by the fact that Irene was treating her like an adult, and talking to her as if she were her equal. People generally tended to think that she was younger than she was; her father still treated her like a little girl, and her stepmother like a rebellious teenager.

Irene was talking now about Lesley. She was working in an art gallery and she had found a nice flat, not far from Chris, where she was doing wonders with the minimum of expense - bright paint work, cushions, a cheap dining room table and chairs from Habitat. Elisabeth, used to buying at jumble sales and junk shops, found it hard to imagine how buying chairs at Habitat could be considered cheap. Irene went on, "You know how clever Lesley is at things like that. She always thinks it out carefully beforehand, never buys anything on impulse, so she never wastes money. The flat's in Camden - do you know it? You should go and see her. Lesley wanted Chelsea, but it was too expensive and anyway Chris's firm is the north side of London. He was hoping to join a firm in the City but they wanted more experience. I expect they'll be getting married before long, and then they can pool their resources and buy a place together. Bertrand will help if they need it. I don't know how long they'll stay in London - we had thought she might come back home for a year or two after she'd finished her course, but I think once you leave home there's no going back, is there? We've always liked Chris. More tea?"

"No, thanks." Elisabeth tried to ignore the stirrings of jealousy at the thought of Chris and Lesley. "How is Heather?"

Irene poured herself some more tea, and stirred it round thoughtfully.

"She's determined to go to Africa to teach. She's doing a short course and the plan is she goes out there in September, for two years. She'll be teaching in a missionary school. We persuaded her against becoming a missionary because that's a commitment for life and we just don't think she's ready for that. She's found teaching quite difficult. The job she's just left was in a tough part of Leeds, where the only thing that has any effect on the children is firm discipline, and discipline is not Heather's strong point. I just hope that African children are more amenable than Yorkshire ones. She'll be coming to see you at the weekend."

"Is there any news of Pattie?"

"Just a card on her mother's birthday."

"Poor Pattie," Elisabeth said without thinking. Glancing at her aunt she said "Well, poor Auntie Phyllis as well, of course. But Pattie somehow - she was always getting into trouble. But she meant well."

Irene put down her cup of tea. "She needed discipline. She always responded well to a firm, steady hand. Phyllis and Allan were too changeable - over-indulgent one minute, and over-strict the next."

Elisabeth supposed she was right. She could remember being irritated by Irene's reasonableness and refusal never to lose her temper, but on the whole it had produced the desired results. Pattie had kept her most outrageous behaviour for home.

"Well now," said Irene, getting to her feet and picking up the tray, "you're on holiday so I'm not expecting any help. Look, the sky's lifting, why don't you go for a walk round the garden? Bertrand will be back in half an hour or so."

Before going out, Elisabeth browsed among the bookshelves. One day she would possess books of her own like these. She picked out one on 17th century Dutch art, and wandered out into the garden with it. The grass was damp but Irene was right, there was a pale lemony sun pushing out faint rays from behind the clouds. She was delighted to see that her favourite perch on one of the apple trees was still there - a gnarled old branch, inviting as an armchair, still stretched horizontally above the grass, just low enough for a person with one and a half arms to clamber on to and make believe she was climbing a tree. Elisabeth was taller now, and able to get herself and her book on to the branch without any difficulty. It was a nice spot, in what had originally been a small orchard - three apple trees, a pear and a damson. Down the far wall were currant bushes, gooseberries, and raspberry canes. Perched a little way above the ground she had a good view of the house and garden. The book was a nuisance - she had to hold on to it to prevent it from slipping to the ground, and she no longer felt like reading. She was quite content to sit.

She heard the sound of a car, then the scrunch of tyres on gravel. She jumped down from her perch and came slowly out of the trees, hesitating on the edge of the lawn. She didn't have to wait long. The French windows opened and Bertrand came striding down the steps, holding out his arms.

"Elisabeth! Let me look at you! Oh, doesn't she bring a breath of fresh air into this place! Just look at her, Irene! At last we've got one of them back!" He gave her a big hug. Irene appeared in the doorway, tea towel in hand, and gave them an ironical but tolerant look.

"I told you he would be pleased to see you," she said.

Bertrand stood back to study his niece. "But you've grown up too," he said, shaking his head sadly. "Why do you all do this? You'll be leaving the nest soon. What am I saying? You are an independent career woman already, aren't you? Tell me about that job of yours," he continued, linking his arm in hers. "Is it better than the last one? I know it's not really what you wanted to do, but you're not unhappy, are you?" He was like her father. He needed to be reassured so that the 'Elisabeth problem' could be put away. What could she do? She had to reassure them. And no, she wasn't unhappy. Not really.

"No, I quite enjoy it. And it's nice to be able to get hold of any book I want."

"Oh, that's good. That's good. I know things aren't quite as easy for you as they might be, but it's not a bad thing to be working and independent. How is your father?"

Elisabeth told her uncle what she thought he wanted to hear about her father and stepmother.

The next few days passed pleasantly enough. She helped her aunt in the house and garden, went shopping with her, and visited her grandmother, who did know who she was although she had very little to say to her. As Elisabeth found it difficult to know what to say to her grandmother, the meeting was awkward but the television was on in the background, and Irene bustled about checking the fridge and making a shopping list, and the time passed. Just as they were getting ready to leave Mrs Lindsey said, "And how's my bad boy?" looking at Elisabeth as she spoke. Elisabeth, puzzled, was turning to her aunt for guidance when her grandmother said, "Hugh. Hugh. Have you forgotten your own father? Is he still bad?"

"Far from it," said Irene, helping out. "He's become a preacher in a church in London. Elisabeth lives with him."

"Ernest always said he was a bad boy. Went his own way."

Elisabeth went over to her grandmother and kissed her cheek. "He's been a good father to me," she said. "I wouldn't change him for the world."

"Poor bad Hugh," said her grandmother, and turned back to the television.

Phyllis called in every day. She looked much older, her eyes seemed sunk into her head, and her hesitant manner and habit of drifting from one topic to another without warning had become more pronounced. Most topics, however, led to Pattie and what she might be doing, and Elisabeth was happy to share memories and her aunt's belief that one day Pattie would come home.

Phyllis also brought her up to date with local gossip, including the rumours that were circulating about the friendship between Heather's friend Cynthia and Mr Maddox, the vicar. Elisabeth had noticed that Irene was more than usually tight lipped when Cynthia was mentioned, but had put it down to the fact that her aunt held her responsible for Heather's enthusiasm for Africa.

"What does Heather say about it?" she asked Phyllis.

"Oh, she won't hear a word against her, says it's all to do with Cynthia becoming an Anglican. She was something else before, I can't remember what. But I did hear that Mrs Maddox went to see her, and now it seems the Maddox's are moving away. The curate is taking over at St Mary's, I believe."

"The clergy do move around," said Elisabeth. She hardly knew Cynthia. "Do you remember that Christmas when she and her parents came? I remember it all felt very awkward."

"Yes - oh, we had some lovely Christmases, didn't we? What about the one when Hugh came, you hadn't been with us very long, that must have been one of the best. We were all together, all so happy. Why did things have to change? Why did Pattie have to leave? I know she and her father argued, but not enough to leave home, surely not enough to leave home. And now where is she? What can she be doing?" Elisabeth could only shake her head.

Irene insisted on taking her to visit Chris's family. Elisabeth would rather not have gone. For one thing, they were bound to talk about Chris and Lesley, and that would cause those uncomfortable feelings of jealousy again. For another Colin, Chris's brother, had, over the years, written to her several times, but she had not replied. The letters had come at a bad time, and she simply had not been able to write back. What could she have said? That she was miserable, distraught, humiliated? In addition, while she was at school she had to ask Rhoda for postage stamps, and Rhoda would then have wanted to see the letter before she sent it. Rather than that, she wrote no letters. Colin's letters had been full of the things he was doing at school, O levels, then A levels, helping his father, his sister's wedding, the news that Chris and Lesley had moved to London. In his letter he said, fairly casually, that he was considering studying for the ministry himself. Elisabeth threw this letter away. No more religion for her. Did Colin but know it, he had put the last nail in the coffin of any friendship they might have had. Religion had caused more grief, more dissension, more wars, than anything, she thought fiercely to herself.

Colin's parents, the Davies's, were the same as they had always been - untidy, pre-occupied, but happy, despite the fact that they were, as they said, living on borrowed time. They should have moved on to another church five years ago, but had pleaded schooling and A levels, and had been allowed to stay on. However, they thought they would be moving away within the next year.

Elisabeth wondered how they could be so happy. She said this, later, to Colin, when he came round to Sycamore Avenue. The meeting was awkward, at first, until Irene sent them out into the garden where they were more relaxed. Elisabeth sat on the apple tree bough, and Colin leaned against the trunk. It meant that they didn't have to meet each other's eyes when the discussion turned into argument.

"Don't tell me it's religion, because it's not that. I know plenty of religious people who are not happy."

"Well," Colin said cautiously. He had matured over the last few years, was more confident, and less gawky. He still blushed too readily, and had the same dislike of conflict, and an inability to do or say anything which might upset people. But he remembered Elisabeth well enough to know that she would not be satisfied with anything less than the truth, as he saw it, and he did his best to give it to her, his open freckled face frowning with the effort.

"It is partly that. No, listen, please - it suits them. No, that sounds silly - it fits them, like a glove. They and their Christianity are the right fit. There's no conflict. And they are fortunate enough to be surrounded by like-minded people. They're not ambitious, they're not evangelists - they are content. They are doing what they love, and they

265

perceive that in doing so they are fulfilling a need. They have their priorities sorted out. They know what's important and what isn't. You might not agree..."

"You do," stated Elisabeth, who was enjoying the first opportunity she had had in years to speak her mind.

"Not on everything. On the big things - yes, we do agree pretty well. I guess I've never really understood what the generation gap was all about," he added with an embarrassed little laugh. He was too nice, Elisabeth thought crossly. She wanted to needle him, but hesitated because, after all, he was nice.

A few, silent minutes later she said, "Uncle Bertrand says you are going to become a minister yourself."

"I think so. Well, I'm sure, really, but in the Methodist church they like you to work for a few years first. So I'm doing a social work diploma, and then I plan to do community work, in a settlement."

Elisabeth disliked the idea of social work almost as much as she did religion. She hated poverty, and was struggling to better herself, but would have died rather than ask anyone for help. She had no patience with people who expected the state to provide for them. Once she had got her life sorted out she never wanted to hear about other people's troubles again. Colin, unaware of this, described the sort of work that was done at settlements, feeding and sheltering the helpless, the homeless, the tramps, people who had been let down by society.

"People who are just too lazy to do anything for themselves," said Elisabeth, who still wanted to needle Colin. "What do you know about poverty, about hardship," she wanted to shout at him, irritated by his wish to experience things that she knew only too well, and was trying to escape. Poverty for the most part was a bore; it meant limited options, being cold, having enough food but only just enough, being stuck at home, narrow houses, narrow lives. And being crippled meant nothing dramatic, just that everything was that much harder and you were regarded as a freak, to be pitied or jeered at, take your pick. Colin was upset at Elisabeth's hostility. His face was red and unhappy. "That's not really fair. OK, you get the odd scrounger, but most of them are sick, or not very bright, or just plain unlucky. Most of them are poor through no fault of their own. Society has abandoned them, and so they come to the settlement."

"Oh, society," Elisabeth said, with bitterness. "It's just a convenient term, letting individuals off the hook."

At that point her uncle came into the garden with drinks, and the argument ended. Afterwards, Elisabeth felt bad about arguing with Colin who was, after all, a nice boy. He just had different views from her. She thought of writing him a note, but the old problem of paper and envelopes and stamps arose, and anyway, what would she say? Better to leave things as they were. If he were as Christian as all that, thought Elisabeth, he would forgive her.

Heather came home on the Friday evening. She was her usual warm, emotional self, and delighted to see her young cousin again. She talked about her teaching, and how much she was looking forward to going to Africa.

"Once Elisabeth has gone home we must talk about it. It's not too late to change your mind," said Irene.

"Oh Mummy, I must go. People there really need schools and teachers, there's so much poverty, the only way out is through education. And God. After two years if it all works out I can come back home and train to be a missionary myself."

"Heather," said her father, "do you remember the school visit to France?"

"Yes, Daddy, but that was different. Monique didn't like me and I was living with her family."

"Where will you be living in Africa?"

"Well, I don't know, in a house attached to the school I think."

"What Daddy means is that you are happiest at home, Heather. You've never really enjoyed being away."

"Cynthia thinks…"

"I really don't see why Cynthia's views take priority over ours."

"No, but she sees things the way I do."

"Leave it for now. We'll talk on Sunday before you go back."

"There are these forms."

"The forms can wait. Now, please, no more talk of Africa. Elisabeth leaves tomorrow, let's make the most of her time with us."

Lesley, London based, decided not to come to Aireton to see Elisabeth but telephoned instead, and said that she would invite her to their new flat once she had it sorted. Elisabeth did not expect to hear anything further.

However, Lesley kept her promise. In October she and Chris threw a party, and invited Elisabeth. A note was added to the bottom of the invitation: "You're welcome to stay the night if you don't mind sharing the sofa!" Elisabeth worried about it for a week, longing for something to break the dreary monotony of her life, but at the same time frightened when the opportunity came. Then there was the difficulty of telling her stepmother that she was invited to a party, when she was still discouraged from making friends outside the Church.

Relations with Rhoda remained precarious; it was all too easy to upset the balance and trigger antagonism. It had taken her a long time to come to terms with Elisabeth leaving the factory to work in a library, and with her desire to study. History was acceptable, but literature! There were those in the church who thought all fiction was the work of the devil and Rhoda herself could not see the point of it. She insisted that Elisabeth continued to attend church twice on Sundays, her hair hidden behind a scarf, pointing out that to do otherwise would be to create problems for them all. Elisabeth submitted, hiding extracts from Shakespeare in her prayer book.

In the end, accepting Lesley's invitation was more to do with establishing her right to do so than from any real wish to be at the party. She worried that her cousin's friends would be smart and sophisticated. She didn't have anything to wear. She worried about her response to Chris, with whom she had always been a little in love. She wanted, very much, to talk to someone about her future and she thought that Chris might be the right person. She imagined herself explaining to him that she had been offered the opportunity to go to library school on secondment, assuming she passed her two A levels. This meant that she would be paid a salary while training, and would work in the library during holidays. She would, however, have to sign an agreement to return to the library for two years after completing her course. The alternative would be to wait until she was 21 and get a grant based on her own earnings. She would then be free to take a job wherever she could find one. She might even go abroad.

And did she in fact want to become a librarian? Would it not be better to try for three A levels and apply to University? But that would mean at least another year. The advantage of a salary over a student grant was obvious; however, it meant that she would be tied to this part of London for the next five years. It was quite a dilemma, and she needed to talk to someone about it. Her father was no good. He would just say 'whatever you think, my clever Mrs Fox'. Chris was different, he would understand, she could imagine his cool blue gaze holding hers, and the little frown he gave whenever he was concentrating on something.

So she went to the party, wearing her everyday skirt and a blouse she had found on a stall in the market near the library, stubbornly telling herself that she had been invited for herself, not for her clothes, an attitude that was difficult to maintain faced with the hard-edged fashion of most of the other guests; the girls long legged and provocative in mini skirts and tight tops; the boys strutting about in bright shirts and white jeans belted low down on their hips. Lesley's artist friends were loud and demonstrative; Chris's friends were quieter, and more conventional, but none of them showed much interest in people who were not part of their set. The odd ones out were Elisabeth, Lesley's cousin Tim from Bath, who was now a student in London, his girlfriend Sheila, and a friend of Tim's from college who had come along, as he put it, for the ride.

At 11pm people were still arriving. Elisabeth had no idea that parties could go on so long. She was ready to go to bed. It was as late as she had ever been out. Her narrow bed in the narrow little house in Hoxton had its attractions.

She dragged her attention back to the party. She stood on the edge of a group and tried to look as if she were participating. She fixed an interested-looking smile on her face, then let her mind wander again. Chris and Lesley had both been very friendly when she had arrived (far too early) but had been preoccupied in getting ready for the party. Elisabeth had helped to open packets of crisps and nuts, and buttered French bread, and had quite enjoyed the early stages when people had arrived slowly enough to be properly introduced and she had handed out food and drink as if she were the hostess. Now, however, introductions were forgotten in the noise and gaiety of it all. Food was forgotten, people helped themselves to wine and the sweet smell of pot drifted in the air.

She was unused to drink, and had clutched the same glass of punch all evening. Chris had come up one or twice to make sure that she was alright, but natural shyness and her consciousness of his attractiveness made her tongue-tied. He had introduced her to people but she could think of little to say to them. She realised that she had no party talk at

269

all. She listened to the group she was on the edge of in an attempt to find out just what people talked about at parties. For the most part it seemed to be about people they knew - so how could she possibly join in? Lesley's friends also discussed current art exhibitions, and Chris's talked about inflation and the failings of the current Labour government. Both groups claimed to enjoy foreign films, most of which Elisabeth had never heard of.

Lesley's cousin and his girlfriend had spoken with her longer than anyone else, partly because they had family in common, but now they were dancing together at the far end of the room, dancing that was getting slower and slower until they came to a halt against the wall and stayed entwined there.

Other couples were also dancing, and Elisabeth could see that she would soon be the only person without a partner. She wished she could find a dark corner to hide herself in, but the flat was small, and her 'bed' was presently occupied by two couples. Perhaps if she could find a book she could curl up somewhere and no-one would notice her. She thought she remembered a book case in the bedroom where she had left her things. She backed away from her group, ready to make an excuse about the bathroom, if challenged, but nobody took any notice of her. She was glad to get out of the room for a while. The smoke and the noise and the effort of concentrating made her head ache. Perhaps she could sit in the bed-room, among the coats, until people started to leave.

She edged out of the room and stood for a moment in the tiny, cold hall. Bedroom to the left, bathroom next, the kitchen straight ahead. She turned left. Opening the door, however, she heard noises indicating that the room was occupied, although in darkness - the rustling of clothes, moans and murmurs.

Innocently (how naive could you be? she asked herself crossly afterwards), she continued to open the door, letting the light from the hall penetrate its darkness. She could then see the two bodies entangled among the coats, the girl's breasts bare and her skirt rucked up around her waist, long pale legs raised. With the light the legs straightened, the girl said "Christ," and a man's voice said "Shut the fucking door."

Elisabeth backed away, closing the door, shocked, and angry at herself for being shocked. She knew well enough what the bumps and creaks from her parents' room meant, why Rhoda sometimes came down in the morning looking thoroughly pleased with herself, what went on behind the lavatories at her old school. Parties were for sex, weren't they? That was why she felt out of place. She didn't want sex, she wanted companionship. She turned towards the kitchen and tentatively tried the door. She couldn't think that anyone could find room to make love in the kitchen, but people were ingenious.

The kitchen did have an occupant, but only one. A man was perched on the work surface between cooker and sink, his head bowed over a book. He looked up quickly as she came in, and caught his head against the edge of the cupboard above.

"Ow!"

"Oh, I'm sorry!"

He jumped down, rubbing his head. He was tall and very thin, with a long sallow face, full of planes and shadows. His hair was blue-black, and his eyes were dark. Elisabeth recognised him as having come with Lesley's cousin Tim. She forgot that she hadn't liked him when she first met him, and now saw him with relief as a friendly face.

"I wanted some water," she said, and found that she did. He bent his long body back so that she could get by.

"What's going on in there?" he asked, jerking his head in the direction of the party.

"Talking. Music. Some dancing."

"Oh God. What a bore."

"Why don't you leave if you're not enjoying it?" Elisabeth was slightly resentful on her cousin's behalf.

"They're giving me a lift."

"Oh."

"What about you?"

"I'm staying here."

"Poor you. Forced to stay until the bitter end."

"I'm enjoying it," she protested.

"It looks like it," he said, looking at her and her water.

"It's just that I don't know anybody."

"You know your cousin."

"Yes, but ... She's busy."

"You came in here to get away," he pronounced.

"It's very hot and noisy," she agreed. "Where did you find the book?"

"In the bedroom. There's a book case."

"Oh."

"What's the matter?"

"I looked in there. It was - occupied."

"Are they still at it? You should have gone ahead. I did."

"I couldn't."

"If people choose to have it off in other people's bedrooms in the middle of a party," he said reasonably, "they must expect to be interrupted. Go back and get what you want."

"No," she said sharply.

"You can't have this one."

"I don't want a book all that much. It was just something to do."

"So you're not enjoying the party."

"I've had enough," she admitted. Embarrassed by his scrutiny, she went back to the tap and re-filled her glass.

"What have you done to your arm?" he asked, curious.

She turned to confront him, her face scarlet. "I haven't done anything. At least, not since I had polio at the age of three."

"I thought polio affected people's legs."

"It can affect any part of you. People die - or used to. I was unlucky. I was just too early for Salk."

"How bad is it?"

Elisabeth was pleased rather than otherwise that Tim hadn't thought to mention her handicap to him. Then it occurred to her that he probably hadn't thought to mention her at all.

"I can't grip things. I can move my fingers and hand, a bit. I used to go to a physiotherapist, and she gave me some exercises to do. It doesn't get any better, but they stop it getting worse."

"What does it look like?"

"Thin and shapeless. Do we have to talk about it?"

"It's fascinating."

"Not to me it isn't. I have to live with it."

Elisabeth was now faced with the dilemma of staying with this disconcerting man, whom she really didn't like, or returning to the party. She didn't want to do either. She wanted to go home, but she had probably missed the last tube and anyway, Chris would be hurt.

Defensive, she attacked: "So why are you in here? Are you not enjoying it?"

"It's boring. All the best looking birds were snapped up in the first five minutes. I thought Sheila might have tired of your cousin by now but the last I saw of them they were stuck together like glue."

Jealous, thought Elisabeth. She said "He's not my cousin. He's Lesley's cousin on her father's side."

"So it's your mothers who are sisters."

"My father and Lesley's mother."

"What does your father do?"

"He's a minister. Church. Non-conformist," said Elisabeth quickly, praying that she would be asked no further questions. The information was usually enough to put people off. It did in this case. The young man - she could not remember his name - said "Christ" and turned back to his book.

Elisabeth dithered. She didn't want a third glass of water.

"I suppose you're training to be a nun, or something."

People with very dark eyes had always disturbed her, she couldn't see what they were thinking. She liked to be able to distinguish the iris.

"No, I'm not. Why are you being so aggressive?"

He looked surprised. "I'm not. I'm just curious. You interest me. I can't make you out. You don't seem to fit in with any of that lot." He jerked his head towards the party again, and a lock of black hair fell across his forehead. He swept it back impatiently.

To prevent him from probing any further, she asked him about himself. He told her that he was studying engineering at one of the polytechnics, but he wasn't enjoying it. He'd rather be doing psychology. He was interested in people. It was his father's fault he was doing engineering, fussing about getting a job.

He talked at some length about himself. This made things easier for Elisabeth. She found a stool tucked away in a corner and sat on this, while he re-seated himself on the work surface. His chief ambition, he said, was to be a writer, but before he could do this he needed a lot more experience of life and the human condition. He hinted at radical political views, but said that he couldn't tell her more now. He sounded as if he expected her to be disappointed. He said that he might tell her more if they got to know each other better. His black eyes were expressionless.

Chris weaved in, his eyes glazed, an empty glass in his hand.

"They've finished the punch and the beer. I don't think we've got anything else. It's all your fault, Lizzie, you've drunk the lot."

"I have not," she protested.

"Well, someone has. Are you alright, little Lizzie? I missed you in there. Are you enjoying yourself?"

"Oh yes," she said, anxious to reassure Chris but aware that too much enthusiasm would be taken as a compliment by her companion -

and she wasn't sure whether she wanted to pay him one. "Only it got a bit hot and noisy." She was pleased that Chris had come in search of her - well, her and the punch.

"It's quieter now. People are leaving. No more booze, you see. Lesley is very annoyed with me. D'you think if I fill a bottle with tap water they'll think it's gin?"

"If they're drunk enough they might," said Lesley's cousin's friend.

Chris eyed him suspiciously. "Are you one of Lesley's friends or one of mine?"

"Neither."

Chris's eyes brightened. "Ah, a gate-crasher."

"No, I'm Antony. I've come with Tim and Sheila."

"Oh. Welcome to the party." He started to hold out his hand, then thought better of it. "Well - come back next door. Help to swell the numbers. Stop Lesley feeling cross." He backed out of the door. The others stayed where they were for a minute or two.

Then Elisabeth said awkwardly, "I'd better go and see what's happening."

"Right, right, right," he said, not looking at her.

In the living room the mood had changed. Procol Harum was playing *A Whiter Shade of Pale,* and two couples were still shuffling round and round in a pretence of dancing. Others were stretched out on the floor, or curled up on chairs, or on the sofa. A small group, including Lesley, were arguing amongst themselves. Someone was wandering around the room, trying to persuade people to go to a night club, the latest place, where it was all happening. Lulu had been seen there.

Some time later the dirty glasses had been joined by coffee mugs. There were still half a dozen or so people left. Lesley, amazingly, had gone to bed (having first ejected the lovers, Elisabeth assumed). Elisabeth herself was nearly dropping with exhaustion. She sat on the floor, her head resting against a chair. The disconcerting young man, whose name was Antony, sat on the chair. His fingers played idly with her hair and neck. She had disliked this, at first, but was now too tired to care. Chris, half asleep, occupied the other chair. Tim and Sheila were squashed up with another couple on the sofa.

The music stopped. Chris stretched out his legs and said, "That's the last record, the last drink and the last coffee. The party's over. Would those of you who are going please go, and the rest find themselves somewhere to sleep. The bedroom's out of bounds."

With much yawning and stretching and complaining they began to disperse. Antony gave Elisabeth a funny sort of salute in lieu of saying goodbye. She had thought that he would ask for her address or phone number, and was disappointed that he did not, although she had found him an uncomfortable companion.

She spent the rest of the night in the armchair. The couple who had been sharing the sofa with Tim and Sheila refused to be separated, and stayed there. Another girl took the second armchair, and a man who looked decidedly the worse for drink took some cushions and a blanket on to the floor. Twice in the night he disturbed everyone by groaning loudly then staggering to the bathroom, where he was noisily sick.

By half past seven the following morning, Elisabeth had had enough. She was cold and stiff. Everyone else appeared to be asleep. She crept out of the room to the kitchen which smelled of stale alcohol. Every surface was covered with dirty glasses, cigarette ends, crusts of French bread, cheese and crisps. She found a coffee mug and washed it under the tap, then searched the cupboards for a jar of coffee. She filled the kettle with water and plugged it in. There was no milk, so she drank the coffee black. What to do now? If she went home she would be forced to go to church. There was nothing else open on a Sunday. She could go for a walk but she didn't know this part of London and it looked to be raining outside. She really ought to say goodbye to Lesley and Chris. She would give it an hour or so, and then go.

She picked up the book which Antony had been reading the night before, *The Divided Self,* by R D Laing, and was deep in it half an hour later when Chris came in, walking carefully like a man with a thick head. He was wearing pyjamas and an old dressing gown tied carelessly round the waist and slipping over his shoulder.

"I didn't know anyone was up. Couldn't you sleep?"

"No," said Elisabeth honestly.

"Nor me. How many are there in there?"

"Four others."

"I'm sorry. There were only intended to be you and Karen. We thought you could top and tail on the sofa."

"Don't worry, I don't suppose I should have slept very well anyway. With all the excitement," she added vaguely.

He was holding on to the work surface so she slipped off her stool and pushed it over to him. He sank on to it gratefully, but winced as the movement jarred his head.

"There's times I wish I'd never taken to drink. It seems impossible to have half measures - you either don't drink at all, or you drink too much. I feel lousy. I don't think I slept more than an hour or two. Lesley is sleeping like a baby and will appear, fresh and glowing, in an hour or two. I don't know how she does it. Is there any coffee?"

Elisabeth indicated the jar. "But there isn't any milk."

"Black's just fine. God, my head. Do you think you could switch the kettle on - quietly if you can." He looked awful - tousle-haired, unshaven, hung over - so different from the clean-cut, conventional Chris she had known. It was at this point that she knew she was in love with him. He was now looking helplessly at the array of dirty mugs and glasses. "There aren't any clean ones?"

"I had to wash one." She took pity on him. "Give me one, I'll do it for you. I can do the rest if there's hot water."

"What is it about women," he demanded, "that they can indulge in the worst forms of debauchery and come up shining and new the next day. Why aren't you feeling lousy?"

"I didn't drink very much. I do feel tired," she admitted.

"We shouldn't have made you sleep on the chair," he looked distraught.

"It was only one night. It was nice of you to ask me."

"I never enjoy parties. I don't know why we keep on having them. Well, I do. You always hope that the next one will be better. That's the thing about parties - they offer possibilities. Never realised, though, in my experience."

She said, hesitantly, because she was happy talking to Chris, "I think perhaps I'll be going now. Now I've seen you. You can go back to bed."

Chris looked shocked. "We're expecting you to stay. Lesley will be upset if you leave now. You must stay a bit longer, I'm not going back to bed, truly. Once up I stay up. What I will do is get a couple of aspirin, and then I suppose I'd better get dressed and buy some bread and milk and things for breakfast."

"I'll get those," offered Elisabeth, "if you tell me where to go."

"There's a shop just down the road, round the corner and on the right. It's run by Indians, they sell all kinds of things. Including newspapers, could you get a paper as well? *The Observer*, if they have it. That's really kind of you, thanks a million."

Elisabeth waited. "I don't think I have enough money," she said at last, stony. She had her bus fare and two pence in case she needed to make a telephone call.

"Oh," said Chris, embarrassed, "of course, I'm sorry." He rummaged around in a drawer. "Let's see – five shillings, that should do?"

The Chris of her imaginings would not have left it to her to ask for the money. He would have realised that if Elisabeth had paid for a Sunday paper out of her own pocket it would have meant a lunchless day next week. The pedestal wobbled very slightly.

As she was leaving he said, in a voice muffled by the coffee mug, "Have you heard anything from Pattie?"

"No," she said, surprised. "I don't think anyone has."

"No. I just thought - maybe you. She was very fond of you."

"I haven't heard anything. I think her mother gets a card from time to time."

"If she - maybe if she contacted you but asked you not to tell anyone - would you do that?"

"It would be difficult," said Elisabeth. "But if I could, I would. Of course I would."

"Not even tell her mother?"

"If she wanted it that way. I might try to persuade her... But I haven't, Chris. Truly."

"She must surface sooner or later. I wouldn't have thought Pattie capable of going to ground and staying there."

"If she's with someone..."

"Since when has Pattie stuck with anyone this long?"

Elisabeth was unable to answer. She was very concerned about her cousin, and couldn't understand why she hadn't returned home. She worried that she was ill, or in some other kind of trouble, but the cards kept coming so they could only assume she was alright. She thought how wonderful it would be if Pattie did come to her for help - her among the whole family, asking for help. Not serious help, Elisabeth amended her fantasy, help perhaps in returning to her family. It wasn't very likely, though. What help could she give, anyway?

Elisabeth stayed with Chris and Lesley until after lunch, which they had in a nearby pub. The girl, Karen, also stayed, but the others left mid-morning. Then she went home to an empty house, to her relief. She struggled to start an essay but she was tired and eventually she gave up and lay on her bed and thought of the party, of the

277

disconcerting young man, and of Chris. She tried not to think too much about Chris. He and Lesley were a couple, they slept together, they had a future together. Talking to him had been wonderful, however, despite his hangover. It was the first time she had talked to him since she was a child. She hoped that they would meet again, soon.

5

A week later there was a telephone call for her in the library. The caller was Antony, the boy she had met at her cousin Lesley's party. She realised as she took the call that she had been half expecting it.

"How did you know where to find me?" she asked.

"You told me where you worked."

"Did I?" She supposed she must have done, although she did not remember.

"And you sounded a bit cagy about where you lived."

"Well - we don't have a telephone at home."

"I'm going to a talk tonight, at Conway Hall, on George Orwell. 'Do you believe our society may one day be like the world depicted in '1984'?' What do you think?"

It wasn't entirely clear what he was asking. "Um," said Elisabeth.

"I thought you might be interested."

Her instinct was to say no, and then she thought again. Tuesday was the day her parents went to the regular meeting of church elders, after which they had supper. They needn't know that she was out. It would mean giving up an evening's study, but just once... The party had made her restless. She wanted more out of life. But with Antony?

"What time does the talk end?"

"Eight, eight-thirty. We could have a drink afterwards."

"As long as I'm back by ten."

"Why, Cinderella?"

"Oh," she couldn't think of a reason she could give, "just because."

After that first meeting they continued to meet every two or three weeks, usually on a Tuesday. Neither of them had much money so they would go to a talk, or a lecture, or occasionally a film. As the weather improved they would sometimes walk: through the City, deserted after 6pm: along the Embankment; over the Hungerford foot bridge to admire the Festival Hall. Elisabeth enjoyed exploring London in this way. Talking was somehow easier when they walked and Antony, a tenacious questioner, quickly found out something of her home life. She was both alarmed and flattered by his interest.

She had feelings of guilt about living a life of deceit. She was back each week just before ten, half an hour before her parents returned. But sooner or later there would be a slip and she couldn't bear to be found out in that way, as if she were doing something wrong. It would humiliate her and also give a false sense of importance to her relationship with Antony. She wasn't even sure why she hadn't told them about him. It had become a way of life to keep things to herself. It avoided arguments.

"But what do you think they would say if you told them you had been seeing me?" asked Antony.

"I can't imagine."

"Perhaps I should come and meet them."

"Oh no!" she said.

"Why not? Are you ashamed of me?"

"Of course not."

"Of them?"

"No - oh, my father would be alright. On his own. She's - she doesn't like anyone who's not a member of her church. She was furious when I got a job in the library because it means that I meet all sorts of people, who aren't. She thinks novels are sinful. We don't even take a newspaper. But I see all these in the library. So she's virtually given up with me, now. She'd like to get rid of me, but finds the money I earn useful."

Antony never sympathised with her. She probably wouldn't tell him these things if he did.

"How fascinating," he said this time.

She didn't really know what their relationship was, and this was unsatisfactory. Did he want her as a companion, an acolyte, a sister, a lover? She didn't know. So far, Antony had not touched her, except accidentally, when handing her a drink or when walking down the street together his arm had brushed hers. She didn't know whether she wanted him to touch her deliberately or not, but she felt that he ought to. She feared that her arm made her repulsive to men. She didn't know what she wanted, either, only that without him she would feel very lonely. He was a distraction, he took her mind off the one man who did interest her, her cousin's boyfriend Chris. It was dangerous to think of him; it would only add to her general unhappiness

It would be hard to go back to the isolation of her life before she met Antony. She was beginning to rely on him, and she realised that she had told him very much more about herself than she had told anyone else. More than she liked. He expected answers to his questions and went on at her until she responded. He wanted to know her reactions to the events in her life, her emotions, her feelings. Nobody had ever asked her such questions before.

"So how did you feel when you were sent to live with your cousins?"

"They were very kind."

"How did you feel?"

"I was grateful," and then, knowing that he expected more, "it was comfortable, I was warm and well fed, I appreciated that."

"Life with your father was hard?"

"We were very poor." She recalled the damp, cold room they shared in Bradford. "I hate poverty," she said, surprising herself with the strength of her feeling.

"You are poor now," he stated.

"Yes. But not like that."

"So part of you was relieved that you had been rescued."

"I suppose so. Yes, of course. But I wished my father had come too."

"Why didn't he?"

"He was looking for work."

"Did you understand that?"

"Sort of. But I couldn't understand why he had to go to London."

"So you were angry with your father?"

"Not angry. Disappointed." They were leaning on the wall on the Embankment looking at the dirty sluggish river with its muddy shore. Elisabeth felt a great melancholy descend on her.

"I think you were angry." She was silent. "And now? Still disappointed and angry? Resentful that the rest of your family has had it easy compared to you?"

"I suppose so."

"Hmm," said Antony. "Fascinating."

Their meetings always ended with Elisabeth feeling exposed and vulnerable, but at the same time she found herself wanting to make confessions. It was strange. She would talk and hate herself for talking, and he would probe and she would tell him more and then hate herself for doing so but at the same time she had an urge to tell more. Antony was like a drug. The more she hated herself for revealing her vulnerability the more she longed to reveal.

They were meeting more frequently now. Elisabeth had let it be known that she was going out with friends, or to meetings related to her studies. Her father showed some interest, her stepmother none at all. Antony was very keen to meet them, and kept pestering her to arrange it. Elisabeth did not want this. She had a strange feeling that she must protect them, even Rhoda, from his scrutiny.

"Why do you want to meet them so much?"

"It will help me to know you better."

Why did he want to do that? He wasn't in love with her.

"You fascinate me."

But she didn't want to be fascinating in that way. Sometimes she felt like breaking things off and going back to her old way of life. Gradually, he seemed to be making decisions for her. He was even chipping away at her academic work, telling her it wasn't necessary to have A levels in order to get a good job.

"You've got them."

"I was at school and it seemed easier to stay on than not. And I wanted to be a doctor. I admit that you need those bits of paper if you want to go into a highly competitive field like medicine. But librarianship! You don't need A levels to stamp books in and out all day. Besides, it's different for a man. He has to earn enough for his dependants. You'll get married and have kids. What's the use of A levels then?"

"No, I won't," Elisabeth said fiercely, betraying herself once more. A few months ago she would have told him that he was old-fashioned and that women had as much right to qualifications and interesting jobs as men.

"Why not? This?" He picked up her left arm and let it drop again. "It's not hereditary."

"It's not just that," she said with difficulty. "I just don't think I'd make a very good wife and mother."

"No worse than anyone else. Once you throw out those hang-ups of yours. Any moves yet on the family front?"

"Yes," she said, having decided that some sort of meeting was inevitable, and she was only prolonging the agony by putting it off. "Next Saturday afternoon. I've lent you some books, and you're returning them. You'd better take them now. And please don't stay too long. An hour at the most. Don't push things. If it works out this time you can come again but you've got to take it slowly. Please. I do know them."

"OK, OK, no need to get into a flap. I'm not accustomed to outstaying my welcome."

She was anxious not to upset him. "No, I know, but they are strange. I feel bad about inviting you to what might not be a friendly

282

reception. It won't be anything to do with you. It would be the same with any stranger."

"Don't worry, I'm thick-skinned," he said.

Elisabeth did not deny this.

But, to her amazement, the visit went off well. Hugh always responded warmly to new acquaintances, and on this occasion had persuaded Rhoda to do the same. She seemed to like Antony's direct way of asking questions, even the ones about the Church, at which Elisabeth cringed. He sat on a chair facing Rhoda and Hugh on the settee, while she sat in a corner, feeling resentful at the mockery which was being made of her earlier fears. He had done his homework and showed an understanding of the origins of their beliefs.

"The Church of England was too worldly?" he asked.

"By the middle of the 19th century it had become perverted," Rhoda told him. "It was full of wrong doers. People who look upon evil are contaminated by that evil. You have to keep apart."

"If someone has been contaminated can they ever become clean again?"

"We believe they can, if they strenuously seek to do so," said Hugh.

"It's hard to avoid the temptations of modern life," said Antony. "My mother is always warning me."

"True salvation may only be possible through complete separation from unbelievers and evil-doers."

"But with a strong church and family life it may not be necessary," Hugh said, quickly.

"Temptation may be too great: 'be ye separate, saith the Lord, and touch not the unclean thing'." Rhoda sat upright on the sofa as she spoke and fixed her eyes on the far wall on which were taped sayings from the Scriptures and a poster exhorting readers to be prepared for the second coming of Christ.

"However, my dear," interposed Hugh, "we are also bidden 'to be gentle unto all men, patient; in meekness instructing those that oppose themselves.'"

"The bit about not touching unclean things sounded like St Paul," remarked Antony.

"2 Corinthians 6. I can give you some further readings that might help you to understand."

"That is very kind."

He sat back with the little smile of satisfaction that Elisabeth was familiar with, while Rhoda sorted out a selection of readings from the

Old and New Testaments, each handwritten on to a separate sheet of paper, and numbered. When he was leaving, she said "I was an unbeliever as a child. When I was twelve I was fostered, and my foster parents introduced me to God. They were very, very strict, because they knew my soul was in danger. One day, I saw the light, and I have never looked back. Truly, the Lord is my salvation, and through me my husband has also seen the light. I rejoice that I have brought another soul to God."

"Amen," said Antony, taking the sheaf of papers, and bidding them farewell.

"You went down very well," Elisabeth told Antony when they next met, trying to sound casual. "You might even be invited again."

"Oh, I shan't need to see them again," he said. "I've got all I wanted."

Elisabeth was deeply hurt by his callousness. She was even hurt for her stepmother. Rhoda had put herself out to be pleasant and, by her standards, had succeeded. She said nothing, however. Some time later he spoke again.

"You are very quiet."

"Am I?"

"I know why. Do you want me to tell you why?"

"Not much," said Elisabeth, aware that she sounded like a sulky twelve year old.

"You're upset because I'm not leaping about with excitement at the thought of meeting your parents again."

Elisabeth pulled in her mouth. "I just don't see what all the fuss was about."

"I told you, I wanted to see them so that I could place you in your own environment. I know that your formative years were spent elsewhere, but it's not so easy to get up to Yorkshire. Unless we go for a weekend. What do you think?"

"Perhaps," said Elisabeth. She had no intention of taking him to Aireton but had learned that there were times when it was better to hide her real feelings.

"I tell you something else."

"What?"

"I think your stepmother is illiterate."

"Of course she's not."

"When have you seen her read a book?"

"She doesn't believe in books. Apart from the Bible."

284

"Does she read that?"

"Well," Elisabeth considered. Rhoda usually asked Hugh to read a passage from the Bible after meals. She had assumed it was because her father had a good speaking voice.

"She can write, she signs things."

"A lot of illiterate people learn to write their names, and sometimes their address. Maybe semi-literate, then, over the years she's learned to hide it."

"What made you think of it?"

"It explains why she doesn't like you working in the library, and studying. And the quotations she gave me were all numbered. I think she'd memorised them."

Elisabeth was interested. Rhoda unable to read or write! But she was not allowed to reflect on this. Antony was ready to move on.

"Tell me about your father. He's the significant one. You're jealous of your stepmother because she took him away from you."

"I'm not!"

"Come on, tell me. I know he was an actor. Was he any good?"

She could never resist the opportunity to talk about her father.

"Yes. Not first-rate, but good." (How did she know? She'd only ever seen him in pantomime. But he had said he was good). "He wasn't determined enough, he gave up too easily."

"Come on, tell me more. You say you're not jealous of your stepmother but you must have been upset when she came to take him away."

"No, I wasn't. I really don't think I was. You see, he'd been away for four years, and at first I saw her as someone who would bring us back together, enable us to live a proper family life. I was old enough to know that a little girl couldn't take the place of a wife, however much she loved him."

"And you loved him."

"I loved him so much. I hardly remember my mother. But I think she loved him, like I did. He was away a lot and we never knew what time he was coming home, and we would wait and wait, and when he did come - oh, I can't describe the excitement. And he always had something for me, however small - a coin, a sweet, a theatre programme, a scrap of material from an actress' dress. I never wanted anything else when he was there. He didn't understood that. He should never have sent me away, I could have put up with anything, just to be with him. That upset me far more than marrying Rhoda did.

I thought it would be the same after he married, when I went back to live with him, but it wasn't."

"You were probably a burden to him," Antony said.

"Very probably," Elisabeth said, lips tight.

"Fascinating," Antony said.

That was what he did to her. Provoked or teased, persuaded or flattered her into talking about herself, insisting on her analysing what might better remain unanalysed. He made her bare her soul then left her, stripped, naked, ashamed. It was unpleasantly like the humiliations she had experienced at church, in the early days, when she had had to stand up and confess her sins in front of everyone. She had done it twice, for her father's sake, but then refused to do it again. Now Antony was putting her through a similar process. Sometimes she felt like a museum specimen, pinned out on a board to be probed and analysed. All she could do was hope that one day they would find whatever it was they were looking for and he would help her to put herself together again. Meanwhile she struggled through the working day, increasingly unhappy and confused. She went through the motions of study - reading, making notes - but the words passed before her eyes without making any sense, and writing essays was such a huge effort that two or three times she abandoned them. She began to wonder if it was possible for a literate person to become illiterate.

Antony was taking control of her life. She was like a puppet, dancing to his commands. She, so proud, so reticent, was letting this man take over her life, find out all her secrets, worm his way into her innermost thoughts. Sometimes she would struggle to express herself and then, looking up, would catch him with a smile of satisfaction on his face, as if he had set up the whole thing in anticipation of her response. At other times he would lecture her on some aspect of popular science, for example the amount of information in the world, and perception, and how people would go mad if they were forced to perceive more than seven things at any one time, and how subconsciously people sifted through this information, accepting some and discarding the rest. It didn't mean that the rest wasn't there. She found it difficult to argue with him when he explained things away like this. He spoke fluently and at length, basing his arguments on knowledge gleaned from the Sunday papers, using long words and jargon which were sometimes inaccurate. (For instance he confused "fraction" with "faction", and "enervating" with "energising".) She often felt that his analysis was somehow out of key, not quite right, but

286

she was unable to pinpoint exactly what was wrong until later, when she lacked the courage to re-introduce the subject and present her challenge.

Having explored her family background, Antony now expressed curiosity about Elisabeth's arm. How had it happened, what treatment had she been given, how much movement did she have, what did it look like? At first she refused to discuss it, until he began to speculate on her reasons for being secretive and reluctant to bring this problem into the open.

"I don't think it's abnormal to be upset because you are disabled."

"That's how you see it. It's your perception of yourself."

"I perceive what is."

He shook his head. "Oh no. You have an arm which doesn't fully function. Now why do you think that makes you disabled as a person."

"That's how society sees me," Elisabeth said, using his language.

"99% of the people you pass in the street wouldn't have any idea. People at work know because you've chosen a job which involves moving piles of heavy books around. Not that you should be doing that anyway. The library service belongs in the Victorian age. Physical drudgery is not necessary. It could all be mechanised." That was one thing about Antony - he could easily be distracted.

"I don't see how mechanisation could sort books out into categories," Elisabeth said, playing on this.

"That's easy - any factory does something similar. A computer readable mark on the spine, and a mechanical arm to pick the books up..."

"But what if all the books were tightly packed and there wasn't any space for a new one?"

"You're just trying to make difficulties," he said. "I haven't worked out all the details, yet. I will if you like, and you can take it to your boss and sell it to him. But mind I mean sell it. If I'm going to put time and effort into this invention, I expect a reward."

"Oh, then you'd better not risk it," she said. "You know how old-fashioned Mr Macfarlane is. It took weeks of persuasion to get him to agree to move the enquiries desk."

He scowled at her. "You're not taking my ideas seriously."

"Oh yes I am," she assured him. "In principle it sounds wonderful. It's just the details that worry me."

"Well of course the details are what I haven't had time to work out. We can do it if you like. I'll need your help. I'll need to know every detail about the classification system and how you shelve books. If it works we could make a fortune. How many libraries are there in the country?"

"Oh, hundreds, I don't know."

"Even if it was only the bigger ones, that would be a fair number. I think it could work."

"Just don't ask Mr Macfarlane to be your guinea-pig."

He was angry again. "You're so bloody negative."

"Realistic."

"Negative. You're caught up in a web of your own making. You see yourself as disabled and repulsive, and you want other people to see you that way because it means you don't have to make an effort. When have you ever gone out of your way to make friends with people? You're bloody self-centred, you just sit there thinking me, me, me all the time, and expect others to do all the running."

"I don't expect anyone to run, as you put it," she said, white faced and tight lipped.

"No, you hope they won't because then you can go on feeling sorry for yourself, and justified in that."

"You are so cruel," she whispered.

"No, I'm realistic," he answered, throwing the word back at her like an insult.

She was crushed and humiliated. She was utterly in his power and she didn't know how she had come to be there. She dreaded seeing him but could not bear it if they didn't meet. By making himself so necessary to her he had undermined some of the props which had previously underpinned her existence and made it tolerable. She had thought that she was tough enough to survive on her own. But her old supports had disintegrated - the Atfields, too distant; Chris, committed to Lesley; her father, too wrapped up in himself to take on her troubles; those one or two teachers who had interested themselves, now out of reach; her academic work, slipping out of her grasp. Now there was only Antony himself to protect her.

And she did not love Antony. She didn't even like him. But she needed him. He was absolutely essential to her. And though she struggled feebly while he pinned her down and tried to dissect her, in the end she knew she would submit.

She would submit to anything he wanted. Because she was weak, because she could no longer survive on her own. He was interested in her. She was important to him. It gave some purpose to her life. But there were times when she wanted to run screaming away from him and never see him again.

He returned to the subject of her arm. She knew he would. The only thing to do was play it down, make it seem less important than it was.

"When were you first aware of it?"

"Always. It happened when I was three."

"No, I mean when were you conscious of it - conscious that you were different from the other kids - not able to play the same games, that sort of thing."

"I never really played with other kids; we moved about too much - oh, alright. I don't know. There was no one occasion. My father used to carry me around on his shoulder, and my arm was in a kind of sling. And he had friends who played with me and would toss me about and my mother would call "Don't do that, you'll hurt her.""

"And did they hurt you?"

"I don't think so. There was one man, I didn't like him much, he had these eyes..." Elisabeth stopped. She had not thought about this man for many years, but now she realised that he had looked like Antony - the same hollow face and black, unreadable eyes. "He never played with me," she went on hurriedly, afraid of Antony's scrutiny. "I think he found my arm repulsive."

"Did they want to look at it?"

"I don't remember. I don't imagine so. Why should they?"

"It's interesting," said Antony. Elisabeth didn't think so. She went on: "Then my mother died and the friends seemed to disappear and we moved again."

"What did your mother die of?"

"Heart attack," Elisabeth said firmly. "She'd always had a weak heart."

Her feelings towards her mother varied from a yearning for the delicate, pretty woman whom she barely remembered, to a feeling of grievance that her mother had not loved her daughter enough to wish to see her grow up. It was true that she barely remembered her. The images she had came mainly from two or three blurred photographs and her father's reminiscences, both of which were unreliable.

"How old were you?"

"Four."

"She must have been young."

"Yes."

"Do you think about her?"

"I wish I'd known her better - known what she was like. It would help to put her in perspective - and me," said Elisabeth. It was always safest to tell Antony part of the truth, like throwing crumbs to a lion.

"If you knew where you came from you'd know better where you were going?"

"Something like that."

"I want to know if she was mad," she thought to herself. This was the poisonous worm of a thought that was always with her. Had her mother always been unbalanced? The delight in playing childish games, the sudden tears, the dressing up, the hysteria, the flouncing out of the house - could Elisabeth really remember that, or was she making it up? She suddenly felt very tired.

"You've gone away," said Antony. He was always accusing her of not concentrating, of only being half there.

"I must go," she said, gathering her things together.

"It's only nine o'clock. What's up? Why are you upset? Is it your mother?"

"I'm not upset, I'm just tired. I've got some work to do when I get home. And I find these conversations tiring, you know I do."

He frowned. "We've still got a long way to go."

"I don't know why you want to go on. Can't we just let it go and - and enjoy ourselves."

"The way you are at present, you're not capable of enjoying yourself."

"That's not true!"

"Think about it," he said. "Is it your turn to pay for the coffee?"

"Yes."

"Then order me another one on your way out, will you?"

He was angry with her. Normally he walked her to the bus stop. She didn't care. She just wanted to get home and into bed and under the bedclothes where all was darkness and nothingness and non-feeling.

She was beginning to feel very strange. It was the effort of keeping all thoughts of her mother from Antony. Now she was alone she could think about her. My mother. How could she do it to me? How could she leave me? Was it deliberate? Was she mad? Mad, or cruel and inhuman, which was worse? But if she was mad, where does that leave me? One thing's certain, I must never have children. Polio might not be hereditary, but madness is. Why me? The decision not to marry and have kids didn't stop you wanting to. She hadn't realised that before. What was happening to her? She had never wallowed in self-pity to this extent before. What was Antony doing to her? He was bringing all these awful things out, and then leaving her to struggle alone. It was like drowning.

She tortured herself most of the night with thoughts of her mother's madness and death and the ruin of her own life. The neglect of her A level work added to her anguish. Her books had always been a consolation to her, but now, when she tried to settle to them, she became so anxious about the ground she had lost that the task of studying became even more difficult. A few months earlier she had been bored with the undemanding nature of her library work; now she found comfort in the routine of stamping books in and out, shelving, fitting plastic sleeves over dust jackets, and writing classification numbers on the spines. The sad old men and women who spent all day among the newspapers, whom she used to avoid, now seemed like kin to her. She wanted, desperately, to talk to someone about her mother before she was forced to confide in Antony.

Her father was no good. He spoke of Fay in sad, romantic tones, which brought her no closer to the real woman. Her death was described as if it were part of a drama in which he had a bit part; he seemed genuinely to have forgotten the true facts. And really, there was no-one else who had known her. She had come from another town, her parents had been killed during the war, and any remaining family had long since disappeared. Her Yorkshire aunts had only seen her once or twice, and could only say that she had been pretty and delicate looking and, Irene had added, the pair of them had looked like a couple of children out of school and far too young to be marrying and setting up a family.

Her father had one or two snapshots among his stage memorabilia but the face, though pretty, had been somehow formless - the sort of face, having seen, one then forgot. One picture showed her mother holding her as a baby, with a strange, blank, withdrawn expression on her face. It could have been the result of unpreparedness for the camera, but Elisabeth now saw in this expression the beginning of her mental disintegration. How old had she been then? Only a few years older than Elisabeth was now. How long before the symptoms showed in her daughter?

She felt she was drowning in a flood of memories and fears, loves and jealousies, with Antony on the bank, pushing her out of her depth.

6

Antony telephoned her one day to say that his parents were going away, and suggested that she spent the weekend with him in their house. Elisabeth had grown used to the existing pattern of meetings, and was not sure that she was prepared for the change in their relationship that this might represent. She said that she had agreed to work a colleague's shift for her on Saturday, and had an essay to finish in the evening. She knew that Antony knew that she was making excuses, but he let her get away with it.

"What about Sunday then? Come for the day."

However, he was annoyed with her and showed his annoyance by not meeting her at the station, leaving her to find her way to his house. She had brought with her one of her text books and he took exception to this, suggesting, with heavy sarcasm, that perhaps she would like to write her essay that day - they had a typewriter. He didn't mind. He also had some work to do.

"Don't be silly," she pleaded. "I only brought it to read on the train."

He allowed himself to be placated. "What is it, then? *Macbeth*? Why does everyone insist you study Shakespeare? What's wrong with modern writers? I dare say Shakespeare was alright in his day, but that was 500 years ago. Most of it's incomprehensible now. Why can't you study something more relevant to today? Don't you agree?"

Elisabeth sighed, but quietly so that Antony didn't hear. She knew that the atmosphere between them would be further soured if she admitted to liking something which he did not understand.

"I found it difficult at first," she compromised, "but now I've had things explained I am enjoying it."

"That's exactly my point. Shakespeare always has to be explained. It's meaningless otherwise. That doesn't seem like very good writing to me. Take someone like John Braine, you always know exactly what he's trying to say."

Antony lived in a semi-detached house in Ealing. Inside everything was neat and spotlessly clean. He and Elisabeth perched on the edges of their chairs, rather than crease the covers. Outside it continued to rain and plans to walk on the Common had to be abandoned. Water dripped off the roof, and off the trees and laurels which surrounded the house and took much of the light. They drank coffee (taking great care to put their cups down on little mats that were scattered around the room, which Antony said his mother had made him promise to use), listened to jazz records and played cards. Elisabeth was careful to let Antony win, not every time, or he would have been suspicious, but often enough. Her tactics paid off. Antony was soon in a pleasanter and more tolerant mood.

Lunch was cold meat, potatoes and tinned peas, followed by tinned rice pudding. Elisabeth peeled the potatoes, and Antony watched with interest as she held each potato down on the chopping board with her weak left arm, and peeled with her right hand, using her thumb as further support.

"You don't let it prevent you from doing much," he said.

"Years of practice," she said, brushing it off, but felt pleased. Antony rarely paid her a compliment.

He produced a bottle of cider, and poured them each a glass. Elisabeth sipped at the sweet, fizzy drink, not enjoying it much, although it helped her to feel more relaxed. Antony finished his glass and had another. He explained why it was important to live away from home during the week even though he could commute from Ealing to his college.

After lunch, he said he wanted to show her his room. He said it was the only room that he was allowed to do what he liked in. It expressed his personality rather than those of his parents. She was uncomfortable but could not think of any good reason for refusing. After all, the house was empty, and there was really no difference between one room and another. Their friendship was a sterile, analytical affair, and it did not seem possible that there should be a sexual element to it. Elisabeth felt no physical attraction towards Antony and as he had never made any move to touch her assumed that he felt the same way. So she followed him up the staircase with its discreetly patterned carpet to his room, uncomfortable but not alarmed. His window overlooked the gabled and bay-fronted houses opposite, although protected at the top with coloured panes and at the bottom by net curtains. It was the room of a boy who was not quite a man. There was a model aeroplane and a collection of matchboxes on the mantelpiece, posters on the wall of the Rolling Stones and George Best, and a shelf of books: blue and white Pelicans, a boy's encyclopaedia, a few text books. A black and white striped scarf was draped over a chair, and a cricket bat propped up in the corner. The divan bed was pushed into an alcove at the side of the chimney breast, which had been painted black and had an open fireplace at its base. The room was cold, and Elisabeth began to shiver.

Antony closed the door. "I want to see your arm."

"Whatever for?"

"I just do. We've talked about it so much. I want to see it. It fascinates me."

"But you can't. I'm sorry, you can't. I haven't let anyone see it since I was a child."

"Am I just anyone?"

"No, of course not, but - I can't. You don't understand how much it would hurt me. Why is it so important?"

"You're the one who is making it so important by making such a bloody fuss about it."

"I'm not making a fuss about it. I prefer to ignore it as much as possible."

"I've got to know you pretty well over the last few months. I've helped you to come to terms with a lot of things that were upsetting you. But one of your major hangups, still, is your paralysed left arm. Now I can't get to the root of this until I see for myself how bad it is. Come on, don't be so stupid. Pretend I'm your doctor."

"But you're not my doctor," she protested, close to tears. In this hateful, empty house, in the hateful, wet and empty Sunday street in the god-forsaken borough of Ealing he could do anything - rape her, murder her, examine her arm.

She said, trying to keep her voice from trembling. "I'm wearing long sleeves. They won't roll up very far."

"Then take off your blouse."

She was shocked. "I can't do that."

"Oh come on. I only want to see your arm."

Defeated, she turned her back on him and slipped off her cardigan, then began to unbutton her blouse. She hesitated, then quickly pulled it down over her shoulders and sat on the bed with her left side towards him, shivering in the chilly air. Her head hung down so that her auburn hair covered her face. He studied it in silence.

"Move it," he said after a minute.

She took her left hand in her right and moved it up and down. The movement of the joint in its socket was clearly visible.

"Can't you move it on its own?"

"Not a lot." She demonstrated. "The hand isn't too bad, but it gets weaker towards the shoulder. I can't lift it up."

"What about these exercises you do?"

"They prevent it from getting worse. They won't make it any better."

"Hm," he said. "Fascinating. It does look weird, but I guess you could get used to it."

He started to knead her shoulder with his hands. She was alarmed. It was the first time that there had been any deliberate physical contact between them. Then he sat on the bed beside her and kissed her shoulder. His mouth was hot and wet. He pressed his teeth into the wasted flesh, and then began to suck and run his tongue all over her upper arm. Elisabeth was revolted.

"What are you doing?" She struggled to get away from his wet, hard, thrusting tongue. He paused for breath.

"God, it turns me on. I thought it would. It really turns me on." He put his hand on her breast, covered by a schoolgirlish cotton vest. "Not exactly Jayne Mansfield, are you? It doesn't matter, though, it really doesn't matter. See what you've done to me." He got hold of her right hand and pulled it down to the hard swelling in his groin. He pushed down the straps of her vest and bra, so that her breasts were exposed and her arms trapped. She lay on the bed and he lay half on top of her, squeezing her breasts and sucking and chewing at her arm. He ignored her pleas for him to stop, telling her, as if she should be pleased, that she was really turning him on. She struggled to get free, but he turned his attention to her breasts, sucking at these instead. This was worse. Her insides squeezed themselves into a tight knot. She shut her eyes and suddenly had an image of Chris standing in the doorway, watching their obscene struggle. She screamed to make Antony hear "Stop, oh please stop!"

He raised his head to look at her. "You don't like that as much as the arm? Neither do I. Funny, isn't it? Let's see how you're feeling down below."

He fumbled inexpertly with her skirt, then said, "You'll have to take some clothes off. Hang on and I'll get a heater to keep us warm." He rolled off her and left the room. When he came back, carrying with him a small electric fire, she was fastening up her blouse.

"What the hell does this mean?" he asked, an ugly expression on his dark face.

"I don't want this. I don't. You wanted to see my arm and I've shown you and now I don't want to show it to you ever again. I want to go back downstairs."

"You stupid bitch," he said slowly. "You think you can work me up like this and then drop me? You bloody cock-teaser."

She didn't know what he meant. "I didn't work you up - or if I did I didn't mean it. Please let me go."

He stood by the door and regarded her sullenly. "I suppose you're frigid on top of everything else."

"Maybe, I don't know." She was desperate to get away.

"You're a virgin?"

"Of course."

"Hasn't anyone tried to fuck you before?"

"No."

"Well," he said, considering, "perhaps I was too hasty. With all the hangups you've got, I should have expected this. Let's start again."

"No." Despite her repugnance she could not bring herself to tell him she didn't want him to touch her again, ever.

"God," he said, "you're about as affectionate as a cat. And as selfish. It seems to me that all you ever want to do is take. It hasn't been easy, you know, taking you on, and you haven't shown any gratitude."

"I'm sorry," she murmured, desperate to get away but anxious not to make him angry, "I am grateful to you for your friendship. I just don't think I'm ready for this."

"I'll make you ready," he promised, excited again by the challenge she set him. "Don't worry, I won't force you to do anything you don't want. You're not on the pill, of course?"

"No. But..."

"So we can't fuck, anyway. Getting you pregnant is not my aim, I can tell you. But there are alternatives. I've been reading some books. Come on, let me see your arm again."

So, out of a mixture of guilt and fear, and passivity in the face of his male superiority, and a longing for anything which might pass as affection or bring it closer, she allowed him to undress her again and explore her unresponsive body with rough, insensitive fingers. In return for the pleasure which he assumed he was giving her, she tried to bring him to a climax as he instructed, with her hands, fighting repugnance. In the end he came against her belly, while sucking obsessively at her shoulder. It was red and sore by the time he allowed her to get dressed again.

"Well," he said, lying contented on the bed, his penis wet and limp between his legs, "it looks like we've got a long way to go. You'd better get yourself fixed up with the pill as soon as possible. You could talk to the doctor about your frigidity. We'll get over it, but they might be able to speed things up a bit."

"I'm sorry," she whispered into the pillow, apologising to herself as much as to him.

"I think I'll have a bath," he announced. "Will you start running it for me? You can get in the end, if you like."

She was longing for a bath, but not if it meant sharing with him. Instead, she found herself soaping his bony, awkward body, scrubbing his back, kneading his shoulders, and soaping gingerly between his legs. Afterwards she cleaned the bath, removing pubic hairs in a piece of toilet paper and flushing them away. She felt that this was a necessary martyrdom although for what, she wasn't sure.

Antony was now in a good mood. He walked Elisabeth to the station after tea.

A few days later, at his insistence, she made an appointment at one of the new birth control clinics which had been set up to help both married and unmarried women. She got an appointment on one of her Wednesday half-days. She waited in miserable silence with half a dozen other young women in a room decorated with posters showing happy, healthy family groups exhorting their readers to plan their families, and others showing young couples with their arms round each other and the warning 'Better to be safe than sorry'. One young man was there with his girlfriend. A nurse moved briskly among them, taking names and giving cards and numbers.

When it was Elisabeth's turn to go into the surgery she felt sick with fear. She couldn't think what she was doing there. Antony's will had propelled her, and it was only fear of his wrath that kept her from running out into the street. The thought crossed her mind that if she were to run into the street and under a passing car she would escape from all the horrors of her life. But the nurse was waiting and she was used to obeying authority, and those who had pretensions to authority, and this carried her to the white painted door with a panel bearing the words 'Surgery no. 4.' She knocked, and prayed that she would be told to go away. But instead a loud, cheerful voice called "Come in!", and her unwilling hand pressed the handle which opened the door. The room into which she stepped was long and narrow with a desk at one end and a high couch at the other. Two people, wearing white coats, were already there, and when Elisabeth came in it looked crowded. The owner of the cheerful voice, a middle-aged woman, said

"Come in dear, and shut the door. That's right. Elisabeth Lindsey? Good. Now just go and sit by the desk and the doctor will have a little chat with you." The second white-coated figure stood up and came from behind his desk to shake her hand. He was a youngish man, younger than Elisabeth had expected. Her alarm increased. How could a man, a young man, understand what she was going through? She felt rigid, puppet-like. Had she any control over her actions she would have said "Stop. This is a terrible mistake. I should never have come here," and left. But she couldn't. Her whole life was being controlled by other people; there was nothing she could do. She was fixed, in this room, with these people, and must continue with the grim charade.

The doctor was small and fair and matter of fact. He asked questions about Antony, and how long she had known him. Elisabeth, weighed down with guilt, lengthened the time and also added a year on to both their ages.

"Any marriage plans?"

"Oh no," she said, so quickly that the doctor raised his eyebrows. "We're both studying," she explained.

"I see, I see," said the doctor, and Elisabeth felt that she had come up with a suitable formula - a responsible young couple, wanting a sexual relationship but not able to offer each other anything permanent at present. She began to feel a little better.

"Have you had full intercourse?"

Elisabeth was humbled again. "No."

"You are still a virgin?"

"Yes."

"Good, good. And what type of contraceptive are you thinking of using?"

Elisabeth looked blank. They (or rather Antony) had only ever talked of using the Pill. The doctor went through the various possibilities open to her.

"On balance, I think the Pill is your best option. As a virgin and in your situation I should be reluctant to insert an IUD, and you would initially have difficulty with the cap. There may be side effects but these affect only a handful of the thousands of women who are now taking it, and I think you will find that its advantages outweigh these minor problems. If taken properly - and the nurse will explain all this to you - it is 99.9 per cent safe. It is easy to use, no mess, no interruption of your or your boyfriend's enjoyment.

"Now let me take your blood pressure, and weigh you, and then we'll have a little look at you."

'A little look at you', she realised as she was led to the high couch where the sister awaited them, meant an internal examination. She was told to draw the curtains round the bed and remove her tights and pants (the curtains seemed an unnecessary modesty considering what was to follow).

She lay on the bed, knees wide apart, and awaited the doctor's hand. It came, covered with plastic, poking and exploring like Antony's finger, but clinical and detached, and holding an instrument. He did not seem to be progressing much better than Antony, for all the detachment. "Come on, relax," he said, stroking her tummy. "Come on, now, relax those muscles. I can't hurt you if you are relaxed."

Eventually he was able to do what he had to do, and withdrew his hand. She lay there, humiliated.

"No obvious problems there, are your periods regular? Then get dressed, please, and I'll give you your prescription."

He explained that she would be given a three months' supply, after which she would come back for a further examination, and a further supply. He explained how she was to take them. She would have to wait until her next period. Elisabeth nodded, not really listening. It wasn't her he was talking to, it was some stranger who was inhabiting her body. He seemed reluctant to let her go. He told her she was under weight and should try to put some weight on. He kept asking if she understood what he was saying. She muttered yes, her eyes on his prescription pad. She could still feel his hand inside her vagina, which now felt enormous and gaping. Why were women constructed in such a way that men could force their way right inside them? Why was it that two men, who until recently had been strangers to her, were so interested in exploring a part of her body which she ignored, apart from a few days each month? She felt invaded. She got away at last when the nurse reminded him that it was time for his next appointment.

"Well, I'll see you in three months' time," he said, with a slight emphasis on the 'I'. "And don't worry. Take your time. If he cares for you, he'll wait."

Elisabeth flushed scarlet with anger and embarrassment. She made a vow never to come to this clinic again. Ungraciously she turned and followed the nurse out of the surgery and to the supplies counter, where the prescription was exchanged for a brown envelope containing three packets of contraceptives. She handed over her money (another incursion into her savings, Antony hadn't offered to pay), and buried the envelope deep in her shopping bag. Then she hurried down the stairs and into the free air of Charlotte Street.

She felt giddy with relief. She never wanted to see the clinic again. For years to come she was unable to go to that part of London without experiencing a feeling of humiliation. She was tempted to throw the brown envelope into the nearest litter bin, but as always fear of Antony prevented her. He ought to pay for it, but he would call her mean if she asked him. He didn't understand how important her savings were to her - they represented freedom and the more she had, the more freedom she could buy. When she had enough she would leave London for ever.

She walked down Charlotte Street towards Goodge Street, thinking of freedom. Some people would say that she had bought herself some freedom today. She could now have sex with whom she liked, as often as she liked, without fear of pregnancy. But she didn't want sex with anyone. She probably was frigid. She didn't mind. She would be quite content to live in celibacy. It was only Antony who had pushed her into this and Antony - she didn't really know why he had decided that they should have sex. Things had been alright before; why did he want to change?

Just before Goodge Street she turned into Tottenham Court Road. She couldn't face going back to Hoxton just yet, to the pile of work waiting to be done. She saw Heal's with its curved glass frontage across the road. She was a little overawed by the grand entrance, but her relief at being outside the clinic gave her the energy to walk through the door held open for her by a uniformed commissionaire, and once inside the store she found that she was able to wander about quite freely without anyone taking any notice of her.

She descended the polished wooden staircase to the basement, and walked among the gleaming pots and pans, and unfamiliar, specialised pieces of equipment which had their function explained by a small notice in front of each shelf: chopsticks and spaghetti tongs and rice steamers and coffee grinders and food mixers. Cooking did not interest her and she was turning back to the staircase when she heard her name called. At first she assumed the call was for another Elisabeth but when she turned, cautiously, she saw Chris coming away from the cash desk with two carrier bags in his hand.

301

Her first reaction was delight, followed by depression. If Chris knew what she had been doing, how shocked and disgusted he would be!

"We were talking about you the other day," he said, smiling at her, "and wondering when we would see you again, but I didn't expect it to be here. What are you doing? Has someone left you a fortune?"

"It's my day off. I'm just wandering around - I've never been in here before. I'm certainly not buying anything!"

"I am," he said, indicating his shopping. "Lesley wanted some storage jars and it seems that Heal's is the only place in the world where they can be found. These things are important to her. Let's go and get some tea."

"Don't you have to get back to work?"

"Visits to clients can take such a long time, don't you know? If anyone sees us, I can always say you are a prospective client."

"Not one who could afford your fees, I'm afraid."

"Oh, anyone who shops in Heal's must be wealthy."

"But I'm not shopping..." she began, then realised that he was joking.

They went up to the cafe on the top floor. Chris bought her a coffee and, despite her protests, a Danish pastry.

"You're looking thin." He was the second person today who had commented on her weight. She thought again of the doctor's hands, and of her brown envelope. She felt vulnerable, every nerve exposed. She couldn't finish the pastry. "I'm sorry, I really can't."

"Are you sure? Well..." and Chris finished it off.

"I'm delighted to have met you today," he told her. "You'll be the third - no, the fourth - well, one of the first people to hear our news. We've decided to get married. We were going to wait until Heather is next home but we don't know when that will be and we thought - why wait? Let's get married, just a quiet do, we thought of just popping into a registry office, but then we reckoned we ought to tell the parents. It would be a bit of a slap in the face for my father if we didn't get married in church so we'll do that, but it'll just be family and we'll have a party later. We're virtually living together now, paying two rents, it's daft. You will come, won't you?"

302

7

For a few moments Elisabeth could see nothing but blackness, a blackness which was then pierced by vicious blinding lights. She thought she was going to faint. She concentrated on raising her glass to her lips. The cool orange helped to steady her. She agreed that it was wonderful. Fortunately Chris was too taken up with his news to notice the strangeness of her manner. She felt utterly consumed with jealousy. Lesley already had the world at her feet, and now she was marrying Chris. Soon she would be having his baby. Not for her the horror of Antony's bedroom, or the doctor's plastic fingers.

She herself was doing the right thing in preventing pregnancy. Of course she was. She could never have a baby, not with her history. How had it ever come about that she was having sex with Antony. She didn't want sex with anyone, least of all Antony. He revolted her. Everything revolted her. She felt an urge to scream.

Chris was still absorbed in his news. "Then we'll have a party in London, for friends. Lesley's planning it now. Lizzie, are you alright? You look very pale."

No, she was not alright. She couldn't say what was wrong except that the blackness and lights were still there, at the periphery of her vision, and a terrible panicky feeling was rushing at her in waves, growing stronger and threatening to engulf her.

"It's hot - I must go." She grabbed her bag to her chest - for God's sake don't leave that behind.

"It is hot in here. Just hang on while I pay the bill and I'll come with you."

"I can't wait." Elisabeth struggled to hold on to herself. "I must go." She made her way through the tables. She knew that she had left Chris puzzled and anxious, but she couldn't help that. She had to get away, away from people. She knew of no refuge and was frightened that Chris would catch up with her. She looked about her in desperation.

Then she spotted it - the 'Ladies Powder Room'. Elisabeth hurried along the rows of mattresses and bedside cabinets towards privacy. Chris couldn't follow her here. Inside there were two smartly dressed women seated at mirrors but, thank God, no attendant. She went into the empty cubicle furthest from the women and locked the door firmly. She put down the toilet lid, dropped her bag on the floor and sat down, leaning forward with her head between her knees. She had a great desire to lie on the floor but there was not enough room. Waves of blackness came over her; she felt very hot and then very cold, and passed out for a few seconds. She came to with the onset of cramp like pains in her bowels. It seemed that she really did need the lavatory. With an effort, she raised the lid, and pulled down her pants and tights. She defecated vigorously and painfully, in little spurts and spasms which seemed to last an age. When it was over she felt weak and drained, but better.

Weak-legged, she emerged from her cubicle and washed her hands, slowly and carefully. Then she sat on a stool by the mirror and pretended to comb her hair. Finally, she gathered her things together and made her way out of the store to the nearest bus stop, hoping that Chris wasn't looking for her. The first bus to come along dropped her half a mile from Hare Street but she walked home from there, unthinking, light-headed. No-one was at home, so fully clothed she climbed on to her bed and slept for two hours, until she was woken up by the sound of her parents returning.

The sleep refreshed her and normality returned. She should have been in the little box they called a kitchen, making the tea, having polished off an essay and read several chapters of the current text book. She leapt off her bed and ran downstairs, to face an aggrieved Rhoda. Following her usual policy of telling as much truth as possible, she said that she had had an upset stomach, but she thought it was better. In fact it felt fine, and she was positively hungry for the first time in ages. She pushed all thoughts of Chris and Lesley to the back of her mind.

When she next saw Antony he wanted to know every detail of her experience at the Family Planning Clinic. Elisabeth allowed him to pick over the unhappiness and embarrassment she had felt while being examined, but was determined to tell him nothing about her meeting with Chris. Fortunately, it did not occur to him to ask what she had done after the clinic.

"When do you start taking them?"

"Five days after my next period."

"When's that?"

"Um - a week - ten days I think."

"So long?"

"Mm." Elisabeth's periods had been light and irregular of late. The clinic doctor had told her that the pill should regularise everything.

"I have to go back in three months. They warned me about side effects," she added. "Headaches, nausea, that sort of thing."

"Sounds like your normal self."

Back home, she wondered yet again why she was going through with it. Because she was afraid of losing him? Was her life was so dreary that Antony was the only person she could claim as a friend? Why couldn't he stay a friend, why did there have to be this mess? She couldn't understand why he was so keen to have sex with her. He wasn't in love with her, he didn't even lust after her with any real passion, he maintained this clinical detachment about it all. He was experimenting with her. So why did she not have the courage to say that it was not what she wanted.

She found excuses not to see him alone. When she ran out of excuses her feet dragged her to his lodgings so slowly that he complained about her lateness. She tried to make coffee, tidy his room, think up new topics of conversation, to take his mind off the inevitable bed. But he wore her down until she once more found herself straddled half naked across his stained and crumpled sheets while he sucked at her breasts and rubbed her clitoris and asked her to describe her sensations. As these were mostly irritation leading to revulsion, she found it difficult. She hedged but could not disguise her lack of enthusiasm. She knew (she read *Nova* and *Honey* in the library) that women were supposed to enjoy sex these days as much as men did, but her reactions seemed to be locked in the Victorian age.

She began to wish they could get full intercourse out of the way as quickly as possible. It couldn't be any worse than this so-called petting, and at least she would have achieved something, have gained some measure of freedom by losing her virginity to somebody who seemed to want it. But her period didn't come. It was now three days late and she had none of the usual pre-menstrual symptoms. Both she and Antony were strung up and frustrated. Although she knew it was impossible she began to wonder if she was pregnant. Life seemed to come to a halt. She did no study. Antony's conversation was limited to enquiries about her physical state.

One day, he telephoned her at the library. After the usual question "Anything happened?" he told her that his friend - Lesley's cousin - had been in touch and suggested that they go out for a meal together. He had a new girlfriend he wanted them to meet. "Only a pizza, nothing expensive," Antony assured her.

305

Elisabeth agreed, trying to sound enthusiastic. She was negative about so many of Antony's ideas that she felt she had to say yes when she could. She had no real wish to meet Lesley's cousin again, she wanted to put all thought of Lesley and Chris out of her mind. Still, it would be a change, she could enjoy Antony's company without worrying about sex, and she willed herself into a more positive state of mind.

Tim was friendly and easy going. Sarah, the new girlfriend, was a tall blonde who used frequent expletives spoken in an impeccable home counties accent. Tim said "Sarah's promised to drink Dettol tonight," and roared with laughter. Sarah wore a mini skirt, a tight high necked sleeveless white top, and knee length white boots. Elisabeth wore a fluffy pink angora sweater, borrowed from a girl at work, over her everyday grey pleated skirt.

She had not anticipated drinks at the bar before they ate. Neither had Antony, but he allowed himself to be treated. Elisabeth asked for bitter lemon and made it last. Sarah concentrated her attention on Antony with the manner of a professional socialite, and Elisabeth talked to Tim. He told her that he was glad that Antony seemed to be settling down. She was puzzled at first, but then decided that he was referring to her relationship with his friend. She started to protest.

"He hasn't had much experience with women. Don't listen to what he says. It's all in the head. My last girlfriend, Sheila, went out with him once or twice before me, and she told me he didn't know the first thing. I expect he's changed since then. We're in different groups this year so I don't see much of him. I expect you're a good influence. He seems a bit more - well - human."

Elisabeth was flattered. She warmed to Tim. Under the casual manner was a sensitive man. She considered that what he had said about Antony was probably true. It explained one or two puzzling things about his behaviour. If they ever had intercourse she would be the first for him, as he was for her. She recognised that she was submissive and non-threatening and totally inexperienced - ideal for someone who did not wish to reveal his own lack of experience.

Now Tim was asking her if she ever saw her cousin.

"Not often. I did see Chris the other day."

"I see them now and again," Tim said. "What do you think of their news?"

"What news? - oh, getting married."

"Sooner them than me. Can't imagine being tied down, you need to have fun while you're young. Although Lesley doesn't make demands. Chris is alright there. But I'd have thought they would have waited a bit longer. Have some fun. She's only, what, 22?"

"I think they couldn't see the point in waiting."

"They seem sure of each other. I don't think Lesley has had another serious boyfriend, not sure about Chris. There were probably girls at university. And wasn't he seeing your other cousin for a while, what's her name, Pattie? "

"I'm not sure." Elisabeth longed to change the subject.

"I've always got on well with Lesley. She knows how to enjoy herself, mucks in, you know. I never had much time for Heather. She's wet - forever crying. Heaven knows how she copes in Africa." (Heather was teaching in Ghana).

They were interrupted by the waiter coming to tell them that their table was ready, and they made their way across the restaurant. Sarah strode across the floor in her white boots, followed by Tim. Antony and Elisabeth trailed along behind.

When the pizza was placed in front of her Elisabeth thought she would never be able to eat it all. "They're big, aren't they?" she murmured, but the others were already sawing through the dough and raising forks, glistening with strands of cheese, to their mouths. Elisabeth sipped her wine, hated the taste, took a deep breath, and began on her pizza.

After two mouthfuls she felt as if she had eaten enough. She ate so little these days that her stomach had shrunk.

"How are you two related?" demanded Sarah, already half way through her pizza and well into her second glass of wine.

"We have cousins in common, that's all. Lesley and Heather. Tim's related on one side and I'm on the other."

"There's another cousin too, isn't there?"

"Pattie." Elisabeth though affectionately of her favourite cousin. "She left home after a row and we don't know where she is. I wish she would come back."

The unaccustomed wine had loosened her tongue. It was nice to be able to talk about her family with people who were interested. She never mentioned them at home.

Sarah related at some length a story about a friend of hers who had run away from home and was found earning fabulous money posing for Playboy. "You can make a fucking bomb."

Elisabeth, still struggling with her pizza, felt a movement within her body. At the same time she realised that the slight abdominal cramp she had been experiencing was not caused by indigestion, as she had thought. She looked across at Antony but he was busy talking and didn't look her way. She could feel the blood trickling down her vagina. There was no doubt about it, her periods had started. Now she could take the pill and sleep with Antony. Oh God. She murmured an excuse and stood up, but no-one took much notice. Embarrassed, she had to ask a waiter for directions to the lavatory. Once inside the cubicle she found one bright spot, red like the wine, staining her pants. She fastened on a towel, washed her hands, and returned to the table, half relieved (she hadn't really thought that she was pregnant, and yet...) and half apprehensive. Another week, and there would be no more excuses.

Sarah was talking about her experiences with a modelling agency when Elisabeth rejoined them. Tim had pulled Elisabeth's plate towards her and was eating her pizza. He pushed it back as she sat down. "Sorry."

"No, have it, please, I couldn't eat any more."

"Oh come on," Antony said, irritation showing.

"No, really, I don't have much appetite and I'd hate to waste it."

Sarah, huffy about being interrupted, continued with her story, but addressed herself exclusively to Antony. Tim winked at Elisabeth, and poured her another glass of wine. "Tell me more about Pattie. I've only had snippets of information. Why did she leave home?"

"I wasn't there at the time, so I've had to piece it together. She had been getting into trouble for some time - late nights, unsuitable boyfriends, that sort of thing."

"What's an unsuitable boyfriend?"

"I don't know - boys her parents disapproved of. She and her friends used to hang around a coffee bar in Bradford which had a bad reputation. They were into music and I heard that she had gone off with them to make a record. I don't really know any more, I'd moved to London. You didn't know Pattie?"

"I met her once or twice."

"She had a light-hearted, happy go lucky attitude to life. She was always crazy about music. I thought she might be in London, I keep looking out for her. I thought she might have got in touch with me though it would be difficult."

"Why difficult?"

Elisabeth hesitated. She didn't want to describe her home life to Tim.

"Can anyone join in your conversation?" enquired Sarah sarcastically, enabling Elisabeth to shake her head and smile at Tim. He took the hint and gave his attention to his girlfriend. Elisabeth, aware that the wine had made her talk far more than usual, watched her tongue and said little further. She was beginning to feel tired. At 10 o'clock they got the bill and divided it into four; Elisabeth, although shocked at the final amount, had been saving up and was able to pay her share. Tim and Sarah said they were going dancing and Antony said he might go too; Elisabeth excused herself on the grounds of tiredness, causing Antony to look annoyed, and say 'Come on' again. It was Tim who suggested they should walk to her bus stop and see her on her way home.

Antony always liked to analyse social events. The next time they met he pointed out that she had talked animatedly with Tim but was silent when the others joined in. Clearly she would have preferred to have spent the evening alone with him. This way of looking at it had not occurred to Elisabeth.

"It's only that I know him a little. We were talking about family."

"Family! I don't understand your obsession with your family. And what possible interest could Sarah have had in your family." He spoke the last two words as if they were an insult.

"That's why we stopped when you joined in. We knew you wouldn't be interested. Anyway, you and Sarah seemed to be talking quite happily."

"Oh we were. Don't you worry about that. But it would have looked better if you had addressed the occasional word to her." He was ready to be mollified. He seemed unaware that Sarah had virtually ignored Elisabeth.

"I'm sorry. To be honest, I found her difficult to talk to."

"Why?"

"She's so" Elisabeth sought for a word to describe her feelings without being over-critical, "sophisticated," she compromised. "Her life style is so different from mine that I didn't feel we had much common ground."

"Couldn't you have shown some interest in this alien life style? You might have learned something."

"I listened. There have to be some listeners in any social group."

Thus encouraged, Antony proceeded to analyse the members of the dinner party and their interactions. Sarah in particular was a phenomenon to be studied. She encapsulated all the good things about the age they were living in – smart, pretty, able to hold her own with any man. Elisabeth, half-listening, looked at his thin dark face, puzzled that he should spend so much time analysing a casual meal with friends. She wondered how he would react if she told him what Tim had said about his lack of experience. She had taken her first pill that morning and thought that her present headache was a result of that.

"I'd like to meet her again." Elisabeth suggested another coffee.

8

Elisabeth's A level work was not going well. Her marks had deteriorated. She had missed one or two classes and several essays. She had a tutorial that week, and worked late into the night, trying to catch up, but it was no good, the more she read the worse it got, the words just would not go into her brain in any meaningful way. She read the same sentences over and over until forced to give up with tears of frustration. She found it hard to concentrate on anything these days, and had started to read light fiction, surreptitiously, pretending to anyone at work who found her checking out these doctor and nurse romances, thrillers, murder stories, that they were for someone else. She devoured them at the rate of two or three a week. Anything else was indigestible.

She did not have the time or the will to get to know her fellow students, and she was not close to any of her colleagues in the library. The girl she had been most friendly with had left, and her affair with Antony took up most of her remaining energies. One of the boys in the reference library had tried to be friendly, and even asked her to the cinema one evening; this had alarmed Elisabeth and she had turned him down with unnecessary vigour. He had been cool ever since, and word seemed to get round that she was to be left alone. Most of the younger staff thought she was bit odd, she knew that. She hadn't minded while her ambition was intact and her friendship with Antony enlivening and relatively undemanding, but now she wished she had a girl friend to whom she could unburden herself.

Sometimes she thought longingly of Aireton, and how different her life would have been if she had remained with the Atfields. These thoughts were like a drug which she was taking more and more frequently, after years of forbidding herself to think of the past. She wondered, however, whether in fact things would have been so different. She had been considered a queer little thing, even then, and had found it difficult to make friends, and there would always have been the humiliation of being dependent on the goodwill of others. She was what she was, the child of her father and her mother, and she could not escape that. She had to be independent, she had to earn enough money to enable her to take control of her own life, and the only way she could see to do this was to go to college and gain a qualification. And so she turned again to her text books and read a few lines before the words once again became meaningless and panic threatened and she turned for comfort to Mills and Boon.

When the time for her tutorial came round she had progressed very little. Brian Whitehead was her tutor, a middle aged man with problems of his own who despite these was interested in Elisabeth and concerned about her current difficulties.

"I wondered at the start if you were taking on too much," he said, after listening patiently to Elisabeth's fumbling excuses for her failure to produce the required work. Elisabeth assured him that it was a short term problem, it was over now, she would take a week's leave from the library and catch up.

"You sounded so determined that I thought you could carry it off, but it seems that it's all too much for you. You've got the brains but you seem to have lost your motivation. Is there anything the matter - problems at home, boyfriend trouble, anything like that?" He sounded kind, if slightly embarrassed, and for a second she was tempted to tell him everything, but she resisted the urge. Where would she start, anyway? "I don't get on with my stepmother. My boyfriend is possessive and demanding. He wants sex and I don't like it." What had that to do with her work? It was a simple matter of concentration, or the lack of it. She tried to explain:

"I read something and it just doesn't go in. I have to read everything several times over and even then I have difficulty making sense of it. And I find it so hard to get down to writing essays. I do try, really."

"It sounds to me as if you are over-tired. Are you busy at work?"

"Yes."

"And things to do at home?"

"Yes."

"And have a boyfriend."

"Well, not - yes."

"Nothing wrong with all that, but you're trying to spread yourself too thinly. Look, it's tough trying to study part time. Most people wouldn't consider it. Some people are so determined to get through that they drop everything else and study all the spare hours God sends them. A few succeed. That's how you were at first. But you couldn't keep it up. No blame on you for that. Circumstances have obviously changed, and so have your priorities..."

"Oh no," said Elisabeth involuntarily, desperately.

Brian stopped for a minute, hearing the desperation but out of his depth. He went on

"I know you don't want to give up, or admit defeat. It's natural. What I'm going to suggest is that you drop one of your subjects. Drop history. A level history is tough and it needs all your attention. Your first love is literature, I think. Concentrate on that, give it your full attention, enjoy it. You could try taking the exam in June but on balance I think you'd do better to wait until Christmas, and leave history altogether until the following year."

He continued to give her good, practical advice. Elisabeth sat silent, numb. Give up history! Postpone the exam! When would she ever get to college now, when would she ever be free? She wished he would stop talking, she just wanted to get away, hide in a corner, die.

"I know it's disappointing for you," he said, worried at her silence. "But it's better to postpone it, give yourself a fair chance, rather than fail which I have to say, on your current performance, you would do."

She kept her head bent so that he would not see her stricken face. She hardly heard him. All she wanted to do was get out of this dreadful classroom and hug her humiliation to herself.

"It's not a failure of ability, I know you have it in you. It's a failure of time, of strength. Don't give up, just make it easier for yourself. Don't worry about the fees, we can sort something out."

He was going on to give her advice about her study skills. The head of the Centre might be able to help. But study problems were not something she normally had. She was going to pieces, losing her mind - her mind, which she had always been so proud of! Clever little Lizzie, they used to call her. Not any longer. She would lose her mind, like her mother.

Now he was talking about the essay she should have brought with her. He was suggesting that they looked at it together, drafting an outline which she could fill in on her own. They began, but it was hopeless. She couldn't hear a word he was saying. Her eyes felt funny, too, as if she was wearing blinkers, with dark shadows at the edges of her vision.

"I think I need glasses," she interrupted him at one point.

He looked at her, good-natured but puzzled.

"Do you get headaches?"

"Sometimes - I'm sorry, I didn't mean to interrupt."

He was talking about colour imagery in Macbeth - red for blood and black for evil. Blood and evil, red and black. She understood that.

Her stepmother was fond of red and black. She wondered what Antony's favourite colour was. She hated red, it clashed with her hair. She had to admit defeat. She could not bring her mind to focus on Macbeth. It would go off on its own tack. She told him, shaking her head so that her hair fell across her face. Brian Whitehead was concerned but at a loss. He said "Why don't you have a holiday? There are only a couple more weeks before the end of term, so give yourself a proper break and relax. Put the books aside for a time and then come back to them afresh. Go away if you can - do you have friends or relatives you could stay with?"

Sitting on the bus after her tutorial, Elisabeth felt the familiar sensation of panic threatening to engulf her. The dark night outside the bus windows seemed like a black doom with only a thin pane of glass between her and it. She peered at the window but the reflections were distorted and peculiar, and her own ugly, distraught face peered back at her. She had to get home. There was nowhere else to go. The hated little room in the hated little house was a haven to her now. She could not think about anything until she had reached that place. She could not allow herself to think of Mr Whitehead, or her studies, or Antony, or her parents, or Chris or anyone, until she was safe. She began to work out the number of bus stops between where she was now and Hare Street. In her mind she took herself from the bus stop, across the road, round the corner, past the mean little terraced houses, to no. 68. She would have to speak a few words to her parents, make some excuse for being late, then say she was tired and going to bed.

She had made it. She alighted at the seventh bus stop from the college, walked past the newsagents and the launderette and the off-licence, crossed the road, round one corner, and down the street to the house. She spoke a few words to Hugh and Rhoda (her voice coming as from a great distance, high-pitched and strange), said that she had a headache, and went up to her room. Once there, she pushed all unpleasant thoughts to the back of her mind, read the latest trashy novel for ten minutes, and then fell into a deep, dreamless sleep which lasted until her alarm went off in the morning but left her tired and unrefreshed. Like an automaton she went through her early morning chores and got ready for work, and it was only as she neared the library she thought of the interview she would have to request with the librarian, to say that she would have to postpone her application to library school. No hurry, she could think about that later.

Intercourse with Antony, when it happened, was a humiliating and painful experience. She knew that her attitude was partly to blame. She saw it almost as a duty, the inevitable next step in their relationship. The opportunity to say no had long passed. She didn't see that she had any choice but to do it, get it over with, sooner rather than later. She had an idea that losing her virginity was a kind of initiation ceremony, which was supposed to liberate her - but for what, she did not know. She didn't want to go around having affairs with men. In fact, she was pretty sure that she never wanted to sleep with anyone ever again.

For Antony, too, the event failed to live up to expectations. "Well," he said, wiping the blood of his penis while Elisabeth lay curled up on her side, trying not to cry, a wad of Kleenex between her legs, "I suppose the first time is never easy. For a woman, I mean."

By now, Elisabeth was sure that Antony, too, had been a virgin. She daren't ask him - he would deny it, and then become huffy because of her suspicions. But it made sense. If only he had trusted her enough to tell her. Then they could have explored the thing together, as equals. But that was not Antony's way. Always, he had to be in control. At the moment, however, he sounded uncharacteristically uncertain. She twisted around to look at the blood stained tissues.

"Have you any more?" she asked.

"No, you've emptied the box. Are you still bleeding?"

"Yes."

"I never expected so much."

"Neither did I."

They stared, fascinated, at the bright red on the pale pink towel she had been lying on. They were in his lodgings, having chosen a time when his landlady was out.

"We've got to keep it off the sheet. I'll get some paper from the bathroom." Padded with toilet paper she struggled into her clothes. Antony sat by the window, smoking - something he rarely did. He said "I need a drink. It'll have to be the pub. Are you ready?"

"Yes."

"Come on then."

They put on their coats and walked to the pub in silence. Inside, there was a comforting fug of cigarette smoke, alcohol, and warm bodies. Antony ordered two whiskies and Elisabeth found seats in a corner. It was the first time that she had drunk spirits, and after the first shock she enjoyed the warmth and stimulation. She began to relax. So did Antony. He said "They say that women never forget their first time."

"I'm sure that's true."

"It'll be better next time. We won't have all this nonsense."

His hand waved vaguely in the direction of female physiology.

She travelled home alone, feeling rather cool and grown up about it all. She had tried sex and she didn't like it. It wouldn't always hurt so much, but there had been nothing to give her any pleasure, despite Antony's assurances that that was why he was doing what he was doing.

She began to wonder if she was being very wicked to have this sort of relationship with someone whom she did not love, sometimes even positively disliked. Perhaps her stepmother was right, she had a devil inside her. It had been one thing to have Antony as a friend, a companion, someone to go to films and pubs with, but quite another to have a sexual relationship with him. Why had she allowed it to happen? Why was she incapable of saying no? When had it all changed? Oh it was her arm, that was what had started it, he wanted to see her arm and that seemed to excite him - how horrible, how gruesome, she turned him on because she was a freak, abnormal, something you might pay to see in a circus. But it had started before that, it hadn't been such a sudden change, he had been stripping her mentally and emotionally long before he had told her to take her clothes off. And where did that leave her now? No longer a virgin, on the pill, probably frigid, with undermined intellectual confidence and serious emotional vulnerability. The loss of her intellectual ability troubled her most. The knowledge that she was brighter than average had always given her the strength to survive hardships. But now she wouldn't be going to college next year - no, she mustn't think about that. She hadn't told Antony yet - it was one of the few secrets she had been able to keep from him. But she must tell him, he would tell her what to do. He would probably say that the system was at fault, exams were unimportant (although he made quite sure that he passed his). What did she want to be a boring librarian for anyway? She could do better than that. She would telephone him tomorrow

Engrossed in her thoughts, she missed her stop and had to go on to the next one and walk back. This meant walking past a pub, which she disliked. As she neared it a group of four young men swayed in front of her and invited her to join them. They encircled her so that she couldn't get away without pushing past them, and she was frightened to do that. They were good-natured, joking, but they smelled of drink. An older couple, going in, said "Let her alone, boys. She's only a kid," while the man put his hand on her back and guided her along the pavement. The lads sniggered, but let her go. Elisabeth ran the rest of the way home, feeling sick and more shaken than the incident warranted. She wished she could retrieve the brief feeling of relaxation that the whisky had brought her.

When she got home she found her father sitting alone in the living room, reading a newspaper. From his air of guilt and the smell of peppermints, she knew that he too had been drinking.

"It's alright, Dad, it's only me. You can get it out again."

With a mixture of slyness and pride he pulled a half bottle of whisky from behind his back.

"You're sharp, Lizzie May. It's not that I drink a lot, it's just that she" he paused, "doesn't like it. Doesn't like it at all. So rather than have an argument - well, there's no point in upsetting the applecart, is there?"

"May I have some?"

He hesitated then handed the bottle to her. She also hesitated. "No glasses? No water?" Her father laughed, shamefaced. She raised the bottle to her lips, and took a drink. The neat alcohol burned and she choked and coughed (Hugh quickly took the bottle from her hand) but when she had recovered she felt a lot stronger. "Do you always drink it like this?"

"It's easier this way. No dirty glasses, no fuss. Now, my favourite, my absolute favourite little tipple is what they call a Calypso special. Oh it's a long time since I've had one of those. There was a little pub, just off Covent Garden, the barman was a good friend of mine, he could make them just so. For a shilling. That was a lot of money in those days. It was when I was in *Bon Appetit,* the revue, you know. I was the waiter, the barman, the awkward guest – not a lot to say, but there was a lot of business - in and out, fetch and carry, pulling faces at the audience, making sure that they could see what was going on even though the main characters couldn't. Oh, it ran and ran, we had a wonderful time. And then I had my accident." Hugh had fallen off a ladder and broken his ankle, and life had never been the same since. "And do you know, Lizzie May, I've never told you this before," (he had, many times,) "they refused to pay me a penny compensation. Said I'd been careless - implied I'd been drinking. Not a penny. And of course, you're out of circulation for a long time with a broken leg. There are not many parts for a one-legged man. You might just about get away with a broken arm, but not a leg. You can't hide a broken leg."

Elisabeth took another drink. She was learning to anticipate the burning, and no longer choked. The soreness between her legs had eased, and the room felt warm and cosy.

"What are you reading?" She picked it up. "*'The Stage'*. Oh, Dad, I thought you had given all that up."

"An actor never gives up," he said with tipsy dignity. "Once a professional, always a professional. One rests, perhaps, one has to look for alternatives in order to keep the roof over the family's head - but one never gives up. Only amateurs do that. They're auditioning for a new play - it's that fringe theatre in Whitechapel, but there's always hope for the West End. I've a good mind to go along and see what's what."

Elisabeth, whisky brave, laughed. "Yes, why don't you? You could still do the church on Sundays."

Hugh looked foxy. "Well, you see Miss Lizzie, there are one or two things you don't know. You've been out of the house so much lately that you won't have noticed that Rhoda and I have been busy too. Where do you think she is now? At another meeting, protecting our interests. There's trouble brewing, you see. And I shan't mind – well, it really wouldn't trouble me – anyway, I pleaded tiredness and the need to prepare my sermon." He shook his bottle and giggled. "But she'll be back soon and we must have a good story ready. You're helping me with some quotations - which play are you studying?"

"The unmentionable one."

"Well done. What about linking Lady M washing her hands with the cleansing of the soul."

"Mm. Dad."

"Hm?"

"You don't really believe in all that, do you? I mean, not really believe, not really."

Hugh looked foxy again. "It's funny you should say that. That's what it's all about, you see."

"What what's all about?"

"The dispute. Doctrine."

"But I don't see - oh, you mean that's why you've been so busy. There's been some kind of dispute at church - over doctrine. Is it serious?"

"Of course. Have you ever known there to be a dispute over doctrine that wasn't serious? It's like arguing the merits of the *First Folio* over later versions. Now, in our case, it's the older ones, the elders, they don't like change, don't like my interpretation of some texts. Well, they were written thousands of years ago, translated from Aramaic into Greek into Hebrew into English - there's room for interpretation. They're all for brimstone and fire, you know, no escape for the wicked, but I've been saying that God in his wisdom allows for some errors on the way. Humans are human, therefore fallible. Couldn't keep up the fire and brimstone, not fair, you know? How would I stand? Rhoda would be alright, she never wavers. You could almost call it a schism," Hugh said proudly.

He now cast an expert eye on the clock. "She'll be back soon. Look after this for me, will you?" He passed her the whisky bottle. She pushed it into her shopping bag. "I'll take it upstairs. Where do you usually hide it?"

"In your wardrobe."

"In my wardrobe?"

"Yes. There's an old schoolbag in the back that you never use."

"What a cheek!" She got to her feet with an effort. Whisky certainly had a nice relaxing effect. She really didn't care about Antony or her exams.

"Watch the door - here, you'd better take a couple of these."

Hugh fished a packet of mints out of his pocket. "Extra strong, they should do the trick. Oh, and put the kettle on when you come down. A cup of strong tea will be just what Rhoda needs when she gets in."

Elisabeth, feeling more than a little unstable, obeyed. She could not take the so-called schism too seriously. There had been disputes before - when Hugh first took over as minister, for example - then everything settled down again. She was feeling better than she had done for weeks. Virginity lost, history postponed, more time for literature. Perhaps it would all turn out for the best. She went back downstairs, filled the kettle and brought it to the boil, then turned off the gas. "I won't make it until she comes," she said, returning to her father, who remarked that she was later than usual. "I wonder if they're giving her a difficult time." There was some problem of her own which needed to be resolved, but she couldn't think what it was.

She gave up and stretched out her legs in front of the gas fire. She felt pleasantly warm and drowsy. Her father passed her the mints again. "Have another? Vodka's the best, of course, but I've always been partial to whisky."

"Best for what?"

"Doesn't smell."

"Oh, I see."

A few companionable minutes later they heard the sound of the key in the front door. They sat up, and Hugh put his paper behind the cushion. Elisabeth vanished into the kitchen to make the tea.

Rhoda came heavy footed into the lounge and sat down in the chair Elisabeth had vacated, still wearing her coat. "It's cold out there. A real March wind." The cold had reddened her usual sallow cheeks and her eyes were bright. There was an energy about her.

"What happened?" asked Hugh.

"Well," Rhoda held out her hands to the fire, her face now shadowed. "There was a lot of talk. I'll tell you when I've had my tea. There'll be a vote on Sunday after the service. I said that Sunday should be kept for the Lord's work, but they said this was the Lord's work."

Elisabeth came in, balancing a tray on her hip. "Do you want me to stay?" The feeling of well-being was evaporating, and a headache was developing.

"You should. It's going to affect you, little interested though you are in the church."

Her father helped her set the tray down on a table, and she poured the tea. Her stepmother continued to gaze into the gas fire. She took her cup, wrapping her hands about it, and began to talk about the meeting. Elisabeth did not listen very closely. Her head was muzzy, and the whisky induced euphoria had disappeared, leaving her with a feeling of depression. She could not see how a silly little religious dispute could affect her. She began to think about Macbeth and colour imagery. She suddenly saw how it could be analysed - red - the red of blood and the black of tragedy - death. What a lot of blood there had been staining the pink towel. Blood and death. Red and black. Blood was life as well, of course. Black - nothing in nature was black. Except coal. Was coal nature, exactly? Her stepmother was almost a figure of tragedy, sitting there, hunched like a crow in her black coat. Elisabeth suddenly saw for the first time how tragedy could come from within, how a person's character, life, whatever made them what they were could be a tragedy for them. It wasn't only external events that affected your happiness. She had never seen it like that before. Rhoda's tragedy was that she could not get on with people, could not be happy, was conditioned to fight against any possibility of happiness. And what about Elisabeth herself? Oh, but she would be happy if she could. She would! Only - it was all so difficult. Oh, concentrate, she told herself, she's bound to ask what you think.

"But I still don't see..." her father was saying.

"Don't be such a fool, Hugh," snapped Rhoda. "If they win the vote do you think they'll let you stay on as minister? You'll be out of a job. Your vocation!"

"Well, they didn't pay much. I'll get something else. We'll manage. In fact, I did think..."

"Is that all the ministry means to you - a salary?" she asked, bitterly. "Then here's something else for you to think about. The house belongs to the church - it goes with the job."

That did give Hugh something to think about, and attracted Elisabeth's wandering attention. She wished now that she had listened more carefully earlier. She would have to ask her father to fill her in.

She heard her him say "Thank goodness for Lizzie. She'll be able to keep us going until I find something else."

"Only until September. She won't be able to do much for us on a student's grant."

"Oh, I shall have found something by then."

Elisabeth felt sick. The trap was closing around her. How could she leave them, how could she abandon him at a time like this? How fortunate for them that she wasn't going to college in September. Some time she would have to tell them.

Her stepmother glanced across. "It's good to see Elisabeth taking an interest at last."

"Of course I am," she managed to say. "It's very upsetting."

"All you two can think about are material things."

"We must think of them, dear. We can't carry on our ministry without a roof over our heads."

"The Son of Man..."

"Yes, dear, but that was Palestine. London in March is a very different thing."

"You are being frivolous. They see in you a weakness – you have to convince them that they are wrong. You have not weakened. There is nothing to worry about. You have one chance on Sunday to bring

321

them back." She looked up at Hugh, her eyes black as coal. "You must do it. I don't care about the money, the house – I do care about the Church. I helped to build it up, here in London. I won't let it go, I won't be kicked out of my own church. You mustn't let them do it. Hugh!"

"Dearest, I'll do what I can. I don't want to lose our home."

"That isn't the issue. The Lord knows we do our best, he will provide."

"The Lord seems to have turned his back on us," thought Elisabeth, but kept the thought to herself.

Hugh put on his ministerial voice. "That of course is what I have been saying. That to do your best and fail is not a sin. It is tragic that these divisions should have arisen." He glanced across at his daughter. "We have of course been aware of a possible impending confrontation. The dispute took its inexorable path and there was little we could do." He gave a little hiccup which he turned into a cough.

"You could have thrashed the devil out of those dogs earlier," broke in Rhoda, unable to contain her anger and bitterness. "You are too weak for this work. I listened to you when you said we could be reconciled - more fool I. Ten years ago I would not have been so weak."

"My wife," Hugh informed his audience, "believes that we could have saved the Church had we pursued the dissidents earlier. She may be right." ("I am," asserted Rhoda). "However that raises certain moral questions about the use of force - I mean moral and, um, legal force, of course," he added, with another glance at Elisabeth.

"And spiritual force."

"And spiritual force, of course. I am not by nature a forceful man. I believe in constructive discussions, the use of friendly persuasion, and I will continue believing in that," he continued, raising his voice a little to counter Rhoda's angry breathing, then giving another little cough to disguise a belch. "I do not have any great faith that we will win our battle tomorrow. I can only assume that the Lord has different plans for us."

Elisabeth looked at her father, standing on the miniscule hearthrug, loving the sound of his own voice, the attention of his family, being on stage again. His sandy hair, thinning now, stood out like a halo around his animated face. How ridiculous he was - and how she loved him. While he needed her she could not abandon him.

322

The flush on Rhoda's face darkened. "Are you out of your mind? We cannot lose. We have not deviated one inch from the path laid down for us. All I am saying is that you – your weakness – your abominable habit of even-handedness. You risk losing everything I - we - have fought for, built up, over the past years."

"No, no, no," said Hugh, losing confidence and seeming to lose stature as he shuffled uncomfortably on the hearthrug, looking for some cue which would enable him to walk off stage. "I wonder if there might be grounds for - er - compromise."

"Compromise! Have we come this far to find a compromise?"

"Is that so wrong?"

"Religious matters are too important to compromise over."

"This dispute is damaging everyone. Surely they will see that. We must discuss and find a way forward."

"I shall not waste my breath arguing any more with you. Things have gone too far. That is the reality. You must make the sort of sermon tomorrow that will stir them, and convince them that you have the Truth in your soul. They will accept no less. You can do it. This is what you must say." Her eyes were fixed on Hugh. Neither of them saw Elisabeth leave the room. She didn't want to hear any more about a stupid church dispute. She knew that the trouble was serious, in that Hugh was being sacked as minister, that they would have to move as the house belonged to the Church. That much she knew. It was enough. She didn't need to know any more. She supposed that she would share in any discussions they might have about their future, although, in a way, that was irrelevant too. She would wait to find out what their plans were, and then decide what she would do. What would she do? No, don't think about it now. One more chapter of her current romance, and then sleep.

9

Elisabeth went reluctantly to church the following morning in order to support her father. She arrived early and sat near the back, hoping to remain unnoticed. She wore a headscarf pulled low over her forehead and kept her eyes downcast, not in humility but in order to keep her thoughts to herself, and with some childish idea that if she could not see people they could not see her. As the church filled, however, she was conscious of people looking in her direction, and knew that although a few were sympathetic most were suspicious. She had never made any effort to ingratiate herself with members of the church, and Rhoda had warned her that her hostility would cause problems for them all. Perhaps she had been right. Near the front of the church was a cluster of men whom she knew to be her father's enemies. The bare red brick building with its cheap benches and chairs had never seemed so harsh and unfriendly. She wished Antony was with her.

Against Rhoda's advice, Hugh preached a sermon based on the Sermon on the Mount, emphasising words like 'merciful', and 'peacemakers'. He spoke of the poverty and ignorance he saw all around him and of his belief that there were people who were led astray as a result, not of wickedness, but of poverty and ignorance.

"I cannot find it in myself to neglect these people," Hugh declared, "or to deny them the opportunity to be saved. Can any one of us claim to be so without sin that we can judge others?

"I myself have erred," Hugh continued, "I have not always been rigorous in following the word of the Lord but was tempted by the primrose path. Then, through my wife Rhoda, I was offered a second chance. She showed mercy in helping me see the error of my ways. That experience, I truly believe, has helped me to be your pastor. Surely we should rejoice that there are so many opportunities for bringing lost sheep into the fold. 'A city that is set on a hill cannot be hid'." There was a pause while Hugh gazed round the congregation. He lifted his arms. "I stand here before you, in all humility, acknowledging my human failings but assuring you that I never have, and never will, neglect you, my people. May God be my witness. Amen." He bowed his head. During the silence that followed Elisabeth knew that Hugh's acting skills had let him down. His passion seemed simulated, the words stale, and formulaic. He did not convince. He would be challenged.

The challenge came from a number of men known as the elders, sitting at the front of the church, who formed the equivalent of a committee overseeing the church and employing Hugh and Rhoda. Their leader was a man called Josiah Turner, who questioned Hugh's sincerity and his understanding of some of the Church's key beliefs, in particular the division, at Judgement Day, of people into the saved and the unsaved.

"This Church believes that salvation is for believers, that the ungodly will perish, thrown into the fires and torments of hell. There is no escape. No amount of remorse will save them. Do you believe this?" Josiah glared at Hugh.

Hugh could not – he simply could not – bring himself to agree with this.

"Jesus was clear that we should be merciful to sinners. He suffered for us, He died on the cross, He cannot have wished…"

"Do you believe that salvation is for the chosen and that the ungodly will perish? That on Judgment Day there will be a division of souls, with sinners cast into everlasting darkness. We believe this to be true. Do you share this belief? Will you put your hand on the Good Book and swear it?" Hugh was pressed on this point, over and over. He could not - he would not give up hope for sinners. How could he, a sinner himself. He pointed out that the Old Testament had been written by and for primitive peoples. The New Testament, through the words of Jesus and his disciples, offered hope of salvation.

"Are you denying the truth of the Old Book?"

"I think we have to acknowledge that things today…"

Josiah raised his arms. "Apostate!" he spat. "You are not fit to be our pastor."

Rhoda, aroused, came to stand by Hugh, accusing the elders of splitting the church in two. Her passion was unfeigned, her belief absolute. She would have made a better preacher than her husband. Her intervention, however, only confirmed the elders in their judgement that both Hugh and she were non-conforming, potentially heretical, a threat to the community. The decision was made. Hugh was to cease being pastor from that moment, and a further meeting, at which they would not be present, would decide whether the two of them should be expelled from the church altogether. Rhoda was outraged but the elders rose and left the church. Hugh took her hand and she stood by his side, her face red and her eyes very dark. One by one the congregation followed the elders out of the Church. Hugh and Rhoda waited until everyone had gone and then walked down the aisle,

325

Elisabeth joining them as they came alongside her. They walked home in silence.

Later, a small number of people called in at the house to offer sympathy, awkward and embarrassed because they had lacked the courage to stand by Hugh and Rhoda in public. Elisabeth felt sick with humiliation and rage - humiliation on behalf of her father, rage that, despite herself, she was unable to prevent herself from being drawn into the dispute. What did any of it matter, they were arguing about words, none of it meant anything. None of it was true. It was just a collection of stories. She handed round tea and slices of bread and margarine but took nothing herself because she felt too sick. She sat with the others in the tiny front room and tried not to listen to what was being said by using some mental tricks: counting up to a hundred and then down again, reciting in her head poetry or speeches from plays. The trick was less successful these days because she could rarely remember more than a couple of lines, and her frown of concentration was becoming increasingly a look of desperation. On this particular occasion that seemed appropriate.

Later that afternoon, she found an excuse to slip out to the telephone kiosk at the end of the street. She wanted to speak to Antony. She knew that he would worm out all the humiliating details and upset her, but she needed him. The red kiosk was the only colour in an otherwise grey street, and for once it was empty and the telephone working. She laid her coins carefully on top of the pile of tattered directories, and as it was the weekend dialled his home number. His mother answered the telephone. Her voice cooled when she heard who it was. "He was in this morning, but he said he was meeting a friend this afternoon. No, I can't tell you who it is."

Elisabeth apologised, and hung up. It was strange that Antony hadn't told her he was meeting someone; he usually took every opportunity to let her know that he was not reliant on her for his social life and also he knew that today was an important day for her. Elisabeth thought of the last time she had seen him and began to wonder if she wanted to speak to him after all. It was too soon. Tomorrow would do. She left the kiosk and walked slowly down the road. Half way back she realised that she had left some coins behind. She went back, but someone else was using the telephone. Peering in, she saw that her coins had disappeared. Sighing, she accepted defeat and went home.

Over the next few days discussions about their predicament continued. Although she knew that this affected her profoundly, Elisabeth's mind wandered off after a few minutes of hearing her stepmother outlining her latest scheme for re-establishing the Church in another part of London, and drifted haphazardly between Macbeth, Chaucer, and Antony. He did not return the message she had left with his mother and although it was difficult, because she had to use the library telephone, she made two or three further attempts. Eventually she managed to contact him in his digs but he said he was in the middle of a long essay and couldn't talk. Elisabeth, whose ability to concentrate on anything was very limited, was only slightly hurt. Presumably he had enjoyed their love-making as little as she had. She had wanted to talk to him that Sunday, to tell him about the trouble she and her family were in. But he had been out. She had coped, she had gone back home, cleared away the dishes, said goodbye to the visitors and sat quietly with Hugh and Rhoda until it was time for bed. She needed him less than she thought she did. She was no longer prepared to be analysed and criticised and then left to cope as best she could. To what purpose? Before she met him she had some sense of herself and what she might make of her life. Now she felt fluid as if she were made up of separate floating molecules. Nothing joined up, nothing made sense. It was like existing in a fog.

Her vagueness and passivity caused certain difficulties - like leaving her money in the telephone kiosk, or getting off at the wrong bus stop, or making mistakes with the reservation cards at work. The advantage was that Elisabeth was more relaxed than she had been for a long time. She was no longer fighting. She was discovering that struggling only prolonged the agony of drowning, and one might just as well lie back and let the water take over.

It was a several days before Elisabeth saw Antony again. Her parents were busy packing up the house and preparing to leave. One of their supporters, a neighbour, had offered to put them up for a time until they had found somewhere else to live, but there was no room for Elisabeth. She, too, must find some temporary digs. Forcing herself to think about this problem she remembered Antony saying that his landlady had a spare room which she rented out from time to time. Antony disliked this, as it meant sharing his bathroom and kitchenette. Elisabeth thought that she might be able to stay there for a week or two, until she could find something more permanent.

She put this to Antony almost as soon as they sat down with their coffee. Antony looked surprised, and then displeased. "I'm not sure that it's free," he muttered, and then, realising that Elisabeth knew that it was, "She doesn't really like having more than one lodger at a time. She only does it when she needs some extra cash."

"It would only be for a week or two. We're - I'm trying to find somewhere else. We have to get out."

"Isn't there anyone at work?"

"I haven't asked. I don't want to have to explain what it's all about."

"You could say you've had a row and want to get away from home."

Elisabeth in her strange passive state was not particularly concerned about Antony's reluctance to have her living with him.

"I could sleep on the floor where my parents are going. But they don't really want me there."

"So you won't be homeless," Antony said, sounding relieved. "Why don't you do that for a few days, then look out for something better? You keep saying you want to move into a flat. My place is too far from your work, anyway."

He had never shown such concern before. Their meetings had always been at places convenient to Antony.

"I thought you might like it," Elisabeth said.

"The fact is," he said, slightly uncomfortable, "it wouldn't suit. I really don't think it would suit. I mean, I have my own life to lead, and knowing you - I mean, I might want to see my friends and you might think - I like to be free, I don't want someone watching everything I do," he said, becoming irritated.

"Oh," Elisabeth said vaguely, not understanding.

"And I think I should tell you," he continued, buoyed up by his irritation, "that I don't think our relationship can continue as it was. I mean, I hope we'll see each other from time to time," (looking uncomfortable again) "but of course if you move to a different part of London it would be more difficult - the fact is, I'm seeing someone else. I was going to tell you. She's a bit possessive," he said smugly, "she doesn't really like me to have other women friends. The fact is, I think she and I are more suited than you and I will ever be. I'm sorry to leave you with your problems but you've always resisted me when I've tried to help. And I don't think you're ready for a sexual relationship just yet."

328

Elisabeth gazed into her coffee cup, trying to take this in.

"I don't understand," she said finally, and truthfully.

"Oh Christ," said Anthony. "Look, I'm going to have to be brutal. I'm seeing another woman. It's Sarah, you know. You met her. I like her a lot - well, she's more my type, we're equals in a way you and I never were. She's exciting, she's got ideas, she's just fun to be with. What I'm really saying is, I can't go on seeing you when I'm seeing her. It's not on."

Elisabeth said nothing.

"You could get in touch with Tim, now they've split up. You seemed to get on – mind you, I think he's met someone else."

Elisabeth set down her coffee cup. She understood that she had been jilted. She opened her bag, took out her purse, and counted out some coins.

"Oh for Christ's sake," said Anthony, "I'll pay for your coffee."

Ignoring him, she set the coins carefully on the table, then replaced the purse in her bag. She reached for her coat and pulled it on.

"Aren't you going to say anything? Look, don't take it so badly. You'll meet someone else. It was good while it lasted, wasn't it? I helped you come to terms with things, didn't I?" Ignoring him, she walked to the door. He came after her. "You're not going to do anything stupid, are you? I'd better come to the bus stop with you. Wait while I pay and get my coat. I'll catch up with you."

He never did. Elisabeth walked unhurriedly to the bus stop, caught the first bus that passed and made her unfeeling, unthinking, trance-like way home.

Once home, she went to that part of the kitchen cupboard where medicines were kept and looked through its contents. There were no sleeping pills, tranquillisers, or fashionable modern drugs - only a tin of Germolene, a roll of bandage, and a packet containing six Anadins. What did life mean when you were too poor to kill yourself?

She found a cup and filled it with water from the tap, then took the Anadins. That part of her mind which was still functioning told her that the most they would do would be to make her sleepy but that was better than nothing.

In bed, she turned over on to her left side, hugging her pillow, and slept. She was still in the same position when her father tried to wake her at 7.30 and again at 8 and 8.30. On this third attempt she did rouse, turn over, and gazed blearily out at a world that was becoming increasingly hostile.

"Darling, you have slept well. You must have been tired. You'll be late for work, you know. Will you get into trouble? Shall I come with you? I could say it was my fault, I forgot to put the alarm on."

"No, I'll get up - oh, I've such a headache."

"Poor darling. Would you like an Anadin? I'll put the kettle on for some tea. Rhoda's gone out."

"No, I haven't time, I'll just get dressed and go."

She had an almost overwhelming desire to put her head back on the pillows and sleep a little longer. Only the thought of upsetting her father made her move. She dragged herself to the bathroom where she was overtaken by nausea. Leaning against the basin she tried to be sick but all she could bring up, painfully, was bitter colourless bile. She had been hot, now she shivered uncontrollably. The tears which had run down her face while she was trying to be sick would not stop. Wet cheeked she staggered downstairs, called goodbye to her father, and left the house. 'Don't think, just don't think. Or think of something painless, a poem or what about that essay I'm supposed to be writing.' Sitting on the bus she gazed out of the window at the grey London streets and thought doggedly about metaphor. Language and meaning. Black and red, images of black and red. Her tutor had told her to think about imagery. It was a Scottish play – the Scottish play. Black velvet jacket and red tartan. Black lace and red nails, red lips - red hair? Black eyes and red lips, that was Rhoda. Rhoda as Lady Macbeth. Black meant sin, evil, guilt – why was Rhoda with her black hair and eyes righteous, and she with her red hair wicked? Guilt wasn't black, it was a more indeterminate colour. Wicked was black, sharp, bright - could black be bright? Yes of course, think of coal, not all coal, those pieces with minerals in. What minerals? No, she was drifting again. Move on to red. Red was blood. My mother killed herself. Blood on hands, those red finger nails again. The blood of a virgin. Blood to a woman meant so much more than it could to a man. Purging, cleansing. Funny that her periods had started again. Could Lady Macbeth have behaved as Shakespeare described it? Yes, of course, she had betrayed her sex, defiled the good blood, the cleansing, healing power with the murderous bloody knife.

Still thinking about literature, she got to her feet just as the bus came to a sudden unexpected stop. She lost her balance and fell against the window, banging her forehead. Someone with two strong arms would have been able to prevent themselves from falling, but her one good arm was holding her bag. She wanted to cry, as much from

330

the humiliation of falling as from the pain, but held it back. A couple of women came to see if she was alright; she muttered that she was and hurried away from them down the road to the library.

In the library cloakroom she took off her coat and put on her green nylon overall. She was only shelving that morning and she hoped that her lateness would go unnoticed. She pushed her trolley down to the far end of the library, and slid Dornford Yates and Emile Zola into their appropriate places. This part of the library was secluded and unpopular – for some reason the most popular authors had names starting with letters in the first part of the alphabet. She didn't know why. It was the sort of thing that would interest Antony – except that Antony wasn't around any more. Well, she wouldn't think about that. Down among these forgotten authors she felt secure. She didn't think she could bear to be on the issue counter at present.

She crouched down to shelve a last book and then stood up. As she did so she felt dizzy, and put her hand on a shelf to steady herself. The shelf felt sticky under her hand. She moved and saw that whatever had been on the shelf had transferred itself to her hand. It was red and sticky and looked like blood. She wiped her hand on her overall and looked at the shelf. It was blood, red, sticky blood, dripping from the shelf and onto the floor. Where had it come from? From her? She touched her head and her fingers came away bloody. Panicking, she wiped her hand again but it seemed that no sooner had she wiped away the blood than more came, now oozing out of her fingers. Her overall was stained with blood. It was everywhere. She reached out, and knocked over a pile of books. They stared up at her from the floor, all in paper covers, all depicting scenes of violence - murder, rape, torture - blood everywhere. Was there no end to the blood? It was trickling down her face, soon she would be drowning in it, it would be in her ears and her eyes. Elisabeth staggered to the opening of the book bay, and collapsed.

The next few days were confused. Real faces were confused with phantoms, nightmares with real journeys to doctors and hospitals. Most of the faces she didn't know. They belonged to bodies with white coats and capable hands. Sometimes they hurt. They pushed needles and tubes into her and made her do things she didn't want to do. They seemed to want her to talk but she had nothing to say. When, to please them, she tried to speak the words came out as gobbledegook. Phrases sometimes passed through her mind, but she was unable to form them with her mouth. Soon she gave up trying.

331

She was afraid, anyway, to open her mouth or her eyes in case the blood started flowing again. She didn't look at her hands. That blackout in the library had been truly black, empty, nothing. She longed to return to that state.

Despite herself, however, the days gradually took on some shape and meaning. She understood that she was in a hospital. She recognised her father and Rhoda when they came to see her, but turned her face away. The librarian's secretary came with flowers. The white coats took on individual faces, she noticed the other patients in the ward. She understood that the white coats were trying to help, trying to find out the cause of her blackout. They kept asking questions, lots of questions, and asked her to do simple tasks. She couldn't understand, she had blacked out because she hadn't had any breakfast that morning - and the blood, of course. She wondered if they had been able to clean it up. She worried about her overall. Would she have to pay to have it cleaned? She should have asked the librarian's secretary, she would know.

She got up, went to the bathroom, ate a little, felt sick. She was able to say if she was hungry, tired, cold. She was frightened to try anything more complicated, and pretended she didn't understand what people were saying to her. She was terrified of comprehension.

The second time her father came he was alone and when she saw him she cried, quietly, undramatically, but without ceasing. She, who used to pride herself on never crying! She could see that the crying upset him but she couldn't stop. One of the doctors, the young, worried-looking one, spoke to him. Hugh, who had tears in his own eyes, turned back to Elisabeth. "Mrs Fox," he began, using his pet name for her. Elisabeth continued to cry. "Darling, the doctor wants me to talk to you. Now, if you carry on crying you'll have me in tears, and that won't do, now will it?" Hugh's eyes glistened and his little sandy moustache quivered. "Now, between us we've come up with such a good idea, little Fox, Rhoda agrees as well, now tell me, just close your eyes and tell me where you'd like to be right now, where in the world would you really like to be?" Elisabeth turned her head into her pillow. Why was he saying this, what choice did she have? "Sweetheart, do try, do listen to me. You're upsetting your father, I can't bear to see you like this. Rhoda's upset, they think you haven't had enough to eat, they think we've neglected you. We told them you're tired, we know that, you've been studying and working and it's been too much. And a boyfriend too – has he been to see you? Now,

Lizzie, please don't start crying again. We're all agreed, hospital isn't the place for you, not any longer. They've done what they can, but they say you're not ill but you're tired, you need a rest. Now, as you know, just at the moment it's a little difficult for us to give you that, so what do you think I've done?" Elisabeth's attention was sliding away. So many words, why did her father use so many words? Hugh, pleased with his new role, the concerned father, concentrated on finding the words, getting the tone right, and failed to notice her lack of attention. He continued talking, eyes bright, lips red and glossy under his moustache. She focused again to hear him say "And Lesley and Chris will drive you there."

"What?"

"They have a little car now, a mini, all the rage, you know."

"No." Elisabeth twisted her head on her pillow.

"Darling..."

"Please..."

"But, darling, I thought you'd be happy. The doctor says you need a rest. We thought you'd like to go to Yorkshire for a while, until Rhoda and I get ourselves sorted out. You can write to your boyfriend, tell him what's happening, I'll post it. Darling, I thought it was the answer. I thought everyone would be happy. Lizzie?" Hugh's shoulders drooped, his eyes lost their brightness, his lips seemed to lose colour.

Elisabeth couldn't bear to disappoint her father. But neither could she bear the thought of Chris seeing her in this state. And Lesley being kind and, oh, patronising. She had always found Lesley patronising. That was so unfair. The thought of being secure and cared for was an enormous relief but it was like going backwards, being a child again, being dependent, admitting she had failed. "I've spoken to Irene, they are looking forward to having you." Her mind ran around inside her head, trying to find a way out. She settled on something that had been worrying her.

"The library?"

"They'll give you leave for three months, so you don't need to worry about that."

She was still worried. "My overall?"

"What?"

"The blood. There was so much blood."

"Darling, you cut your head, we don't know how, do you remember? Then it must have bled, I expect you got some on your overall. Someone will have washed it, don't worry about that."

"But.." Elisabeth was confused about what had happened but she was sure about the blood. There had been a lot of it. Just as there had been when she and Antony had sex. She'd been thinking about Lady Macbeth, who had red finger nails – no, that didn't make sense. None of it made sense. She closed her eyes again. The only thing that did make sense was that she was going home to Aireton.

10

Lesley and Chris collected Elisabeth from the hospital and drove her to Yorkshire. Her father came with them to the hospital, bringing a suitcase. He hugged her and fussed over her, telling her he would see her again soon, and she wasn't to worry, and she must give his love to Irene and Phyllis. It was like ten years ago all over again.

The journey was a nightmare. The car was a mini, small, noisy and uncomfortable. Every bump in the road could be felt. Elisabeth's limbs ached and her head ached and at times she felt overcome with claustrophobia because of the smallness of the car and the enormity of the vehicles around them. The only good thing about it was that it was too noisy to hear what was said in the front and Chris and Lesley soon abandoned attempts at making polite conversation. Elisabeth lay on the back seat, pulling a rug over her head, and tried to forget everything.

Their arrival, in the dark, was confusion. Her aunt Irene was there to meet her and she was bundled upstairs into bed; time passed and she was conscious of little other than light, dark, unwelcome food and the occasional need, which she put off for as long as possible, to drag herself out of bed and to the bathroom. She was still afraid that she might start bleeding again. She remembered little of what had actually happened but was very conscious of the fact that she had been as low as she had ever been – sick, tearful, unable to look after herself - and had been rescued by Lesley and Chris. Thinking of it was intolerable so she pushed the memory away. She continued to feel sick. Her aunt came and went, her uncle looked in, then went away. A doctor came - she knew it was a doctor from the faint smell of antiseptic that came into the room with him. She kept her eyes closed and said nothing. She was given pills that were hard to swallow and made her gag but she took them because she was told to. She was no longer capable of making decisions for herself.

Some time later (she had lost all track of time) she woke up without her usual feeling of dread and fear. She had slept well with no dreams that she could recall and felt rested for the first time in months. It was late - 10 o'clock she saw from the clock by her bed - and the house was silent. There was something different about the day. She lay still, mentally tasting the strangeness and wondering what it was. She noticed a bar of golden light on her pillow. Slowly she put out a finger and touched it. It felt warm. Pulling herself up she ran her tongue round the inside of her mouth, which felt rough and dry and swallowed with difficulty and distaste. She followed the bar of light to a gap in the curtains. She crawled to the edge of her bed, peered through the gap and looked out onto a garden. The sun shone from a newly washed pale blue sky, across which trailed a few strands of white cloud. Looking down she saw yellow flowers, which after some effort she identified as daffodils, nodding about the edges of the lawn, and a great splash of more strident yellow she remembered was forsythia. Other trees and shrubs, encouraged by the warmth of the sun, bore delicate nets of palest green. From somewhere came memories of April, fragments of poetry "when that fair April with her showers sweet...." "oh to be in England..."

Across the blackness of Elisabeth's misery and despair lay a thin, fragile band of light, like the sunshine on her pillow. So fragile that even as she looked it moved away, leaving only the dark. But it had been there. She looked out of the window again, letting the peace of the view soothe her and comfort her. She gazed again at the spring garden, knowing it to belong to the house in Sycamore Avenue, unable to resist memories of other springs, when she had been just an innocent child. She was back with the Atfields, back in her old attic bedroom. Tears started to form, but tears coming from an appreciation of beauty, and nostalgia, rather than grief.

To her left was the roof of the back porch. Gazing down, she could just make out what appeared to be a pair of feet, sticking out from the doorway. A hand appeared from time to time, hovering over a white bowl which stood fully in the sunshine. As she watched church bells began to ring. Elisabeth drew back her head, caught in a complex mesh of emotions - distaste, nostalgia, love, pity - sadness for herself. Of course it was Sunday, and not only was it Sunday, she remembered her aunt telling her last night that it was Easter Sunday. No wonder the house was quiet - they were all at church. All except for the person sitting in the doorway. Curiosity created another chink of light as she wondered who it was. Lesley? Her aunt? Her grandmother? But Irene rarely missed church, and had she been at home would surely have been up to see Elisabeth by now. They were certainly female legs. Heather was away. She wasn't sure whether Lesley had returned to London. Perhaps a neighbour had agreed to come in to keep an eye on her while they were all out. How humiliating that would be!

As she watched the legs withdrew, and then the whole figure moved into view, into the sunshine, stretched and yawned. It was

Phyllis, her aunt Phyllis. Elisabeth felt relief. Phyllis was gentle and undemanding, and Elisabeth loved her without reserve. (Her feelings for Irene were always mixed). She wanted to speak to her, but shrank from attempting it. She sat on her bed and worried. The thought of going downstairs filled her with panic, and yet she did want to see her aunt. And it was time for another pill. Two had been laid out beside a glass of water on the dressing table. That must be Auntie Irene's doing; she was taking no chances. She picked them up, laid them on her palm, and studied them. White, oval - no, oblong with rounded corners. Pretty little innocent little pills. Were these what her mother had taken? Elisabeth picked up the capsules, put them on her tongue, then took a gulp of water. She sat back against the pillows, and waited for the panic to subside, her heartbeat to slow down, the tension to leave her head. She would feel calmer soon. She wondered what to do next. Should she get up and surprise her aunt? That would mean leaving the safety of her little attic room. She could start by getting dressed. She supposed she had brought some clothes with her. Still undecided, she swung her feet off the bed, intending to go to the bathroom. As she opened her door she heard footsteps coming up the stairs, and Phyllis's fluffy fair head, now tinged with grey, appeared over the banister rail. She gave a great start to see Elisabeth standing in her nightie in the doorway.

"Oh, Elisabeth dear, you gave me a shock. You look like a little ghost standing there. I came tiptoeing up to see if you were still asleep - I didn't expect you to be up."

"I'm sorry - bathroom - I didn't mean - I'm sorry," Elisabeth, shocked at her aunt's shock, became tearful. She retreated to her bed. Phyllis followed her and sat down at the foot.

"It's silly of me, I somehow thought you'd be asleep, my nerves are all on edge, I haven't seen you for such a long time and you look - oh, Elisabeth, you look so ill. What have they done to you, you poor little thing. You were just a child when you left, all those years ago. You mustn't ever go away again, we need you here. I can't bear the way everyone has gone - just Irene and me and Bertrand and Allan plodding on. And Mother of course." Elisabeth began to cry, and Phyllis took her in her arms - the first time in a long while that anyone had shown her such natural, instinctive affection. They wept together, and talked of Pattie.

"We think she's in London – I thought she might try to contact you. She's never given an address. Lesley thought she saw her on Top of the Pops but it was only a glimpse. Irene wrote to the BBC but they didn't reply. For a time I thought – oh, you can imagine. All the horrors you read about, I thought they might be happening to her. It's her father, I know - she won't come back because she thinks he'll be angry with her. If only she knew, he's a different man now - so quiet. He didn't realise – they just worked each other up. She can't be so hard hearted, she must know what I'm suffering – I just feel so helpless. If she only knew how it brings everything back! We've tried everything. All those years we've missed! Oh, my baby!"

After a while, Phyllis sat up, sniffing and feeling up her sleeve for a handkerchief. "This won't do, I'm supposed to be looking after you, not the other way round. It's just, looking at you - we've all changed so much, do you remember how happy we were, when you were all children? I'll make a cup of tea - do you want it up here or downstairs? Irene said I should encourage you to come down if you feel like it. I've been sitting in the porch - it's sunny and sheltered there. You can come in your dressing gown if you like."

Elisabeth hesitated. "The others?"

"They'll be an hour or so. You can come back upstairs then if they're too much for you."

Elisabeth consented to have her coat put round her shoulders and to be led downstairs, through the kitchen to the porch. It was good sitting there in the sun, with no noise to disturb but the sounds of distant children playing and the songs of the birds.

"We're going to have a good summer this year, to make up for the last few, I'm sure of it," said her aunt, returning with the tea. "Just listen to the birds, they think so too."

She sat beside Elisabeth, talking nervously and intermittently. Elisabeth said little but felt - if not at peace, as if peace might be a possibility. That feeling lasted perhaps twenty minutes. Then, she began to feel nervous about facing the rest of the family. She jumped up when she heard a car and scurried back upstairs.

That day was the start of Elisabeth's recovery. Progress was slow but gradually she grew stronger, and less fearful. The outside world no longer seemed overwhelming, chaotic, terrifying, but divided into areas in which she needed to take an interest, and others. The morning light woke her and when her aunt flung open the curtains, as she always did, she noticed the day, whether it was grey or bright, breezy or still, and the sounds which she had heard but taken little account of became associated with people leaving for work, her aunt clattering dishes in the kitchen, visitors, the telephone. Her daily absorption in the patterns in the wall paper, and the texture of her bed cover, moved, almost against her will, to an interest in the leaves on the tree outside her bedroom, the songs of the birds, and the pattern of the sunlight. Outside her window was a birch tree and she observed the fat little catkins and the fresh green of the young leaves. Spring, ridiculous, glorious spring was all about her and it was hard to resist. Re-awakening was painful, however. The soft unfurling of the early leaves, the joyful birds, the soft spring sunlight, were at times almost more than she could bear and the unnameable, unspeakable anguish returned, a burning mixture of anger and jealousy and misery and desolation. There was also a kind of terror that she had lost something which had been very precious to her, something to do with her sense of self. It manifested itself in an inability to do those things that she had once enjoyed – to think rationally, to act independently, and to read and take pleasure in learning. There were some days when, if the house was empty of visitors, she could get up and go downstairs, but there were also other days when she kept to her bed as the only safe place in a tormented and tormenting world. The first time she regressed, her aunt Irene, practised in dealing with physical illness but unused to mental problems, told her she must get up; later she became more sympathetic. She made efforts to be more understanding and her rational, undemonstrative, practical good sense helped Elisabeth's recovery. Her uncle Bertrand, though friendly, kept his distance. He had always been uncomfortable with illness of any kind, and there was a tacit understanding that dealing with men was something she might have difficulty with. Her father had come once, she thought, during the bad time; she seemed to remember him giving her a hug and yet again she had burst into heavy weeping that wouldn't stop. At one time she would have taken any opportunity to see him, but now she felt distanced from him; much as she loved him he was part of the bad times. It was unfair, it was almost intolerable, but it was so. She had no idea how things were with Rhoda and the church, and didn't want to know. Her life was separated into before and after breakdown, and for the time being she wanted to keep it that way.

The doctor she saw was not the one she had known as a child, but young and energetic and modern in outlook. He didn't regard her breakdown as being shameful, but as an illness that needed treatment in order for her to get better. He told her that just as there was pain associated with the knitting together of flesh and bones after an accident, so there was pain in mending mental wounds. This image made sense to Irene and was something Elisabeth could accept, although it left a great deal unclear. He took away some of her pills and gave her different ones to help her to eat. She still found it difficult to swallow food, and was extremely thin. She was so alarmed at the suggestion that she might see a psychiatrist that he didn't pursue it, although he told her she would eventually have to come to terms with the events that had led to her breakdown. This seemed too close to Antony and his brutal attack on her sensitivities (which she had told nobody about). She wasn't ready for further intrusion although she was aware that Antony had been a clumsy amateur and talking to a professional could be very different. Irene, whose view was that Elisabeth's collapse was entirely due to over work, poor living conditions and difficulties with Rhoda and her father, intervened to say that she was sure that a quiet summer with the family would make all the difference.

Phyllis visited regularly and stayed when Irene went to London to visit Lesley and Chris. She treated her niece gently, almost timidly, but seemed to enjoy talking to her and rarely demanded a response, unlike her more forthright sister. She talked of herself, her husband, her job, Pattie. She spoke with innocent candour and Elisabeth learned that Bernard was having problems at work, and Irene was worried about Heather, now teaching in Africa, that Mrs Lindsey was getting increasingly forgetful. Pattie's continued absence, of course, caused grief to the whole family. Only Lesley and Chris, now married, were secure, settled, and successful.

Between them, the sisters were able to give Elisabeth some peace and security. She was less comfortable with her uncles (indeed, she saw Allan only once during her first month at Sycamore Avenue). However, she found ways of being useful to Bertrand and with a role she relaxed more. He had always been careless and his worries at work caused him to become more absent minded at home. One day he lost his spectacles, and turned the house upside down searching for them. It was Elisabeth who found them, on top of a large flower pot in the corner of the patio where he had earlier been reading the newspaper and enjoying the spring sunshine. After that she became the finder of mislaid articles, and the writer of reminder notes, even, sometimes, checking his diary.

She went with Irene to visit her grandmother in her flat. Initially Mrs Lindsey had difficulty remembering who Elisabeth was; when she

340

did remember she made critical comments about Hugh, referring to him as 'that wicked boy'. It was some time before the visit was repeated.

Later, Irene encouraged Elisabeth to speak to the people who called at the house, neighbours and friends from church, who remembered her as a child. The story they gave was that she had become over tired in London and needed a complete rest. This was accepted; local people knew full well that London was a terrible place to live. Returning to the north was the only sensible thing to do, and there was an assumption that this was where she would stay. Elisabeth found these meetings difficult, but people remembered her shyness and were not surprised when she slipped away after a few minutes. The fact that she was able to meet them at all was a sign that the world hadn't stopped and there was life outside her bedroom. Chris's parents, who had moved to York, came to Aireton one day. They knew something of the background, and were sensitive and tactful, and responsive to any hesitations or cues provided by either Elisabeth or Irene. She found this exquisite tact both touching and irritating. Cynthia, now engaged to the ex-curate, now vicar, at Aireton parish church, came one day, spoke patronisingly to Elisabeth, expressed admiration for Heather, spoke at length about the many demands on her time, and drifted off. Irene, who always blamed her for Heather's decision to teach abroad, did not encourage her to stay.

The weather stayed fine. Elisabeth walked in the garden and enjoyed the sun on her face. She absorbed the warmth and felt herself expand. Her aunt, hating to see anyone idle, set her to gardening work, and Elisabeth, after an initial panic that she didn't know what to do, became almost obsessively caught up with it. Irene and Bertrand were relieved to see her happily employed. They found a bed that needed digging over, and she was told that she could fill it with whatever plants she wanted. She ventured into town with her aunt and bought several packets of seeds in Woolworths – lupins, lobelias, nasturtiums, stock. Her uncle showed her how to sow the seeds in trays before transplanting them, and she got real pleasure from laying them in the compost (she handled even the tiniest of seeds one at a time; scattering from the packet was too coarse a method for her). The feel of the soil in her fingers was satisfying. She visited her trays every day, and was thrilled when she saw the first green shoots, so fine that they were almost invisible unless you looked at them from an angle. Bertrand had always been the gardener in the family, and

Elisabeth's new enthusiasm brought them closer together. It was a distraction from the things she could no longer do, like reading. Books gave her a kind of vertigo. Thoughts of her abandoned A levels caused real panic so she put them out of her mind.

One evening Irene had a telephone call from Chris's parents to say that their other son, Colin, who was a trainee social worker, wanted to know if he could see Elisabeth. For once Irene chose to ignore Elisabeth's pleading face and said "That would be nice - we haven't seen him for a while. Just a short visit, mind - Elisabeth tires easily."

Some evenings she and Bertrand played simple games together, like snakes and ladders, and snap, and old maid, while Irene sewed or knitted. Bertrand said he enjoyed playing as it took his mind off work. It was on one of these evenings that Colin joined them. Elisabeth's first reaction was resentment at this intrusion into her quiet uneventful life. Colin, however, was at least as nervous as she was, so anxious to do and say the right thing that he became clumsy, tripping over the rug and jolting the table with his knee as he sat down so that the dice which they had been shaking fell onto the floor and under the settee. He blushed, furiously, as they all got up and pushed the settee back so that the dice could be retrieved. Elisabeth found herself feeling sorry for him, and forgot her resentment, and gradually they both relaxed and played their games with the enthusiasm of children, while Bertrand quietly withdrew into his study.

A few days later Colin called again, bringing with him a book on gardens. Elisabeth took little notice at first, but her uncle was soon drawing her attention to the illustrations "Look at this! formal borders enclosing cottage garden planting. And this archway made out of a yew hedge, with a statue at the end - I wonder if Lesley could make us one. We must have a yew hedge." When Bertrand was enthusiastic he was hard to resist. "What do you think, Elisabeth?"

"Perhaps the rough patch at the bottom could be a kind of grotto, with a winding path leading to it." Elisabeth pointed to another illustration.

"Hidden by shrubs and trees - good idea! Irene..." and he was away, his old self again, work forgotten. Elisabeth persuaded herself that Colin's visits were helpful to her uncle, and viewed them more favourably. She looked through the pictures in his book with interest. Then she read the notes on the pictures to see where the gardens were. Then, one day, she asked if she might take the book up to her room at night, and gradually began dipping into the text. The book was undemanding, and she was relieved to find that the words no longer jumped around on the page. Finishing it, and finding herself hungry for more information, she asked her aunt if she could borrow more gardening books from the library, and was soon absorbed in these. Colin went back to work, but Elisabeth's reading continued.

11

By the time she had been with the Atfields for three months, Elisabeth was looking much better. Although her appetite remained small she was eating and not feeling sick after every meal. She was able to go shopping with Irene, and talk to people outside her immediate family. The tranquillisers and sleeping pills had been reduced. The panic attacks occurred less frequently. She still cried, too easily, particularly at night when she wrapped the bedclothes over her head so that no one could hear. A period of bad weather, when she could not go into the garden, induced a black depression which was difficult to cope with.

During this time Mrs Lindsey fell and broke her hip; just as Irene was making plans for bringing her to live permanently at Sycamore Avenue she had a stroke, and died in hospital. This was a great shock to everyone, and Elisabeth was forced out of her self absorption. Her feelings were mixed; she was as shocked as the rest of the family by the relative suddenness of her grandmother's death, although guiltily relieved that they would not be living in the same house. She had resented Mrs Lindsey's frequent criticisms of Hugh. It was, however, hard to imagine a world without her, despite the fact that they had not been close and her own sadness was no more than this. Unable to pretend to feelings she did not have, she busied herself with practical activities, and did what she could to help her grieving aunts.

She kept to herself worries about her own future. The library had initially given her three months' sick leave, which had been extended to four. She was now starting the fourth month and before long a decision would have to be made. Should she go back to her old job or - what? She hated the thought of returning, but she couldn't stay with the Atfields for ever. Whatever she did she had to pay her way, and this meant a job. But a job meant finding somewhere to live. She worried about this, lost her appetite again and slept badly. The panic attacks grew worse, but she couldn't tell anyone what was causing them. She became obsessed with the idea of becoming financially independent.

She knew, however, that she did not want to go back. The memory of what she had left filled her with dread - that grubby, grey, deprived area of London with its boarded-up windows, hopeless looking people, sordid pubs, dirty streets, and the library with its grubby dog-eared books. But she couldn't stay where she was, dependent on other people. She had to earn her living.

One grey, cool day, with dampness in the air and low horizons, she and Colin went for a walk. They both wore raincoats. Elisabeth was unenthusiastic about the walk. She would have preferred to stay indoors, leafing through gardening catalogues. Since her illness she had difficulty in disguising her feelings and she trudged along, hands in pockets, head down, red hair swinging in front of her face, making no effort at conversation. Colin glanced down at her as they walked along, but he respected her silence. (His tact irritated her sometimes but his ability to keep quiet was, she had to admit, was one of his strongest points).

Out on the moor they rested on a seat for a while. It was a place she used to love, on the grassy lower slopes, with the high heather- and bracken-clad moors behind and fields in front. Between moor and fields was a rocky decline, then an old farm built of stone with scattered out-buildings and dry stone walls enclosing fields. Beyond the farm were woods and although it couldn't be seen, a peaty brown stream. In the spring the woods were full of bluebells.

Today, however, the view failed to bring her peace. She swung her feet and gazed at the ground immediately in front of the seat which had been scuffed by many hundreds of feet over the years. Further away the quaking grass was covered with tiny specks of moisture, adding a lace-like quality. Nothing moved, apart from some hikers against the sky on the hill, and the only sound was from the sheep or the occasional, distant, car. Colin said to her gently in his flat Northern voice "You seem a bit down in the dumps. I know you are upset about your grandmother. Is there anything else?"

"No," said Elisabeth, then, feeling the need to say something more, "I'm alright."

"Gloomy weather," said Colin, trying to feel her mood.

"I like it," said Elisabeth perversely, pulling up the hood of her macintosh.

"Suits your mood?"

"Maybe."

"Anything I can do to improve matters?"

"I don't suppose even you can make the sun shine."

"No. I suppose that was a silly thing to say. Is there anything you want to talk about, or shall we just discuss the weather?"

"If you've brought me here because you feel sorry for me you can just take me straight back again," Elisabeth said with sudden annoyance. But she stayed seated, scuffing her feet in the sandy soil.

"I'm not here because I'm sorry for you but because I enjoy your company. Only I don't think you're enjoying mine at the moment."

"It's not that," Elisabeth said with difficulty. She nearly said "I like you as much as anyone," which would have been true, but she didn't want to encourage him. Better all round if he would just go away and leave her alone. She said, trying it out:

"I shall be going away soon - this might be our last walk."

"What do you mean? Where are you going?"

"Back to London. I've got to go back to work."

"You can't go back there," he said, shocked.

"Why not?"

"Well - I suppose I assumed you'd settled here. And anyway - you weren't very happy, were you? Surely you're happier here."

Inside her mac Elisabeth shrugged thin shoulders. "That's irrelevant. It's where I live. It's where my job is. I have to work."

"I hadn't thought - but where will you live? Where are your father - and stepmother - now?"

"I shan't live with them. I'll find somewhere to live. I have to earn my living."

"Your uncle and aunt..."

Elisabeth's lips set in a stubborn line. "They've done too much for me already. I can't be dependent on them any longer."

"But they want you - they miss having family around. I think your aunt was really quite worried about your uncle at one point. He's been much more cheerful since you arrived."

The sky was overcast and as she turned her head away from him she saw a band of dark cloud moving across the moor from the north. Elisabeth pulled her hood forward. Sometimes the moors were too dark, too massive, too dominating.

"It's going to rain, we'd better move."

Colin remained seated. "Lizzie, tell me the truth - I won't pass it on or try to make you do anything but - do you really want to leave? I mean, I can understand you want to be independent but - if there were a choice of jobs, here and in London, which would you choose?"

Well, what would she do? Here there was fresh air and space, but also a kind of exposure; people knew her – or thought they knew her – too well. There was noise and dirt and anonymity. Here was safety, security, kindness, but on her side, dependency. In London was her father, and Chris, though she did her best not to think of him. And perhaps Pattie was also there. But also her stepmother, Antony – no, she wouldn't think of him. "I don't know. Don't ask me." She was crying, angry with herself for her weakness. Awkwardly, Colin put his arm round her and patted her damp plastic shoulder. The top of the hood rubbed against his face.

"Lizzie, it's too soon. You've been ill. Maybe you can cope with a job but not a job and London. Perhaps you can get something part-time here, something not too demanding, just to get you back into work. I know your uncle and aunt love having you. Their whole life was their children and now they've gone. They rattle about in that big house, you know that, they love having you there. And since your grandmother died..."

The plastic hood nodded and scratched his chin.

"It's like convalescence for you now - you're frustrated because it's slow and it's painful but it is necessary for the future. You need longer. Trust me, Lizzie, please."

She pulled herself out of his arms but stayed close while she felt in her pocket for a handkerchief. Then she said, not looking at him, "I'm frightened, you see. I don't know if I can cope at work. I have to try. I thought it might be easier to go back to the old job - I might remember. I'm scared - my mind doesn't seem to work properly. I'm not quiet because I'm unhappy - not always anyway - but because I can't talk. I can't. I have nothing to say. I can't think like I used to."

"You will. Just think convalescence, think "I'm getting better." Set yourself little tasks, little challenges. Read things that are easy, short - poetry maybe. And Lizzie - don't be cross but why not talk to your doctor again? See if he can find anyone for you to talk to - a therapist or someone like that. It might help you to - I dunno - pull things together a bit."

"Maybe." Elisabeth was beginning to regret she had said so much. And yet - it hadn't hurt, really, talking to Colin. And she had expressed herself reasonably clearly. But it was enough. She stood up.

"It's time to go back."

"OK." He followed her down the rocky path to the old iron gate which led off the moors. They walked back through the fields in the fine rain, Colin talking of his work and the people he met while out in the community helping his father, and Elisabeth thought of her life and how to get it back together, and how it all seemed far too much for one person to deal with.

Between 5-6pm was always a quiet time in the library, between the shoppers and the students, now going home for tea, and the office and shop workers, still covering typewriters and tills and putting files away. The library assistants, in green overalls, moved unhurriedly between the high wooden shelves, sorting and straightening. One girl, small and slim with a pale grave face and long auburn hair, sat at the enquiries desk talking to an elderly man with a keen interest in railways. Why, he wanted to know, did the library not stock a larger selection of books on railways? By the very nature of things they traversed the country so why nothing on cuttings in Devon and Cornwall, not to mention the Settle line north of Carlisle? Elisabeth replied patiently that they had to stock books according to the needs of the local community, and on the whole people in Bradford were not much interested in reading about railways. Yes, she agreed, it was odd. However, she added, not for the first time, books not in stock could generally be ordered from another library. Next time he came into the library he should bring with him his railway enthusiasts' magazine, and they would look at the book reviews together. The old man, who lived alone and whose interest was as much in conversation with another human being as in railways finally shuffled off, satisfied.

Elisabeth stood up and stretched. That particular old man came in two or three times a week, and always made a beeline for Elisabeth. He liked her quietness and willingness to listen. It was difficult sometimes when she was at the issue desk at busy times of the day, but he had come to know the library timetable quite well by now, and waited for her to be free to talk to him.

She had written to her old library, saying that she felt unable to return, and giving in her notice. Instead, she had found part-time work first of all in the Aireton branch library, and then in the central library in Bradford. She had extended her hours and intended to work full time as soon as she could. This meant that she would be able to pay her way at home.

Elisabeth's health had continued to improve in the months since she had started work. She had not followed Colin's advice about seeing her doctor again, but she had found a book about overcoming depression, and although she found it difficult to read, Colin had helped her to work through some of the suggestions it made. She had started to keep a diary in which she recorded anything that occurred to her during the day, from small domestic irritations to reflections on her own psychological and mental state. Physically, she was better than she had been for years. She would always have her slight build, but there was flesh on her limbs and her cheeks were no longer hollow and sunken. She would always be pale but the bloodless pallor of earlier days had changed to a healthy looking ivory skin. In the opinion of most people, she had returned to normal. London was blamed by many people for Elisabeth's breakdown, London and her unstable father and peculiar stepmother.

Only those who knew Elisabeth very well knew how much she had changed. Phyllis said "Elisabeth doesn't have any go any more." The strong will she had shown as a child had weakened under the strain of her years in London. She was no longer sure of her own wants and needs, and was, on the whole, content to follow other people. To say that she had lost her interest in living did not mean that she wanted to die, but she had no real interest in life. Being kind to old men was easy, on balance she preferred people to be happy rather than unhappy, but it was of no real concern to her. She could not understand Colin's drive to help people and improve the world.

She continued to worry about what she felt was a kind of softening of the brain, an inability to think clearly. Colin was convinced that her present lack of intellectual curiosity was the result of eroded confidence, and would return. He was trying to nudge her into taking up her A Level studies again, but Elisabeth was reluctant to do this.

After the rift in the church, the relationship between Hugh and Rhoda had deteriorated. Rhoda wanted to move to Essex, and reform the church from there. Hugh did not want to do this. As his daughter suspected, religious belief did not go very deep with him. One day, shortly after Elisabeth's breakdown, he met an old actor friend in a pub who had pointed out to him that in middle age he could become a 'type', with fewer competitors and potentially more interesting parts than the young romantic hero he had always aspired to be. He acted on the advice, visited his old agent, went to some auditions and to his surprise and delight a new career opened up for him, primarily in television. The husband next door, the bumbling detective, the hapless father of teenagers, the luckless employee - never the lead but always memorable in the roles. He had just signed a contract for a comedy series, which looked as if it could have a long run. The series was about girls living in a flat and Hugh played the father of one of them, a soft touch, someone to be called on in the middle of the night to rescue the girls from the scrapes they kept falling into. Rhoda had gone to Essex and he was living the way he knew best, out of a suitcase. He came to Aireton for his mother's funeral and they talked of Elisabeth spending a weekend with him without making firm plans. She was content.

As she got up from the enquiries desk and stretched, she noticed a woman talking to Gerry, on the issue counter. Gerry was pointing to her. The woman, blonde, wearing high heels and a fake fur jacket, had a small child strapped to her back and was holding a little boy by the hand. She came across the floor towards Elisabeth, who froze. For a moment she wondered if she were suffering another mental collapse.

"Pattie!" she said. "My God, Pattie, is it really you?"

"Hi there," Pattie said, as if she had only been gone a few days. "How're ya doin'? This is Paul. Say hello to your aunt Elis'beth, Paul. Bet that makes you feel old. Oh don't be silly, he can say it perfectly well when he wants. This one's Nalini." She turned so that Elisabeth could see her, then pulled the sling off her shoulders. "I'll put her down, she's getting heavy, so's my bag. There you are, petal. Paulie, why don't you go and look at some books - is there somewhere he can play?"

"There's a children's corner," said Elisabeth, weakly. "Oh Pattie! I thought I might never see you again." She had gone very pale. She put her arm round her cousin's neck and clung to her, tears flowing down her cheeks. Pattie let go of Paul's hand gave her a big hug in return, stepping carefully over the baby on the floor.

"Sorry," said Elisabeth, feeling in her overall pocket for a handkerchief. "How did you know I was here?"

"I bumped into your father."

"My *father*?"

"Yeah. I was going to Top of the Pops and got to the studios early so I went to the canteen and there was your dad. I recognised him straightaway, because of the telly. He's making quite a name for himself, isn't he? Anyway, he brought me up to date with everything. I'm sorry about Granny, I should've come to see her."

"It's been difficult." Elisabeth felt as if she were in one of her father's domestic dramas herself. "Look, Pattie, if we stay here we'll be interrupted - there's a tea room, we should be able to find a corner to ourselves. Only I've only got 15 minutes."

"Okey dokey. Shall I bring him?"

Paul was sucking the corner of a book.

"You'd better."

Upstairs in the tea room, Elisabeth gazed at her cousin. Pattie looked older than her - Elisabeth worked it out - 24 years. She was thin, and looked pale under the carelessly applied makeup. Elisabeth could see little lines under her eyes and around her mouth. But the eyes themselves were as blue and bright as ever as she looked round the room, talked to the children, threw in vague references to her life, and finally brought her attention to rest on her cousin.

"Your dad said you'd been ill?"

"Yes - but I'm alright now. That's why I'm here - it all happened at once - my parents - they left the church they were in, and then they split up and I became ill. I think that's how it happened. It's all a bit hazy. I prefer not to think about it. I'm glad to be out of London."

"I like London - well, when I've got some money. It's not so good when you haven't." Elisabeth had found some milk for Paul, which he was now dribbling on to the table and spreading with his fingers. Pattie regarded him with affection. The little girl was gurgling to herself. Pattie reached down to tickle her ear.

"I'll have to get back to work soon," Elisabeth said. She reached out to touch her cousin – she wanted to hug her again but the bleak tea room with its formica topped tables and chipped blue crockery, and inquisitive glances from regular users stopped her. "Oh Pattie - why did you never get in touch? We all - I missed you so much. We tried to reach you. We did everything we could think of. We even tried the Sally Army, and had a record played for you on Radio Luxembourg."

"Did you?" Pattie said, impressed. "I had a boyfriend once who worked for Radio Luxembourg. Well, I say boyfriend, I only saw him twice. Don't put it on your hair or you'll have to wash it." This to Paul, who was dribbling milk on to his hair. Other staff were coming in and casting disapproving glances in their direction.

Pattie lifted wide blue eyes to her cousin. "You know how it is, I kept meaning to but the time was never quite right, and then time went on and I thought - well, what can I say? I knew my dad would be angry and I didn't want to upset my mum. I did send her postcards to let her know I wasn't dead or anything, but even then I couldn't think what to say. I was never any good at writing. And then I had to keep moving around, you know, to dodge the welfare."

Elisabeth felt a great sadness for Pattie, but all she said was:

"Have you been home?"

"Yeah, well - no, I thought I'd see you first, just see how things are. I wasn't sure what sort of a reception I'd get. Your dad said it might be best."

"Your father doesn't get so angry about things. I think he sees - well, that it's your mother who suffers. She's been so unhappy. It'll be a shock for them."

"Yes, I s'pose. P'raps I should have written first. Only, well, seeing your dad and hearing about Granny, and then money was getting a bit low. And I thought, it's been a long time, I've got kids now, time to come back. Thought I'd surprise everyone."

"It's been so long. Oh Pattie we've missed you! Your poor mother."

"Yeah. I never meant to leave it so long. I'm going there now, I thought you might come with me. It's the kids really. I don't know how they'll take it. Especially the baby. Her father is Indian, you see, and she looks like him. He had to go back to his family in India, but he wants me to join him. So I've got to find some work and save up enough money to go."

"And Paul's father?" Elisabeth asked tentatively, glancing down at the blue eyed, blond haired boy, who seemed full of the nervous energy that Pattie herself had probably displayed as a child. He was now trying to pour tea from his mother's cup on to the table. People were watching, and Elisabeth was distracted.

"Look, I can't just leave. I have to do my shift. Let me think - there's a phonebox in the hall, why don't you telephone your mother. Or, wait - phone Auntie Irene first, maybe even ask her to phone your mother. And perhaps you can all meet up there - there's more room and Auntie Irene will keep things under control. Heather's not there, she's due back from Ghana soon - I suppose my father told you about that too. She'll be so pleased." Elisabeth felt close to tears again.

"Yeah, he told me. And Les and Chris are married."

"Yes, they're living in London. Oh, we were all there and we didn't know! Pattie, I have to go."

"OK, I'll phone Auntie Irene, like you said. D'you have any money?" Elisabeth hunted for some coins while Pattie sorted out her bags and her children and eventually made her way down the old stone steps to the entrance hall, Elisabeth helping as best she could.

"I'll see you later." She was relieved to see them go; the reappearance of her long lost cousin was a considerable shock. She felt shaky, and sat down on a chair in the hall for a few minutes. Pattie

352

returned, with two children - now it all began to make sense. Pattie must have run away when she found she was pregnant. But there were two children - clearly different fathers. One mistake you could understand, but two! If she was shocked, how would Pattie's parents react? And the Atfields? Her break was over, she must get back to the library. But Pattie had come home! Elisabeth's loyalty, once given, rarely wavered and she had always rooted for her cousin, who had done her misguided best to help her when they were both children. She was sure that whatever Pattie had done was out of generosity and with the best of intentions. As her legs returned from cotton wool to flesh and bone and muscle, she determined that she would help her in any way she could.

ELISABETH AND PATTIE

1

Elisabeth was on a late shift that evening, and Phyllis and Allan had arrived when she got home; Allan's Ford Anglia was in the drive. Rather than disturb them she went round the side of the house to the door to the kitchen where she found Irene gazing out of the window and drumming her fingers on the sink. She glanced up when Elisabeth came in, then turned back to the window. Elisabeth put down her bags and went over to her aunt. Her shoulders were drooped and Elisabeth noticed white hairs among the short dark hair at the nape of her neck; she had never noticed them before. She wasn't sure what to say - the event was so momentous that any comment she could make would seem banal.

"They're here?"

"Yes." Elisabeth noticed that her eyes were wet and she was folding then pursing her lips. Emotion was rare in Irene, and Elisabeth was unnerved. "I gather you've seen her - them, I should say."

"She came to the library."

"I don't know why..." Irene stopped. "I wish Bertrand was back. We should phone Lesley. What do you make of it all?"

From the direction of the living room came the sound of voices. Elisabeth considered her words carefully. She sat down at the table and pulled a chair out for her aunt. Irene sighed, then turned from the window and sat down.

"Well? What do you think?"

"She looks older," said Elisabeth, not quite answering the question. "Of course she is. It's a long time since I saw her."

"Over four years since she left."

"She sounded just the same. I was so surprised - I couldn't believe it was Pattie. Isn't it just like her, to turn up without warning, after all this time." Elisabeth tried to speak lightly but not flippantly; it was important to get the tone right.

"Over four years, no word apart from the odd card, and now she turns up without warning. What was she thinking of? What did she tell you?"

"Not a lot, there wasn't time. Oh, she met my father in London. That's how she knew where I worked. She wanted to surprise us, but then I think she got cold feet. I told her to come here first, I thought it might be best. She should have telephoned first."

"Oh, yes, she did that. It's funny, I think I half knew who it was when the phone rang, and then when I realised it was a public box. I told her to get a taxi and come round here." Irene sat back and examined her finger nails. "Then I had the job of telling Phyllis, who was in a great dither of excitement and wanted to come round straight away and then she thought it would be better to wait and tell Allan so they could come together. So she talked to Pattie on the telephone. And then she phoned and went through it all again. And then again. The two of them came round about an hour ago. I stayed for a few minutes but they were so - Phyl was so agitated - I thought it better to leave them to themselves. So I came in here."

"How were they?" Elisabeth really meant Allan.

Irene's thumb worried away at a rough piece of skin on her finger. "Tears and hysteria from Phyl. Allan didn't say much but then he never does - he gave her a hug."

This had to be good. Allan's reaction to events was always of concern. "The children?"

"Well, the excitement got them excited so that added to the general hubbub. I tried to bring the little boy in here but he ran back. He didn't want to be left out, and I thought, well, they have to get used to each other. I'm afraid that when they think about it all, they won't be so happy. I mean two children, Elisabeth, what was she thinking of? I suppose there's no talk of getting married."

Elisabeth shook her head. Irene put both hands on the table and pushed herself upright. She seemed awkward in her movements. "I think it's time to interrupt them," she said. "I'll make some tea, and we can take it in together." Elisabeth realised that for the first time she could remember, her aunt was unsure what to do.

When they went in with the tray, the Mitchells were sitting down with Paul leaning against his mother's legs. He and Pattie were talking non-stop while Nalini gurgled on a nest of cushions on the floor.

Phyllis looked up, eyes bright. "We can build an extension - will Bertrand do it for us? Meanwhile we'll use the box room; Pattie can have that and the children her room. We'll need to buy a cot for the baby."

"They can stay here while you get sorted out," said Irene, pouring tea.

"No! You've done enough. They belong with us."

"Well, you know there is always space here if it's needed. Now, Pattie, will you please tell us what you've been doing all these years? And whyever you didn't you get in touch? Did you never think that we'd be worried? And why didn't Hugh let us know he'd seen you?"

Pattie talked, words tumbling out of her mouth, people, places, years jumbled together in an incoherent rush. Phyllis interrupted, and Allan shook his head, while Irene said "But I don't quite see..." and Paul raced round the living room until Elisabeth took him outside and got him to race up and down the drive. When they came back Irene was saying "Well, Pattie, there's still a lot I don't understand. But enough for now. Phyl, what do you want to do about eating? There are three extra mouths to feed."

"We'll manage."

"Well, come into the kitchen and I'll see what I have spare, to get you over tonight and tomorrow morning. I can give you some eggs, and half a loaf." The sisters moved into the kitchen. Elisabeth let Paul go and retreated to her usual armchair while he flung himself onto the hearthrug and made faces at Nalini. Pattie snuggled up to her father. "Daddy? We won't be a nuisance. Paul will be going to school and I'll find some work."

"Doing what?" asked Allan, but his tone was friendly.

"Singing...or maybe hairdressing," said Pattie quickly, seeing his face change.

"Shame to waste that training."

"Yeah, well, there's someone I know, told me there's a new salon in Leeds, it's very trendy, all sorts of famous people go there. You know, the scene's moved from Liverpool, it's all happening here."

"I don't know about any scene. Your mother hasn't been the same since you left. You know she's been ill."

"Yes, Uncle Hugh told me."

"All this worry over you, it pulled her down. Whatever you do, don't go upsetting her again, making her ill. I won't have it."

"No, Daddy."

"I mean it. She's not strong."

"No, Daddy."

"And your grandmother died, not knowing where you were. Your mother had to make up stories, said you were working away."

"Uncle Hugh told me, I'm really sorry."

"I don't know what we're going to do about these two," he said, indicating the children. "What are people going to say? Where's the father?"

"Not around any more."

"The blighter should be made to pay."

"It's over and done with, Daddy."

"Not for you."

"We do alright." Pattie pulled her son into her arms. Paul yelled and tried to turn it into a game, punching her playfully on her arm.

"Ow, Paulie!" "He'll take some handling," said Allan, with what sounded like admiration in his voice. Paul launched himself onto his grandfather's knee.

"Yeah, well, he'll be going to school soon."

"They'll want to know who his dad is."

"Maybe."

"This isn't London, you know. And what about the other one?"

"Her father had to go to India. He wants me to go out there."

"India?"

"Yes."

"What do you want to go to India for?"

"That's where he's from."

"You'd be better off staying here."

The Mitchells left, squeezing into a car that was full of sheets and pillows and a fold up bed that Irene had found in the attic. "Well," she said, "let's hope it all works out."

It was not long before Phyllis and Allan came round again. Two weeks of living together had caused old tensions to resurface and new ones to arise. Phyllis, who was easily agitated, wanted to talk it through with her sister and had brought a reluctant Allan with her. He was in his work clothes. It was late afternoon, Bertrand was still at work but Elisabeth had a half day and was in a corner of the living room reading.

Allan was angry with Pattie for her casual attitude towards her children. "She seems to think she can leave them with us whenever she wants to go out. She wants to go dancing again. I'm not having it. What will people think, with that half-caste child of hers."

Phyllis was tearful and agitated. She walked around the living room wringing her hands. Irene, with a glance towards Elisabeth's corner, said "Like it or not, she is your granddaughter."

359

"I'm not having it. What are people going to say? She belongs down Lumb Lane, that's what they'll say."

"People are delighted that Pattie is safe. This is the nineteen-sixties, people aren't so easily shocked."

"At least we know why she didn't get in touch with us. Too ashamed. She should stay ashamed, stay at home with her children, not go out dancing."

Phyllis broke in "She's your daughter, Allan. Allan!" She took him by the arm and shook him. He shrugged her off. "You can't turn her away."

"She disappeared without a word, made you ill with worry, now she's turned up again. Well she's not going to upset you again. She either fits in with us or she finds somewhere else to live."

Elisabeth, abandoning any pretence that she was reading her book, detected in his face some of the strong passion and inability to articulate that passion that she had seen in her stepmother, Rhoda. For both, anger was the only expression available to them. Allan was now standing by the door, indicating by his stance that he had had enough of talking.

"I'm not losing my daughter again! Or giving up my grandchildren! You might give some thought to me!"

"You are the person I'm thinking about. I'm not having you upset again. Look at you now."

"I'll be more upset if I lose my child. I've lost one, I won't do it again. If she goes I go with her."

Irene, with another glance at Elisabeth, said "Phyl…"

Phyllis turned on her. "You knew and did nothing to help me. He knew. I was supposed to be grateful that he took me. I'd rather have kept the baby! I would!" She started to cry, noisily, unbearably. Elisabeth felt embarrassed to be witnessing her aunt's distress, but she couldn't leave without drawing attention to herself. And she wanted to know more; what did Phyllis mean by another child, a baby? Had she heard it right? She was desperately sorry for Phyllis, so kind and gentle, caught as ever in the cross fire between her husband and her daughter.

Irene rose from her chair and tried to put her arms round her sister. "Lovey, do sit down. Calm yourself." Phyllis pushed her away. "No! It's too late." Irene stepped back and her arms dropped to her sides. Phyllis turned and blundered towards the door, where Allan was standing. As she reached him he put his hands on her arms. She

360

struggled to free herself and then put her head on his shoulder and continued to sob. Allan's arms went round her and his head bent over hers. Irene remained where she was. Then she turned, saw Elisabeth, and gestured with her head towards the door. Elisabeth uncurled herself and slipped out of the room and Irene followed her into the kitchen.

They were both shocked and silent. Irene went over to the kettle. "Tea, I think," she said but her voice trembled and her hand shook. Elisabeth had been the centre of some stormy family rows herself and in any case knew nothing of what Phyllis was referring to. She was less shaken than her aunt. She took the kettle. "I'll make it." Irene sat down at the table, and gazed at her clasped hands. Her mouth was working again, her lips folding and unfolding. The lines on her forehead were very marked.

She said, "She's wrong to say I knew. I didn't. I knew she'd been in some trouble with a man, went away, to get away from him, I thought. We were innocent in those days, I never suspected she'd had a child. My mother told me, before she died. Perhaps by then I'd guessed. When she came back she was unhappy, I could have helped more, but I'd married Bertrand and was expecting Heather. Then she married Allan - I did wonder, he's always loved her, there's no question of that, but she was always nervous ... She never used to be like that. She loved dancing, singing, was a great flirt... It was as if she had lost her nerve. I knew there was something wrong but I thought with time - I've always tried to be there for her. And help with Pattie. My poor little sister. And she was so fond of Hugh and he let her down - let us all down. Poor Phyllis. Poor, poor Phyllis."

Elisabeth pushed a mug of tea towards her aunt.

"My father?"

"Hugh and Phyllis were so close. But he quarrelled with your grandfather, went off, didn't give a thought to those left behind."

"And the baby?"

"Adopted. In those days it was decided very quickly. And of course it was war time, things were disrupted, people disappeared and reappeared. Nobody thought much of it. People didn't have telephones, travel was difficult, newspapers were scarce."

Elisabeth was intensely curious. "Uncle Allan?"

"He'd always been keen on her and when she got back he was there."

"So he wasn't the man?"

361

"No, no, I don't know who it was. Some GI I imagine. You know what they used to say, over sexed and…" Her voice trailed off, challenged by the word 'sex'.

"Does Uncle Bertrand know?"

Irene shook her head. "No. He's fond of Phyl, I could have told him, but it was her story, if anyone told him it should be her. But of course it didn't arise, it was twenty five years ago, until my mother told me I'd forgotten all about Phyllis going away. Not that I thought very much of it at the time, we were both working, I just understood that she was unwell and had gone away for a rest. I tell you we were innocent in those days. And now look at Pattie, two illegitimate children, no father in sight, and she shows not a scrap of shame or remorse. Things have changed so much, there's no morality any more. I can understand that Allan is upset. It's a relief your grandmother isn't here, what she would have made of it I don't know. I'm sorry that you've had to hear it all, you must put it aside, don't think about it any more. It was all a very long time ago."

"And now Pattie."

"Yes. She and Phyl – oh dear. It's like a terrible pattern. No, I mustn't think that way, and neither must you. Thank goodness Lesley is settled, and Heather – well, perhaps Heather will marry one day. And you are stable and getting stronger, now you're with us. We can all help Phyl by looking after Pattie."

"Will Uncle Allan come round?"

"I imagine so, for Phyl's sake. But I don't think they can go on living there. The house is too small for five people and Pattie and Allan have always clashed. We'll have to have them here."

"You're very good," said Elisabeth, thinking of Phyllis's desire to keep her daughter with her. "Perhaps Auntie Phyllis would like…"

"It's a big house, Bertrand won't mind, he likes to have people around him. He would have liked a bigger family but two was quite enough for me." Elisabeth blinked at this further revelation.

"Now then, how is it to be? Phyllis will be upset but it will give Allan a chance to come to terms with things and they can come over here whenever they like. They'll have to go into the room we made for Granny. I need to keep Lesley's room for her and Chris. Heather - I don't know her plans but we must keep her room for the time being."

"Auntie Irene…"

"And you will of course stay in your room. So Granny's room it will be."

The door opened and Bertrand swept in. "Irene, really, you must do something about that brother in law of yours. He is the limit, stormed out of the house without a word to me, dragging Phyllis with him. It is my home, after all, not an hotel. We give sanctuary to his wife and children - and grandchildren - and what do I get? Cold shoulder. In my own house!"

"Bertrand, dear…"

"Sorry, Elisabeth, but you've been here long enough to know - the efforts I've made to bring him into the family, the evenings we've spent together struggling to make conversation - the man doesn't have any! It's quite apparent that Phyllis brightens up when he's not there and gets that browbeaten look when he is. Sorry, my dears, but really! He has no social graces. No culture. What is he interested in? Football. And cricket," admitted Bertrand.

"He doesn't know what to do about Pattie," Irene said, more calmly. "And he's worried about Phyl. As we all are. She's not strong. Now, Bertrand, sit down and listen to the plan that Elisabeth and I have been hatching. We think it best for Pattie and her children to stay with us for a while, until Allan and Phyllis are better able to cope. Their place is too small anyway, there are only two bedrooms and that tiny box room. They can go in the extension you built for Mother." Bertrand protested that it was Irene's sewing room, but Elisabeth could see his eyes brighten at the thought of a new project. Faced with a practical problem, Irene too became her normal competent self. She left them talking it through and went up to her room, where she leaned against the window and looked out over the garden, a view that always calmed her. She was distressed by what she had heard, and found it hard to take it in. Poor dear Auntie Phyllis. What a terrible secret to bear. She wondered where her child was now. If the same thing had happened to her she couldn't imagine not trying to find out. But how could you find out? She supposed the nursing home or wherever she had given birth would have records. But as Irene had pointed out, it was war time. Records went missing, people went missing. She wondered who Phyllis's lover had been. She wondered how she could find out more. Her mind tried out one or two possible scenarios. She thought about Pattie, and wondered if she would be told about her lost brother. Her own lost cousin! How strange that first Phyllis, and then Pattie - giving birth to illegitimate children wasn't something you inherited, exactly, but perhaps there was something about their relationships with men. Elisabeth began to brood about family relationships, and how the mistakes in one generation could get passed down to the next. If you could call them mistakes. If you were to remain childless, of course, you could avoid that. Inevitably, Elisabeth's thoughts turned to her own mother.

Along with sympathy for her aunt was a curiosity and a desire to understand. She didn't want to upset her by asking questions. However, Phyllis knew that she knew, and they had become close during Elisabeth's illness. Elisabeth too had been through difficult times, and had lost her mother, whereas Phyllis had lost her child. Elisabeth persuaded herself that her aunt might want to talk, finding an opportunity when the others were busy and Phyllis was sitting quietly in a patch of sunshine in the garden, Nalini sleeping on a rug at her feet. However, when she tried to raise the subject she was gently rebuffed.

"Allan said I shouldn't talk about it. I should put it behind me again, as I have for the past 25 years. He's right, there's no point, it's too late to do anything. And please don't say anything to Pattie, Allan and Irene and I all agree, there's no reason for her to know. She'll only get excited and want to find... I shouldn't have spoken in front of you, I hadn't noticed... Oh, Elisabeth, dear, never ever give up a child. Never whatever happens. You don't forget, you don't ever really put it behind you. If I could just know, for certain, that he was alright, well cared for. I wouldn't want any more. Not after all this time. Just to know that he's alright." Phyllis started to cry. Awkwardly, Elisabeth put out her hand and touched her aunt's arm. She didn't know how to respond and regretted that curiosity had overruled discretion.

"I'm so sorry. I'm sure he would be well looked after, I'm sure he would." What did she know, thought Elisabeth to herself, these were just words. How stupid she was, to think that she could handle revelations like this!

"I wonder, sometimes, if he knows about me. If he wonders what I'm like. But it's no good thinking that way, I have to stop myself. I'm so happy that Pattie has come back with her babies. When I think - oh I'm so glad. I'll do anything to keep her here, I won't let her go away again. I couldn't bear it. If she goes, I go with her. I guessed, you know. I guessed it was something like that. I couldn't have borne it if she'd given her child up too. Why couldn't she have told me, oh why? I'm not like my mother, I'd have understood." Phyllis was crying and laughing at the same time; tears were streaming down her face. Elisabeth, remorseful, came closer, and put her arm around her.

"I'm sorry," she said. "Dear Auntie Phyl."

Phyllis sniffed, and wiped her face. "Pattie mustn't know. I've kept quiet all these years, it was just the shock, you know. You mustn't say anything. Just forget you ever knew. You must." She was beginning to get agitated, creases appearing on her soft tear-stained face.

"Of course I won't say anything."

"I must pull myself together before the others get back. It helps, you know, pretending, putting on a brave face. You don't forget but you manage."

Elisabeth squeezed her aunt's hand. "I'm sorry."

"Please forget it. Forget all about it. Talk about something – please talk about something else. I can't bear – it upsets me too much."

"Well – this is painful too. For me. But all this family talk – I'll stop if it upsets you, but I wanted to ask about my mother. I think about her so much, but no-one ever talks about her. I was four when she died, I ought to remember her but I don't. Sometimes I dream of her, but I don't know if my dream mother is anything like the real person. How well did you know her?"

"I met her two or three times, that's all. I didn't really know her."

"It's hard, not knowing. Daddy just gets sentimental when I ask."

"None of us knew her well. Hugh met her when he was touring, she wasn't from round here. He should talk to you more, of course you want to know. Dear, oh dear, this family. Nobody would believe the tangles."

"Can you tell me what she was like?"

"Let me see." Phyllis sighed, put away her handkerchief, and pulled herself into a more upright position.

"She was pretty, dark hair, and big dark eyes. You don't look like her, you take after Hugh. She was someone who was always up and down, you know, sometimes laughing, sometimes crying. She had a lovely singing voice, although I remember one time - I don't remember the details, but I do remember she tried to sing and couldn't and was very upset. I remember that very clearly. I don't know what the problem was. Daddy wouldn't let me go to the wedding, I was sorry about that. He was still angry with Hugh. He felt he had let him down by not following him into the mill. And the stage was frowned upon, and especially ladies on the stage - they were thought to be no good, you know, not respectable. It's all so different now. Hugh was no good at keeping in touch, and Irene and I were just married. Heather may have been born, I can't remember, and of course I had my own problems. We all met once, though, when we were on holiday. You were just a baby, you won't remember. There may be a photograph. You'd better ask Heather, she has all the family photographs. She might remember, she'd have been about five or six at the time of that holiday."

"If she was - up and down, like you say - might she have - well, I've thought perhaps she took her own life. When she was feeling low. Because of me, because of my father." Elisabeth's voice trailed off. It was the first time she had voiced her fears. As she spoke she realised what a shocking thing she was saying. Certainly Phyllis was shocked.

"Oh no, oh my dear no. Is that what you thought? Oh dear, no, it was a heart attack. Poor thing, she was so young."

"I thought she drowned. Like Ophelia, Daddy said."

"I don't know, I don't know, your father said something, no, it was a heart attack. It's better to think that. I really don't know." Phyllis shook her fluffy head, and twisted her handkerchief in her hand. "It's dreadful to think about, she was so young. It was winter, you know, and cold. She wouldn't have known anything, not after the heart attack. Even now, I can hardly bear to think about it. I was so sad when I heard. Poor Fay, poor Hugh. Poor you. Oh dear, oh dear, this family. Dear, you must talk to your father. You know what he's like, he likes to put things behind him, but he should talk to you. He did his best to bring you up, you know, it can't have been easy. Oh dear," Phyllis started to cry. Elisabeth put her arm around her again. "Sorry, Auntie Phyl. I shouldn't have brought it up."

"I'd tell you more if I could. We just accepted it, we didn't ask questions. You can try Irene but I don't think she knows any more. You must talk to Hugh."

2

On hearing that there was once again conflict between Pattie and her parents, Heather decided to intervene. She was home on leave from her teaching job in Ghana, distraught not to have seen her grandmother before she died, but delighted that both Elisabeth and Pattie had returned to live in Aireton. She was thinner, and admitted that she found the African climate difficult. The teaching was wonderful, the children so keen to learn, but there was so little to teach with, few books, and hardly any of the teaching aids that she had been used to. But the people were lovely, and she really felt she was doing some good. The opportunity to help the family and put things right, as she saw it, brought back some of her old energy and enthusiasm. She was keen to see everyone settled before she went back to Ghana.

"I'm just so pleased that Pattie came back when I was here," she said to Elisabeth, eyes glistening with happy tears. "It's almost as if she planned it. So I really feel I ought to do something for her."

"What sort of something?"

"Well, help her to see her parents' point of view. Help her to plan her future. I'm sure that's the key, I mean nobody quite knows - how serious is she about India? Is she in touch with Nalini's father? It might be that he was called back to marry someone chosen by his family – it's common among Indian families. We ought to warn her."

"She must know that's a possibility. She doesn't talk about it very often."

"And then there's the clubs and discos, apparently she's trying to get work as a singer, but of course all Uncle Allan sees is that she's out partying again. Auntie Phyl was round at Mum's yesterday when you were at work."

"She had some success in London. I suppose she doesn't want to let it go."

"She can't become a singer, not commercially, not with two small children. She might be able to sing at parties, you know, private functions. St Mary's would be delighted if she joined the choir, but I don't suppose she'd be interested in that."

"Pattie likes rock 'n' roll."

They arrived at the Mitchells' bungalow at ten o'clock in the morning to find Pattie still in bed with her children playing around her. Phyllis was out.

"Plans," Pattie said vaguely, after Heather had delivered a speech in which jobs, schools, building an extension, Pattie's father, the upbringing of children and the likely outcome of the next election all featured. She lounged back on the bed, her legs over the side in a gesture towards getting up.

"I don't have any plans. Whenever I try something gets in the way."

Heather opened her mouth to speak again but was distracted by Paul, who was trying to pull the buckle off her new sandals. Elisabeth stepped over Nalini to sit on Pattie's bed.

"Heather's keen to help you settle down before she goes back to Ghana," she said, while Heather tried to free her foot from her nephew's grasp. "We know things aren't easy."

"I'll bite your foot off," screamed Paul in delight, applying small pearly teeth to the task.

"Oh, darling, don't do that, it hurts!" gasped Heather, stumbling against the bookcase and knocking a couple of books to the floor. One of them caught Nalini on the shoulder. It was only a soft paperback but her eyes opened in shocked surprise before her face crumpled and she began to cry. Elisabeth bent down and picked her up, enjoying the feel of her warm sturdy body and sweet baby smell. She bounced her up and down and Nalini stopped crying and beamed at her with tears like jewels on her long dark lashes.

"Come on, it's time you got up. We'll take the children down while you get dressed."

"Yeah!" shouted Paul, and dashed down the stairs ahead of them. "I'm a tiger, I'm a tiger!"

"We haven't talked," said Heather, but she followed Paul while Elisabeth went carefully downstairs with Nalini, who put a chubby, trusting little arm round her aunt's neck. Elisabeth felt a rush of love for this gentle, innocent little girl. She thought about her aunt and the child who had been taken from her. It was hard to imagine the pain she must have felt, and how terrible it must have been for her when Pattie ran off. No wonder she wanted to spend as much time as possible with her grandchildren. She felt uncomfortable about keeping the story a secret from Pattie. She herself was finding it impossible to forget the lost child. She lay in bed at night and thought about Phyllis, forced to keep her secret for so many years past, and for many years to come. She herself could never – it was unimaginable.

While Pattie was getting up she and Heather sat on garden chairs outside the kitchen door and watched the children were playing in the garden. Heather said, "I'll be so happy to think of you all here when I'm back in Ghana. If only Pattie were more settled. Paul, keep off the roses or Grandad will be upset." She bent down and allowed Paul to jump on her.

"Goodness, what a fierce tiger!" Paul jumped off and wriggled on his tummy across the lawn. "I hope Pattie comes soon, I'm worried about those plants."

"You are going back?"

"Yes. It's a commitment, you can't just drop it. And I have friends there, people I'm close to. At the moment I think I am meant to stay. I've talked it all through with Cynthia. She understands. You know, initially we were both going to become missionaries. I'm so lucky to have a friend like her." Heather beamed.

"She hasn't gone to Ghana though."

"No, she has her role here. We each do what is right for us. She tells me she is very proud of what I am doing."

"And are you sure that Africa right for you?"

"It's what God wants me to do."

"Then I just hope he knows what he's doing," said Elisabeth, concerned for her cousin and angry at the power of religion to turn people's lives upside down.

Heather looked hurt and Elisabeth felt remorseful. It was extraordinary that Heather, who had been such a home lover, should be working abroad. She was about to ask about her friends (were they English, Ghanaian, men, women?) but they were interrupted by Pattie. Paul rushed over and his mother picked him up and swung him round. "Golly, Paul, you're getting to be a big boy." He laughed and kicked out at her.

"Ow, Paulie!"

"Is there any news of your stepmother?" Heather asked Elisabeth, postponing attempts to pin Pattie down to a discussion of her plans.

"All I know is she's gone to Essex. We're completely out of touch and I intend to keep it that way."

Heather had hinted once or twice that something "ought to be done" about Rhoda so Elisabeth continued hurriedly, "My father never talks about her. I think he's met someone else," she added.

"Do you mind?" Heather asked.

"As long as she's not Rhoda I can live with it."

"You have to grow away from your parents," Pattie said. "Fathers particularly. That's what lovers are for. That's what you both need."

Heather opened her mouth to protest but Elisabeth got in first, "You were never close to your father."

"No," Pattie said, "I wanted to be but my mother always came first. And I loved her too. So I couldn't be jealous. So I had to find someone of my own."

"Goodness," said Heather, "you've thought a lot about it."

"I went out with this psychology student once," Pattie said, off hand.

Heather shook her head. She went across the lawn to detach Paul from the roses. "You'll have to do something with him if you stay here, he's wrecking the garden."

"Yeah, I know. There's this man I met at the Mecca, he said there's someone, he's just bought a couple of clubs, he's looking for talent. He wanted to know if I was interested."

"What sort of talent?"

"Singing."

"Who'll look after the children?"

"I'll sort something out."

"I don't like the sound of it," Heather said. "Who is this man?"

Pattie shrugged.

"Just a man. I've got to earn some money. I can't stay here. I get up Dad's nose, and then Mum gets upset. I need somewhere where I can do my own thing, bring up the kids, you know."

"Your mum would like you to stay here," Elisabeth said.

"Yeah. I know. I'm not keen on this man, to be honest, but he knows people. Don't suppose you'd want to share a place, would you? I wouldn't mind if you brought fellas back."

"You'd have me baby sitting all the time."

"I wouldn't!"

"I don't know - I don't think it would work. We'd fall out."

"Just an idea."

Pattie's future remained uncertain and Heather turned her attention to Elisabeth. An opportunity to step in came when Colin, Chris's brother, called round to bring information about child benefits for Pattie. After he had gone the family congregated in the kitchen; Bertrand was looking at a picture book with Nalini, Pattie had her son held firmly between her knees and was trying to cut his hair, and Elisabeth was writing a shopping list. Heather stood gazing out of the window, a thoughtful expression on her face. "Colin's grown into a nice young man," she remarked.

370

"If you don't stop wriggling it'll come out lopsided and then you'll be sorry," Pattie threatened Paul. He wailed that he didn't want his hair cut. Nalini gurgled in sympathy.

"Is he your age, Lizzie? Or a little older?"

"Mm? Who? Oh, Colin. I don't know, a year or so older I think. Why?"

"And he's finished his course?"

"Yes, he's working now. Why?"

"He's quieter than Chris, not that Chris is noisy, but somehow you notice him when you don't always notice Colin. He seems very fond of you, Lizzie, he always asked about you when you were away and Mummy said he came to see you when you were ill."

Elisabeth looked up suspiciously. "That's his job," she said. "He's a do-gooder."

"But he still comes to see you and you're not ill now."

"He comes to see us all. He's a nice boy, he's Chris's brother."

Heather smiled. "You're missing the point."

"What are you trying to say, Heather?" enquired Pattie. "Paul, will you keep still! If my scissors slip your hair will go a funny shape and then everyone will laugh at you."

Paul scowled, then pouted and submitted. He could not bear the idea of being laughed at. "The quieter you sit the sooner I'll be finished," promised Pattie. "Just turn your head a little - that's right. Go on, Heather."

Bertrand raised his head to listen. "Oh well," said Heather, coy again, "I don't want to seem to be - well, manipulating, but Colin and Elisabeth are such good friends and it just occurred to me how nice it would be if they were more than friends - I think that's what Colin would like."

Elisabeth reddened and drew in her breath to respond.

"You mean you think they ought to shack up together?" asked Pattie, scissors poised over her son's head.

"I don't mean that at all. I just thought that their relationship might develop - they seem well suited."

"Well we're not," Elisabeth said shortly. "We disagree fundamentally on a lot of things."

"That doesn't matter," said Pattie. "It's more important to have a good time in bed and still be able to talk to each other the next morning."

"Oh Pattie! I just thought - it would be nice to think of your

371

relationship developing while I'm away. I shall miss you all."

"I'm sorry we can't all be neat and tidy to fit in with your wishes," said Elisabeth sharply. "But I shall have to disappoint you. Colin and I are friends, but at a deeper level we are completely incompatible."

"I'm sorry I mentioned it," said Heather, hurt. "It's difficult when you go away, you lose touch. I was only trying to be helpful. I thought you wanted some encouragement."

"Well I don't," Elisabeth said. "I'm going shopping, is anyone coming with me?"

Pattie set Paul on his feet. "There we are, very smart. If you can hang on a minute, I'll come with you. I need some ciggies."

"That's a good haircut, Pattie," Bertrand said, taking Paul by the shoulders and turning him round. "You've got the shape very well."

"Yes, hasn't she," said Heather, admiring. "I need to get mine cut before I go back but I don't really want to go to one of those smart salons in Leeds. I don't suppose you would do it? I don't want anything fancy, but it needs to be short."

"I can do it when I get back. You'll need to wash it, it cuts better wet."

"She could open a salon," said Heather, still keen to plan her cousin's future. "She could use the extension you built for Granny, there's a wash basin …"

"Nice idea," Bertrand said, "but you'd need permission. You can't just set up a business in a private house. And I'm not sure I'd want all and sundry beating a path to my front door. But you ought to go back to hairdressing, Pattie, you've got a talent. Why don't you see if one of the smart salons that Heather was talking about can take you on part time?"

"Yeah, maybe. If Mum can look after the kids."

"Or go to people's homes, you know, take your scissors and use their bathrooms."

"Yeah," Pattie brightened. "I could get a car."

"Hmm."

Hearing about this conversation, Irene went to see Joan Mason of Snips and Scissors in the village, whom she knew was looking for an assistant. The hairdresser thought she was losing clients because she was considered old-fashioned; the young people were going into Leeds to have their hair cut, and a young hair stylist who could introduce some modern styles might bring them back, while she continued to work with her old clients who wanted the same cuts they had always had. "So I mentioned you, Pattie. She was interested, she'd like to meet you. Now you'll have to fit in with her, make sure you get to work on time, all that sort of thing. She only wants part time, I expect she'll want Saturdays, as that's her busy time, but the rest can be discussed. The good thing is that she has a room at the back of the salon which she's turned into a kind of playroom, so that mums can keep an eye on their children while they are having their hair done. So you may be able to have the children there, though Paul will need to behave himself."

Elisabeth would have resented this organisation of her life, but Pattie was relaxed about it. "Sounds fab, Auntie. Thanks a million."

Irene had also come to a decision about where Pattie should live. She shared this with Elisabeth when they were both in the conservatory, Elisabeth watering plants and her aunt doing some darning, sitting on a chair by the window, her feet stretched out in the late summer sun.

Elisabeth finished her watering and sat down opposite her aunt in the old wicker chair, while Irene told her that she and Bertrand had been talking about Pattie coming to live with them and had come to the conclusion that it wouldn't do.

"We've had a difficult time with Mother, and Pattie herself is a responsibility, let alone her children. I really don't want to take on two small children, just when Bertrand and I are starting to think about having an easier life. And Phyl wouldn't like it. An extension to the bungalow is a possibility, Bertrand's firm can do it and he'll make sure the costs are kept down. But I'm not sure that even that will solve the problem."

Elisabeth had to agree. She had seen Allan getting irritable, Phyllis looking tense, and Paul frustrated, and therefore naughty, because of the restrictions on his games. She listened carefully, interested that Irene was taking her into her confidence.

Irene picked up some darning which had been left on a stool. "It's important to keep her here. We don't want her wandering off again. If the hairdressing works out she'll have a bit of money, but she needs somewhere to live. So, just a day or two ago I thought of Granny's flat. It hasn't been sold yet, I've been meaning to do something about it but there have been too many other things to think about. It's not ideal, there are only two bedrooms and most of the other residents are elderly, although there's a young couple just moved in on the ground floor. What do you think?"

"She needs a place of her own," Elisabeth said, thinking about it.

"The intention was to sell it with the proceeds forming part of the overall estate so we'd have to get everyone's agreement if we were to do anything different."

"It sounds like a good idea to me."

"She would have to pay rent, it shouldn't be a gift, but we could work out something affordable. Bertrand's in agreement, and I expect Heather will be. I'll mention it to Lesley next time I speak to her. Don't say anything to Pattie for the time being." Irene picked up her darning again.

"She needs a place of her own," Elisabeth continued her train of thought. "She said the other day she couldn't stay in the bungalow."

"And we don't want her running off again."

"She wouldn't."

"She might. Oh, Elisabeth, I know, her heart's in the right place – too much heart, perhaps." Irene frowned, folding in her lips in the way she had when she was thinking. "We could try the flat for a year, delay the sale, see how things go. It might not work out. She's so scatterbrained, can she be trusted to look after the children?"

"I thought the other day how well she's taken to motherhood. The last few years can't have been easy but she's coped."

Irene bit off the end of her wool. "She doesn't give much away about those years."

"No, she doesn't." It was true. Pattie, normally so open and carefree, was capable of keeping things to herself when she chose.

"She keeps her mouth very tightly shut on the subject of Paul's father. As for Nalini – do you think her father will come back?"

"No."

"Well, I hope Pattie has learned her lesson and will act more sensibly in future. Now, dear, I have some news for you too. I haven't mentioned it before because I wanted to check with the solicitor that I had understood it properly. Your grandmother left you a small legacy in her will. Properly it's not yours until you are 21 but that's not far off and he agreed that I could tell you now and you can give some thought to what you want to do with it."

Elisabeth had not expected this.

"Phyllis and I get a third each, but she divided your father's share in two, so you are getting half of his. She worried that he wouldn't use the money sensibly, and she was anxious to do right by you. Now, Elisabeth, don't get ideas about giving it to Hugh. He's doing well, from what I hear, and Mother was clear that you were to benefit. It won't be a great deal, by the time everything's paid for, and of course there'll be less if we don't sell the flat."

Elisabeth was surprised and touched. She had not been close to her grandmother, but that hadn't stopped her grandmother thinking about her. It was hard that her father's inheritance was reduced as a result, but at least he had been remembered, not cut out, as he had from her grandfather's will. And it was true, his acting career seemed to be taking off with the new television series, which was very popular. The girls in the library were watching it, and were amazed when she said that the man who played the father was her father. Her status had risen considerably since she told them.

Irene gave her more details and she began to feel quite excited. She had never had any money of her own before. She would buy her father a present, she couldn't think what, but she would find something. She could think about going to university, travelling, buying a car, even putting a deposit on a place of her own. The world began to open up for her. Suddenly, she had a future. She wanted to be on her own to think about it. She put the watering can down, and went towards the door, then on an impulse turned to her aunt and planted a shy kiss on her cheek. Irene looked up, surprised.

"You must miss Granny," Elisabeth said.

"Yes, I do. So many little things - I think, oh I'll tell Mother about that, then I realise she isn't here any more."

"I'm sorry. I'm sorry I wasn't closer to her."

"Just because she was old doesn't make it any easier. I thought we'd have her for a few more years."

The following Sunday afternoon Elisabeth and Pattie took the children to the playground. It was a mild day in late summer; Heather was getting ready to return to Ghana and a gentle end of summer melancholy had settled on the rest of the family. The cousins sat on swings while Nalini played in the sandpit and Paul flung himself on and off roundabouts and slides and squabbled with the other children playing there. It was the first time they had had together without someone else being present, and Elisabeth took the opportunity to ask about Pattie's life in London, about which she was intensely curious.

"I try to imagine how it must have been, living on your own all that time."

"I wasn't on my own, there were always other people. It was fab, no-one to tell you off for doing things."

"How did you come to leave home? I wasn't around, I never really knew."

Pattie swung her legs. "The group I was with, we were getting offers, only Dad got mad when I was in late, and there wasn't much happening in Bradford, then someone said 'let's go to Liverpool, anyone can play in the Cavern, you just have to turn up,' but when I told Dad he got mad again and Mum started to cry, and I just knew I had to get out of there. I mean anything I wanted to do caused trouble. I thought if we were a big success it would be OK. I could go back, you know, with money and clothes and my picture in the papers. So we went to Liverpool and played a few clubs but then we reckoned if we wanted to make a record we'd have to go to London, that was where it was all happening. It was really exciting. I used to go to these shows, Ready Steady Go and Top of the Pops. But then people started going off, did their own thing, so there wasn't a group any more. I did some modelling. It was good money. It's amazing what they'll pay you for giving a silly smile and sticking your tits out. There was so much going on, you were in London, you know. The scene. Swinging London. It was fab, really fab."

"My London was a bit different to yours," Elisabeth said. "If only I'd known you were there."

"Yeah, I thought of getting in touch but I'd lost your address. Then I found out about Paul. That settled it, I couldn't come home. Dad would've given me hell. I was going to have an abortion, I got as far as this woman but then I looked at her and I looked at her stuff and I thought no, not me, I'm gonna have this baby. I always wanted a baby, you know? I used to tell Mum I wanted a baby sister. So I went ahead and had him and golly aren't I glad I did?" They watched Paul racing around the playground, shrieking loudly.

"How ever did you manage? I mean bringing up a baby, on your own."

"There was a group of us living in this house, there was always someone to keep an eye on him. Then I met Nalini's father - golly he was beautiful. So-o sexy, with that lovely brown skin and eyes that made you just melt." Pattie had a dreamy look on her face. "I moved in with him and while I was with him I never looked at another man. Not once. Not seriously. Trouble was, he didn't like me being on the pill. Didn't like the modelling, and anyway I wasn't as trim as I was." Pattie sighed and pulled in her stomach. "So there wasn't much work. I did a bit of singing now and again, student discos, you know. He was a student so he didn't have much money either. Then when he finished his course he got a call to go back home. Family business. He had to go, they wouldn't send him any more money. The plan is I join him when he's settled down."

"India?"

"Yeah, it'll be great. The Beatles have been, now everyone wants to go. It's the place to be. They say George will stay."

Elisabeth didn't know what to say. How serious was she? There was so much she didn't understand.

"And Paul's father – was he one of the group you went off with?"

Pattie jumped off her swing and ran across to rescue her daughter who was having sand poured into her wellington boots by another child. They came back to the swings together and Pattie sat Nalini on her lap.

"Golly," said Pattie, shaking her soft blond head, and swinging gently back and forth, "I was wild in those days. It wasn't any one man, it was any man, I was in love with them all as long as they were good looking and good fun."

"Pat…"

"Men seem to think that all women want is a man - one man - and they're satisfied. It's not like that for them, so why should it be for us? That's what I think anyway," said Pattie, with a return to her usual vague manner.

"That's not what the women's magazines say."

"Then they're fooling everyone," said Pattie. "Golly, I had a good time! Parties every night - my poor parents couldn't cope. I had to leave. Oh, it was fun - I only have to hear one of those old songs and it brings it all back." She started to sing "Please please me". Then she said "Oh golly, look at Paul." She handed Nalini to Elisabeth and ran over to where her tough young son was fighting a group of children a year or so older than him with hands and feet and teeth.

3

Pattie had been back for five weeks and Lesley and Chris had not been to see her. They had come for Mrs Lindsey's funeral and spent a few days in Aireton earlier in the summer, after which it seemed that they were both very busy. Then Lesley telephoned to say that she would come by train, on her own, and then she rang again to say she thought she might stay with Carol in Sheffield; finally it was agreed that they would both come north and Chris would spend time with his parents in York, dropping Lesley off in Aireton on the Saturday and collecting her the following day. It would give Lesley time to spend with her sister before she returned to Ghana, as well as seeing her cousin. Irene commented that it all seemed rather complicated, but she supposed they knew what they were doing. She said she thought Lesley hadn't forgiven her cousin for upsetting the family so much. "They'll be alright once they meet; they were great friends as children."

The two of them arrived early on Saturday afternoon. Pattie ran out of the front door as soon as she heard the car turning into the drive. Elisabeth, watching from the house, saw Lesley climb out and the two cousins met in an brief embrace before going into the house. Chris stayed outside to show off his new car to Bertrand, who had wandered out in his Saturday pullover and corduroy trousers. Irene offered tea but Chris said he would rather get on with his journey and he would see them all the next day. "The traffic on the ring road can be bad on Saturdays," he said, to no one in particular.

"Five minutes won't hurt, surely," said Irene. As he hesitated, Pattie ran out again, and threw her arms around him. "Hiya, Chris!" He gave her a hug. Pattie hung on. "It's so good to see you again."

"Good to see you too, Pat. Sorry we couldn't come before." Then Heather came up with her arms held out and Pattie was forced to move away. Chris stepped back so that he was free of both cousins, "The thing is, if I stay I won't get away. I'll be back tomorrow, mid morning."

"We were planning to be at church," Irene said.

"I won't go," Pattie said. "I'll look after you. Mum and Dad will bring the kiddies over later. You can tell me about all the famous cases you've solved." Chris opened his mouth to put her right, then thought better of it. He gave a little shrug and an apologetic smile, and said to Irene, "I really think I should go."

378

"It's all planned, Mum," said Lesley, who had now joined everyone else on the drive. "You've got me to yourself today, and Chris and me tomorrow." She went over to her husband and gave him a kiss. "Give my love to everyone," she said. Chris got into the car and began to back out of the drive, with Bertrand standing by the gate waving him on.

Elisabeth watched all this from the doorway. The whole thing seemed managed, and Chris appeared ill at ease. The germ of an idea planted itself in her mind.

When he had gone everyone went back into the house, and gathered in the sitting room. Elisabeth was conscious of an edginess about the family, as if no-one quite knew how to behave. No-one except Lesley, who was her normal calm self. She sat next to Pattie on the settee, listening to her cousin's excited chatter. When Irene said, again, that it was a pity they weren't going to see more of Chris, she moved across the room to give her a hug, and asked when she and Bertrand were going to spend a weekend with them.

"I've got a couple of pictures in an exhibition, I told you, you must come and see it. It opens in October."

"We'll certainly come for that," Bertrand said.

"Maybe Elisabeth can come and bring Uncle Hugh."

"Me too!" said Pattie.

"It seems a long way to come for two days," Irene said, still thinking of Chris. "Couldn't you go back on Monday?"

"We've got things on. We'll have more time in the autumn. I've brought some wine, Dad, I hope you like it. How're things at work, did that block of flats get built?"

Bertrand told her, at some length, and then Pattie wanted to know what concerts she'd been to recently, and what did she think of Pink Floyd, and were the Beatles really going to split up. Irene was interested in the gallery where she worked.

"Do you think you could get time off to come to the airport with me next week?" asked Heather.

"I should think so, if someone can cover for me. I'll ask. Why don't you come the day before and stay the night with us?"

Later, after Pattie had left, Lesley turned her attention to Elisabeth. "We haven't seen you for ages, you must come and spend a weekend with us sometime soon."

"Yes, thank you," said Elisabeth, who was sure that she did not want to do this.

"Mum was saying she's so glad you are here, especially with Heather going back to Ghana. I think she hoped she would stay, especially after Granny died. And the Pattie business has been quite a shock for her."

"It's been a shock for all of us," said Elisabeth.

"And poor Auntie Phyl, she's aged so much over the last few years. Has she said anything to you? Pattie I mean."

"Nothing significant."

"Heather is surprisingly relaxed about it all, and Mum seems to be coping. I can't help feeling annoyed with Pattie; she's upset everyone and now she's back as if nothing had happened. That's really why we didn't come rushing up to see her the minute she returned. I'm being silly, I know. She's always done her own thing. I suppose I'll get over it. Will you give me a ring sometime and we can talk properly? I'll come up again once the exhibition's over. Your father's doing well, isn't he? We always watch 'Girls at Large'."

The following morning Chris arrived while Irene, Bertrand and Heather were at church. Pattie was still at her parents' bungalow. Elisabeth found some chores to do, leaving him and Lesley alone, but after a while Lesley went into the garden to pick flowers. When Elisabeth came into the kitchen from polishing the dining room table she found Chris in the kitchen reading the *Observer*. He saw her hesitating in the doorway and pulled out a chair.

"Don't run away, stay and talk." As usual, his good looks disturbed her, and she kept her head down and tried to hide her shyness behind her long hair. He was more relaxed than he had been the day before. He put the paper down and told her that he was looking into the possibility of partnerships. He lounged back in a chair, his long legs thrust under the kitchen table.

"I guess it will work out," said Chris, "but a lot of these firms expect you to bring money into a partnership, and I don't have any. It will be the same wherever I go. You have to be born rich to succeed at this game."

"But you're doing very well," Elisabeth said, surprised to hear a note of discontent in his voice. "People don't usually get partnerships until they're much older than you, surely?"

"I guess so. I'm impatient, I want to get on. And then we need to buy a place to live, we can't go on renting."

"Will you stay in London?"

"Not sure. We had thought of moving somewhere a bit leafier, now Lesley's focusing on the natural world, flowers and trees, you know. She'd like to replicate this," he waved his hand in the air. "But who can afford a house like this these days? And she's doing well, it's coming together for her, London is the centre of the art world, it would be a bit silly to move out into the sticks. And of course all the big legal firms are there. Do you think I might have a drink?"

"I'll make some coffee."

"Ah, coffee, yes, please."

As she was spooning the coffee powder into mugs Pattie came down the path that ran round the side of the house and into the kitchen, carrying Nalini on her hip. Paul dashed in and then out again, heading for the garden. "Hiya, Chris, how's things? That was Paul, he's a bit lively today. Is there some coffee for me? Goodie. Can Nali have some milk? Nali, give Uncle Chris a kiss." She acted as if everything was perfectly normal. Elisabeth was half impressed, half shocked.

"Do I have to?"

"I thought you'd like kissing her," said Pattie. "Most people do."

"I think she's adorable, especially at a distance. I saw my sister yesterday and I'm up to here in kids. I'd just like some sensible adult conversation for a change."

"Okey dokey. D'you know I'm working now?"

"Hairdressing. I heard. Are you enjoying it?"

"S'alright. They're all wanting perms."

"Perms?"

"Yeah, straight is out, curls are in. Do you fancy having your hair cut? I could do you a nice modern style. Special rates for family."

"What's a modern style these days?"

"Not mop top any more. Long, like John and George. You've got nice hair, just a bit of curl. Lemme see." Pattie ran her fingers through Chris's hair. "Just a bit of shaping, perhaps, let it grow a bit. So it curls into your neck. That's really sexy."

"Pattie, I'm a lawyer. City type. We don't have long hair."

"Boring!"

"That's what I am."

"You're too sexy to be boring."

Nalini, feeling neglected, began to whimper.

"Don't cry, petal, why don't you go and sit on Uncle Chris' knee – oh, go on, just while I make my coffee. There you are. Where's Paul gone? Heck, I'd better go and find him."

Chris, holding Nalini gingerly on his knee, shook his head and smiled. "You haven't changed." She reached the door as Lesley came in to say that Paul was trying to climb the apple tree.

"I'm going." Elisabeth, alert to everything that affected Chris, noticed the look that passed between him and Lesley before she turned and followed Pattie into the garden.

"Take the baby, will you?" said Chris, lifting her onto Elisabeth's knee. Elisabeth bent her head over her niece's silky dark curls.

"You must have known Pattie quite well, when you all lived here. Didn't you go around with her?" she asked, trying to sound casual then, deciding some kind of explanation was necessary, "I missed a lot when I was in London."

"Oh, years ago. It didn't last long – I was working and studying, all she wanted to do was dance and party. It was hopeless. She thought I was very dull.

"Now, Lizzie, talking of that sort of thing, and whilst we're alone, you'll say it's none of my business, but I'm fond of my kid brother, and he was sounding a bit down when I saw him earlier. I gather you were sounding off about something – religion I guess – and he took it a bit personally."

Elisabeth was annoyed. "Does Colin tell you everything I say to him?"

"No, no, but he's worrying about his future, whether to go for his local preacher exams. He knows that won't impress you very much."

"It's nothing to do with me whether he does his exams or not."

"Well, you see, he thinks it does. I mean he'd like you to be happy with what he does."

"I don't know why he should do that."

"Lizzie, he's very fond of you. He gets depressed because you don't take him seriously. He's my kid brother, I look out for him."

"I do take him seriously. As a friend."

"Hmm. Sorry, Lizzie, I don't mean to interfere. He doesn't know I've spoken to you, by the way."

"Good. Leave it, please Chris."

Of course she loved Colin. How could she not love someone who was so transparently good, who had helped her so much? But to think that she could love him as a lover, or he her, was just not possible.

"Have you been in love, Lizzie?"

"Yes."

"And?"

"He was married."

"Oh, I'm sorry. How tactless. Sorry, Lizzie. But, well – hopeless then?"

"Yes."

Interference was to be expected from Heather, but it was difficult to take from Chris. She supposed that it was proof, if proof were needed, that he himself had no feelings for her. She felt depressed, but resigned. It was a fact that her feelings were no longer as intense as they had been before her illness. The emotional drain of unrequited love, and the knowledge that Chris would never see her as anything other than his wife's little cousin, had, over time, eroded her passion. Days now passed without her thinking of him. She was able to hear his name without blushing and talk to him without becoming tongue-tied. Perhaps it had been a childish or adolescent passion, something she had needed when there was little else to give meaning to her life. She had loved him as a boy, and as a young man, and had been bitterly unhappy when she had heard that he was to marry Lesley, even though she had expected it. She hadn't gone to the wedding. Her stepmother wasn't keen and for once Elisabeth sided with her, rather than her father. She pleaded poverty; the real reason she kept to herself. Her father never knew of her feelings.

And Chris had changed. The man she now knew was very different from the boy who had first entered their lives nearly ten years ago. That boy had been an ideal, a hero, someone to bring colour to her dreary teenage years, not the real, flawed, flesh and blood human being who was now married to her cousin and had also dated her other cousin. What if her suspicions were true? The timing was right, as far as she could tell, and Paul looked as if he might develop Chris's fair good looks. And he and Lesley were not quite at ease. It was possible. Had he known, had he suspected? Had Pattie left because of him? If it were true and if he had left her to sort it out for herself he could no longer be her hero. And yet, and yet - her heart still did a little flip when he came into the room. Elisabeth sighed. If passion was waning she rather regretted its loss. Falling out of love might be almost as painful as falling in love. What would take its place? What excuse did she now have for keeping Colin at a distance?

Because Colin was a good friend, a very good friend. Was it not possible for a man and woman to be friends, without all the romantic and sexual complications? He was not as tall as his brother, and his features were less regular, but he had a pleasant, open face and, unlike

Chris, gave the impression of being at ease with himself. His once fiery red hair had mellowed to a golden red and the freckles were less prominent. He was intelligent, empathetic, caring. He liked her, and as far as she could tell was indifferent to her disability. She liked him. Why did everyone seem to think there should be more? Because it would be a neat solution to the Elisabeth problem? Because, if she was honest, they could see what she knew but didn't want to admit, that he wanted to be more than a friend. She knew that he was unlikely to say anything without a hint from her. This made her self-conscious, which meant that she was less able to confide in him about the things which concerned her, about which she could talk to no-one else. It was frustrating.

There again, they disagreed on so much, could they even be friends? She had never subscribed to organised religion, even before Hoxton, whereas Methodism was a significant part of Colin's life and she knew that he gained strength from his beliefs. For him, it was a force for good and it was within that framework that he made sense of the world. Because she liked him, Elisabeth tolerated views in him that would have been intolerable in anyone else. Her own opinion was that organised religion was at the root of many of the world's problems and that she, personally, had been seriously damaged by it. For these reasons religion was something they rarely talked about and it was a real barrier to their relationship.

It was a shame, because his easy, undemanding friendship had helped her in the months during and following her illness. His experience of doing social work meant that he could understand what she was going through better than her close family. He dealt with the despair and anger that terrified her and frightened her family, saying matter of factly that she had to get it out of her system, that it would take time, but she would get there. In this way he helped her to see that she might have a future. She was grateful and as time passed and she became stronger their relationship became more equal, and she felt more his friend and less his client. He was almost a member of the family. Another cousin, perhaps.

Of course she loved Colin, how could she not love someone who was so transparently good, who had helped her so much, who was a supportive, understanding companion. They shared many interests, loved gardening and the countryside and enjoyed the same films. She felt she knew him through and through, leaving no mystery, no unknown, no possibility of passion.

384

Even Pattie had a go at her. Elisabeth and Colin came in from a walk one Saturday to find her moping in the kitchen. She had asked Irene if she would look after the children while she went to Manchester to audition for the friend of the man she had met at the Mecca ballroom, but Irene had said no. She was safely back in Aireton, everyone was very willing to help her and her children settle down, and she must not give it all up for some questionable work in a sleazy night club. She got Bertrand to reinforce the message. "And do not breathe a word of this to your mother," was Bertrand's final word.

Subdued, she sat in the kitchen over a mug of cold coffee, while Bertrand took the children into the garden to help him gather up the autumn leaves. Elisabeth tried to cheer her by saying she might be able to do some singing locally.

"Yeah, but I need a group. I can't sing on my own." Pattie gave a big sigh.

"When Nalini goes to school…"

"Do you know how old I'll be then? 27. 27!" She shook her head in dismay.

"You could try folk singing," suggested Colin, who was making fresh coffee. "It would suit your voice, and you don't need a group."

"You mean like Joan Baez? Don't I need a guitar?"

"You've got one, haven't you? I remember Chris giving you and Lesley lessons."

"Mm."

"I can play a bit. We could try out some songs. And, well, people who are into folk music are nice, genuine people. These night clubs, they can be pretty rough."

"Yeah, well, maybe." She sighed again, resting her chin on her hands.

"Pattie," said Colin, putting a coffee mug in front of her, "why did you leave London?"

"Ran out of money."

"That all?"

"Missed my mum. Heard about Granny."

"You can't do anything about your grandmother but you can do something for your mother. You know how happy she is to have you back."

"S'pose."

"Any other reason?"

"Better for the kids," Pattie said after a pause. "And me," she added, after a further pause. "S'pose I'm not going to Manchester. But," with a renewal of energy, "I gotta have a life of my own. That was the great thing about London, you could do your own thing and nobody bothered you."

"Nobody helped you either," said Elisabeth.

"You have to grab things when you can. But I don't want to upset Mum again. I hadn't realised - well, you know, you don't when you're a kid. But now I've got two of my own... So I reckon I'm staying put for a bit, but not too close, you know. Auntie Irene said I might be able to live in Granny's flat. You could come and share."

"There wouldn't be room."

"Just an idea."

"What about India?"

"Yeah." Pattie brightened. "They have big families there, like Heather said in Africa, so there'd be loads of people to look after the children. Mum might come with me, she's never been abroad."

"Have you heard from Ranjit?"

"No, well, he's got to talk to his family. D'you know, my Dad's started calling her Nelly. He never could bring himself to say Nalini. But he says Nelly quite happily and she responds."

Colin got to his feet. "I must be going. Look after yourself, Pattie, you've got a lot going for you. Don't forget about the folk singing."

"OK. Thanks, Colin, you're a good man." She got up from the table and gave him a hug and a kiss. "Thanks a lot."

Elisabeth went to the door to see him off. When she returned Pattie was rinsing her mug at the sink. She said "I'd better see how Uncle Bertie's getting on with Paul." Then she added "I love them to bits but I'd have chosen a few years without. So bear that in mind when you and Colin finally go to bed together."

"Pattie!"

"Well, he fancies you and I reckon he'd be a good lover, thoughtful, you know."

"I just wish everyone would stop managing my affairs for me," said Elisabeth, annoyed. She had expected better of Pattie.

"If you turn him down too many times he might start looking elsewhere. He looks like a man who's ready for love."

"He's not like that, he's not interested in casual affairs. Neither am I."

"Sex doesn't have to lead to marriage."

"I know that. But there has to be love. Even if it's not for ever."

Pattie went off to find her son and Elisabeth was left wondering how she would feel if Colin had a relationship with someone else. It might even be Pattie, if they played folk music together. Pattie would flirt with him, and if as she said he thought he and Elisabeth weren't getting anywhere he might respond. Bother Pattie, it was no good, her remark had gone home. Would she be jealous? She thought it over. She was still a little in love with Chris. She was not in love with Colin. But she would be annoyed if Pattie muscled in on what she considered to be her territory. Had Pattie's flirtation with Chris gone beyond flirtation? Had Lesley minded?

Along with all of this, Elisabeth was worrying about her own future again. Family pressures felt overwhelming at times, and left her little time for herself. That was one thing about Colin, she had to admit, he never put pressure on her. She believed that she had recovered from her illness, and she was no longer satisfied with her present life. She was bored with routine library work. She loved the house at Sycamore Avenue, and was reasonably comfortable with the arrangement now that she was paying for her bed and board. Despite this, at times she felt angry and resentful, feelings which she knew to be unreasonable and tried to keep to herself. It was time to plan for the future. And now she knew that she would have some money, to provide some independence, her aunt had said. But what to do with that independence? where to go next? She had no clear idea but she knew she had to create a life for herself.

She thought again about her father's offer of a bedsit in his block of flats. It might suit her for a time, but it would mean giving up her job here and finding another one. Or doing a course. But somehow the thought of going to college or university had lost its appeal; she felt too old, too many things had happened to her. Without a qualification, however, she would be stuck with routine jobs. It was all very difficult, and Elisabeth started to feel weighed down with problems. She feared the approach of another period of depression. If that were to happen she knew the only person who could help her was Colin. She couldn't give up his friendship.

4

One day in mid September, Elisabeth and Colin went for a walk and headed for their usual seat on the moors, overlooking the valley. It was a day to lift the spirits with a warm sun and a soft blue haze over the moors, still purple with heather. Despite the day, Elisabeth was feeling irritable and resentful. She nearly said she didn't feel like a walk, but then decided that it was an opportunity to discuss the nature of her relationship with Colin. It needed to be discussed. It was an unsatisfactory element in her unsatisfactory life and it was time to sort it out. She was tired of the fact that everyone except the two people most concerned were discussing their relationship. She was irritated by Colin's tact and refusal to put himself first. Everything about him annoyed her, his good humour, the way he walked, the ill fitting maroon jumper he wore which looked terrible with his red hair, but it had been knitted for him by an elderly aunt, so he wore it. 'You don't need to wear it when she's not there,' Elisabeth had argued, but he said that wasn't the point. She felt prickly and argumentative, and wanted to goad him out of his normal tact and kindness. She was silent at first, thinking about how she might do this. Before they reached the seat she stopped, so that he was forced to face her, and she asked him outright what he wanted (unaware that three years ago Lesley had asked Chris a similar question)."

"How do you mean, what I want?"

She prevaricated. "Out of life."

He treated her question seriously, as he always did. "I want a good life. A life with purpose, but also fun. A life with friends, and family. Parents, brother and sister, and in time my own family."

"Like your parents. Following tradition."

"I haven't found anything better."

"Have you tried?"

"I've seen other people try."

"It's not what I want."

"What do you want?"

Elisabeth was silent. That, indeed, was the question. But not that, not the conventional family, mum at home looking after the kids, doing the cooking, while dad did interesting work and went to the pub with his mates. What sort of a life was that? She pushed these thoughts to one side. This was looking too far ahead.

"What do you want out of this?"

"What do you mean, this?"

"You and me." It was difficult but it had to be said.

"You know damn well," he said.

"Tell me." Elisabeth was wearing her stubborn face.

"I want you," he said. "I want you whatever way I can have you. If this is all I can have," he indicated the space between them, "well, I'll put up with that. I'll try to be satisfied. I'd rather have that than nothing."

"And never ask for more?"

"I'm afraid of frightening you off," he said. He tried to look at her but she had turned away and was gazing out over the moors. "I know you've been hurt. I know you love my brother. I know you don't like the work I do. What can I do - what can I offer you? Maybe you won't be unhappy to know that I love you and I want you to be happy."

There was a pause. Elisabeth gazed out over the valley. A declaration of feelings was what she had asked for, and now she wished she hadn't. She didn't know how to deal with it. And he knew she loved Chris. How many other people knew? Her mood had changed and she regretted forcing the issue. He went on, "Chris – I love him too. Of course I do, he's my brother. It's difficult to handle. I know that if we're in a room together you're seeing him, not me."

"I didn't know you knew."

"It's easy to see, when you care for someone."

"Does Lesley know?"

"Probably not."

There was a silence. It was her opportunity to break off the relationship with Colin. All she had to do was say, yes, I love your brother, that won't ever change. So I think you'd better find someone else. But she didn't, and the silence continued. After a pause she found herself saying, "There is still something there. But - it doesn't hurt as much. It is hard to let it go, even though I know it's hopeless. But I'm coming to realise that I'm not prepared to go scrabbling for crumbs for the rest of my life. It's hard though. I've felt this way for so long. It sounds silly but – it's been a kind of lifeline."

"When you were unhappy?"

"Yes. A kind of daydream."

"Which you no longer need?"

"Perhaps I need it less than I did."

"So – might there be room for someone else?"

"I don't think of that. It's too soon. And I'm better on my own."

Colin closed his eyes, briefly. Then he said

"Are you happy on your own?"

"I don't think I'll ever be happy." As she spoke, Elisabeth knew this to be true. Happiness simply wasn't in her nature. It was strange how different she was from her father; he could be happy anywhere. She must take after her mother. Anyone else would have told her not to be silly, would have pointed out all the things that might cause her to be happy. Colin simply acknowledged that this was how she felt, and she was grateful for that.

"Anything else we need to discuss? You don't like my job?"

"It's not for me to say."

"Come on, you wanted to talk things through. What specifically don't you like?"

"I've known poverty," Elisabeth said. "I've known what it's like to be hungry and cold, and I've known what it's like to scrape by. I don't like it. I don't want to be reminded of it."

"I get paid. I don't live in poverty. I try to get other people out of it."

"I know. But you are – oh, interested in it. You'd talk about it if it weren't for the fact that I don't want to."

Colin sighed. "So how do you see your future?"

"I don't want to be rich but I do want to be comfortable. And independent. I need to find a place of my own. Soon I'll have a bit of money, something my grandmother left me, it's not much but enough to put a deposit on a place. If that's what I want to do. My father is more stable now, he tells me I could go and live with him again, not actually with him but apparently there's a bedsitter in his block that I could have. It's tempting but I'm not sure. I don't really want to live in London. And I think - perhaps – I'm wary about getting too close to him again." She thought about what Pattie had once said, that her father wanted to know she was settled so that he could live his own life. "It seems easier to know what I don't want than what I do." The anger and tension had gone, and she wanted to confide in her friend. They moved over to the seat and sat down.

"The money will help. Give you some options."

"Yes, it will."

Colin said, "I've been thinking quite a lot about my future. Whether to go on with my religious studies or not."

"You can't give up!"

390

"Yes, I can. If they're getting in the way of other things. And I don't have to give it all up, I can still be involved in the church. It's a lot to do on top of my job. I had thought that in time I'd do more of that and less of the day job. But I'm no longer sure that's what I want."

"But it's your life."

"Part of my life. But I begin to think there are other ways in which one might serve. I don't know, Lizzie, I'm still thinking it through. But, well, you do come into it."

Elisabeth said, "I don't mean to upset you with all of this. I just felt – some things were never getting said."

"You're right. Perhaps I've been too careful not to upset you."

"I've been aware of that."

"And what about your feelings for me?"

Elisabeth gazed out over the valley. This was a good spot, a place they often visited. The mistiness of early autumn was beautiful, and sad. Winter would soon follow. How was she to respond to Colin, be truthful without being hurtful. And what actually was the answer? What were her feelings?

"It's not easy to say. Well, to be completely honest, it's not easy to know. You are very important to me, there's no question of that. And everyone knows that and expects – things. I don't want to go along with that just for that reason, but on the other hand I don't want to throw it away out of contrariness. Do you see? It's so hard to explain. I'm only 20, I don't want my future planned for me, I'm not ready. When I was ill you helped me, probably more than anyone else. I'm grateful, eternally grateful, and you know me so well. And I miss you when you're away. I suppose I just don't know if that's enough. I think I need to find a bit of space to think it all through. I'd like to get away for a while from everything, but I don't think London is the right place to go. Too many bad things happened in London. "

It was a relief to have said all that. She might have said too much, but she didn't really care. For the first time that afternoon Elisabeth relaxed and enjoyed the warm sun on her face. She unfastened the neck of her jacket.

Colin said, leaning forward, elbows on his knees, "I'm glad we're talking, you're right, the unsaid things were becoming an obstacle. I was afraid – well, like I said I didn't want to frighten you off. There are differences between us: I can never give up my beliefs, any more than you can give up yours. But, Lizzie, it seems to me that you have to find security in yourself. Until you do that you won't be happy with me, your father, or the rest of your family. Maybe you do need to go away, but I don't know, I don't like to think of you living on your own. Just don't shut me out, please, unless – well, don't shut me out. Because whatever happens I'll always be your friend. Other than that, well, I've been clear about my feelings. It's over to you."

"Can you wait? Until I know better what I want?"

"Of course."

"I want us to stay friends."

He put out his hands and pushed her hair away from her face. Then he leaned forward and kissed her gently. It felt good and Elisabeth did not draw back. He kissed her again. They were uncomfortable, squeezed together on the wooden seat, and their knees got in the way, but the kiss was warm and satisfying and she felt herself relax. He held her in a way that made her feel safe. It was good to feel around her the arms of someone who truly loved her. She had had little of that; her aunts were kind but Irene was not demonstrative and Phyllis's gentle embraces seemed like an expression of her own need for support. Only Pattie - but she wouldn't think of Pattie. Colin worked his hands under her coat but Elisabeth soon pulled back. She wasn't ready for anything more. But it was good to be in his arms, and to feel his love. He sighed, and she put her good hand in his. "Close friends," she said.

"I guess that will do for now," said Colin, kissing her again.

Elisabeth came home from the library one wet and windy afternoon a few weeks later to find Pattie in the sitting room, picking out the notes of a song on the piano. Because of the piano she continued to spend time at Sycamore Avenue although she and the children had moved into the flat. She was full of excitement because her favourite Bradford haunt the Mecca Ballroom was organising a talent competition, and the winner would be offered a singing contract. "'Puppet on a String', what do you think, will they like it? It'll have to be a ballad, I can't do rock without a group. The thing is, I can't tell Auntie Irene, she'll be mad, but there's no harm, no problem, if I win it would be just be one evening a week, two songs, only half an hour. Only it could take off, you know, there'll be scouts there."

"What about the hairdressing?"

"I can work round that, I need the money, I won't give it up but singing's what I really really want to do. If it works out I'll tell Auntie Irene but there's no point in telling her if I don't need to. You'll cover for me, won't you Elis'beth, the night of the competion? You don't need to say anything, just say you're spending the evening in the flat. If anyone asks I've gone for a drink with friends."

Elisabeth was tired. Her mood had darkened with the weather and she could no longer relieve stress with gardening. She sat down without taking her coat off. "I'm not going to start telling lies for you."

"If it takes off I'll work something else out. Oh please, please, please."

"I'll do it this once," Elisabeth said reluctantly. "But if they want you to continue you'll have to come clean." She felt things closing in around her again, and old feelings of panic lurked at the edge of her consciousness.

"Yeah, yeah that's great!" Pattie got up from the piano and gave Elisabeth a big hug. Elisabeth, not happy, submitted rather than responded, and went upstairs to change. When she came back, Pattie had left the piano and was singing and dancing with her children. She held Nalini under her arms and jigged her about, while Paul danced the way he'd seen people on television, twisting his little body and making grimaces.

"Just take Nali will you, I want to put a record on. Paul, that's fantastic, you're a fab dancer!" She clapped her hands. Paul laughed, and tried to pull the records out of his mother's hands.

Elisabeth picked the child up and wondered if Nalini would ever see her father again. She looked at tough little fair haired Paul, and once again wondered if Chris was his father. It was becoming an obsession with her even though she knew when she was being rational that it was really no business of hers. She loved the people concerned and she couldn't get her own life sorted out until she knew. She felt the same way she had with Colin, that some things had to be brought into the open. He and she had had a good talk, perhaps Pattie was ready to open up, and here was an ideal opportunity to ask, when nobody else was around. She had agreed to do something for her cousin, it was only right that Pattie should do something for her. She hesitated, trying to find the right words. When it came to it, it was an impossible question to ask.

"He's a good dancer, he must get that from you. I – what does he get from his father?" It was a clumsy attempt.

"Dunno," said Pattie, crouched over the record player, but giving her cousin a sharp look.

"You don't know?"

Pattie sat back on her heels. "What is it, Elisabeth?"

"You've talked about Ranjit, but you haven't said anything about Paul's father. I'm just curious and I expect he will be when he's older." As usual, Elisabeth hid her face behind her long hair. Pattie turned to the record player again. "I don't know who his father is."

"Oh," Elisabeth said. She put the wriggling Nalini onto the floor.

"Why d'you want to know?"

"He shouldn't have abandoned you," Elisabeth said, trying to find her way.

"Nobody abandoned me. I took myself off. Anyway it's history."

"A boy needs a father."

"He's got me. And a grandfather and uncles and aunts."

"Fathers have a responsibility for their children!" said Elisabeth.

Pattie shrugged. She chose a record and slid it out of its cover. "No, Paulie, let me do it, I don't want to scratch it. Get ready to dance again." To Elisabeth she said "You try to make 'em. I prefer it my way. Let it go."

Now she had started Elisabeth couldn't let it go. "He - whoever it was - must have known - I mean the possibility."

Pattie put the record on the turntable. "Elis'beth, let it go. It's loving the kiddies when they're here that matters, not knowing who produced the sperm."

Elisabeth was shocked. "But if ..."

"None of them wanted to become fathers. I was careless. That's all there is to it. And I wouldn't want it any other way. No-one's going to tell me how to bring up my kids."

She held the needle over the record and allowed it to rest on the black shiny disk.

"Listen to this, isn't it fab? Come here, Nali, bang your little hand up and down, see, she likes music too. Now start dancing, Paulie, clap your hands, yes baby. 'I'm just a puppet on a string...' Yeah, that's right! I was only a kid myself at the time. I was scared when I found out I was pregnant. I knew if the family knew they'd try to find out who the father was and get me married. Just like you're doing. So I kept away. And that's all there is to know."

"I'm sorry," said Elisabeth, still dissatisfied but not seeing any alternative to letting it go.

"It seems to me," continued Pattie, "that the trouble with men is that they're frustrated. They can do everything except have babies. Only women can do that. And they get mad because it's one thing they can't control. They can never be absolutely sure that their children are theirs."

Elisabeth let it go. Her mood had shifted again and she wondered about her own need to know. Because she believed Chris was involved and she was jealous? Because she could no longer love a man who had made her cousin pregnant and then abandoned her? Because her own father was so unsatisfactory? Her motives were so mixed and she didn't feel up to analysing them. Pattie was probably right, better let it rest. If she could.

She left Pattie and the children and went up to her attic bedroom where she took a moody pleasure in hearing the rain beating against the window, and seeing the fat rain drops moving slowly down the glass. There was so much happening and with it a danger that she would get swept up into everybody else's affairs when there was her own future to think about. She couldn't allow herself to get trapped by her family's demands, as she had said to Colin she needed some space, somewhere where she could just be herself and think about what was right for her. She remembered what Colin had said about needing to find security in herself. He was right, and she reckoned she couldn't do that until she had become reconciled with the past. That meant finding out all she could about her mother, and her mother's death. She would have to talk to her father again but he was as bad as Pattie, impossible to pin down. His acting was going well, the new series was successful, and there were hints of a new girlfriend. He never talked of Rhoda; it was as if she had never been part of his life. Elisabeth had assumed that they would divorce but maybe they would just separate, lose touch. Her father had always found it easy to leave the past behind. He was like a gypsy, living for the moment. He had moved house so often that he had very few personal records, other than theatrical mementoes. Just the one photograph of her mother that Elisabeth now had, under the glass top on her dressing table. How much could he tell her? He had probably genuinely forgotten much of the detail. Still, she would try. She would take some leave and spend a week with him in London. That might help her to decide whether or not to move closer to him.

There was another photograph that Heather had found, showing the whole family at the seaside when Elisabeth was just a baby. She

395

believed her father had been performing in a pier show that summer. But it appeared that the family hadn't met again until after Fay had died. Long after she had died. And all she knew about her mother's death was that she had gone out one winter night and not returned, and was found dead the next morning. She had understood her to have drowned, but Phyllis said it was a heart attack. She supposed there would have been an inquest, there would be records, she would be able to find them. When she was in London she could go to the Register of Births, Marriages and Deaths.

Sitting there, brooding, while the rain lashed the window, she thought of Phyllis and realised that her aunt's story had put her own into perspective. Nothing, she thought, could be as terrible as having to give up your child. And if Pattie was not interested in identifying the father of her son, why should she care? The important thing was where she was, where they all were, now, and what they were going to do with the rest of their lives. And yet – she was going round in circles. She had to investigate the past, or she would never be happy, would never have a future.

When she was recovering from her breakdown her doctor had suggested she keep a diary recording her thoughts and feelings, however confused. She had done so, intermittently. At that time all her thoughts centred on her mother, what she was like, whether her death had been accident or suicide. She couldn't get beyond that, her writing just dried up when she tried. She tried to piece together the scraps of information she had, but they didn't amount to much, and it depressed her to think that there was no real substance to her mother's life. Now she began to wonder if there was another way. 'Why not write about how my mother might have been,' she thought. 'I'll put down what I know and then fill in the gaps, and build up a picture that way.' But somehow that felt uncomfortably like Antony's approach. He would have lifted each layer of understanding like a surgeon with a scalpel, to reveal the weaknesses in Elisabeth that had led her to imagine her mother in the way she had.

Elisabeth moved restlessly from the window. Thinking about Antony had unsettled her. She had managed to put him out of her mind, she hadn't spoken about him to anyone; just told her father, who had met him, that they had lost touch. To other people she said there had been a relationship that hadn't worked out. Maybe that was what her father had done with thoughts about Rhoda, just put her aside as a relationship that hadn't worked out. And her mother. Poor mother. Rhoda deserved to be put aside, but not Fay.

Still, she felt like writing. During her illness, with Colin's help, she had tried writing poetry and continued to do so from time to time, but poetry wasn't what she needed now. She wanted something less intense, more diluted, all-encompassing, which would allow her to follow the story through all its winding paths.

She thought again about her mother. Instead of trying to put together the facts, why not start with the idea of her mother, and write around that. It didn't have to be factual. Her real mother had failed to come to life so why not try fiction, a story, not biography. In the process she might come to terms with the real events. It would be liberating. It could also be dangerous, but if she found it upsetting she would stop. Her mother would simply be a catalyst, the germ of the story. Someone resembling her mother would be her main character, someone with a life of her own. Maybe her father would come into it, maybe he wouldn't. She might even change the period in which she lived, make it historical. Her real mother would have been born around 1925. The fictional "Fay" would be born at the turn of the century, her father could be killed in the first world war, perhaps her mother would have died in the 1918 flu epidemic.

And then, and then – Elisabeth still gazed out of the window but her eyes no longer saw the rain. The issue of children and their parents or lack of them would be an important theme. But the story would have to be readable, entertaining, something that other people would enjoy. She thought she had it, a delicate child, from a poor background, with a talent for singing. Because she was poor and without a family she was exploited, failed to get the tuition that her small talent needed in order to develop. Her fictional character sang in music halls, met an actor, they lived together, he became successful, and dropped her. She went back into obscurity and, well, a gloomy tale, thought Elisabeth, I'll have to think a bit more. But the tale had possibilities. She had a rush of energy and took a turn around the room. Yes, but what about making it even earlier, towards the end of the 19th century, which would take it further away from reality. The actor – he would be called George – would perform on the music halls. Yes, that was it! From nowhere a scene came into her mind, of a young girl in a ballet costume (maybe she would be a dancer, not a singer) meeting her future lover for the first time, back stage, all gas lights and greasepaint.

Yes! She picked up her notebook and pen from the bedside table. She would have liked to start a new notebook but there wasn't time, so instead she turned it around so that she could start on the blank back page. She took a deep breath, pen held over the page, conscious of the enormity of what she was about to do, and then she started writing. Get some description first, just broad brush, atmosphere, how it might feel to be back stage in a Victorian music hall. She could check the details later. Then Fay (but she wouldn't be called Fay), uncertain, seeing George for the first time, his face soft in the candlelight, her eyes like stars. Falling in love. It was slow at first, she laboured over each individual word, and then the writing took over and her confidence grew and it was late at night before she stopped, having sketched out her first scene, and with a clear idea of her main characters and how they were. The plot would come out of the characters' lives. Fay (no, another name, what about Marie) and George were easy, they were just there, already they had lives of their own. All she had to do was observe.

Pattie and her children left, noisily, and a little later Irene and Bertrand called up their goodbyes as they went out for the evening. Elisabeth didn't hear them. She continued to write, lost in her work. She had found her space, and she knew what she wanted to do with the rest of her life.

Finished 17/11/15

Lightning Source UK Ltd.
Milton Keynes UK
UKOW02f1906061014

239697UK00002B/113/P

9 781784 073114